BOOMERVILLE AT BALLYMEGILLE

CAROLINE JAMES

THE PUBLISH HUB LIMITED

COPYRIGHT

**First Published in Great Britain
by The Publish Hub 2020**

Caroline James has asserted her right under the Copyright, Designs and Patent Acts 1988 to be identified as the author of this work, No part of this publication may be replaced, stored in a retrieval system, or transmitted, in any form or by any means, electronic, mechanical, photocopying, recording or otherwise, without the prior permission in writing of the publisher, nor be otherwise circulated in any form of binding or cover other than that in which it is published and without a similar condition including this condition being imposed on the subsequent purchaser.
This book is a work of fiction. Incidents, names, characters and places, other than those clearly in the public domain, are either a product of the author's imagination or are used fictitiously.

Copyright © 2020 Caroline James

A CIP catalogue record for this book is available from the British Library

ISBN 9781916338548

Cover illustration and design by Alli Smith

CONTENTS

Reviews	v
About the Author	vii
Books by Caroline James	ix
Chapter 1	1
Chapter 2	11
Chapter 3	22
Chapter 4	31
Chapter 5	40
Chapter 6	53
Chapter 7	64
Chapter 8	78
Chapter 9	86
Chapter 10	93
Chapter 11	102
Chapter 12	108
Chapter 13	120
Chapter 14	127
Chapter 15	132
Chapter 16	142
Chapter 17	151
Chapter 18	161
Chapter 19	172
Chapter 20	187
Chapter 21	196
Chapter 22	206
Chapter 23	214
Chapter 24	225
Chapter 25	235
Chapter 26	244
Chapter 27	256
Chapter 28	267
Chapter 29	278

Chapter 30	286
Chapter 31	299
Chapter 32	309
Chapter 33	313
Chapter 34	322
Chapter 35	331
Chapter 36	339
Chapter 37	351
Chapter 38	363
Chapter 39	373
Chapter 40	381
Chapter 41	387
Thank you	399
Hattie Goes To Hollywood	401
Contact Caroline	403
Further Reading	405

REVIEWS

What people are saying about Boomerville at Ballymegille...

"*Boomerville is Britain's answer to the Marigold Hotel - Fabulous!*" Netgalley Review

"*Caroline writes quite beautifully - a perfect escape read.*" Cathy B Book Reviews

"*Devoured this one! Absolutely loved the first in the series and this one didn't disappoint either. Highly recommend 5**" Nicola Mitchel Reviews

"*A highly recommended and enjoyable read. A book with feeling, warmth, hope, tears, smiles and a clever reflection on life.*" NetGalley Reviewer

"*Caroline has a gift and is a natural story-teller.*" **Judges, The Write Stuff, London Book Fair.**

ABOUT THE AUTHOR

Caroline James currently lives in Lancashire with her husband and Fred, their Westie. Her hobbies include mountain walks, sipping raspberry gin and supporting Blackburn Rovers. Caroline's writing is inspired by her travels and a career in the hospitality industry and she likes to write about life, love and friendships.

BOOKS BY CAROLINE JAMES

All of Caroline's books are stand-alone reads but can be read in the following order:

Coffee Tea the Gypsy & Me

Coffee Tea the Chef & Me

Coffee Tea the Caribbean & Me

Jungle Rock

The Best Boomerville Hotel

Boomerville at Ballymegille

Hattie Goes to Hollywood

DEDICATION

*For my sisters, Vicky and Cathy,
the best and bravest "Boomers" I know.*

With my love, always.

1

On a cold day in late March, the morning sun, having no alternative, rose high over the Church of St Edmond. It disappeared behind steel-grey clouds, casting a muted light on everything that lay beneath and, as a thin blanket of mist descended on the Herefordshire village of Markham, a funeral cortege made its sombre journey through the aged tombstones, to stand by an open grave.

The harsh cry of a raven, eyes trained on the newly-turned soil, echoed as it glided down and perched on a monument. No one looked up. As if caught in a sepia photo, the mourners, with bowed heads, stood silently whilst prayers were read and the coffin was lowered into the ground.

Hattie Mulberry peeped from under the wide brim of her black felt hat and eyeballed the raven. It strutted and flapped as its beady eyes met her own and she wondered if the bird's presence was a sign. For somewhere in her memory, she recalled her beloved Hugo telling her that the raven was a symbol of good luck and not to be feared. After all, his family seat, Raven Hall, had been named after these feathered friends.

'We commend our brother Hugo to God's love and mercy.' The minister spoke softly. 'We now commit his body to the ground.'

A hand slipped into Hattie's and tightened reassuringly, as the gentle sobs of a woman close by were drowned out by the nervous cough of the man next to her.

'Earth to earth, ashes to ashes, dust to dust...'

Hattie held a single red rose. She raised it to her lips and, with a kiss, tossed it into the grave. It fluttered softly onto the coffin, the thick leaves a caress on polished wood.

'In the sure and certain hope of the resurrection to eternal life.'

Hattie stood back, and her friend, Jo Docherty, loosened her hand-hold as she, too, gently threw a rose. Other mourners came forward and followed suit then drifted away from the churchyard. It was a subdued procession that headed to Raven Hall, where refreshments were waiting at a reception in commemoration of Hugo's life.

'Are you okay?' Jo asked.

'Just give me a moment,' Hattie replied. 'I'll be along soon.'

Standing alone in the damp grey churchyard, the tears spilled over Hattie's freckled face. She choked back a sob and had the urge to bawl and scream, to kick at the mound of dark earth piled on one side.

Soon it would cover her darling Hugo.

His smiling face would never light up her life again. Their few short months together had been some of her happiest and now, in the wake of his death, Hattie wondered what the hell she had to live for. What would she do without him?

'Take my arm, my dear.' The elderly minister came alongside. 'It's understandable to be upset, Hugo was a good fellow.' He held out a handkerchief and Hattie dabbed at her eyes. 'The Mulberrys are a fine family,' he said, as they stepped onto the path that wound through rows of tombstones, many crumbling and weathered.

Hattie walked slowly. A carpet of the dead, she thought, as they left generations of Mulberrys to their lonely resting place.

'The Mulberry cider distillery has been the backbone of this county for decades,' the minister continued, 'and I'm sure, with young Geoffrey at the helm, it's in safe hands for many more.' He patted Hattie's hand and guided her through wooden gates and into the village, to walk to Raven Hall.

Hattie thought about the family that the minister spoke of so fondly. Hugo's nephew, "young" Geoffrey Mulberry, at fifty-two, was, in Hattie's opinion, an arrogant shite, who couldn't wait to turf her out of the family pile. With no good reason to stay, Hattie knew that she couldn't linger. Hugo had made sure that on his death, his wife would have an allowance and, thankfully, she wanted nothing more from the family. Hattie had a house in Cumbria but when she'd married, she'd rented it out and now, with this sudden turn of events, she knew she must make up her mind about her future.

'At last,' the minister said, 'the mist is clearing.'

They'd arrived at Raven Hall and Hattie stared at the imposing Victorian mansion. She'd never liked the place and during her marriage to Hugo they'd spent most of their time on a ship. Hugo wanted to show her as much of the world as possible and cruising was the perfect choice. The happy couple woke to sea stretching endlessly over the horizon, where a mighty sun rose each day.

How she'd loved visiting exotic places as their ship docked in exciting locations and, with Hugo by her side, she'd discovered the capitals of Europe, steeped in ancient history, and enjoyed café culture as they'd people-watched locals and tourists alike. In the far east, the market delights of jasmine, incense and fried curried leaves had enchanted Hattie and the scents still permeated the clothes that she'd bought there. In Australia, they'd discovered the Great Barrier Reef and marvelled at the Coral Sea as they swam with turtles, had hiked through a rain forest and even tried hot-air ballooning. With more than two decades between them, Hattie, who had the energy of a thirty-year-old despite being in her mid-fifties, had been amazed by the stamina of her older partner. How satisfying their life had been, she thought fondly, as she crunched across the gravel to gloomy old Raven Hall, the formidable building that was far removed from the colourful destinations they'd visited during their travelling days.

'There you are,' Jo said from the shelter of the doorway, as Hattie approached. She saw the minister shake off his surplice and hand it to a uniformed maid; he'd spotted a tray of sherry on a console table in the hallway and hastened forward to help himself.

Hattie was relieved to see Jo. She reached out and wrapped her arms around her closest friend and the two women hugged. Jo had been indispensable since

Hugo died and Hattie wondered how she would have managed without her. Their friendship went back many years, to the day when Hattie had turned up on Jo's doorstep, hoping for a job at the hotel Jo was about to open. The success of the business over the years that followed was due to their ability to work well together, nurturing and caring for their guests, and they had become a team that overcame many obstacles, both personal and professional.

'Let me get you a drink.' Jo reached for a sherry and placed the glass in Hattie's hand. She took one for herself.

'We'd better get this over.' Hattie nodded towards the open doors of the library, where the minister had begun to circulate and people gathered in groups, relieved that the service was behind them. She knocked back her drink and reached for another. 'I need a couple of bracers before I can face that lot.'

'You don't have to face anything if you're not up to it.'

Hattie knew that Jo was studying her tired face, wondering if she would hold up. But she'd had to be stoic and strong to make the complicated arrangements to accompany her husband's body back to the UK, where Hugo's will was read and actioned, and now she must ensure that the funeral was a fitting tribute to the man she'd loved.

Hattie placed her empty glass on a silver tray and reached into her bag for a lipstick. She smoothed red gloss over her lips and stuck her ample chest out while smoothing her cashmere coat over her shapely body. 'Let's give the old boy a good send-off,' she said and, taking Jo's arm, stepped forward to greet the guests.

Jo watched Hattie and wondered how long she would keep up the performance. The quiet and submissive Hattie wandering around the room, shaking hands and smiling with Hugo's ageing contemporaries and family, whom she loathed, was a far cry from the fun-loving and boisterous person who'd arrived at this house some ten months before.

Hugo's death had knocked the stuffing out of her.

She watched Hattie exchange pleasantries with an elderly cousin who looked scathingly at the recently bereaved wife. In the days leading up to Hugo's funeral, the cousin had questioned Hattie about her future. The Mulberry family were affluent and had lived in the village for generations, where their cider business employed many of the working population. Raven Hall, in its day, had enjoyed a full complement of staff, from a butler and house-staff, to gardeners and farm-workers tenanted on the estate.

Jo knew that Mulberry offspring married into families of similar standing. They had been shocked when Hugo and his brother, Sir Henry, a widower, vacationed at Jo's hotel in Cumbria and ripples of discontent soon turned into a flood as Sir Henry became engaged to Lucinda, a bohemian art teacher, and Hugo married Hattie, the hotel manager.

As Jo studied the mourners, she thought that it seemed such a short time since she'd stood on this very same spot, to attend Sir Henry's funeral the previous year. She wondered if her business had contributed to the brothers' demise, for both had fully participated in their Boomerville experience. The hotel, in the village of

Kirkton Sowerby, was a retreat that encouraged learning and new hobbies for those in the middle and later years and Hugo and Henry had embraced everything with gusto.

When Hugo proposed to Hattie, no one could have been more surprised than Jo. She hadn't seen it coming and had been shocked when she'd realised that Hattie would be leaving and heading south to live at Raven Hall.

But Jo had given her blessing and now, as she watched Hattie move away from the odious cousin and help herself to another drink, her heart went out to her friend.

Hattie was lost.

Lost in in a world that she didn't want to be a part of. Life without Hugo in this rambling old pile had no meaning and, with relatives that didn't warm to the widow, things looked bleak. Jo wanted to scoop Hattie up and take her back to Cumbria but Hattie was stubborn and for all Jo knew, she had other plans.

She looked around at the faces in the room. A few were familiar, friends and guests from the hotel who'd known Hugo and Hattie. Seated on a chair, by a window overlooking the garden, Lucinda Brown held court. Flame-coloured hair billowed around her angular face and her pale skin, accentuated by rouged cheeks, folded in lines at the corners of her eyes. She held an unlit cigarette, placed in an elegant holder and, with long legs crossed, exposed a thin thigh beneath a silk tunic. A ruby engagement ring encased in diamonds, a Mulberry family heirloom, gleamed on the artist's bony finger.

Jo watched Hattie lean in to talk to Lucinda. Geoffrey Mulberry stood nearby and Jo could see that his brow was furrowed and his eyes half-closed, as he glared at the two women. She knew that he thought his father and uncle had been bewitched and could almost feel his pent-up anger.

How would things have turned out if the brothers had lived?

But Sir Henry had died of a heart attack on the night of his engagement to Lucinda, and Hugo, suffering a fatal stroke, had landed face down in his dinner at the captain's table, during a Caribbean cruise with Hattie. Jo thought that Geoffrey must be thanking all the cider angels in brewery heaven that Lucinda and Hattie hadn't become permanent fixtures at Raven Hall. Imagine the upheaval to Mulberry life!

Fortunately for Geoffrey, Lucinda had returned to Cumbria and made a life under Jo's roof, teaching art. Jo's intuition told her that now he was intent on removing Hattie too, thus ensuring Raven Hall remained safely intact for his overpowering family.

Jo sighed; she needed to speak to Hattie. Moving forward, she reached out to touch her arm. 'Can I have a word?' she asked.

Hattie turned and, excusing herself from Lucinda, followed Jo from the room. They went out of the house and across the drive, to sit on a bench overlooking the immaculate garden.

Two ravens appeared and perched on the stone wall.

'They mate for life,' Hattie said and nodded towards the birds. 'Hugo told me they live in pairs in a fixed territory.'

'Just like the Mulberry family,' Jo replied.

'Aye, that's true.' Hattie chuckled.

'Has Geoffrey spoken to you about the future?'

'He thinks I should move on, go back to Cumbria.' She grimaced as she thought about their conversation the previous day. 'He was very aggressive.'

'Geoffrey certainly hasn't inherited any good genes from his father,' Jo said. 'Sir Henry would be turning in his grave if he knew how his sister-in-law was being treated.'

They watched the ravens parade; silent sentries on guard.

Hattie felt their piercing glare. 'I know what you're going to say,' she said, 'this place isn't right for me.'

'I hate the thought of you being stuck here.' Jo reached down and picked up a pebble; she tossed it towards the ravens.

Neither bird moved.

'Will you come back to Boomerville?' Jo asked, her tone almost pleading. 'Cumbria is your home and we need you.'

'You're very kind, not like the selfish buggers here, who can't wait to see the back of me.'

Hattie glanced at the library window, where Geoffrey stood, glass in hand, his stare disdainful as he looked out.

'I know that nothing will ever replace Hugo and your time together.'

'No.' Hattie sighed. 'We had some wonderful experiences and it's a shame we couldn't have had a few more.'

'Perhaps you need to keep busy?'

It was a tentative suggestion and Jo didn't want Hattie to recoil, but she was convinced that if she could get Hattie back to the hotel and installed in her previous position as manager, work would take over and help her friend heal.

Hattie was thoughtful as she looked around the vast garden. 'These last few months with Hugo were like a dream, a delightful episode in my life.' She shuffled in her seat.

'No one can take that away; you'll always remember the good times with Hugo.'

Hattie sat up. 'You're right, they can't.' She shook her head. 'But it's no good feeling sorry for myself and isn't it the motto of Boomerville to get some more memories in the bank, for the days when you no longer can?' She smiled.

'Are you saying what I think you're saying?' Jo stared at her friend.

'Aye, where else would I go and, after all, who wants to be cooped up here with the Grim Reaper and his gang hovering day and night?' Hattie nodded towards Geoffrey and the ravens. 'I'll come back on a temporary basis, but I'm making no promises about staying on.'

Jo reached out and, taking Hattie's hand, began to relax. The sun had broken through the mist and felt warm on her face. She closed her eyes and said a silent prayer of thanks to whatever guardian angel was sitting on their shoulders.

Hattie was coming home.

2

Melissa stared at the advert for a house-sitting job. She wondered if hiding away for a month in a remote cottage in Cornwall would be sufficient to get her out of the mess she was in. Fluffy, a ten-year old Siamese cat, needed a sitter to brush her twice daily and massage her to sleep. The homeowner, advertising on Mind A House Services, was most specific in their demands, which included litter-cleaning and housework. But Melissa didn't like cats and as housework was low on her list of priorities, it was a job that she wouldn't be applying for.

She sighed. Everything seemed so hopeless and, in her heart, Melissa knew that running away to a remote house-sit wasn't the remedy that would sort out her complicated life.

Beyond open windows overlooking an immaculate garden, a lawnmower chugged back and forth across an expanse of grass and Melissa leaned back in her chair to look out. The gardener had his attention focussed on the first cut of the year and the neat lines he'd created.

Following a winter of high winds and heavy rain, which had threatened to uproot trees and flatten shrubs and plants, Pendleton House had been fortunate and had withstood the battering.

Melissa loved this garden and she'd enjoyed the challenge of turning the overgrown site into a formal affair. The old manor house in Cheshire had been as tired as the landscape when they'd moved in three years ago. Weathered and in need of a helping hand, she'd transformed it into what it was today, a stunning home with every conceivable luxury and a garden good enough to be opened to the public.

Melissa felt a tightness in her chest. Life had been so perfect then.

A new bride embarking on marriage with excitement and hope, she'd created a sanctuary for her husband, Malcolm, a place where he could relax and unwind. Pendleton House was home too for their offspring when they visited. Malcolm and Melissa each had a son from previous relationships and now she thought of Patrick, her own beloved son, handsome and kind Patrick, who lived in London and worked long hours in his business. He was so different to Giles, the arrogant, cocky young man who spent most of his time in Spain with his father.

Melissa knew little about her husband's work. Malcolm's businesses operated between Spain, the UK and Ireland, destinations that he visited on a regular basis. She knew that he dealt in property and the stock market but he repeatedly told her that she mustn't trouble herself with either. Being a good wife was her priority. When Malcolm disappeared into his office for hours at a time, Melissa was on hand to dispense refreshments during the visits of his lawyer, accountant and men whom he said were his 'right hand'. They employed a live-in housekeeper too and a security team manned the grounds. But with renovations complete and the garden orderly, the running of the property took little of Melissa's time and she spent most of her days on her own, wondering what to do to fill the lonely hours. She had no friends, for Malcolm discouraged any social activity that didn't involve him, and he didn't like her going out on her own.

Melissa knew that she was trapped. At fifty-one she was trapped in a relationship with a man who held her prisoner at this fortress-like house. He controlled both her finances and her emotions in a farcical sham of a marriage. She rubbed at the faded bruises on her arms and stroked the soft fabric of a blouse that covered sore and aching ribs. This wasn't what she'd signed up for when she'd fallen in love, in a nightclub in Marbella.

Malcolm wasn't the loving husband he'd promised to be and Melissa wanted out.

She turned from the garden. Tears blurred her eyes and she choked back a sob. It had been a rash decision to marry Malcolm and now she wondered what the hell she was going to do. Malcolm was due back that evening. His flight from Spain landed at Manchester at seven-thirty and he would be home by nine. Melissa prayed that he'd had a successful trip. If business hadn't run as smoothly as he'd hoped there was every chance that he'd be in a foul mood and her life for the next few days would be hell.

She hadn't accompanied him to Spain for some time. Their villa in Marbella, in the foothills of the Sierra Blanca, had stunning views of the Mediterranean Sea, and on a clear day the Straights of Gibraltar could be seen. Melissa missed the sunshine and luxurious lifestyle but in recent months Malcolm hadn't wanted her to go with him. He was too busy, he said, with no time to escort Melissa around the restaurants, shops and playgrounds of the well-heeled residents. Melissa was more than happy to spend time in Spain on her own but she had to admit that on her last two trips she had been un-nerved by the characters that came to the house and the shady-looking staff who hovered close by.

Melissa wiped her eyes. Despite the warmth of the spring sun latticing across her desk, she felt cold and she shivered. Living with Malcolm when his wrath exploded was like being held captive whilst a gale raged. Cunning and careful, in the outside world he was charming and kind to his wife and displayed a great deal of affection. But these days, behind closed doors he was a monster and his temper escalated whenever they were on their own.

There were times when Melissa feared for her life. She felt weak and helpless and afraid to stand up to the brute who knew how to hurt with maximum pain but minimum marks to exposed areas of her body. If his dinner wasn't perfect, or his shirt pressed neatly enough, his eyes would half close as he reached for the brandy decanter to pour a large measure. The drunker he became the more he taunted. On one occasion he'd even tied Melissa to the leg of a table, so he didn't need to stoop when his carefully aimed kicks connected with her stomach and ribs.

Wind rattled a window and Melissa flinched.

Turning back to her laptop, she began to type. Earlier, a website for a holiday hotel had caught her eye.

It was called Hotel Boomerville and was discreetly located in a village called Kirkton Sowerby, in the peaceful countryside of Cumbria. The marketing pitch explained that the facility offered courses for mid-lifers in need of a change. She gazed at the list and thought of the tranquillity of meditation in a yoga studio overlooking the fells or learning how to craft metals into saleable items. There was a pool too and Melissa imagined how beneficial a swim in warm soothing waters would be. She scrolled around until she found an online booking form and stared at the page.

Taking a deep breath, she resumed typing.

Her heart hammered as she pressed the *send* key and waited. Minutes felt like hours and she was about to close the screen when a new message popped up in her inbox. The email was from the reception manager who said that there had been an unexpected cancellation and a room had become available at Boomerville.

Melissa's fingers shook as she typed post code details into a route finder. Kirkton Sowerby was less than a three-hour drive from Pendleton House. She glanced at her watch and bit her lip. Beads of perspiration broke out on her forehead and, clenching her hands into fists, Melissa felt sick. Would she walk out and could she really get away from Malcolm?

Gritting her teeth, she typed on.

In moments, the booking form was complete. Melissa closed her laptop and stood up. Hotel Boomerville would be better than a remote house-sitting job and, with any luck, she'd bought herself some breathing space and time to sort out her life.

In a place that Malcolm would never find.

BILL LOOKED up from his morning paper. He'd almost completed the crossword but a noise outside disturbed him and as he cocked his head to one side to listen, he heard a group of boys shouting to each other. Their voices rose above the tarmac path that separated his Victorian villa from the park in the centre of the town. The boys kicked an empty can and it clattered on the hard surface, the sound as harsh as their expletives as they sent it soaring high into the air, to land with a crack on the window of Bill's basement kitchen.

Bill cursed and, shoving the crossword to one side, raced to the door and thrust it open. 'You'll pay for this!' he yelled and shook his fist as the boys, leaning over his railings, stared down the steep steps and laughed.

'Sod off, you silly old git!' a pimply-faced youth replied and pulled a face. He held two fingers up in defiance then leapt on a brand-new mountain bike and cycled away. Another youth picked up a stone and hurled it towards Bill.

Bill ducked as the stone spun through the open doorway, skimming across the black and white tiles that flagged the kitchen floor. It came to rest beside the ageing AGA. Bill sighed as he closed the door and reached down to pick it up. He winced when a pain shot across his back.

Too many years of lifting his mother from her bed into a wheelchair.

He stumbled to the table and gripped it tightly, waiting for the spasm to pass. 'Bloody kids!' Bill muttered, as the pain eased.

Thank goodness his mother wasn't here to witness the mindless violence that had become a day to day occurrence in Amberley Place. She would turn in her grave if she knew that her only son was being subjected to bullying by immature teenagers. Bill stared at the window where a crack had appeared. At least it wasn't broken but, at some point, he'd have to mend it.

Footsteps echoed on the staircase at the back of the kitchen and a woman bustled into the room. She was rake-thin and wore an overall knotted tightly around her waist. 'Not those boys again?' she asked as she placed a bucket in the sink, turned on the ancient tap, and began to fill the bucket with hot water.

Bill looked up.

Kathy shook her head. Her dull blonde hair was greasy and hung limp. Like cold soggy chips, Bill thought as she heaved the bucket out of the sink and added a dash of detergent.

'You need to be firmer with them,' Kathy said, 'never mind waving your fist, 'tis a damn good hiding that's needed with that lot.'

Bill knew that Kathy had witnessed the scene from an upstairs window and would now spend the remainder of her shift telling him how his mother would have dealt with such behaviour and what he should do next.

'Your dear mother wouldn't have put up with it,' Kathy said. She placed the bucket on the floor and water slopped onto the tiles. 'She'd phone the police and have them arrested.'

Bill thought it highly unlikely that the local police would dash to the scene of a recent window crack, nor respond to a few hurled insults from kids who should be in school. They had far more important crimes to worry about in the busy Merseyside town of Creston, which was close to the motorway network and, with the soaring crime rate, difficult to control. It was the perfect place for undesirables to circulate.

'I'll be needing a bottle of window cleaner, put it on your shopping list,' Kathy said as she reached into a cupboard and bought out a mop. 'You can hardly see through to the park in your mother's room.' She plunged the mop into the bucket, squeezed hard and began to attack the floor. Bill raised his feet as Kathy thrust out in his direction.

Given an audience, Kathy worked like a trooper and Bill knew that it was difficult to fault her as she bustled about the room, tidying and cleaning. But beyond his gaze, he was aware that the rest of the house had hardly been touched that day and Kathy had spent her time poking about in his mother's jewellery box, or running her fingers over the coats and gowns that hung in the dressing room on the second floor.

If he had any sense, he would have let the cleaner go when his mother died. But Bill hadn't felt capable of making any decisions and now, a few months later, Kathy was still in his employment. She was part of the fixtures and fittings in the rambling pile, which at times felt to Bill like a giant prison, full of dark and dreary furniture, useless bric-a-brac and forgotten memorabilia that he should have cleared out in the weeks following his mother's death.

Bill knew that he was gutless. His mother had told him often enough. She could never understand that her only son's job, as historian at Creston Museum, had fulfilled his limited ambition. Combined with a love of quizzes, Bill appeared to want little more out of life and, as her health deteriorated, she'd become reliant on his care and insisted that he give up work to tend to her needs. Middle-aged and with a modest pension, Bill had reluctantly agreed. The only help his mother had allowed in the house came from Kathy, on three mornings a week.

'Add bleach to the list too,' Kathy said as she straightened up and poured the contents of the bucket into the sink. 'I'll give the yard a going over on Friday.'

Bill reached for his paper and stared at the print. It was neatly folded around an advert in the classified holiday section. He thought of the website he'd discovered after reading the advert. A hotel called Boomerville, in a village in Cumbria, was offering holidays with courses tailored for those of a certain age. The retreat looked comfortable and inviting and as he'd flicked through the site, Bill had suddenly become inspired to break out of his boring routine. With his mother gone, there was nothing to stop him. To his astonishment, within minutes of filling in the online form, a reply had popped up his inbox. Due to an unforeseen cancellation, his booking at Boomerville had been accepted!

'The yard can wait,' Bill said.

'Well, maybe 'til next week, but no longer.' Kathy put the mop and bucket away.

'I'm having a holiday,' Bill said, 'and you can too.'

'What did you say?'

Bill could see that Kathy was shocked. In all the twenty odd years that she'd worked in the Bradbury household, Bill had never been away. Not unless you counted the annual trip to Eastbourne with his mother but that hadn't happened for at least a decade.

'I've left your pay on the side, with extra to cover my absence and I'll let you know when I decide to come back.' Bill stood. He gestured to a brown envelope which lay on the dresser. It was thick with cash. 'You won't be needing your key while I'm away,' he said and reached out to pocket the key that Kathy had left on the table when she'd arrived and made her first cup of tea for the day.

'B...but,' Kathy said as she grabbed her cash and stared at Bill with fresh eyes.

'Enjoy your break,' Bill said. He held her coat and bag and, before she had time to digest his news and protest, Bill had guided her to the door. 'I'm sure you'll like having some time off.'

He ushered Kathy out and slid the bolt into place, then, pleased that his home was secure, stood and watched her trudge reluctantly up the basement steps.

Bill smiled. His case would soon be packed and he'd be on his way.

'I won't be seeing you for a while,' he called out to the house as he made his way through the kitchen and into the gloomy hall. The long and narrow corridor led him past doors shielding equally dismal rooms, cluttered with heavy dark furniture, reminding Bill of silhouettes in a black and white movie.

As uninteresting as his life.

Upstairs, the door to his mother's room was open and he looked in. Everything was in place, exactly as it had been when she was alive. Faded old tapestry panels hung on the walls. The muddy brown carpet was dingy and worn. By the side of a candlewick-covered bed, a pair of discoloured slippers lay and Bill visualised his mother's ugly feet, the skin yellow and scaly, scrabbling about for the comfort of the only footwear she'd worn in years. He turned away and, gripping the handle, closed the door. 'And I won't be seeing you either, you old bat.'

With a smile, Bill began to prepare for his trip to Hotel Boomerville.

3

The road heading to Marland was clear of Saturday traffic as Hattie turned off the motorway and drove her Mini Clubman towards her old home. Her previous vehicle, which was battered and well-used, could have made the journey on its own, so accustomed was it to the familiar route. But Hugo had insisted on buying a new car for Hattie and now she was pleased with his choice. She'd been able to pack most of her belongings into the Clubman when she'd left Hereford that morning.

Not that her belongings at Hugo's home amounted to much.

When Hattie married Hugo, she'd left behind a house full of furniture and stored any personal possessions. She didn't think her pottery creations, lovingly made in the workshop at Boomerville, would fit in with the precious antiques at Raven Hall. A colourful homemade clay pot was no match for a rare Japanese cloisonné vase, nor were her tired old garden gnomes suitable for the landscaped acres of Hugo's magnificent home. The only items she'd returned with were a collection of colourful clothes, bought for the cruises.

Hattie glanced at the clock on the dashboard. She'd made good time. Her plan was to go straight to her house in Marland and drop off her things, make up a bed and settle back in. Later, if there was time, she'd head over to Boomerville and catch up with Jo. Hattie's house had been rented out while she lived with Hugo, but the tenants had moved out a couple of weeks ago. They hadn't completed their tenancy and, keen to know why, Hattie needed to speak to Alf, who'd been managing things on her behalf.

Alf and Hattie went way back, to the days when they'd both started work for Jo at her hotel in Kirkton Sowerby. Alf had stayed on as handyman when the hotel became Boomerville and assured Hattie that he would take care of her property too. She'd asked Alf to meet her and, as she headed into the familiar cul-de-sac, was pleased to see his tall, well-built figure leaning against an old four-wheel drive parked outside.

'Now then, Alf,' Hattie said, 'what have you done to my tenants?'

Alf touched his cap and nodded. He wore moleskin trousers and rocked on the heels of sturdy boots. Placing two fingers to his lips he let out a sharp whistle and smiled when a dog came hurtling through the open gate of Hattie's house and onto the path, to skid to a halt by her master's feet. 'There's my beauty,' Alf muttered and he scratched the dog's head.

'I was hoping you'd leave the mutt at home.' Hattie scowled.

'Wouldn't dream of it, where Ness goes, there go I.'

He reached behind his ear and produced a roll-up, then struck a match and began to puff.

Hattie had no time for pets, least of all an old black and white sheepdog who looked like she could do with a hot soapy bath.

As Alf looked away from the dog, his expression changed and, frowning, he announced, 'Things aren't looking good.'

'Eh? What do you mean?'

'The folk who were renting have done a bunk.'

'Aye, you said on the phone.' Hattie waited for Alf to continue. In truth, she was secretly pleased. No tenants meant she could have her house back straight away.

'Aye, well, I think they may not have left it quite how they found it.' Alf inhaled deeply then pinched the butt and put it in his pocket. 'Best brace yourself for the worst.'

'Oh, I'm sure we'll soon have it back to normal.' Hattie dug in a pocket for her keys and, striding ahead, made her way to the front door. 'There's nothing a bit of soap and hot water won't sort out.' But as she thrust her key in the lock and turned, Hattie hardly had time to step into the hallway when the devastation hit her.

The house had been trashed.

What was left of her furniture was broken and piled into heaps at the sides of the room. Walls that had been neatly painted in plain soothing colours were scrawled with graffiti and in both the dining and living room, the fireplaces had been ripped out. In the kitchen, a new double-drainer had gone, together with the cooker and dishwasher. The utility room was bare, with gaps where a washing machine and tumble dryer had once stood.

'Don't go upstairs,' Alf said and, taking Hattie's arm, opened the back door and led her out into the garden.

'Did you know?' Hattie was trembling as she sat down on the wall.

'No, of course not.' Alf shook his head. 'If I did, I'd have been around here with my shotgun.'

'It'll cost thousands to repair all the damage.'

Hattie was shocked at the vindictiveness. The tenants had come with glowing references which she now assumed had been fake. It was all her own fault for not putting the property with a managing agent.

'I should have checked on it more often,' Alf said.

'You weren't to know.' Hattie sighed. 'It's my fault not yours.'

Ness appeared beside them. She began to wag her tail then shot off and came to a stop beside the garden shed. Scrambling at the ground with her paws, she began to bark.

'What's bothering her?' Hattie looked up.

'I'll have a look.' Alf strode across the ankle-deep grass and tugged at the padlock on the shed door. It fell away and Ness shot inside. Curious, Hattie followed.

As she peered in and her eyes became accustomed to the darkness, Hattie gasped. Ness had begun to whimper and was sniffing in one corner of the room. The shed was bare, save for a ragged blanket, and the stench of animal excrement and urine, which covered the wooden floor, was overpowering. Hattie's eyes began to smart.

'What have we got here?' Alf whispered and, bending down, he tugged at the collar around Ness's neck and pulled her to one side. 'Oh my goodness.' His voice trailed off as he reached out and pulled an object into his arms.

Hattie backed away. She stood in the garden, her heart pounding, as she waited for Alf to come out. 'What is it?' she yelled. 'What have you found?'

Alf appeared in the doorway. His huge hands cradled a filthy bundle of fur and Hattie could see that he was biting down hard on his wind-cracked lips. 'It's a puppy.'

'Dead?'

'Aye.'

'Dear lord,' Hattie gasped. 'Who would do such a thing?'

'I don't know but I'll string 'em up when I find 'em.' Alf rubbed at the fur with his thumbs and shook his head.

Tears trickled down Hattie's cheeks. She thought of the animal's misery and her heart ached with pain. 'We'd best bury it,' she said and dabbed at her eyes with a tissue. 'But not here, not where it suffered. We'll take it to the meadow at Boomerville.' She thought of the doggy graveyard at the end of the garden in Kirkton Sowerby where Jo's beloved pets were all lovingly laid to rest.

'Just a minute…'

Alf stood still, rotating his thumbs across the chest of the puppy, and caressed its head with his fingers. 'I think its breathing,' he whispered. He held his ear to the little black nose and a smile spread across his face.

'Don't stand there like a dummy.' Hattie grabbed his arm and within moments had Alf, Ness and puppy seated in the back of her car. She thrust the vehicle into reverse and narrowly avoided a delivery van at the house next door.

'Try not to kill us all before we save this 'un's life,' Alf exclaimed as he reached for the seat-belt and strapped the dogs in.

'Hold tight,' Hattie called out as they careered out of the cul-de-sac. 'Let's get the poor thing to the vet!'

∼

SERGEANT HARRY KNOWLES loved his job and, as a shadowy observer of situations, there was nothing he liked more in his war on crime than to swoop in when least expected to utter the phrase, 'You're nicked!' Not that there was much opportunity for swooping in the market town of Marland. The most serious crimes consisted of an occasional drunk staggering home from the pub or a tourist speeding through the town, but Harry found a crime around every corner and made it his duty to investigate each lost kitten and reprimand anyone dropping litter.

At the station that morning, Harry was busy straightening posters on the noticeboard. In the corner of the room, Constable Derek Jones sat behind a battered old desk. He held a pencil and nibbled at the rubber on the end. A crossword book was open and he studied the clues, frowning with frustration.

'Nine letters; lake beginning with 'T',' Derek said.

'Thirlmere,' Harry replied. 'Thought you'd get that, you're slipping.' Harry raised his eyebrows, Derek was normally an expert when it came to crossword clues, a passion that had won him many a competition.

'My brain's going dead with nowt to do.' Derek

filled in the answer then took a biscuit from a half-opened packet.

'Yes, we could do with some action,' Harry agreed.

SUDDENLY, the front door burst open and a woman bustled into the station. She swept up to the front desk and drummed her fingers on the counter. 'Anyone here?'

Derek ambled to his feet, the buttons of his uniform shirt straining over his paunch. 'What can we do for you, madam?'

'Is Harry the Helmet at home?'

'Hello, Hattie,' Harry called out, wishing that Hattie wouldn't be so familiar.

'I want to have a word.' She glanced at Derek. 'Haven't you got something to do? Crime won't crack itself, constable.'

'Grab a seat in here,' Harry said, and he opened the door of a side room.

'Two teas, when you've a moment,' Hattie called out to Derek as she followed Harry.

'So, you're back.'

'State the bleedin' obvious,' Hattie replied. 'Hardly needs a copper to suss that out.'

Harry looked at Hattie. She was still attractive and vivacious in middle-age, with lovely ginger curls enhancing her pretty face. He watched her ample chest bounce as she settled herself.

Derek appeared with tea and biscuits laid out on a china plate. As the door closed behind him, Hattie began.

'My house has been trashed and I want you to find the good-for-nothings who did it.'

Harry braced his shoulders. At last! Something he could get his teeth into. He whipped out a notebook. 'I thought you'd rented it out?'

'I did.'

'It's a civil matter then.' He closed the notebook.

'Aye, it probably is and my own fault for not putting it with an agent but what I'm concerned about is a puppy.'

'A puppy?'

'Half-starved and as good as dead when me and Alf found it in my old shed.'

'Animal cruelty, a job for the RSPCA.'

'No, Harry, it's a job for you.' Hattie was adamant. 'The vet says the puppy will live if properly looked after. He's got it on a drip and antibiotics and is hopeful it will recover. We found it just in time but I want whoever is responsible for almost murdering an animal and trashing my house to be prosecuted. Criminal damage, animal cruelty, whatever you can throw at them. I'll give you what details I have of the tenants.'

'They'll all be false,' Harry said, doubtful that the tenants could ever be traced. He took a sip of tea. 'Very well, but before you start, tell me what you're up to now. Where are you going to live?'

'I'm going back to Boomerville,' Hattie said. 'Jo seems to think it can't run without me and I'll find a bed there while my place is being put back together.'

'Boomerville busy, is it?' Harry dunked a biscuit and began to chew.

'Booming I hear, you should pay us a call sometime,

come and teach the old 'uns a bit of road safety.' Hattie grinned. 'I can set up a course.'

'I'd like that.' Harry returned the smile; he'd jump at the chance of a few hours at Boomerville, anything to break the monotony here. There was always a livener and a warm welcome, if Hattie was in the mood.

'Is Jo keeping well?' he asked.

'Aye, grand and glad to have me back.'

'She's still with Pete, I see.' Harry nodded his head.

'More blindingly obvious police work. Hardly rocket science to know they're still a couple, although I can't for the life of me see what the attraction is.' Hattie had never been a fan of Pete Parks and thought he was punching way above his weight when it came to Jo.

'I'll be on my way,' Hattie said. 'I need to find a new home for the puppy but I've no doubt Jo will have room for another; she's daft when it comes to dogs.'

'She'll have it running about the place in no time.' Harry followed Hattie through the station, where Derek, suddenly occupied, was busy cracking crime as he spoke to a cyclist at the desk. 'Don't forget to have a word about me running a course there.'

'Aye, I will. You know where to find me.' Hattie nodded to both. 'I'll be back at Boomerville.'

4

Jo Docherty smoothed the cover on the bed and tweaked at the matching curtains before straightening the cushions that were neatly placed on the window seat overlooking the garden at Boomerville. The house was large and spacious and in the past, Hattie had often stayed there.

Satisfied that the room was ready for Hattie whenever she needed to sleep over, Jo skipped down the stairs then went through a panelled door in her living room that led into the hotel. She walked through the restaurant and bar and came to reception, where she took a seat at the desk and flicked a computer into life. Due to a couple of unexpected cancellations, there were guests arriving that day and as she studied the booking forms to see who would be joining the courses, Jo hoped that the new arrivals would be in time for the welcoming cocktail party that was held each Saturday night.

Jo smiled. Boomerville was booming.

As soon as rooms became vacant they were filled

with guests who wanted to experience a holiday at Jo's retreat for mid-lifers. Boomerville was now entering its third year under the new regime, where courses were offered to invigorate and re-awaken minds that may have gone into hibernation. Previous guests, having benefitted from their stay, had left to write novels, paint a masterpiece or enjoy better health after participating in the many fitness programmes available. There were a wide choice of classes and Jo was delighted with the way her business had developed. She'd wanted to do something to help maturing adults, as she herself advanced in years and now, as she moved further into her fifties, felt that her vision was working. Jo had rolled the concept out to a smaller property in Bath too, which was run by her dear friend Bob Puddicombe, together with his partner, Anthony, and Jo knew that her little west country business was in safe hands.

But now, she felt that it was time to expand.

Jo was itching to begin another venture and spread the Boomerville message further afield and for weeks had searched through agent's listings for suitable properties until one had caught her eye.

Hattie's return had come at the right time. Jo was planning a lengthy trip and as she tidied the desk, she wondered if her friend would run things in Cumbria while she was away. Work might help Hattie overcome her loss.

A car skidded across the gravel outside and curious to see who'd arrived, Jo went into the hallway, where she pulled the blind to one side and stared out of the window.

A shiny new Mini Clubman, packed full of cases and bags, had careered to a halt by the side entrance. To her delight, Jo saw Hattie fling open the driver's door and place two kitten-heels solidly on the ground. Abandoning the car, she crunched purposefully across the drive.

'Never mind peeping!' Hattie called out. 'Find someone to give me a hand.'

Jo opened the door and, stepping out, flung her arms around Hattie. 'You're early,' she said, as she steered Hattie into the hotel. 'I wasn't expecting you so soon.'

'It looks like I'll be moving in for a bit.' Hattie unbuttoned her jacket and let it slide off her shoulders. 'My house is out of action for the foreseeable and I'll be needing a bed.'

'What's happened? I thought your tenants had moved out?'

'Don't ask.' Hattie shook her head. 'I'll need a stiff drink before I tell you what I found in Marland. Alf will have his work cut out over the next few weeks.' Hattie looked around. 'Where's Bunty?' she asked.

Jo's faithful Labrador was normally within inches of her mistresses' heels.

'She's flat out on her bed in the house. I took her for a long walk earlier.'

'And Pete?' Hattie asked, curious to know if the man in Jo's life was flat out too.

'He's probably on his precious tractor somewhere, possibly ploughing the fields surrounding his house.' Jo was vague. 'But let's get you unpacked and settled.'

Jo went to find a porter to help unload Hattie's car. Her slim hips swayed under a perfectly tailored dress and her hair, still a glorious auburn, bounced on shapely shoulders.

As soon as she'd gone, Hattie looked around.

Nothing seemed to have changed in the time that she'd been away. Boomerville was as inviting as ever, from the honey-coloured stone building to the golden heads of daffodils, as they swayed in large urns circling the house where herbaceous plants packed the borders beneath tall stone walls. In the hallway, Hattie smiled as she saw fires blazing in cast iron grates in both the Red Room and Green Room; elegant areas where guests could relax and unwind.

She climbed the sweeping staircase to the galleried landing and walked down the corridor. Long case windows overlooked three acres of neatly kept gardens and as Hattie looked out she could see that there'd been changes.

The old Victorian greenhouse had gone and a new building stood in its place. Tastefully mirroring the previous structure with ornate ironwork supporting huge glass panes, Hattie stared at an indoor swimming pool. She could see that an aquarobics class was in full flow.

Whatever next? Hattie thought as she trooped down the stairs, where she found Jo, arms full of cases and a porter teetering behind.

'Soon have you settled,' Jo said, 'and you're here in time for the welcoming party.' She smiled as they made their way through to the house. 'We've got a lot of catching up to do.'

∼

MELISSA WAS NERVOUS. The excitement that she'd felt as she'd left Pendelton House had begun to wear off. The housekeeper had the day off and it had been easy to pack and put her cases in her car and the security guard had waved as she'd driven out of the gates. But after speeding along the motorway to Cumbria and arriving at Hotel Boomerville, the thrill of being welcomed by the friendly owner and shown to a delightful bedroom, overlooking the garden at the front of the hotel, had faded.

Now, she sat at a dining table in the Rose Room restaurant and thought about Malcolm. She wondered if he'd arrived back from his trip.

Melissa hadn't left a note and in her haste to depart had packed as many suitcases as she could fit in her car then, without a backward glance, she'd fled from Pendleton House. She knew that Malcolm would be furious and the rage to follow would know no bounds. His wife wasn't at his beck and call from the moment his Bentley convertible drove through the electronic gates of their home and he would realise that the welcoming lights she'd left on were simply illuminating an empty household.

Malcolm would look for her and she wondered where he would begin. She had no friends. Any that she'd had before their marriage had slid into the shadows soon after.

She'd removed her email account and texts from her mobile phone and any information that she thought might trace her steps, then placed the phone in her bedside drawer, where Malcolm would find it. God willing, she'd bought some time and, with luck, safely tucked away at Boomerville, she would be able to think clearly and work out what to do next.

But now, as she sat in the candle-lit room and

glanced around at her fellow diners, Melissa's heart began to thump and she felt her hands shake. Malcolm would be raging and his presence seemed to penetrate the walls, suffocating the life in the room. She felt light-headed and, reaching for her drink, took a deep slug to calm her nerves.

As the wine hit her empty stomach, she began to close her eyes but flinched when a hand touched her arm. Hattie, the manager, stood by Melissa's side.

'Are you alright? You look a little shaky.'

'I'm f-f-fine,' Melissa stuttered. 'Just tired from my journey and I've not eaten all day.'

'Soon have that sorted.' Hattie held a plate of canapés. 'Try one of these while I go and grab someone interesting to sit next to you.'

Melissa watched Hattie move away, the confident figure of a woman in her prime. Well-groomed and beautifully dressed with a flattering hair style, Hattie exuded confidence. Melissa felt envious and wished that she could change places.

She glanced at the canapés and popped one into her mouth.

The warm pastry crumbled and tangy cheese, with a slither of smoked ham, melted onto her tongue. Melissa couldn't remember the last time that she'd eaten, such was her anxiety, and now the combination of wine and pastry felt like lead in her mouth. Reaching for a napkin, it was all she could do not to gag.

∼

BILL STOOD in the doorway of the restaurant and stared at the unfamiliar faces. Everyone seemed to be talking at once, confident as they took their places and settled themselves in. He wondered what to do and pulled at the lapels of his suit and nervously straightened his tie for the umpteenth time. Having avoided the welcoming party, Bill was uncomfortable and wished that he'd stayed in his room and ordered dinner from room service.

Bill had never been a social animal. Years of pandering to his mother had meant friendships were out of the question and when he'd had a job, he'd gone straight home after a working day, his mother's demands too dominating to be questioned. The only respite was a weekly quiz at his local pub, a place where he felt safe amongst fellow quizzers who saw winning as their mission in life.

But this was no quiz and his mother was dead.

'Here you are,' a voice called out and Bill saw a woman bounce across the room. He looked over his shoulder, unsure of her target, but soon realised that she was heading his way.

'Hattie Mulberry at your service.' The woman reached out a hand. 'I'm the manager,' she said and taking Bill's hand, shook it firmly. 'We missed you at the welcoming party.'

'Sorry about that.' Bill grimaced as his fingers crunched in Hattie's palm. 'I was tired after the journey.'

'Well, we're very happy to have your company. Come with me.'

Hattie guided Bill through the room and came to a stop at a long table. Several faces looked up as Hattie made the introductions. 'This is Melissa,' Hattie said, 'you'll be sitting next to her tonight.' She pulled out a chair and Bill sat down. 'Melissa is a new starter too. I'm sure you'll have lots to talk about.' She gave Bill a pat on the back and moved away.

Bill stared at the woman sitting next to him. Melissa didn't look a day over forty. The soft blonde locks that curled on her shoulders were probably tinted, he thought, and her porcelain skin no doubt fed with the most expensive creams. She had crumbs on her mouth and dabbed at them with a linen napkin, leaving traces of pink lipstick. His mother would have been horrified to see her son sitting next to such a "fancy piece", and he almost heard her whispering from her grave.

Don't go getting any ideas! You're not cut out for women, wine and dining.

'Are you alright?' the woman asked. She pushed a plate forward and offered Bill a canapé. 'You must be hungry if you've just arrived. These are quite tasty.'

Bill stared in fascination as she picked up her glass, her manicured nails, painted pearly pink, a contrast to the clear amber liquid.

'Would you like some?' She reached for the half-empty bottle and began to pour.

'I think I'll stick with water.' Bill grabbed a pitcher and winced as iced water slopped and a damp stain pooled on the cloth. He felt his mother's imaginary hand swipe at his head and heard her whisper, *Clumsy boy!*

'Are you here for long?' Bill asked.

'I'm not sure, perhaps a week or two; what about you?'

'I've booked for a week but I provisionally reserved another, in case I happen to like any of the courses.'

Bill stared at Melissa. She'd lost interest in their

conversation and glanced anxiously around the room. Gripping her glass in one hand, her fingers drummed on the table with the other and he wondered if she was a little tipsy. Trust him to get landed with a drunk as soon as he'd arrived. There were empty seats at his end of the table and he wondered who the hell the manager would put there. He didn't have long to find out as Hattie appeared again and broke the awkward silence.

'Shove up a bit, Bill,' Hattie called out. 'I've got a bunch of Boomerville Babes to join you for dinner.' She grinned as she pulled out chairs and settled a group of rosy-faced women around the table. 'They've been practicing dance routines in the pool all afternoon and have worked up a hearty appetite.'

Bill shrank back as hands reached out. He struggled to catch names and stared in horror at the women. The Boomerville Babes were an aquatic team, recently formed from local ladies from the village, headed up by a farmer's wife named Audrey. In addition to their training, they enjoyed dining with hotel guests after a session in the pool.

Bill visualised the rotund middle-agers in spandex suits and little else. Blushing, he turned to Melissa for help but her seat was empty and her slim, elegant figure could be seen leaving the dining room.

Bill picked up a canapé and, as he began to eat, he wondered what the hell he'd let himself in for.

5

The following morning, Jo rose early. She dug out a tracksuit and as she slipped it on, heard gentle snores rippling from Hattie's room. Tiptoeing past, she went downstairs. Bunty was asleep in the living room, sprawled on a window seat with one paw dangling. As the dog sensed her mistress approach, her tail thumped on the padded cushion and she opened one eye.

Reaching out, Jo stroked the silky brown fur. 'Good morning, my darling,' she said as Bunty raised her head and nuzzled into the familiar hand.

A pair of discarded trainers lay on the floor and Jo tugged them on then grabbed a fleecy jacket from the back of a chair. Bunty slid to the floor and raced into the utility room where she stood by the door and woofed.

'I'm coming,' Jo said.

Outside, the sky was mostly grey but a band of salmon pink cut through the cloud and as Jo marched across the gravel path, with Bunty bounding ahead, she looked out towards the fells. A hazy mist was lifting and Jo felt her spirits rise as the familiar scene beckoned. She loved her early morning walk; it was the perfect start to the day and gave her an opportunity to put her thoughts in order. She'd much to think about and plan and Hattie's return could not have come at a better time.

Jo unlatched the gate leading to the meadow at the end of the garden and Bunty, nose to the ground, followed a scent where a baby rabbit lolloped ahead, its earthen coat undetected by the canine predator. A white tail bobbed as it moved across the springy ground and, sensing her prey, Bunty looked up. She woofed as she gave chase but the rabbit shot off and soon found safety by plunging deep into a nearby warren.

Reaching into her pocket, Jo felt the soft leather binding of a notebook. Folded neatly into the pages lay a copy of an email she'd received the previous day. It contained confirmation that her offer on a property in Southern Ireland had gone through and her solicitors, instructed by her request, had completed the sale. A member of staff who had managed the house for the previous owner would stay on to hand over the property, and Jo's vision of rolling her business out to another location was soon to become reality. If Hattie was prepared to take up the temporary post of manager in Cumbria, Jo could head off and begin the process of opening another Boomerville.

At the end of the meadow she climbed over a stile, where a well-trodden path led to the foot of the fells. A thick brown stitching of walls, crafted by Cumbrian stonemasons over the centuries, zigzagged across the fields and Bunty bounded over the familiar territory.

Jo had the urge to run. She wasn't sure what she was

running from or perhaps, she wondered as she picked up her pace, what she might be running to. Instinct was telling her to do something new, to practice what she preached at Boomerville and not settle for the sedentary life that she could so easily fall into as the years rolled by. Another business would keep her occupied with fresh ideas and motivation, a formula she'd perfected with retreats for mid-lifers and was keen to roll out.

But as she began to jog, there was something else on her mind.

Her relationship with Pete felt different. He'd been distant in the last couple of weeks and she wondered if there was something wrong. She'd tried to liven things up by suggesting new places to visit or perhaps a holiday to an exotic location, and even a bit more adventure in the bedroom.

But he hadn't been interested.

Her beautiful underwear and the recent purchase of a silky negligee were a waste of time and Jo wondered if he was experiencing some sort of "men's trouble", for Pete wasn't interested in making love. Perhaps it was his age? She'd heard that middle aged men often struggled with their libido. Pete had always been an enthusiastic and affectionate lover, but recently all he wanted to do was tinker about on his vintage tractors and attend steam engine rallies. Pete was kind and good-looking and she'd known him for many years before they got together and in her own way she was terribly fond of him, but whatever was bothering him needed to be discussed.

As she jogged with Bunty alongside, she made her mind up to talk to Pete. She had much to do in her new venture and would be spending a considerable amount of time away; it could put further strain on their relationship.

She began to retrace her steps. When she reached the meadow, she turned to look for Bunty. The dog bounded across the meadow, which was a patchwork of green, shadowed by passing clouds. As the sun peeked out, a beam fell gently on the gracious old building ahead. Bathed in a pinkish and mauve light, with Great Gun Fell a magnificent backdrop, the hotel stood proudly and Jo felt her heart swell. She knew that her decision was right and her vision for another Boomerville was about to become reality.

She watched Bunty wriggle through the hole underneath the stile and, as Jo leapt over, she called out, 'Come on, we've got a job to do!' and together they sprinted across the lawn.

~

'I HEARD YOU GO OUT,' Hattie said when Jo and Bunty bounced into the kitchen. The dog began to paw at her bowl and demand breakfast.

'Sorry, I thought you were asleep.'

'Hardly, there's things I need to do.' Hattie reached for the kettle and flicked a switch. 'Coffee?' she asked.

'Black, please.'

'Aye, I haven't forgotten.'

Hattie spooned instant coffee and pushed a steaming mug towards Jo.

'I must talk to you,' Jo began.

'No need, I've seen the paperwork on your desk.'

Hattie rummaged about in the pocket of her dressing gown. She pulled out a fluff-covered biscuit and took a bite. 'Have you got a completion date?'

Jo, who'd opened the fridge and found a plate of left-over meat, looked up. Hattie never ceased to surprise. 'The sale has just gone through,' she replied.

'Nice one.' Hattie looked thoughtful as she munched. 'I'll hold the fort, you needn't worry. Boomerville will be in safe hands while you set the new place up, but you'll need to think about replacing me when you're up and running.'

Bunty began to bark and Jo filled a bowl with meat and placed it on the floor. She gazed out of the window and sighed with relief. Her friend had agreed to take over, even if only on a temporary basis.

Hattie left the kitchen and settled herself on a rocker in the living room. 'Come on then,' she said, 'let's hear all about it.'

Leaving Bunty to her breakfast, Jo followed. 'You won't mind me being away?'

As she unzipped her fleece, the notebook fell out of the pocket, sending the email fluttering across the floor.

'I think I can cope.' Hattie leaned over and picked up the email. As she read, she let out a long whistle.

Jo sat on the window seat, Bunty by her side.

'It's a steal, you've got a bargain,' Hattie said. 'Flatterly Manor will make a brilliant Boomerville.'

'Yes, it certainly is a bargain.'

'But can you handle the ghosts?'

Hattie sipped her coffee and watched Jo, who was gazing out of the window, her eyes studying the distant fells. Hattie wondered if memories of a Caribbean holiday, some years ago, were still as firmly imprinted in Jo's head as they were in her own.

For the holiday had changed the course of Jo's life.

It had sown the first seeds for Jo's new business and, as the tropical sun set on their final day on the beach in Barbados, the idea for Boomerville had been born. The thought of bringing her deserted and fading old hotel back to life, as a retreat for mid-lifers, following the sudden death of her husband, had ended a year of mourning for Jo and, together, they'd sipped cocktails and made plans.

Hattie was thoughtful as she rocked in her chair and remembered a very different Jo who'd returned from the Caribbean. The grieving widow was gone and determined to get on with her life; she'd started again and created Hotel Boomerville. But Hattie was acutely aware that something else had happened during their holiday.

Both women had found excitement and romance, Hattie in the arms of Mattie, a handsome local, whose intense eyes and delicious dark skin, combined with an eclectic personality and passion for Hattie, had bowled her over. For Jo, a holiday romance had hit her like the hurricanes that raged through the islands in the autumn months of the year. Jo had fallen for an ageing rock star, who'd swept her off her feet. Long Tom Hendry had been performing concerts on the island and from their first meeting the attraction was electrifying, sending volts of emotion surging through Jo to remind her that she could still attract love in her life.

Hattie reached into her pocket and found another biscuit. As she sipped her coffee and munched, she sighed. She'd never understood how Jo's romance had ended. Despite Long Tom urging Jo to take a leap of faith and live with him, she'd returned to Cumbria and into the arms of Pete.

'I presume the seller of Flatterly Manor is Long Tom Hendry?' Hattie raised her eyebrows. 'It's an incredible quirk of fate that the property belongs to your old lover.'

'It is an interesting fluke but I honestly had no idea.'

'But you knew he lived in Ireland?'

'I haven't chased him down over the years, our relationship was short-lived.' Jo fidgeted in her seat. 'I'm told that since his last marriage broke up he lives in Los Angeles. Flatterly Manor has been empty for some time.'

'Aye, that's just as well.' Hattie drained her mug. 'You don't want to be starting all that up again, not now that Pete has his mucky old boots firmly under your table.'

Jo stood up and took the email from Hattie. 'Pete spends all his time with his tractors,' she said. 'I doubt he'll notice my absence, he seems so distant these days.' She placed the correspondence on her desk. 'And Long Tom is the last person I want to see.'

Hattie had found a box of fudge on the table. She popped a chunk into her mouth and began to chew. 'When are you going?' she asked, as the thick creamy substance melted on her tongue.

'I want to go as soon as possible. There's a former employee looking after the property since the sale; he'll do a hand-over but it's a big place to stand empty and I need to be there. Will you be alright to take over here?'

'Why not? I've nowt else to occupy myself with.'

Hattie poked at her teeth with a finger. 'My house is a mess but I've builders there sorting it out.'

'Then I'll leave as soon as I can book a flight. I need to make plans.'

'Aye, get yourself away.' Hattie took another piece of fudge. 'And make sure it's not all work; a bit of Irish craic will do you the world of good.'

Jo moved about the room, gathering paperwork before plonking herself down in front of her laptop. Hattie chewed on the fudge. As she watched Jo scan the internet for flights to Ireland she thought about her friend's relationship with Pete. Hattie had a suspicion that Pete was doing far more than tinkering around on his tractors, when he wasn't spending time with Jo, and she would make it her mission to find out what was going on.

'I could leave tomorrow; there's a flight to Cork from Manchester in the morning. Would that work for you?' Jo asked.

'Bleedin' hell, I thought you might see the week out.' Hattie smiled. 'Of course it is, get your arse booked on a seat, then go and get your cases packed.' She looked around. 'I'd better get myself up to date with this place.'

'Nothing's changed,' Jo said as she typed in her credit card details. 'You'll be back in the swing of things in no time.'

'No change? You've a bloody great pool out the back that has half the village's women folk splashing about in it, under the illusion that they're set for an Olympic gold medal, and there's a list of new courses that I've never even heard of.'

'You'll be busy but Bunty will keep you company.'

'Oh, hell, I'd forgotten about the mutt.'

Hattie sighed but suddenly remembered the puppy. It was a perfect opportunity for Hattie to offload it. Once bonded with Bunty there wasn't a prayer that Jo would turn the abandoned dog out.

'Bunty will be fine with me.' Hattie leaned down to ruffle Bunty's fur.

'I'm going to pack for the trip.' Jo stood by the stairs. 'Is it cold in Ireland at this time of year?'

'There'll be a cool March wind,' Hattie said. 'Pack your woolly knickers and don't forget a vest.'

'I hardly think I'll need things like that.' Jo laughed and disappeared into her dressing room.

'Aye, maybe not but don't forget your confidence and a case full of courage,' Hattie added under her breath. 'If history is anything to go by, you're certainly going to need them.'

∼

MELISSA STARED out of the window overlooking the front of the hotel. She studied every car in the road below and, with her fingers crossed, prayed that Malcolm wouldn't find her.

She'd been told that Sunday was a quiet day at Boomerville and with no courses taking place and guests free to do as they pleased, Melissa hadn't ventured far. Hattie had asked if Melissa would be joining everyone for Sunday lunch, which was popular with locals and residents alike. But Melissa had no desire to rub shoulders and socialise. If Malcolm was going to find her, he'd be using his contacts to track her down and she needed time before she felt confident enough to join in.

Melissa prayed that Malcolm would let her go and agree to their relationship ending. They'd been unhappy for so long, surely, she thought, he'd be glad to see the back of his wife. There was an abundance of younger women ready to step into her shoes and Melissa knew that Malcolm enjoyed extra marital affairs. Her absence might be just what he needed.

A vehicle crunched across the gravel and she peered around the curtains to see Bill, the man who'd sat beside her the previous evening. She watched as he climbed out of an old Toyota tourer, the windows grainy in the morning sun. Wandering around the car, Bill checked that all the doors were locked, before straightening the lapels of his jacket. He ran his fingers through strands of thinning hair, then disappeared into the hotel. She wondered if he was having lunch; being stuck with Bill, as they ploughed through roast beef and all the trimmings, was the last thing she wanted. Turning from the window, Melissa reached for a tin of biscuits, on a tray beside tea and coffee sachets.

The phone on the desk rang and, startled, she stood motionless, staring at the vibrating object. The ringing stopped and, with relief, she reached for the biscuits. Her hands shook as she took a shortbread but a wave of nausea made her dizzy and she slumped down on the bed.

As Melissa's stomach growled, she closed her eyes. An image of Malcolm appeared, his face angry, eyes bulging as his hands reached out to grab her throat. Melissa gasped and the biscuit fell to the floor, crumbling into the thick pile of an oriental rug.

He would find her. How foolish she was to think that he wouldn't track her down!

A control freak both in his personal and professional life, no one got the better of Malcolm, certainly not his wife. Tears pricked the corners of her eyes and began to trickle over the soft skin of her cheeks. Melissa shook and sobs punched at her chest. Her life was crumbling. She'd felt exhilarated when she'd driven north and encouraged by booking into Boomerville, where no one knew anything about her, but this couldn't last and she was sure that Malcolm would find her.

A knock sounded and, startled, Melissa's eyes darted to the door.

'Only me,' Hattie called. 'Are you coming down for lunch?'

Melissa caught her breath and, gripping the side of the bed, hoped that Hattie would go away.

'Hello? Anyone there?'

Melissa heard a key rattle in the lock. Her eyes were wide as the door handle turned and before she had an opportunity to move and hide, Hattie came into the room.

'Oh dear,' Hattie said. 'I was worried about you.' She stared at Melissa's wet cheeks and puffy eyes. 'I tried ringing but got no answer.'

Melissa had the urge to run to the bathroom but her legs felt like jelly and she couldn't move.

Hattie closed the door and padded softly across the carpet, where her foot landed on the biscuit. 'Now, what's all this about?' Hattie placed a hand on Melissa's shoulder and patted her thin frame. 'A problem shared is a problem halved.'

Melissa felt exhausted and words refused to form.

'Folks come here for all sorts of reasons,' Hattie said, her arm circling her guest. 'We don't question or look for answers and sometimes it's good to have a bit of space.'

Melissa felt weak. Hattie's arm was the most comforting thing she'd felt in ages and it was all she could do not to fall into the contours of Hattie's soft warm body and sob her heart out.

'I expect you feel exhausted.' Instinct told Hattie that Melissa was in no condition to talk. Whatever had happened had shattered her and if Boomerville was the place where she sought shelter, then Hattie would do all she could to help. 'Why don't you relax and have a warm bath and, when you're ready, I'll arrange for some food to be brought up to your room?'

Melissa nodded and Hattie went into the bathroom to run hot water into the bath. She added scoops of scented crystals and placed a fluffy towel nearby.

'All ready and I'll look in shortly,' Hattie said. 'You might prefer to slip into bed when you're done; there's no reason to come down today.'

Without a word, Melissa stepped hesitantly forward and disappeared into the bathroom.

Hattie watched the door close and shook her head.

What on earth had this woman been through? Melissa was a wreck. Hattie gritted her teeth as she busied about the room, closing the curtains, pulling down bed covers and plumping up pillows. She remembered how Melissa had flinched when she'd touched her arm and wondered if there were bruises beneath her clothing. No doubt there was a man behind it all, Hattie would bet her life on it. She dimmed the lights and, satisfied the room was comfortable, crept out. Locking the door behind her, Hattie ran down the stairs. She'd ask Sandra, the hotel cook, to make something light and appetising for their guest.

Bloody men! Hattie cursed as she went about her business.

6

The following morning was full of sunshine with blue skies that gave promise for the summer to come and, as Bill sat in the Rose Room restaurant and looked out, his eyes wandered over the climbing plants on the garden walls. Buds with tiny green shoots were sprouting in the warmth of the April day, reminding Bill of his home in Amberley Place. There was no garden at the Victorian villa, only the basement courtyard where a few straggling branches from old climbing plants hung limply. Withered shrubs in cracked earthenware pots, lifeless from lack of water, lay abandoned from years of neglect.

Like his mother, Bill had no interest in gardening. His father had been keen and Bill had vague childhood recollections of pots of pretty flowers in a colourful courtyard, where climbers burst garlands of vibrant blossoms and hanging baskets trailed sweetly scented blooms. But his father had died when Bill was a teen, his death sudden and violent. The man had fallen from the pavement, down steep steps, to lie broken amongst the plethora of plants that he'd so lovingly nurtured.

'Would you like more coffee?' a waiter asked and Bill nodded for his cup to be filled.

He remembered his mother's screams, as she ran out of the kitchen door to find her husband lifeless on the courtyard floor. She'd implored Bill to do something to help, as her son slowly descended the steps in a trance-like state. He'd reached down to feel for a pulse, but his father was as dead as a doornail.

Bill sipped his coffee and, pushing his plate to one side, thought about his father. His death had meant nothing to Bill, in fact he'd been pleased that the man who'd shown no affection or love to his only son had died. Throughout his life, Bill had kept out of this father's way, for fear of being beaten with the heavy leather belt that hung on a hook in the hallway, his father's hand never far from reaching out to thrash his son for the slightest misdemeanour.

Bill shook his head to rid himself of the memories.

His breakfast of fried eggs, crispy bacon and juicy Cumberland sausage was filling and Bill felt stuffed. Rubbing his stomach, he contemplated the day and picked up a neatly-typed itinerary, placed in a folder that had been pushed under his door that morning, that listed his courses for the week. He scanned the pages and saw that the day would begin with an hour of one-to-one contemplation in a tepee with a resident Shaman.

Bill sighed. It seemed like a load of old nonsense.

Hattie the manager had suggested this addition to Bill's schedule and assured the new guest that it would 'set him up nicely'. Bill didn't agree. He would prefer to go straight to the mid-morning silver class and get stuck into something that might be useful in the future, but he'd been too timid to change Hattie's plan.

He pushed the paper to one side.

Sunshine poured through the window, latticing the room with bright light. A woman stopped at his table and Bill looked up. She was tall and thin and stood in shadow and he squinted as he peered at her face. Silhouetted, it appeared dark and stern and Bill wished that she'd move away, but the woman, dressed in a paint-covered smock, stood firm.

This must be Lucinda Brown, Bill thought, the resident artist whom he'd heard other residents discussing.

'My art class begins on Wednesday evening,' Lucinda said. She held a fountain pen in one hand and a leather notebook in the other. 'What's your name? I'll put you on the list.'

'No thanks, I don't want to do art,' Bill said. He stared at her vivid red hair, piled high, and her pointed features; she reminded Bill of a crow.

'Nonsense, it will bring out your creative side. Now spell out your surname.'

'Bradbury, with a "b". My first name is Bill.'

'Bill Bradbury,' Lucinda said. 'Six o'clock sharp and don't be late.'

Bill cursed the woman as she walked away and wondered why on earth he'd let himself be bamboozled into agreeing to everything that the women at Boomerville suggested. His mother had always bossed him and Bill felt disgruntled that it was continuing.

You've no guts, Bill Bradbury. You're a wimp and always will be, as long as you walk on this planet.

Grabbing a napkin, Bill wiped his mouth and, crumpling the crisp linen into a ball, flung it across the table. He pushed back his chair and stormed out of the dining room.

As he went past reception, Hattie looked up. 'Looking forward to your session with the Shaman?' she asked.

'I'd sooner stick pins in my eyes.'

Bracing his shoulders, Bill marched past and, as he reached the foot of the stairs, he smiled. That's better, he told himself, be more assertive! Pleased that he'd answered Hattie back, Bill knew that he would go to the Shaman's class, his courage wasn't strong enough to get out of it, but at least he'd made a start.

He went up to his room to retrieve a jacket; it might be cool in the tepee and he'd take a scarf too. With a sigh, Bill began to prepare for the day ahead.

∼

JO WAS deep in thought as she hurried into reception and accidentally collided with Hattie, who was manoeuvring her body through the doorway to the kitchen.

'Watch out,' Hattie said, balancing a loaded tray on her hip. 'These eggs are poached not scrambled.'

Bunty looked hopeful as a silver dome slid off a plate to reveal two perfectly cooked eggs and slices of thinly buttered toast. She wagged her tail and pawed at Hattie's feet.

'You can get lost,' Hattie said and pushed the cover back into place.

'Room service?' Jo asked.

'Aye, I'll be back in a bit.'

Hattie wriggled through reception and disappeared down the hall.

Jo pulled out a chair and sat at the desk, then flicked the computer to life to check through the bookings and diary for the coming weeks. To her delight, the hotel was full and Hattie would be busy.

The kitchen door opened again and she turned to see Alf step into the room.

'Mornin',' he said. 'Is Hattie around?'

His boots were muddy and Jo grimaced as she watched clumps of caked earth fall on the carpet. Bunty, who'd settled by Jo's feet, sniffed with interest.

'She's upstairs but will be back in moment; can I help?'

'Er, no, I'll pop back in a bit.' Alf looked uncomfortable and clutched his quilted jacket.

But a movement in the fabric had caught Jo's eye. Alf had something in his pocket and it seemed to be wriggling about. Fearful that a ferret was about to be rehomed at Boomerville, Jo pushed her chair back.

'What have you got there?' she asked and pointed at the bouncing bump. Bunty leapt up and began to whine.

'Nowt,' Alf said. 'Nothing for you to worry about; it was Hattie I wanted to see.'

'Did I hear my name?' Hattie appeared but stopped in her tracks when she saw Alf. 'Bugger,' she mumbled under her breath as Bunty circled excitedly.

Alf looked uncomfortable. A dark wet stain was seeping through the lining on his jacket and a faint woof could be heard.

'That wouldn't be a puppy pissing in your pocket by any chance?' Hattie said in exasperation.

Alf's timing couldn't be worse. If only he'd turned up a bit later when Jo had left for Ireland. Hattie would have put the puppy in Bunty's box and left the two to bond, with Jo none the wiser.

'A puppy?' Jo asked. Her face was incredulous as she looked from one to the other.

'It's a long story,' Hattie said.

'I'm all ears.' Jo folded her arms.

'The tenants who trashed my house left a puppy in the shed. We thought it was dead but there was a glimmer of life and we took it to the vet.' Hattie glared. 'Alf has taken it on himself to collect and deliver the puppy earlier than I expected.'

Hattie and Jo stared as Alf dug into his pocket and retrieved a small furry bundle.

'What is it?' Jo asked.

'Some sort of terrier,' Alf said as he held the dog out, his huge hands a warm platform for the quivering animal. 'A grizzle and tan.'

The skin at the corners of Alf's eyes crinkled and he broke into a broad smile as he ran his weathered fingers over the short dense coat where patches of fur were missing. Bunty sat at Alf's feet, tail thumping, as he leaned down and placed the puppy between her paws. In seconds, she was sniffing then gently licking the little dog's head.

'Oh, bloody hell.' Jo pushed her chair back and fell to her knees. She had tears in her eyes as she watched the puppy snuggle against Bunty's tummy.

'Lil' dog looks comfortable,' Alf said.

Hattie crossed her fingers behind her back. She glanced at Alf and the two nodded. Alf gave a wink then pulled himself to his feet.

'I'll be off,' he said. 'Let me know if tha' needs owt.'
He opened the door and was gone.

'I was going to mention it to you,' Hattie began, but Jo held up her hand. She stroked the puppy's head and made soft cooing noises as his eyes closed and he fell asleep.

Bunty licked gently at his raw skin.

'He's like a tiny bear,' Jo whispered as she gently touched the dog's thin frame. 'We'll call him Teddy.'

Hattie tip-toed out of reception and, uncrossing her fingers, let out a deep sigh.

One puppy safely rehomed.

Hattie back at the helm of Boomerville.

Things were working out.

~

MELISSA SAT up in bed and pushed the tray to one side. To her surprise, she'd enjoyed a delicious breakfast and felt a little better.

The hotel manager had been so kind.

Melissa hadn't been asked to explain herself and Hattie had told the guest that she should take her time and stay in her room for as long as she wanted.

No one need know that she was there.

If only that were possible, Melissa thought as she sank back in the downy pillows. She closed her eyes and felt like she was floating, drifting to a world she could only imagine. A world without Malcolm, safe, secure and welcoming. If only she could stay at Boomerville forever, in this lovely hotel, surrounded by people who, like her, wanted to escape from their humdrum lives.

She thought of her son, Patrick. He'd travelled in his gap year, after university, and she'd wondered if he'd settle down, and now, to her delight, he had his own wholesale business and at twenty-six, was making a go of things. Melissa decided that she would contact him and tell him that she was safe, but for the moment she didn't want anyone to know her location. Not until she'd made decisions and had breathing space away from Malcolm.

In the corridor outside her room, she could hear a group of residents chatting.

'See you at the silver class,' a woman called out and a man grumbled that he had a meeting with the Shaman, the pushy manager had insisted that he give it a go.

'You'll love it,' the woman replied. 'The Shaman sets you up for the start of your journey at Boomerville.'

Their voices faded and Melissa thought about her own plans for the day.

She felt refreshed after food and a good night's sleep. Perhaps she should venture out? Maybe to the pool for a swim, while everyone was at class. Melissa loved to swim, it reminded of her childhood, growing up in Cornwall, where her family were live-in managers of a hotel in the seaside town of Newquay.

She smiled as she remembered the days of package holidays, which consisted of full board and lodging and entertainment at night. With her mum and dad behind the bar, until the early hours, guests enjoyed a variety of cabaret acts by singers who spent their summers in British seaside towns and winters in bars on the Costas.

Melissa often took to the stage too.

She learnt how to sing, dance and entertain a bawdy

crowd. The experience gave her the courage to leave home and join an agency that provided acts for cruise ships and she'd spent many years travelling the world, singing her way from one continent to another.

She threw back the covers and swung her legs over the side of the bed. The memories had sparked a sudden urge to sing. As she crossed the room, Melissa wondered if she could hit any notes. Had she still got a voice?

She stood by the window and tweaked the curtain. Glancing out to the hills in the distance, Melissa remembered the night she met Malcolm.

As the main act in a night club in Marbella, she'd stepped onto the stage in a dazzling silver gown which accentuated her slim curves and long tanned legs. Malcolm was sitting at a table by the front with a group of bawdy men, drinking and laughing loudly. But when Melissa began to sing, the room suddenly became quiet. She remembered the moment when Malcolm looked up and their eyes had met. Locked in a pool of blue, Melissa was lost, drowning slowly in the vast and stormy sea that was Malcolm Mercer.

Business man and playboy. The man of her dreams.

Melissa stared at the sprawling fells that lay beyond the village nestling in the tiny hamlet and, as sunshine warmed her face, she closed her eyes and thought how she'd shone when she first met Malcolm.

As she remembered their happy times together, Melissa began to sing.

~

Hattie stood on the driveway and opened the door of the taxi that had arrived to take Jo to the airport. 'Morning, Biddu,' she said to the driver. 'How's that lovely family of yours?'

'Morning, Hattie.' The driver beamed. 'It's a pleasure to see you again.'

Biddu, who drove taxis during the day, owned the Bengal Balti in Marland which was a favourite dining spot for Hattie. His handsome face, olive skinned and framed with shining black hair, was alight with pleasure as he began to update Hattie with tales of his wife and two fine sons.

'Aye, that's great,' Hattie said. 'I want to catch up with you all, especially the boys and I'll be seeing you at the restaurant, now that I'm back.'

Hattie heard footsteps on the drive and turned to see Jo.

'Good morning, Biddu,' Jo called out, as he came forward to take her case and place it in the back of the car.

Hattie reached out and pulled Jo into a hug. The two women held each other for a few moments until Hattie broke away.

'I'll call you when I get there.' Jo eased into the car. 'Look after Teddy, he'll need a lot of care and attention.'

'Aye, don't you worry, the little dog will be safe with me.'

'Make sure the place is still standing by the time I get back.' Jo wagged a finger. 'No mischief, Hattie, behave yourself.'

'Mischief?' Hattie scoffed. 'As if; I'm getting far too old to be getting up to any capers.'

'You said that twenty years ago and look at all that's happened.'

'Enjoy your trip, give my love to the new place and warn the locals that I'll be over for a visit very soon.'

Hattie watched Jo's car pull away, but as she turned to go back into the hotel, she stopped. Someone was singing! A voice, as clear as a bell and just as tuneful, sang out and Hattie looked up beyond the ivy-clad walls, to the windows on the first floor. The sound was coming from the room that Melissa occupied.

Joining in with a whistle, Hattie smiled as she ran up the steps. 'By heck,' she whispered to herself, 'that lass can certainly sing.'

7

On the Aer Lingus Flight from Manchester to Cork, Jo felt her pulse quicken, as the captain announced that they'd begun their descent and would soon be landing. If passengers cared to look out of the window as the plane banked left, they would see the coastline of Southern Ireland.

She stared through the small oval window at steely grey waters below, where spumes of white surf bounced across waves rolling in to the shore. Hamlets and villages lay clustered along their route and, as a coastal town came into view, Jo could see a deep estuary with tiny boats bobbing about the harbour like leaves on a pond. It was the port of Kindale and only a few miles away lay the property that would become her new Boomerville.

Jo was now the official owner of Flatterley Manor.

She'd purchased an old manor house without a viewing and it was the most reckless thing she'd ever done. But with the success of her businesses in Cumbria and Bath, she'd money for a decent deposit and her bank had co-operated when she'd asked for a loan for the balance of the asking price. She'd never extended herself to this extent and her heart beat a great deal faster as she thought about what she'd done.

'Are you sure you want to have high borrowings at your time of life?' Pete had asked when he'd queried her need to buy another hotel. Jo knew he thought she was insane and wanted her to settle for quieter days.

As the plane descended, she remembered the discussion they'd had the previous evening, when she'd asked Pete to come to Ireland to see her new venture.

'I don't think so,' he'd said, 'but I wish you luck with it. Keep in touch while you're away.'

Jo had been hurt but had kept her feelings to herself. She'd decided that she would put Pete out of her mind and not let him dull her enthusiasm. Instinct told her that it was right and she was a great believer in following a gut feeling.

Jo began to visualise the property from the sales particulars and images she'd seen online and her anticipation built as she imagined her first glimpse of the place.

She couldn't wait to get started!

The flight landed smoothly and Jo found her case and wheeled it out to the taxi rank. Feeling slightly giddy, she crossed her fingers as she waited for a cab. She forced herself to stay calm as a driver pulled up and she settled in the back of his vehicle.

'Good day to you,' he said. 'I'm Finbar Murphy, at your service. Where would you like to go on this glorious afternoon?'

'Good morning, Finbar,' Jo replied. 'Do you know a place called Flatterley Manor?"

'Oh, to be sure.' He grinned as he stared at Jo through the rear-view mirror. 'It's a grand old place in the hamlet of Ballymegille. I'll have you there in a jiffy.'

He started the engine and pulled off at speed.

Cork to Kindale was a pretty journey of approximately twenty miles and the countryside whizzed by as Finbar negotiated the road. Jo looked out of the window at hills and fields recently bathed with rain. The green grass, rough and shaggy in places, contrasted sharply with the rich tones of dark damp earth. Every now and again, high hedges and a long driveway would suggest a property tucked away in the undulating countryside and Finbar took pains to inform Jo of the occupants beyond the gated communities. Hamlets, like Ballymegille and the surrounding area, he explained, were home to an abundance of private and corporate wealth and many famous people had made this area their permanent residence, including a rock star named Long Tom Hendry who, much to the disappointment of the locals, had sold up and moved to Los Angeles.

Jo tensed at the mention of Long Tom's name. Thank goodness he was on the other side of the world and no one here need have any knowledge of their brief affair.

'Everyone liked Long Tom,' Finbar continued, 'an ex-alcoholic, he was a recluse until, out of the blue, he had a massive hit again, got his rocking shoes back on and toured.'

Jo remembered the hit.

No More War had a reggae theme and was Long Tom's reason for come-back concerts in the Caribbean. When they'd met in Barbados, he was relishing his reincarnated status.

'But everything changed when he married and bought his wife here.'

'In what way?' Jo leaned forward, curious to know what had happened to her ex-lover.

'We never liked the wife, she didn't fit in, but Long Tom was a hero, ploughing money into schools and charities.'

Finbar slowed down as he turned off the road and pulled up on a private drive. He lowered his window and reached out to an intercom hidden in the wall. 'He's stayed sober though, by all accounts.' Pressing a buzzer, he sat back. 'We miss the fella, he was a great guy to have around.'

The gates swung open and the vehicle edged forward.

Jo was wide-eyed as she stared out at the shrubberies and trees that surrounded the drive and remembered the information on the sales details. The manor was built on the lands of Flatterley Friary, a derelict monastery of the Franciscan order, whose slender mediaeval church tower could be seen from the avenue that led to the house. Long Tom Hendry had rescued the property from dereliction and restored it, in keeping with its historic character. Jo could see that the garden was overgrown and wondered if the house was in a bad way too. Perhaps that was the reason she'd got such a great deal on the purchase price.

She bit her lip as the car stopped at the front of the building.

Ivy climbed around a honey-coloured stone façade and Jo noticed shrubs nestling under ground floor windows. The house stood tall, an impressive building with a lake to one side.

'Welcome to your new home,' Finbar said and opened the taxi door.

'How did you know I was the one who'd bought it?' Jo asked and she felt a fluttering in her stomach.

'We knew you were coming from the moment your plane touched down.' Finbar leaned forward and winked. 'Tis the fairies that told us,' he whispered and took the money that Jo held out, bundling it into his pocket. 'I wish you happiness here,' he said, 'and whatever you do with this fine manor, remember one thing…'

Finbar's fiery green eyes met hers and he began to sing.

'May the Irish hills caress you.
May her lakes and rivers bless you.
May the luck of the Irish enfold you.
And may the blessings of Saint Patrick behold you.'

His voice, clear, melodic and beautiful, stunned Jo. She stared as Finbar squeezed her hand, then with a cheery wave, leapt into his taxi.

Welcome to Ballymegille, she thought as she stood alone on the driveway and watched Finbar leave. The sun was low in the sky, silhouetting his vehicle against the lush countryside.

She looked at the garden at the front of the manor and saw an untidy hedge. The lawn was long and a mass of brilliant yellow as buttercups burst through the grass. Jo made a mental note to find a gardener as soon as possible. She picked up her cases and began to walk, her boots crunching across the gravel.

She'd arranged to meet the previous employee who'd agreed to stay on for the hand-over. It seemed an unusual arrangement but given the fact that she was in a strange environment, she'd told herself to go with the flow and be grateful. Now, as she stood on the yellow sandstone steps, where two large terracotta pots lay either side of the doorway, she wondered where the house-sitter was.

As she stepped forward, the door swung open and a tall, distinguished man appeared.

'Hello, Mrs Docherty, my name is James. Welcome to Flatterley Manor.'

~

It was late in the afternoon when Melissa locked the door of her room and dropped the key into her bag. Dressed in a tracksuit and trainers she made her way through the hotel. Feeling stronger after sleep, food and a burst of song, the thought of a lap or two in the comfort of a warm pool had encouraged her to leave her room.

There was no one about. Melissa slipped out of the conservatory door and turned into the courtyard. Classes were busy in a variety of converted buildings and there was a delicious smell of freshly baked bread wafting from the cookery school, as she made her way across the cobbles.

As Melissa stepped into the reception area, a young girl looked up. 'Are you here for a swim?' she asked.

'Yes, please.' Melissa peered through the glass-panelled wall, where several swimmers could be seen in the pool. 'Is there an activity taking place?'

'It's the Boomerville Babes, our local aquatic team, they'll be finished soon.' The girl handed over a fluffy white towel. 'You'll find a sauna, steam room and Jacuzzi through the main doors.'

Melissa went into the changing room and slipped into her bathing suit. Clutching her towel, she ventured out to the pool, where a tall, robust-looking woman, wearing a wetsuit, paced one end and issued commands to eight women. Mature and a variety of shapes and sizes, they wore bright Lycra suits with rubber flowered headgear and created a whirl of colour in the water.

Melissa sat down on a lounger to watch.

'It's harder than it looks.' An elderly lady who reclined nearby turned to Melissa. 'You need exceptional lung capacity.'

Together, they stared at eight upturned bouncing bottoms as they wobbled about, expanses of pink and mottled flesh in full view, as the Babes stood on their hands in the pool.

'Timing is critical,' the woman continued as a body teetered sideways and disappeared under the water.

They watched the instructor leap from the side of the pool.

'Resuscitation skills come in handy too.'

Melissa leaned forward to see what was causing the commotion. A woman was being hoisted out of the water and placed on the tiled surround.

'Come on, old girl,' the instructor yelled and pounded on the prone swimmer's back. 'You've just done a bit too much.'

Surrounded, the ailing swimmer began to recover and, with assistance, sat up. She ripped off her hat, revealing closely cropped grey hair.

'Blast and damn, Audrey,' she said, 'I nearly had that back tuck in the bag before I blacked out.'

The Boomerville Babes pulled her to her feet.

'You'll crack it next time,' Audrey, the instructor, said. She glanced at a clock on the wall. 'I've got to go, or I'll miss milking. Well done, ladies.'

Melissa watched the group troop past. Animated from their class, they chatted as they tugged on their swimming caps and reached for towels.

'They want to enter a regional competition,' the woman said. She yawned and, wrapping her robe tightly, lay back on her bed. 'If you're new here, you might want to join them.'

She closed her eyes and was asleep in moments.

With an empty pool, Melissa sat on the side and slid in. The water was warm and felt like silk against her skin. She moved with robotic precision, stroke after stroke. In this safe place she had no worries. Swimming was her therapist and Melissa gave in.

∼

AFTER A BUSY DAY, Bill sat in the bar at Boomerville and ordered a well-deserved drink. It had begun that morning, in a tepee, when he'd sat cross-legged on a straw mat and faced the resident shaman.

Bill shook his head as he thought about the events that followed.

The Shaman held a bunch of smouldering twigs and, with eyes closed, waved them in a circular motion.

As smoke wafted across Bill's face, his breathing became difficult and his eyes watered.

'There is a spirit, recently passed, who is watching you,' the Shaman said.

Bill had felt foolish as he rubbed at his eyelids. This man, with his wrinkled weathered skin and strange headgear of feathers and beads, was, in Bill's opinion, barking mad. Bill heard him droning on about spirits who'd left this mortal plane and he'd yawned as he wondered how soon he could escape. The tent-like structure was dark and oppressive and he'd longed to be out in the garden, making his way to the silver class to work with something solid and real.

'Be rid of your anger,' the Shaman had whispered and Bill opened his eyes to see the man standing with arms crossed against his tattooed torso. His bare feet poked out of baggy cotton trousers as he stared down at Bill. 'Namaste,' he said, placing his palms together.

Bill had scrambled to his feet.

The Shaman moved to an opening in the canvas and held the flap back. 'Be rid of your anger,' he whispered as Bill hurried out into the meadow.

'Weirdo!' Bill muttered and brushed furiously at his clothes to remove pieces of straw. A potent smell of burning herbs clung to the fabric.

Stay away from that crack-pot; don't get involved with all the nonsense!

Bill imagined his mother's scornful spirit hovering over the tepee. He shook his head to clear it of the experience and strode to the gate that led to the garden.

'Off to your next class?' A woman came towards him and Bill recognised the hotel manager.

'I most certainly am,' Bill replied.

'Has the Shaman sorted you out?' Hattie asked.

'He's crazy. Why on earth do you send people to him?'

'Aye, he's as mad as a box of frogs, but some folk swear by his sessions.'

'I shan't be going back; don't put me down for any more.'

'Just as you like,' Hattie said. She glanced at her watch. 'Don't be late, you've a date with the silversmith in a few minutes.'

Bill left Hattie on the path and turned to walk through an archway that led to the courtyard. A building with a red door faced him. A sign read, "Silver Class".

'Ah, Bill Bradbury with two 'b's,' I believe.' Lucinda studied the new arrival.

Bill had the urge to turn on his heel and escape as he recognised the tutor, the dreadful woman who had recruited him to her art class, and now, here she was doubling up to teach silver.

'Don't look so terrified,' Lucinda said. 'Sit down and pay attention.' She pointed to an empty seat. Wearing an industrial cotton coat, daubed with dark stains, Lucinda walked over to a table laid out with odd looking instruments.

Bill shuddered as he joined the other students. He could hear his mother scoffing, *You're wasting your time with this lot!* and thought of her pleasure at seeing him humiliated and not standing his ground.

Lucinda explained to the class that to begin, they would be making a bracelet, using oval wire. She pointed to her tools and explained that she would be showing techniques that involved filing, soldering, sanding, shaping and hammering.

Bill listened to her instructions and thought that he'd like to take a hammer to Lucinda's hawk-shaped face and rearrange her features. But as he slid his arms into the cotton coat folded neatly on his table, he remembered how much he'd paid for the privilege of attending the session and determined that he would get the most out of it.

Now, after the events of a long and tiring day, Bill sipped a refreshing pint of bitter. He looked around and saw other guests gathering to discuss their classes and hoped that no one joined him. As he reflected, Bill realised that he'd enjoyed himself. The bracelet that he'd produced in the silver class was wrapped around his wrist and he felt quite jaunty to be embellishing his body with jewellery.

His mother would turn in her grave.

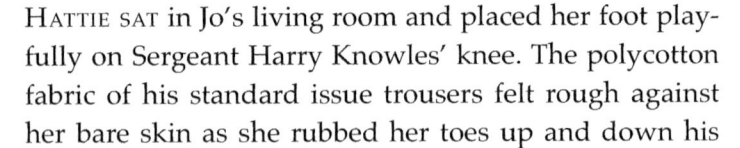

∼

HATTIE SAT in Jo's living room and placed her foot playfully on Sergeant Harry Knowles' knee. The polycotton fabric of his standard issue trousers felt rough against her bare skin as she rubbed her toes up and down his thigh.

'Now then, Harriet, don't be starting all that up again,' Harry said as he bit into a slice of carrot cake and sipped from a mug of tea. 'I'm on duty.'

Hattie raised an eyebrow. 'Duty?' she asked. 'Where have you been for the last hour?'

'Doing my duty.' Harry gave her a wink. 'Policemen are entitled to a lunch break.'

He put his mug on the table then brushed crumbs off the front of his shirt and, lifting her foot, began to caress her toes, making Hattie squirm.

Hattie removed her foot and slid into a pair of court shoes. She'd arranged for Harry to run classes for the guests. Earlier, they'd agreed that road safety was too run of the mill for the residents and Harry would be far better placed to pass on his experience of personal protection, security and self-defence, but if he was to be a regular caller to Boomerville she knew that she'd be needing a few lessons in self-defence herself.

'So when would you like me to start the classes?'

'As soon as you like.' Hattie stood up. She smoothed her skirt over her hips and reached into her blouse to whip a lipstick out of her bra. Striding to a mirror above the fireplace, she leaned in and painted her lips. 'The residents will be queuing to get on your course,' she said as she watched Harry retrieve his jacket from the back of a chair, 'but make sure no one puts a hip out or buggers their back up, or Jo will haul me over the coals.' She turned to fasten his gleaming buttons and, tweaking at the brim, placed Harry's hat on his head.

'A most informative afternoon, Mrs Mulberry,' Harry said, running his hand over Hattie's bottom. 'I'll let you know if there's any follow up to our investigation on your ex-tenants. I'm glad to see that little Teddy has settled in well.'

They stared at the bed under the stairs, where the puppy was snuggled against Bunty. The dogs were deep in sleep after an outing with Alf and Ness. Teddy's paws twitched as he chased imaginary rabbits, while Bunty snored and thumped her tail.

'Aye, be on your way,' Hattie said and blew Harry a

kiss. 'Crime won't crack itself, as you need to keep reminding that daft constable of yours'.

'Derek was the pub's leading quiz scorer last month,' Harry replied. 'Have you ever thought about putting a Boomerville team together?'

'More work,' Hattie said, bustling Harry out of the side door. 'As if I haven't got enough to do.'

She watched him cross the gravel to his squad car. In truth, Hattie thought, as Harry pulled away, a quiz night was a great idea and she remembered that one of their current residents, Bill Bradbury, had included his enjoyment of quizzes on his application form.

Closing the door, Hattie eyed the carrot cake on the table and cut another slice. As she began to munch, she thought of Bill. She'd noticed that he had a habit of talking to himself, as if he was responding to an imaginary voice. He didn't seem to be mixing very well and Hattie wondered what she might do to ease him more fully into the Boomerville experience.

A quiz team might be the perfect thing. The next quiz night at the pub was in a few days and if she added a note to the residents' daily bulletin, there was a good chance that they'd find enough guests to make up a team.

As Hattie dusted cake crumbs from her mouth, her thoughts drifted to a conversation she'd had with Harry, when she'd asked him if he'd seen much of Pete. The men had been friends for many years. She'd learnt that Pete had attended a steam rally the previous week, and, in Harry's opinion, Pete had acted out of character. As Harry greeted his friend, Pete had stared blankly and tears welled at the corner of his eyes. He'd mumbled something unintelligible then hurried away.

The plot thickens, Hattie thought and she determined to find out more. In the meantime, she had a hotel to run, hungry guests and a dinner service to oversee.

Feeling invigorated from her afternoon activity, Hattie set off to do her rounds.

8

The main hotel in the town of Kindale was a fine old building named Kindale House. Built in 1860, it was originally the home of a local family, who enjoyed the water-side location. Successful traders, aware of an opportunity, they purchased the adjoining buildings and opened a hotel. As the first of its kind in Kindale, it was now a flourishing business with extensive leisure facilities and a conference centre.

Jo sat in a cosy corner of the hotel foyer and sipped an Americano. The drink was refreshing and with a good shot of caffeine, welcome after her restless night. She watched the locals and visitors who'd gathered for refreshments, their voices animated as they discussed an event that was taking place. Uniformed staff, efficient in smart uniforms, took orders and dispensed drinks and for a moment, Jo was caught up in the activity. She strained to listen to conversations and it soon became clear that the All Ireland Chowder Cook Off was being held at Kindale House that day. Thirty-two talented chefs were busy in the function room, putting the final touches to their entries, which were to be judged by the visiting public.

A delicious aroma of seafood, nestling in rich sauces, made Jo's mouth water. She'd not eaten breakfast and now, several hours later, was hungry. On the table, a local newspaper lay open. A section called "What's On in Kindale" had caught Jo's attention and she'd noted that the town bustled with activities and events that attracted tourism for most weeks of the year. From jazz nights at local venues, to wine tastings and guided beach walks, there was something for everyone and these local excursions would create extra events for her guests.

Outside, puffs of cloud drifted in a pale blue sky and Jo could hear gulls squawking as they swooped through the air on unseen thermals, above fishing boats making their way in and out of the tiny harbour. Kindale was fundamentally a fishing port but also a haven for tourism. Following her earlier walk around the gift shops and art galleries, Jo had delighted in the upmarket stores, offering everything from designer clothes to the finest Irish whiskies. Within a short drive of Flatterley Manor, the town would provide a perfect distraction for guests.

Feeling excited, Jo longed to tell someone about her findings and, knowing that Hattie would be busy, she decided to call Pete. He was always interested in everything she did and often came up with good ideas and suggestions. Digging into her bag for her mobile phone, she had begun to dial when a voice called out,

'And how are you, on this fine day?'

Jo looked up. Finbar was approaching. The taxi

driver was as smart as paint in a crisp cotton shirt, tailored trousers and polished brogues.

'Hello, Finbar,' Jo said, 'how nice to see you.'

'What would a lovely woman like yourself be doing, sitting alone in a place like this?' Finbar asked, his eyes twinkling.

'Well,' Jo began, 'after yesterday evening and a full morning at Flatterley Manor, I found it all a bit overwhelming and I wanted to get out and see what Kindale has to offer.' She placed the phone back in her bag. 'Will you join me for a coffee?'

Finbar sat down. He ran fingers through curls of thick dark hair. 'As much as I would love to enjoy your company, I'm working.'

'Oh, are you collecting a fare?' Jo looked around.

Finbar laughed and pearly white teeth flashed across his handsome face. 'No,' he said. 'I'm the host for the day, at the chowder championship, and later tonight I'll be singing.'

'Forgive me, I didn't realise, you're a man of many talents.'

'To name but a few.'

Finbar winked and Jo felt her cheeks redden. Clearly she has misjudged the mystery man who had delivered her to Flatterley Manor.

'My main job is cabaret singing,' Finbar said. 'I've worked all over the world, mostly on cruise ships but I've had residencies at some of the finest clubs on the Costas.'

'So, Kindale is your home town?'

'To be sure. My mam is still alive, God bless her, and I've friends here. Kindale is a place that draws you back.' Finbar paused. 'Believe me, you'll always return to this beautiful place.'

'Is your wife an entertainer too?' Jo asked, curious to know more.

'Mary is long gone.'

'Oh, I'm so sorry.' Jo felt uncomfortable as she watched Finbar stare out of the window, his eyes looking out to the harbour where the water flowed to the distant sea.

'Yes, it was many years ago.'

'I'm so sorry, I shouldn't have asked; I had no idea that you'd lost your wife.'

Finbar stared at his hands.

Suddenly, with a smile as wide as the sky outside, he said, 'She went off with an American tourist and hasn't been seen since. My friends tell me that she's settled in a suburb of Sacramento.' He laughed. 'And I wish her nothing but luck.'

'Oh, I see.'

'It was best for both of us,' he said. 'We married far too young.'

Jo felt slightly foolish and decided to change the subject. 'What does your job entail today?' she asked.

Finbar glanced at his watch. 'In a short while,' he said, 'ticket holders will flood into the ballroom and enjoy tastings of the best chowder in Ireland, then they'll complete a voting slip and tonight, at a finalist's dinner, the winner will be announced.' He grinned. 'Yours truly will be entertaining the guests.'

'Oh, how exciting, will you sing?'

'Why don't you come along and find out?'

'I haven't got a ticket, and I'm sure it's a sell-out.'

She wasn't sure that she was comfortable attending an event on her own.

'You have now. I'll find you a seat with the friendliest folk in Kindale and you will be made most welcome.' Finbar stood. 'Now, I must go, I have a job to do. Why don't you come and taste the chowders?'

Jo felt her tummy rumble and remembered that she was hungry. It was way past lunch time and she needed to eat. 'Thank you,' she said, gathering her jacket and bag. 'I'd love to.'

∽

Bill watched with interest at Melissa poured milk into two china cups then, taking a spoon, stirred a pot of tea.

'Sugar?' she asked as she poured the steaming liquid.

'Not for me.'

It was the afternoon break at Boomerville and as light refreshments were served, guests gathered to discuss their classes. Chatter was lively as they heard about the others' experiences. Bill wondered how he'd ended up next to Melissa; he'd wanted to avoid company, but the only spare seat was beside her.

'Did you have a good day?' Melissa asked.

'It started off badly. I had to go and see that Shaman person.'

'The Shaman?'

'A complete fraud, if you ask me. I can't get the smell of his wretched twigs off my clothes; it's lingered all day.'

'Did you do anything else?'

'I went to the silver class, that crow of a woman, the artist, was the teacher.'

'I haven't met her.'

Bill began to explain how Lucinda doubled up to tutor the silver class and was an artist too who'd roped him in to her art class the next day. 'Are you taking art?' he asked.

'I haven't decided yet.'

Bill felt uncomfortable sitting next to a woman. Melissa seemed nervous, putting him on edge. Having grown up in a dysfunctional household Bill had never been interested in women and, with parents who hated each other, their legacy put paid to any thoughts of romance. As he drank his tea and gave sideways glances towards Melissa, Bill recognised something of himself.

She was a shy person struggling to fit in.

He reached for a scone and forced himself to make conversation. 'What did you do today?' he asked.

'Oh, nothing much. I've been quite tired since I arrived and haven't begun any courses.'

Bill wondered how this guest had managed to avoid Hattie's demanding schedule. 'I thought we were all here to participate,' he said. 'I didn't think Boomerville was for rehabs.'

As soon as he'd said the words, Bill regretted them.

Melissa eyed the exit. She placed her cup on its saucer, the china clattering, then grabbed the arms of her chair.

'Hell, I'm sorry, I didn't mean that,' Bill said. 'I only meant that I didn't think people came here to rest, more to energise themselves.' He pushed the plate of scones forward. 'Don't go, please stay and have something to eat.'

Bill began to sweat; he felt stupid and knew he was making a fool of himself. He could hear his mother's cackle and imagined her contempt.

Idiot, you can't possibly think this woman wants to talk to you?

But Melissa had relaxed her grip and, leaning back in the chair, shook her head to the offer of scones.

At least she hadn't bolted.

'Did you go for a walk or anything?' Bill began again. He'd noted that Melissa wore trainers and a track suit and he wondered if she'd been out of the hotel.

'I went for a swim.'

'Oh, I don't swim.'

'It's tranquil in the pool and enables me to think.'

Suddenly, a ball of fur shot across the room and in seconds had landed on Bill's knee. Horrified, Bill shoved his chair back to push the object away.

'Oh, don't do that.' Melissa jumped up and, as she reached out to catch Teddy, brushed her hand against Bill's thigh. Pulling sharply away, she cradled the little dog in her arms.

'I'm so sorry!' Hattie called out as she raced into the room. 'All my fault, where is the little blighter?'

She placed her hands on her hips and looked around. Bunty, hot on Hattie's heels, had her nose glued to the carpet and began to scoff at crumbs.

'It's okay,' Melissa called out. 'He's here, I've got him.'

Bill sat down. He was flummoxed. Melissa's touch had sent shockwaves through his body and now, as he watched her nurse the puppy, he felt a stirring of emotion.

'Little devil,' Hattie moved forward. 'Let me take him.'

'Oh no, he's fine, can I look after him for a while?' Melissa stroked Teddy's head and let him lick at her wrist, his baby teeth nibbling the soft skin.

'Well, if you're sure.' Hattie took hold of Bunty's collar and jerked the dog away from a cake stand, teetering with scones. 'I'll be in reception; drop him off when you've had enough.'

Bill stared at Melissa. Her features had softened as she spoke to the dog and he realised that she was a very pretty woman. His mouth felt dry and he was tongue-tied.

Lost for words and feeling uncomfortable, Bill stood and stomped out of the room.

9

Jo woke early. Rain bounced against the bedroom window and pellets of water cascaded off the sill, ricocheting to the pathway below. It was a strangely comforting sound and as she listened to the elements, she felt a surge of happiness.

On reflection, everything was good in her life.

Both her sons were well. In Cumbria, Boomerville was booming and Hattie, dear Hattie, was back and Jo's business was in safe hands. Hattie would liven things up, for her friend was a force to be dealt with, full of crazy ideas and schemes to amuse the residents. Jo knew too, that she was lucky at her time of life to have found a relationship with a man who loved her. Pete gave her strength and enabled her to do all that she did. Jo sighed with pleasure and snuggled into the soft down of the duvet. She wished that Pete was sharing the deliciously comfortable bed and felt smug as she traced her fingers over the silk of her negligee. She thought about their lovemaking and her body squirmed as she imagined him by her side.

But there was so much to be done at Flatterley Manor and it was time to get up and get on with her day. Jo threw back the cover, swung her legs out of bed, and walked over to the window to open the curtains.

A diffused grey light greeted her. It came from a dark sky, softened by green tones on the east-facing garden below. As Jo looked out, she could see that even in heavy rain and under thick cloud, Flatterley Manor was a beautiful property.

A place to bring joy to many future guests.

She hoped that everyone who came here would feel as happy as she did at that moment and find a balance in their life to take forward in whatever they chose to do. Many damaged souls had passed through Boomerville's doors since she'd opened the revamped business and Jo thought of guests who, having tried new experiences, had gone on to find joy, even love, in the later years of their lives.

Jo wriggled her toes and felt the soft pile of carpet underfoot. Flatterley Manor had many features, including expensive furnishings, and Jo had been astonished when James took her on a tour to familiarise her with the building and its contents. She'd known that a certain amount of fixtures were included in the deal but had no idea that the house was more or less as the previous owner had left it.

'None of this was appropriate to ship out to Los Angeles,' James had explained. 'The lifestyle is very different there.'

Jo still couldn't believe that she'd bagged such a bargain.

A knock on the door startled her and she slipped on her robe then padded across the room. 'Who is it?'

'It's James, with your tea.'

'Oh, James, you don't have to do this.' Jo opened the door and reached for the tray.

'Did you enjoy the chowder evening?'

'It was entertaining.'

'Is there anything special I can prepare for your breakfast?'

'James, I can look after myself.'

'It's my pleasure, madam, I'm quite used to it.'

'But I'm not.'

James retreated and Jo closed the door. She sat down and sipped her tea, thinking about the previous evening. Finbar was a skilled host, keeping the guests entertained, and after a delicious dinner, he'd announced the winners of the competition. There was much rivalry between the chefs and the trophy for the best chowder was a coveted prize. When a local band took to the stage and Finbar began a repertoire of songs, his versatility shone with wide-ranging hits from Elvis to Irish folk.

Jo was impressed and had thoroughly enjoyed her evening.

She made her bed and began to plan a list of jobs. Having poked her head into every nook and cranny of the building, she'd been pleasantly surprised by her findings. The manor was more or less ready to open to the public and there were meetings lined up with the council, Environmental Health and the Fire Officer, who were keen to allow the necessary permissions for the building to be used as a hotel. It would create jobs and encourage tourists to the area. She wondered if the previous owner had put things in place with the expectation of many parties, catering for multiple guests, for the kitchen was a dream, with every conceivable appliance.

Jo dressed carefully then brushed her hair and applied some light make-up.

She was ready for the day. When she reached the galleried landing, she ran her fingers along the polished bannister of the grand curving staircase that led to the hall, and imagined guests arriving at the front door to be greeted at a reception desk, before checking into one of the lovely bedrooms. Refreshments would be enjoyed in the elegant reception rooms overlooking the gardens.

Making her way to the kitchen, Jo thought about recruitment. James had indicated that he'd stay on for a week or so and Jo imagined that he probably knew many of the locals who'd worked at the manor over the years. There was a cottage in the grounds that had been used for staff accommodation but it needed a thorough clean and a coat of paint before it could be used.

Despite the lavish dinner the night before, Jo was hungry. She rummaged about in a fridge and found a pot of yogurt then cut a slice from a loaf. Placing it in the toaster, she searched for a spoon and plate. She thought about Pete. Strangely, she hadn't heard from him. He normally called several times a day and sent silly texts covered in emojis. She dug into a pocket for her phone. As she looked at the screen, Jo smiled.

There *was* a text from Pete.

She remembered that she'd turned her mobile to silent mode the previous evening and had forgotten to turn it back on.

But Jo was puzzled as she read the words.

Something has happened and I need to talk to you. Don't worry, haven't been arrested or anything xx

She pressed Pete's number.

'Hello?'

'Hello, that was a strange text to send, is everything alright?'

Jo cupped the phone under her ear as she buttered the toast. Taking her breakfast to the table, she peeled the foil off the yogurt.

'Jo, something has happened.'

'So you said, what is it?' Jo frowned and hoped Pete hadn't been in an accident.

'I went to a steam rally last week.' Pete's voice was low, the tone measured.

'Yes, I remember.'

'I met someone.'

'Anyone I know?' Jo thought of the gaggle of men who met at these events and the bored wives who trailed alongside.

'No, you don't know her.'

Jo felt her heart tighten. The silence was thick as she waited for Pete to continue.

'Someone I met seven years ago, when I was away on the annual golf trip with the lads from the pub.'

'I see.'

'We met again, four years ago, and had a one night stand. She's called Amanda, Mandy.'

Jo had a vague recollection of Pete mentioning a Mandy, someone he'd said he'd liked but nothing had ever come of it.

'And?' Jo pushed her breakfast to one side.

'She was married then. She's not now.'

'What are you saying?'

'It's completely undone me.'

'What do you mean?' Jo's hand shook as she gripped the phone.

'I'm a mess.'

'I don't understand. What about us?'

'There is no "us".'

Jo could hear Pete babbling about his feelings for Mandy and how he knew that he'd never loved anyone else and only now did he realise this when she'd suddenly turned up in his life again. He went on to say that although he thought the world of Jo, he knew that he couldn't go on with their relationship.

Jo felt as though she was listening to a stranger. This wasn't the man she loved, and, as he droned on, she found the phone slipping from her hand. She watched it slide onto the stainless steel table and, as if in a trance, she reached down and ended the call.

The kitchen was silent, the table icy as she gripped the edge for support.

Her heart thumped hard and heavy. She took long slow breaths to try and ease the panic that was rising throughout her body.

The bastard.

A one night stand she could handle. But to have been in love with someone else all these years? Every day Pete told Jo how much he loved her, how she rocked his world and how he loved being with her. And now this? Jo was poleaxed and didn't know what to do.

She closed her eyes and felt his strong arms around her, his warm and tender hands, capable of giving so much pleasure. His face, kind and loving as he lay next to her in bed, when they were wrapped in each other's arms. She could smell his skin, feel his touch.

Jo shivered and had to fight for breath as realisation dawned.

Every man in her life left her. From her first husband taking off with a younger model to her beloved John dying. Now Pete, so suddenly and abruptly ending their love, for a woman he barely knew. It made a mockery of all that they'd had.

Jo slumped forward and held her head in her hands. Pain shot through her body and she shook uncontrollably. Tears welled and with huge shudders that wracked every muscle, Jo began to sob.

10

Hattie ended the call. As her fingers drummed heavily against the polished surface of the desk, she took a deep breath and slowly exhaled.

Revenge, as the saying went, was a dish best served cold.

But right at that moment the dish was piping hot and Hattie had no intention of letting it cool any further. She stormed out of reception and went through the hotel. When she got to Jo's house, she stomped into the kitchen. Rummaging about under the sink, she found what she wanted and set about her task.

In less than an hour, she'd completed her job.

Hattie was waiting on the driveway when Harry pulled up. As he climbed out of the squad car and walked towards her, Hattie held up her hand.

'Don't get comfy,' she said, 'you're not stopping.' She pointed to a pile of bulging trash bags. 'You can be responsible for that lot.'

'Hang on a minute,' Harry began. 'For one thing I'm

on duty, and for another, I don't see what it's got to do with me.' He frowned as he stared at the mound, where coat hangers poked out amongst shoes, toiletries and items of Pete's clothing.

'He's your mate and it's all in the line of duty, sergeant.' Hattie folded her arms. 'Otherwise I'll have Alf take it to the local refuse station.' She glanced at her watch. 'He's out the back and can have it loaded on his truck in minutes.'

'Oh, bloody hell...' Harry scowled but knew that Hattie meant business, and began to gather Pete's belongings into the car.

'And you can tell the feckless bastard that he'd better not show his two-timing, lying face around here ever again.'

'Tell me how you really feel,' Harry muttered. There was a strange smell coming from one of the bags and Harry knew that the sooner he got the goods offloaded at Pete's, the better.

Hattie turned on her heel and marched back into the hotel.

She went through to the bar and poured herself a measure of gin. Adding a splash of tonic, Hattie took a swig then went through to the conservatory where she sat and stared out at the garden.

'What a bastard!'

All these years and he'd been holding a candle for a woman called Amanda? Pete had certainly had Hattie fooled. When Jo had called, it had been hard not to drop everything and jump on a plane to Cork, to head straight to Flatterley Manor, to comfort her best friend. Jo had sounded devastated and it had been difficult to make out her words. God willing, Jo had calmed down now and that fella, James, was keeping an eye on her. It was impossible for Hattie to leave here with a hotel full of residents and Jo had refused to come back.

What on earth was Pete playing at? He wasn't operating on a full deck in Hattie's opinion and there must be something more to the tale. But there was a fair chance they'd never know what had caused him to act so out of character. Thank goodness she'd got rid of everything he'd left in Jo's house and there were no reminders. She raised her glass and knocked back the last of her drink.

'Excuse me.'

Hattie stood up. 'Hello, Bill,' she said. 'What can I do for you?'

'You mentioned last night, at dinner, that you were putting a quiz team together?'

'Aye, I did, there's a game at the pub tonight; are you in?'

'I'd be happy to give it a go.' Bill came into the conservatory. 'I've done a bit of quizzing in my time.'

Bill looked smug and at that moment Hattie tried hard not to dislike him and every member of the male species. Instead, she gave him one of her best smiles. 'Well, I say we make you captain.' She beamed. 'Guests who want to take part have been asked to assemble in the Red Room at six-thirty and you can make your team choice.'

'Oh, I don't know about that,' Bill stammered, his hands floundering about in the air. 'I'm not a leader or anything.'

'Nonsense, Captain Bradbury, the pub won't know what's hit it when the Boomerville Brains turn up.' She slapped Bill on the back and almost sent him flying. 'I'll ask chef to arrange an early dinner.'

Hattie picked up her glass and straightened a cushion and before Bill had time to further his argument, she glided out of the room.

∼

MELISSA WAS out on the fells. She'd taken a route recommended by Hattie that led out of the meadow at the end of the garden and, walking briskly, she kept to the well-trodden path. Bunty ambled alongside while Teddy darted ahead. Bunty was familiar with the territory and Melissa felt safe with her furry companion, who stayed close - as if sensing apprehension around this lady who'd taken it upon herself to exercise with the dogs. Teddy sprang forward. In constant motion, he ran, wriggled and jumped and Melissa smiled as she watched the puppy discover the joys of the countryside. Occasionally, Bunty nuzzled Teddy and gave him a shove, if he showed too much interest in a stagnant pool or the remains of a dead bird. The older dog's mothering instincts amused Melissa and she realised that their antics made her walk more pleasurable.

Melissa was beginning to relax.

She'd been at Boomerville for several days and, so far, there'd been no word from Malcolm. Was it possible that he couldn't trace her or even that he no longer wanted to? Perhaps he was thankful that she'd left their loveless relationship. Melissa prayed that this was the case – it would mean she could decide what she wanted to do with the rest of her life. She'd managed to squirrel away money during her marriage but knew that it wouldn't last long. Kept in a metal box, hidden in the garage, the contents were now in a safe at Boomerville, together with pieces of expensive jewellery that Malcolm had bought for her. She didn't want to keep the watches, bracelets and earrings and would sell them as soon as she got a chance.

The spring sun was warm on Melissa's face and she thought of the daffodils that would be flowering at Pendelton House. The garden was lovely at this time of year, trees heavy with blossom, crocuses and wallflowers blooming bright in the borders. But as she stared at the meadow where dandelions sprouted gold amongst the green, Melissa didn't miss her former home. She felt safe at Boomerville, where Hattie had wrapped a protective arm around her.

Hattie hadn't asked any probing questions but had given Melissa a mobile phone.

'It's a pay-as-you-go and not registered.'

Melissa had used it to call Patrick. He was relieved to hear from his mother and even more pleased to learn that she'd left Malcolm. Happy that she was safe, he didn't ask where she was but told her to let him know when she was settled.

As she walked, Melissa thought about her son. Patrick was the result of a brief romance when Melissa was a young singer on a Mediterranean cruise, and although her pregnancy was shameful at the time, her parents had stepped in to help and raised Patrick when Melissa was working away.

She wandered alongside a patch of bluebells, and wondered when she would see him again, for Patrick was the only family she had. Her parents were long gone, Mum from cancer and Dad, having never recovered from the death of his wife, had a sudden heart attack and his friends were convinced that he'd died of a broken heart.

Teddy was yapping. He'd found a stick and teased Bunty. The older dog gripped one end and Teddy the other and the puppy spun into air. Melissa watched as the dogs danced around, tails thumping as they pounced and played. She began to laugh and as sunshine broke through a cloud and flowed over the fells, Melissa had a strange sensation.

It was joy. A long forgotten feeling. With tears in her eyes she tried to remember the last time she'd laughed or felt this way. Could something so simple as a walk with a dog make her feel so good?

Whatever was happening, Boomerville was weaving its spell. With a flutter of excitement, she wondered if it was time to join a class or go on an outing. She called to the dogs and as they turned to retrace their steps, Melissa made up her mind. She'd take a class that would enable her to learn a new skill. Something that would be useful in the future.

Picking up a stick and tossing it, she smiled as she watched the dogs chase ahead. She couldn't wait to get back and find the list of classes that Hattie had left in her room.

~

IN THE CONSERVATORY, Bill held half a pint of locally-brewed beer. He sipped the syrupy liquid and wiped a layer of froth from his top lip.

Drinking now and being idle? What's to become of you, Bill Bradbury?

Bill scowled. His mother had never approved of alcohol in the house but Bill knew that his father had a secret stash of whisky in his flower pots in the courtyard. When the geraniums were watered, the old man made sure that he was replenished too. Bill was in a foul mood and the daytime drink felt rebellious. He was surrounded by women who constantly told him what to do. From that bossy manager who'd made him captain of a quiz team, to the artist who'd insisted he join her art class.

Bill closed his eyes. His experience in the art class would haunt him for days.

No one had told him that it was a life class and that the students would be subjected to such a disgusting experience. The woman that had lain prostrate across a chaise, completely naked, had caused Bill to drop his pencil, sending his drawing pad flying. He'd spluttered an excuse and with cheeks burning with shame, had fled from the room. He was sure that the other students sniggered as he grabbed his jacket and slammed the door.

Lucinda hadn't muttered a word.

She'd merely watched, her eyes amused as Bill took flight.

A man-hating lesbian! She's made a fool of you!

Bill wondered what the hell he was doing at Boomerville. This was supposed to be a holiday but so far, he'd spent most of the time in fear of what might happen next.

The conservatory door was open and as Bill reached for his drink, a gentle breeze ruffled the pages of a newspaper nearby. Outside, bright sunshine highlighted a herbaceous border, a riot of colour beneath the garden wall. Bill sipped his pint and watched a collie dog run alongside a man, who moved backwards and forwards behind a mower as he cut the lawn, his pace steady, creating neat stripes in the lush grass.

Voices could be heard and Bill looked up to see a group of women, clutching towels and bags as they came into view on the pathway.

Bill was tempted to bolt. The last thing he needed was the Boomerville Babes, fresh from a session in the pool, adding to his misery. He finished his drink and stood up to leave but the women had veered off the path to disappear through the courtyard gates, away from the hotel.

'Nice back tuck, Audrey!' one of the women called out.

He settled back in his chair and contemplated another beer. A waiter appeared and picked up Bill's glass. As he ordered, Bill knew that his mother would be turning in her grave and, feeling cocky, he asked for a whisky chaser too. Bill nibbled a handful of nuts and noted that the gardener had finished the lawn and, as he manoeuvred his machine over the path, two dogs bounced into the garden and began to play with the collie.

Like a dog's home! What are you doing there? You should be taking care of the villa! Dirty animals, keep well away!

Melissa stood at the top of the steps. She held Teddy's little harness and trotted down the treads to exchange a word with the gardener.

Fascinated, Bill ignored his mother's voice.

Melissa's hair was loose and, silhouetted by the sunshine, shone like a halo. She wore a close-fitting shirt and blue jeans with a sweater knotted around her waist. Bill had never studied a female form but he could see an air of fragility around Melissa, as though she might break. He was spellbound and remembered her touch when she'd rescued Teddy from his lap.

'Ah, there you are.' Hattie came into the room. She strolled over to the door and closed it. 'Don't want you catching a chill before the big night.'

Bill glared at Hattie and wondered what the hell she wanted now.

'Feeling nervous?' Hattie carried Bill's drink. 'Don't worry, the quiz won't be hard.'

'I'm not nervous!'

'I'm sure you'll get some of the questions right,' Hattie continued, as she straightened the papers and tidied the table.

Bill wanted to pour his beer over Hattie's head. The stupid woman had no idea he was a quiz champion in his local area and had scores of trophies in a cupboard at home. He picked up the whisky and knocked it back.

'Aye, a bit of Dutch courage, good idea,' Hattie said. 'See you at six-thirty sharp.'

'Old bag,' Bill mumbled as Hattie left the room. 'I'll show you!'

11

Hattie looked at the crowd of guests assembled in the Red Room and wondered if the pub was ready to be bombarded by the Boomerville Brains, who were now overflowing into the hallway as the room filled up. She knew that a quiz team consisted of five members and looking at this lot, told herself that they could make up at least six teams. She hoped there was room in the pub and having made an earlier call, had given the landlord the heads up. Delighted for the increase in trade, he'd assured Hattie that all would be in order.

'Let's have a bit of hush!' Hattie called out and bashed a dinner bell on the hall table. The loud gong quietened the crowd.

'Now it might be a bit of a squeeze in the pub,' Hattie said, 'but I'm assured that we'll all be made welcome and I think it would be an idea before we head over, to get yourselves in teams and appoint a captain.' She glanced at Bill and took his arm. 'If anyone has any questions, we have an expert in our midst; Captain Bill Bradbury is the overall representative of the Boomerville Brains.'

Bill snatched his arm away. He had to stop himself from slapping Hattie but the buzz of the quiz was getting to him and, boosted by the whisky, Bill was feeling confident in familiar territory. He soon formed his own team, Boomerville Brains One, and began to discuss tactics.

Teams consisting of Boomerville Two, Three, Four and Five also took shape, with captains appointed.

'All set?' Hattie called out and, waving a wide brimmed hat, summoned everyone to follow her out of the hotel to the pub.

It was an assorted crowd who stopped the traffic and crossed the road. The Boomerville Babes had formed Team Two and Audrey was their captain. They wore their flowered rubber hats and strode confidently behind Bill's Team One. Melissa, who'd decided to come out of her room and give the quiz night a go, was amazed to find that she had been chosen as captain for Team Three which consisted of cookery students from a biscuit-making class, wearing tall chefs' hats. Alf had been dragged out of his potting shed by Hattie and told to captain Team Four and he led a confused group of guests, many with twigs in their hair, who'd spent the afternoon in the tepee with the Shaman. Bringing up the rear was Harry, off duty and dressed casually in jeans. His team included Biddu and his wife and sons from the Bengal Balti. They looked resplendent in traditional Indian robes and had arrived with a huge pot of curry, which Hattie had laid on as a post-quiz supper.

Hattie held the door as the quizzers trooped in and made themselves comfortable in the crowded pub. 'Another successful evening,' Hattie said with a smile and went to find the landlord, who would be supplying her throughout the evening with drinks on the house.

~

FAR FROM THE rolling fells of Cumbria, across the Irish sea, Jo wandered around the grounds at Flatterley Manor, where the damp garden appeared as sorrowful as Jo's mood.

The previous evening, sitting at the kitchen table with James, she'd heard how Hilary, Long Tom's wife, had loved to potter and plant. As James served a simple meal of steamed mussels, salad and soda bread, he'd explained that Hilary had spent a considerable amount of her time and copious amounts of her husband's money on the garden. It was clear to everyone but Long Tom that Hilary had more than a passing interest in the head gardener. Jo had listened to James recount tales of Hilary's infidelities and wondered if Long Tom had been upset when he found out. She felt a wave of sympathy.

Deceit cut deep, as she well knew.

The mussels were delicious and she was surprised that she'd finished the lot. She didn't think she had any appetite but James was skilled in the kitchen and the meal had been perfect. As she'd carried their plates to the sink, Jo asked, 'What happened to Hilary?'

'She ran off with the gardener,' James said and began to rinse the dishes. 'They moved to her home in

Kensington and she became his agent. He made a name for himself as a gardening expert on internet TV.'

The memory of this conversation tumbled through Jo's mind as she stood by the edge of the ornamental lake. Weeds choked the side of the banks and, as if reflecting her feelings, the water looked muddy and grim. Jo wondered if Hilary was happy. Had her affair with the gardener worked out? Would Pete's affair with Amanda work out too? Jo's vision blurred and tears fell as she remembered her text with Pete that morning. He'd made it clear that there was no going back.

He was in love with Amanda.

Jo wanted to be angry, to kick out and scream but the feeling of loss hurt. Jo felt drained, sucked of energy and hope. Her body ached for Pete, as though the break up hadn't happened and they were still together and loving each other. Jo had tried to explain this to an angry Hattie. Her friend was chomping at the bit to get her hands on Pete. But Hattie was kind and told Jo to try and relax at Flatterley Manor while all this sank in. She was in shock, Hattie said. A relationship ending was like a death and Jo needed to grieve. What better place than away from the scene of the crime in a beautiful part of Ireland? Jo knew Hattie was right. Time would no doubt heal but right at this moment the pain was too raw.

A voice called out and Jo turned.

'I thought you might be cold.' James appeared wearing a wool coat, buttoned tightly. 'There's a sharp wind coming off the sea, I think we might be in for a storm.' He held out a blanket.

'James, you don't need to worry about me, but

thank you, the wind is cutting.' Jo hoped that he hadn't noticed her tears.

'It really is no trouble,' he said and wrapped the soft wool around her shoulders.

Jo watched the tall figure walk back across the lawn and suddenly felt angry. What on earth was she doing, moping about when there was so much to be done? This place wouldn't self-finance and Flatterly Manor needed to generate revenue as soon as possible. She shrugged the blanket off, rolled it into a ball and stamped her feet on the damp grass. She had a vision of Pete's face and stamped even harder. Blast the man! Pete bloody Parks would not spoil her plans for Flatterley Manor! She could cry over him at the end of a working day, if she still had any energy. Tucking the blanket under her arm, Jo ran across the lawn to the manor, where James stood by the door, deadheading a pot of tired-looking daffodils. He turned when he heard Jo's footsteps.

'James,' Jo said as she caught up, 'I need your help.'

'What can I do?'

'You know the area, how do I set about finding decent staff?'

'Any particular category of employee, madam?'

'A manager has to be a priority. I wondered if that might be something you'd be interested in?'

'Me?'

'You'd be perfect, with your knowledge of the house, and the guests would adore you.'

'It's a flattering proposition, I'll give it some thought.'

'Oh, I'd be so thrilled if you would; I'd love to have you by my side as we start this adventure.'

'I'll let you know my decision in a day or so.'

'That would be marvellous and, in the meantime, I need to recruit a gardener.'

'A gardener?' James asked with a smile.

'As the previous gardener is otherwise engaged we must set about finding a new one.'

James reached for the blanket and folded it neatly. 'Indeed, madam,' he said. 'I'll see what I can do.'

12

Bill was alone in his bedroom. Pacing up and down, he grimaced as he held his hands to his rumbling stomach and wondered if it was safe to go downstairs. His tummy was doing a dance and it wasn't a pleasurable experience. Throughout the night it had gurgled and tumbled, like the fast spin on a washing machine.

That wretched Hattie!

The woman had insisted that he join the Boomerville Brains for a curry supper when they all trooped back from the pub. Bill didn't like curry but Hattie had told him not to let his team down. She'd said that in the wake of them losing the quiz, Bill must use his position of team captain to raise spirits over a heartening dish of Biddu's delicious dhal and dhansak. Reluctantly Bill had agreed and tucked in, but he'd been up for half the night with an upset stomach and now regretted his decision.

You've always had a weak belly, just like your father!

His mother's voice followed him as he paced the

room. Bill's foul mood wasn't helped by the fact that he was hungry. He wasn't sure if the gnawing pains he was experiencing were a craving for his breakfast or warning signs of another trip to the bathroom. None of this would feel so bad if his team had won. Bill had never been on a losing side and the humiliation had been hard to bear.

To his amazement Melissa had captained the winning side, with Bill's team in third place and Bill shook his head as he thought about his useless team members, who'd argued over every answer. He determined that it wouldn't happen again.

Bill stopped pacing and looked out of the window where a car had had turned onto the driveway and stopped outside the hotel. It was long and sleek and piqued Bill's curiosity.

A Bentley convertible! Dream on, you stupid boy, it's out of your league Bill Bradley!

A well-dressed man, tall and dark-haired, stepped out of the car. He looked up and Bill darted back. After a moment, Bill leaned forward again to see that the man had disappeared into the hotel. Bill was curious. The stranger was obviously wealthy and had an assertive air. Bill wondered if the Boomerville ranks were about to be swelled by such a guest. One never knew and it was a mixed bunch that resided under this roof.

He rubbed his stomach. The gurgling had stopped and things appeared to have settled down. Bill decided to venture downstairs and eat a slice of toast. He glanced at his watch; breakfast was still being served and if he hurried, he would just make it.

It was also an opportunity to have a look at the newcomer.

～

Hattie lay in the bath in Jo's house, luxuriating in deep warm water, softly scented with oils from a selection in the bathroom cabinet. She hadn't slept very well and her stomach, which was normally capable of digesting whatever she put into it, gurgled threateningly. Biddu's supper had been delicious but Hattie wondered if the seasoning had been too strong and had the dish, which had travelled from Biddu's Marland restaurant, been reheated more than once? Whatever was causing the upset had delayed Hattie's day and she'd instructed the reception staff to expect her a little later than normal that morning.

Hattie closed her eyes.

She'd had a conversation with Jo and was delighted to hear that for the time being, Jo had put the business with Pete to one side and was gearing herself up to put things in motion at Flatterley Manor. It was music to Hattie's ears for she couldn't bear to think of Jo so upset, and if work was a way of getting through the pain of parting, then Hattie applauded her friend. Men were so unpredictable, Hattie thought as she fiddled with the bath tap, wrapping her toes around the cool metal to trickle hot water into her bath. Pete was an absolute dick if he thought that this woman, Saint Amanda, was the woman of his dreams. In Hattie's opinion, the relationship was a fantasy which would come crashing down in time and she hoped that Jo wouldn't be picking up Pete's pieces. Thank goodness she had a new project and wasn't here at Boomerville, moping around, wondering where Pete was and what he was up to.

She closed her eyes and remembered Hugo. This time last year they'd been in the Mediterranean, eating tapas and sipping wine on the balcony of their suite on the Monarch of the Waves, as the ship sailed through gentle waters. They'd spent a lot of time in their suite on that cruise and Hattie smiled as she thought of the old boy's bedroom energy. At least his last days were happy and he'd spend eternity with a smile that would light his heavens and beyond.

How she missed that lovely man.

Hattie sat up. It was no good day dreaming of what might have been, she told herself. Their time together had been short but she was grateful that she'd had it, and now, like Jo, she too must move on. One never knew who was going to walk through the Boomerville door and she liked to keep her options open.

Her stomach seemed to have settled down and Hattie stepped out of the bath and reached for a towel. The thick cotton was soft and, as she rubbed her skin dry, she thought about breakfast.

A slumbering mound lay across the bedroom doorway and Hattie almost tripped over the dormant dog. Bunty's tail began to thump.

'Where's Teddy?' Hattie asked and gave Bunty a nudge with her toe. The dog looked up but Teddy was nowhere to be seen.

Together they went to search for the puppy but when they got to the top of the stairs, Hattie stopped and drew her towel tightly around her body. A terrible smell wafted up from the lounge and she wrinkled her nose as Bunty shot ahead. Following tentatively, Hattie tiptoed down.

She gasped when she saw the sight that greeted

them. The carpet was covered with piles of vomit and poo.

'Teddy?' Hattie called anxiously.

Bunty began to bark as Hattie carefully stepped her way through to the kitchen where Teddy lay motionless on the cold tiles. His little body was lifeless.

Remnants of the curry supper were spread on the table and Hattie realised that the puppy must have climbed on a chair during the night and tucked in.

'Oh, hell!' Hattie said. She spun around to find her phone on the worksurface and frantically searched for Alf's number. 'Emergency!' she yelled as soon as Alf picked up. 'Mayday! It's Teddy! Get over to Jo's now!'

∽

MELISSA SAT in the breakfast room and pushed her plate to one side. She smiled as a waiter came forward to take it away.

'Can I get you anything else?' he asked.

'No, that was absolutely delicious, thank you.'

She'd enjoyed her breakfast, in fact, she'd enjoyed it more than any meal she'd attempted to eat in a very long time. Perfectly poached eggs with slices of smoked salmon and piping hot coffee with frothy milk.

It was wonderful.

Melissa sat back and looked beyond the French windows where all was still and spring shoots appeared in the wide borders that nestled under the walled garden. Clematis climbed through the nooks and crannies, wrapping around knobbly cherry trees, pruned to spread their branches wide.

As Melissa stared out, she realised that she felt

different. Tension was lifting from her shoulders and the anxiety that had gripped her for months had let go its hold. The bruises on her arms and ribs were fading and her appetite had returned, as had an interest in life. She'd enjoyed the quiz, the evening before, and had relished being amongst others who were friendly and kind, characteristics that she'd almost forgotten existed. It has been astonishing to learn that her team had scooped first prize, and the biscuit makers, so elated with their winnings, had bought wine for everyone to enjoy with the curry supper. Melissa didn't eat meat and had declined the dhansak, preferring instead to nibble on the dahl, while enjoying her wine and the company of the quizzers as they celebrated the evening.

She looked around at the empty dining room and wondered where everyone was. Perhaps most of the guests were preparing for classes. A list of courses, neatly typed on hotel stationary, lay on the table and Melissa picked up a pen and began to read through the details. She decided to select something she'd never tried before and would ask Hattie if there were any spaces.

Engrossed, Melissa didn't hear Bill come into the room but when he muttered a gruff, 'Good morning', she looked up. Bill had been most put out by coming third in the quiz and as he took a seat at a corner table, she wondered what sort of mood he was in.

Melissa gave a cheery wave and Bill responded with a curt nod.

'Morning, Melissa,' a group of ladies called out, as they strode to the buffet table. 'Cracking result last night.'

'I was surprised that we won,' Melissa said as she

watched the swimming team slather butter and marmalade over slices of toast.

'You gave Bill a run for his money,' Audrey said.

Melissa saw Bill wince and for a moment, she felt sorry for the man.

'Never mind, there's always next week,' Audrey said as she piled her plate high and smiled at Bill. Turning to her team, she continued, 'Come on, girls, we need to perfect our back tucks today.'

They trooped out of the dining room to head to the pool.

Melissa returned to her notes. The cookery class looked inviting and as she'd never been very good behind a stove, she considered giving it a go. The biscuit makers had been keen for her to join them and today's schedule included iced buns and fancy cakes. It would be an achievement to acquire a new skill.

Melissa put a tick against the course and poured another cup of coffee. She looked for something to do that morning, toying between a visit to the Shaman in his tepee, or art with Lucinda in the conservatory.

Deep in thought, Melissa didn't notice a stranger appear at the door.

On the other side of the room, Bill was eating a slice of toast, relieved that the starchy substance had calmed his stomach. He looked up and recognised the man from the car park. Bill watched him walk across the room and stop when he reached Melissa's table.

'Good morning, darling,' Malcolm Mercer said. 'There you are. I've found you at last.'

Bill saw the colour drain from Melissa's face and her pen dropped to the floor.

'Malcolm!' she gasped.

Malcolm pulled out a chair and made himself comfortable. Crossing his legs, he clicked his fingers to summon a waiter. 'More coffee over here,' he said as he stared at Melissa.

From his corner table, Bill watched as the waiter bought a fresh cup to Melissa's table and began to pour.

'This seems like a quaint place,' Malcolm said. 'A bit off the beaten track, but that's probably why you chose it.'

Melissa's eyes were wide and she covered her mouth with her hand.

Without stopping to consider his actions, Bill stood and carefully edged around the table. There was no one else about and he moved closer to hear what the man was saying. Bill instinctively felt that the visitor was trouble and his calm and menacing demeanour was clearly upsetting Melissa.

'H...how did you find me?' Melissa asked.

'Hardly rocket science, my dear.' Malcolm smiled. 'I have a tracker on your car. It gave me your location immediately.'

'B...but I've been here for days.'

'I thought I'd let you have a little holiday.'

Silence hung thick as their eyes met.

'I'm not coming back,' Melissa said.

'Of course you are, we need to get you to a doctor, you're obviously unwell.' Malcolm picked his coffee up and, with a glacial stare, began to sip.

Suddenly, the French doors were wrenched open from the outside, the frames crashing back on their hinges. Bill's head whipped round and he was astonished to see Alf running into the room. Speeding across the carpet with Ness at his heels, clods of soil scattered from Alf's boots as he hurled himself towards Jo's house and disappeared.

'A resident?' Malcolm raised an eyebrow.

'The handyman,' Melissa replied and winced. Fear was making her stomach cramp and she longed to stand up and run with Alf too. But there was nowhere to go; Malcolm would track her down like a predator hunts its prey.

'Finish your breakfast then we can pack your things.' Malcolm ignored Alf. He tweaked the cuff of his shirt and glanced at a gold Rolex.

'I'm not coming back.' Melissa's voice shook. 'Our marriage is over.'

'That's for me to decide,' Malcolm said. 'Now be a good girl and get your things.'

Malcolm drained his coffee, stood up, and reached out and grabbed her arm.

'No!' Melissa shouted, and as she pulled away her chair crashed against the wall. Gripping the table to steady herself, crockery clattered to the floor. But Malcolm held on, his fingers like a vice on her soft pale skin.

Bill was horrified by the unfolding scene and leapt forward. Without stopping to consider his actions, he ran across the dining room and forced himself between Malcolm and Melissa.

'Oh no, you don't!' Bill cried out and he lunged, surprising Malcolm.

'What the hell?' Malcolm yelled, as Bill grabbed his arm and twisted it painfully back.

Melissa slumped and stared at the grappling men.

At that moment, Alf reappeared. In his hands, wrapped in a towel, lay a limp and prostrate Teddy.

Bunty and Ness stood alongside and Alf raised his bushy eyebrows as he took in the scene.

Suddenly, Hattie, who was bustling past in her haste to get the puppy to the vet, stopped at the dining room door. Dressed in a novelty woolly onesie and resembling an over-large sheep, she'd heard the commotion too.

'What the hell is going on?' Hattie asked, as Bill, crunching china underfoot, clung onto Malcolm.

'It's Malcolm,' Melissa said and she rubbed her arm. 'He wants me to go with him.'

'Do you want to?'

'Never!'

'Then I suggest that Bill releases Malcolm, so that he can be on his way.'

'Who the hell are you, to interfere with my wife's decision?' Malcolm said. Angrily, he pushed Bill away and straightened his jacket. 'This place is a mad house.'

'Just one moment.' Hattie tossed a bunch of keys at Alf and held up her hand. 'Alf, start my car and get the dogs settled, so we can get off to the vet as fast as possible. I'll be along shortly.'

Reaching into a pocket, Hattie pulled out her mobile. She scrolled through the contact list and tapped a number, then, tugging on a lopsided woollen ear, removed the hood of her onesie.

'Sergeant Knowles?' Hattie said when the phone was answered. 'We have a domestic incident at Hotel Boomerville. I've just witnessed physical abuse against one of our residents and require your immediate attendance.'

Very calmly, Hattie replaced the phone in her pocket.

'What the devil do you think you're doing?' Malcolm raised his eyebrows as beads of sweat broke out on his brow. 'You've just made that up, you didn't see a thing.'

'No, but I did.' Bill stepped forward and puffed out his chest.

'What?' Malcolm asked, incredulously. '*You* assaulted me!' He rubbed at his arm in protest.

'Now, I suggest that you get on your way.' Hattie fiddled with her zip and wished she'd had time to put a bra on. 'Or if you prefer, stay here and be arrested.'

'You're all quite mad.' Malcolm shook his head and turned to his wife. 'Melissa, I'll give you twenty-four hours to come home. I'm sure you know that if you don't, I'll find you, wherever you end up.' Turning to Bill, Malcolm pushed him aside. 'Get out of my way, you ugly little arsehole.'

Bill took a swipe but Malcolm was too fast and Bill fell onto the table.

Hattie put her arm around Melissa and together they watched Malcolm stride out of the dining room. He didn't look back.

Melissa was worryingly pale and Bill was red in the face from his exertions.

'Captain Bradbury,' Hattie said, 'I'm leaving you in charge of this lady, stay with her. I don't think that monster will be back but Sergeant Knowles is on his way, just in case.'

'Where are you going?' Bill asked.

'I have a very poorly puppy to save.'

'Not Teddy, surely?' Melissa cried out. 'Not poor little Teddy?'

'Aye, he's got a bad bout of the Delhi belly.'

'He's not the only one.' Bill rubbed his stomach.

'I'm coming with you,' Melissa said.

'Then I'm coming too.' Bill looked at Melissa. 'To protect you.'

'Oh, bloody hell.' Hattie shook her head as she realised that the rescue party had swelled. 'Everyone in my car and let's hope we're not too late!'

13

It had been a week since Pete had broken the news that their romance was over and, to stop herself from dwelling on the pain of rejection, Jo was hard at work. The cobwebs were flying at Flatterly Manor and with housekeeping staff recruited, the old place was undergoing a shake up as room by room, spring cleaning took place. To Jo's relief, James had agreed to stay on for two months while his employer, Long Tom, was on a tour of the Far East to promote a new album. Jo found that she now had a payroll to fund. James didn't come cheap and together with the new housekeeper, who'd worked at Flatterly Manor in the past, and the gardening staff, the hours already added up.

Jo sat at a desk in the uninviting study. It had little furniture and the heavy floor length curtains brushed over a polished wood floor. The room wouldn't be used by guests and was last on the list for refurbishment. Jo longed to have her comfy old rocker nestled by the fireplace, with Bunty curled on her blanket alongside. She thought of the shabby chair, where Hattie had flopped out at the end of the day with a glass of gin as they plotted and made plans. Since she'd been in Ireland, Jo missed her friend and wished that Hattie was beside her. Two heads were so much better than one. But at least Jo had James and he was proving invaluable as he set about interviewing and employing staff and supervising the preparations for paying guests.

As Jo made notes, she silently thanked her predecessor, Hilary, who'd restored the house when she married Long Tom, and ensured that facilities included an ultra-modern kitchen capable of catering for big numbers. All sixteen guest bedrooms had their own bathrooms and although fire regulations were in the process of being upgraded, the fundamentals were in place.

Studying the list on her notepad, Jo ticked off some of the tasks. She'd made a plan for the countdown to opening and was working her way through it. New mattresses were being delivered today and a laundry service was in place. Additional crockery, cutlery, linens, bathroom essentials and glassware, suitable for hotel use, were also on the way and supplier accounts had been set up.

A mower could be heard in the garden and Jo looked out of the window to see Declan, the gardener, walking purposefully up and down the lawn. His thick sandy hair was gathered in a pony tail and well-muscled forearms gripped the mower. Grass clippings billowed as he trudged on, determination set in the lines of his chiselled face.

Declan was cousin to Finbar and lived in Kindale.

Finbar had assured Jo that Declan Murphy was to gardening what Gordon Ramsey was to cooking and the estate would be fit for public tours in no time at all.

Jo thought it was a tall order but on Finbar's recommendation, she'd employed Declan on the spot. Aware that the garden was the first thing a guest would see, Declan had said that, together with his twin sons, they'd soon have things tidied up.

Finbar assured Jo that there was a plentiful supply of Murphys lined up to step into the vacant positions in the kitchen and dining room too.

'Might as well keep it in the family,' Finbar said as his nephew, a chef, came forward. A talented lad, with excellent references, who'd trained in the best restaurants in Ireland, Connor Murphy had recently returned from a stint at a Michelin-starred establishment in London. His family lived on the other side of Ballymegille and he'd told Jo that the position at Flatterly Manor was a great opportunity; he'd make it his duty to create a fine restaurant that would attract folk from miles around.

Having sampled Connor's signature dishes, Jo was impressed.

James came into the study. 'I thought you might like some refreshment, Chef is baking,' he said and placed a tray down before leaving the room.

Jo stared at the buttered scone and pushed the plate to one side. She wasn't hungry.

Staring out of the window, Jo fiddled with her pen. She found it hard not to think about Pete, who invaded her thoughts when she least expected him to.

She'd heard nothing from him.

Not a word nor a call. He'd dropped her like a stone and Jo felt devastated that after all this time, their relationship meant so little. Pete had moved on. As hard as she tried not to think about him, her heart ached and there was a knot in her stomach that wouldn't go away. Jo was angry with Pete for depriving her of the pleasure she should be feeling as she set up her new business. Keeping busy was crucial for it stopped the emotional clock, but when Jo lay awake in the early hours, she found herself sobbing into her pillow and longed for the comfort of his embrace and his voice telling her that it was all a mistake. Pride stopped her from phoning, even though she yearned to hear his voice. It was over and now she was on her own again.

The phone rang, rousing Jo from her thoughts and she saw that it was Hattie's number.

'Hello,' Jo said. 'I'm glad it's you, I could do with a chat.'

~

HATTIE PUT THE PHONE DOWN. She sat at the reception desk in the hotel and frowned. Jo was still in a bad place emotionally and as flippant as Hattie might be about picking yourself up and moving on, she knew that only time would heal the wounds of Jo's broken relationship.

Time and perhaps a new romance?

Hattie thought it unlikely that her friend would find a new lover so soon after Pete had packed up and pissed off, but she felt sure that there would be someone in Ireland willing to oblige and it would probably do Jo good. If only Long Tom was in the vicinity. A few notes strummed on his aged guitar and a couple of bars of a love song crooning in her ear and Pete would be a distant memory. Not that Jo would recognise romance, and if Cupid shot an arrow directly into her heart, she'd reach for an indigestion tablet. Her friend was drowning in a river of grief and it was one that looked set to flow for some time.

Thank goodness Teddy hadn't been mentioned. News of the little dog nearly slipping into permanent oblivion might have had Jo heading back to Cumbria. Fortunately, after two days on a saline drip and more antibiotics, the puppy had pulled through. Teddy was back in Bunty's box and faring well as he snuggled up to his older companion.

Unlike Melissa, who was proving to be an ongoing problem and Hattie wasn't sure what to do about her. Melissa had gone into meltdown following Malcolm's visit and hardly ventured out of her room. Audrey and the Babes had been supportive, when news of the domestic upset rippled through the airwaves at Boomerville and, with encouragement, Melissa had ventured into the pool. But it was her only daily excursion and after swimming in silence for an hour or so, she would return to the hotel and take meals in her room. Hattie wanted to wrench Melissa out of her self-imposed exile and thrust her onto some courses, but Melissa was not to be moved. Malcolm had left instruction that he'd had to return to Spain and would pick up her account for the time being.

It was stalemate and Hattie didn't know how it would end.

As she pondered the problem, Hattie's nose began to twitch. A waft of spicy perfume was drifting down the hallway and she leaned over the reception desk to see Lucinda, draped in meters of white cheesecloth from head to toe. The artist was heading Hattie's way and though it was tempting to hide under the counter,

Hattie called out, 'Good morning, Lucinda. Are you all set for this evening's session?'

'The class is full,' Lucinda replied, 'and we'll need blankets with our easels. I want my artists to be warm as the wind of creativity wraps around them.'

'Aye, all sorted,' Hattie said.

The wind that was forecast to whip down off the fells that evening looked set to be gale force and Hattie thought that it would take more than a few old travel rugs to keep Lucinda's class from catching severe hyperthermia, as they attempted to capture a Westmarland sunset. She'd get Alf to set things up in the meadow, including flasks heavily laced with brandy. The Shaman had been instructed to have a fire going outside his tepee, and those not carried away by creativity could warm their digits and drink themselves doolally.

'Leave it all to me,' Hattie said as she followed Lucinda through the bar and into the conservatory.

Tall and aloof and shrouded in fabric as transparent as the sunbeams that poured through the conservatory windows, Lucinda stepped out of the door. She sailed past Audrey and the Boomerville Babes, who were trudging across the patio, returning from the pool.

'Off to knock up another masterpiece?' Audrey called out. 'There's always room for another Babe in the team if you're not too busy painting; we've got a spare cozzie and cap, if you change your mind.'

Lucinda stopped and reached into a pocket for a cigarette. She placed it in a holder and lit up, puffing smoke rings over Audrey's head.

'She can't swim,' Hattie said as Audrey joined her. She thought back to the perilous night when heavy rains had devastated Marland and the hotel became flooded. Lucinda had been rescued by the Shaman in his paddle boat.

'Neither could most of the gang when we started, but an hour or two in the pool and her confidence would build.'

Lucinda didn't need a confidence boost, Hattie thought, in fact there was very little that Lucinda appeared to need at all, now that she'd settled comfortably into life at Boomerville. Cosied up for most of her time in a room above the studios with Paul, the pottery teacher, Lucinda had, for the time being, found her spiritual home. Hattie suspected that nothing would shake her out of it.

'Now here's someone who does need a bit of confidence,' Audrey whispered and held up a hand to wave to Melissa.

Hattie sighed. Melissa's face, devoid of makeup, appeared tense. With her hair scraped back into a ponytail, her skin was taut and pale.

'Hello,' Audrey said and she wrapped a protective arm around her new protégée. 'I've a new routine that will take a bit of mastering, perhaps you might be persuaded to join us tomorrow?'

Walking away, Hattie thought that Audrey hadn't a hope in hell of achieving that particular miracle and had no doubt that Melissa would swim alone for an hour then return to her room.

Hattie's tummy was rumbling and she licked her lips. With any luck, there might be a bit of breakfast still on the go.

14

At Flatterley Manor, Jo sat at the leather-topped desk in reception and studied a computer screen. The new systems were up and running and security cameras had been installed around the hotel. Jo gazed at images that included the garden, grounds and reception areas and thought that it was rather high tech and unnecessary.

But Hattie had talked her into it.

Jo thought that Hattie's love of snooping and seeing what everyone was up to overtook her concern for security. She imagined Hattie enjoying the footage from the comfort of an armchair, with a gin in one hand and plate of nibbles in the other.

A notepad lay on the desk and Jo began to scribble. She wondered whether to change the name of the manor to reflect her business. In Cumbria, Kirkton House had become Hotel Boomerville but would the name work in Ireland? Jo doodled on her pad and formed the words, *Boomerville Manor* across the top of the page.

She stared at the script and smiled. The name worked well.

Turning the page, Jo considered courses. She needed to think outside the box and come up with new ideas for Ireland. She began to make a list.

Self-Defence
Public Speaking
Singing
Gardening
Life Coaching
Cookery

Diverse courses at each destination might encourage guests to travel from one Boomerville to another, thus increasing bookings and spreading the word.

Cookery was always popular and here, so close to the town of Kindale, the coast was part of the Wild Atlantic Way on the West Cork food trail. She'd spoken to Chef Connor and he was busy putting together ideas for afternoon classes that included fresh fish and locally sourced ingredients. The guests could learn how to prepare and cook dishes, then enjoy the fruits of their labour at dinner.

The newly formed in-house team could contribute too. Declan would host gardening to coincide with the regeneration of the grounds and Finbar might take a singing class in the music room, which had wonderful acoustics and was an ideal venue. As an after dinner speaker at events for the Institute of Professional Butlers, James had volunteered to tutor public speaking, a skill many boomers might utilise.

Jo had set an opening date for early June and would begin with a weekend of taster sessions. This would be marketed on the current mailing list to regular

Boomerville guests. The Manor website and social media accounts were ready to roll out and she would also advertise within the Kindale and Cork area. They'd have an official opening day and invite local people.

Engrossed in her plans, Jo didn't notice Finbar slip through the front door and make his way across the hallway.

'May God bless you, on this beautiful morning,' he said.

'Hello, Finbar.' Jo pushed her notepad to one side. 'I'm glad you're here, I've something to ask you.'

Grabbing a chair, Finbar straddled the seat and gazed at Jo. 'May the most you wish for be the least you get,' he said.

'Er, thank you.'

Finbar's eyes twinkled, disarming Jo, reminding her of the captivating colour of emeralds, flecked with strands of gold.

'And what is your question?'

'Do you think you could run a singing class.'

'At Flatterley Manor?'

'Yes, although I've renamed it Boomerville Manor.'

''Tis a grand name.'

'I thought you could use the music room.'

'The music room?' Finbar stood and pushed the chair to one side. 'You want me to hold singing classes in the music room?'

'It seems an ideal place.'

'The music room?' Finbar repeated with eyes wide.

'Well, the acoustics are good in there and might inspire your students.' Jo wondered if she'd made a mistake.

'My God, Jo, there is nothing in the world that I

would like more!' Finbar rushed over and pulled Jo to her feet. 'Imagine! Singing in the room where the great Long Tom Hendry composed some of his finest songs.'

'I hadn't thought about it like that.'

'I'll find new talent and roll it out.' Finbar grabbed Jo's hands. 'I could become an agent sending singers all over the world.'

'Possibly not to begin with.' Jo admired his enthusiasm but visualised her elderly guests forming nothing more taxing than a Can't Sing Choir. 'But feel free to use the music room whenever you like, to practice and put sessions together.'

Finbar's voice softened. 'It will be my honour to perform this service for you,' he said, 'and in tribute to the great man himself, we'll sing songs by Long Tom too.'

'Let's keep it varied,' Jo said, visualizing her boomers bumping and grinding to the reggae or rock versions of Long Tom's hits. It might put a few hips and knees out of action and her public liability insurance was agonisingly expensive. 'I'll leave it all in your capable hands,' she said.

'You won't regret it.' Finbar beamed. 'When will the manor open?'

'I've a date in mind for the middle of June, perhaps with a fete on opening day.'

'That will be grand.'

'It's only a few weeks away and there's a lot to be done.'

'It's not a fish until it's on the bank, but we'll have all hands on the deck.'

'Yes, quite,' Jo replied. 'Let's find James and make

plans.' She picked up the phone and in moments her temporary manager appeared.

'Ah, James,' Jo said. 'Finbar and I are discussing the opening and we need your input.'

'It will be my pleasure,' James said and with their enthusiastic brains, Jo soon formed an action plan to be carried out in the run-up to the opening.

Boomerville Manor was taking shape.

15

Like a tide that doesn't stop, spring pushed April into May and occasional damp and misty mornings became warm and sunny days. Plants burst through the herbaceous borders at Hotel Boomerville and branches of evergreen vines sprouted with buds, as they began their summer ascent over the walls of the enclosed garden.

Sprawled on the lawn, on a bright afternoon, Bunty thumped her tail from side to side, while Teddy tossed a ball in the air, teasing the older dog into play.

On a bench by the pond, Bill watched the puppy wriggling and jumping until finally, spurred into movement, Bunty chased the terrier up the steps to disappear into the meadow. Looking up at the sky, Bill saw birds circling. A swallow swooped down to the water and in one graceful movement, lunged at an insect then soared away.

Much to his surprise, Bill had discovered that he enjoyed being at Boomerville. He even liked Lucinda's painting class and having endured the outdoor session at dusk, where he'd been frozen to the bone despite layers of blankets and buckets of brandy, Bill had been secretly delighted by his effort. His finished work, entitled "A Cumbrian Sunset", took pride of place in the little gallery in the courtyard. Locals and tourists were frequent visitors and paintings, pottery and jewellery, produced by the Boomers, were available to purchase. Bill's painting had been replicated into postcards and notelets and he was as proud as punch that sales had been good.

Lucinda commented that Bill had a talent that could be nurtured with regular instruction. Bill had an inkling that Lucinda might be stringing him along to keep bums on seats, where numbers were sporadic, depending on how many pupils she'd offended that week. But he found that he enjoyed painting; his work was passable and he wanted to do more.

Bill had been at Boomerville for far longer than he'd originally intended. Easter weekend had come and gone and as days turned into weeks, he found that he'd settled into a routine. For the first time in his life, he felt a sense of contentment.

You're going soft; this fancy lifestyle is costing too much!

His mother's nagging was still a constant companion, but Bill didn't care. He'd no desire to return to the gloomy depths of the old Victorian villa, where the ghosts of his parents penetrated every dark nook and cranny. At Hotel Boomerville he'd found a new confidence which, despite his initial reserve, had come on leaps and bounds.

He reached down, picked up a pebble and skimmed it across the pond. Bill thought about Hattie. She was a strong force with persuasion tactics comparable to a military action, and in the early days Bill had been terrified of the manager. But now, with her encouragement, Bill found himself joining in; he liked to be involved and even looked forward to sessions with the Shaman. Following meditation each morning, he would skip out of the tepee with a smile on his face, as he made his way to his next class.

Quiz nights were Bill's favourite part of the week and he was secretly thrilled that whatever team he captained, they were on a winning roll. The prize money was celebrated with several rounds of drinks and it was a tipsy Captain Bradley who staggered happily back from the pub, arms linked with his team members.

As he settled his account each week, Bill was aware that this lifestyle was costing a bomb. He'd already decided that he was going to sell the villa and downsize. It would be good to get away from the memories that lingered in the foreboding Victorian walls that had haunted him for most of his miserable life. His new life was presenting opportunities he'd never dreamed of and Bill was eager to learn more.

But something else had happened too.

For the first time in his life, Bill had feelings of a romantic nature and was drawn to Melissa. He knew that a woman like that would never look in his direction, but there were occasions when their time at Boomerville coincided and it was with trepidation and a brave heart that he sought her company.

Secretly, Bill stalked Melissa and knew her routine. She'd rarely ventured out of her room since her husband had turned up at the hotel, but Bill knew that Melissa allowed herself an hour in the pool each day and occasionally took the dogs for a walk. Now, he deliberately placed himself in situations where their paths would collide and loitered on the off-chance of catching a few moments in her company.

He wondered about Melissa's marriage. To his knowledge, Malcolm hadn't appeared again and Bill hoped that the bullying man had given up the chase. Melissa had extended her stay too; perhaps the relationship *was* over? He wished he had the courage to find out and considered asking Hattie, for Hattie knew what everyone was doing before they knew themselves.

Footsteps crunched on the gravel and he looked up. Melissa was heading towards him.

Bill unbuttoned the top of his shirt and scraped a hand through his hair as Bunty and Teddy danced around, ecstatic to have found their walking partner.

'Are you going for a walk?' he asked.

'No, I'm tired,' Melissa said. 'I've been swimming.' Reaching down, she stroked Teddy as he chewed at her hand.

'The dogs will be disappointed.'

'Maybe later.'

Melissa carried on walking and headed for the hotel. Bill longed to follow to ask if she might join him for a coffee but his feet were set in stone.

Never in a month of Sundays, Bill Bradley, a taunting voice cackled. *You're punching way above your weight!*

As Melissa wandered away, Bill stared at her slim and willowy figure and, with a heavy heart, knew that the ghost of his mother was, as always, right.

Hattie sat on the window seat in Jo's bedroom and thought about her lunch. She was hungry as she stared out at the garden, where Alf was loitering by the courtyard gate. Hattie could see Ness, the scruffy mongrel, asleep at his feet.

Alf had a spade in one hand and a roll-up in the other and as he leant on the wrought ironwork, he turned his face to the sun and closed his eyes.

'Oi! Alan Titchmarch!' Hattie knocked on the glass and yelled through the open window. 'There's work to be done!'

'Keep your hair on,' Alf yelled back. Dragging deeply on the butt, he flicked it into a border. With a grin and a half salute, Alf turned to open the gate and Ness, sensing activity, sprung to her feet and followed, her tail wagging in time to Alf's rolling gait.

Hattie watched the handyman and hoped that he was heading for the herb garden, which was in dire need of a good sort out. Hattie knew that the Shaman dipped his fingers into the precious supplies and she'd also noticed some very healthy plants in the greenhouse that the Shaman was cultivating. It wasn't rocket science to work out what they might be, but the Shaman's classes were a sell-out and whatever aids he used to brighten up the lives of the old codgers, she decided to leave well alone. She wondered if Alf had made any progress with the repairs to her home in Marland and decided that she'd chase him for an update on the builders later that morning. Hattie wasn't in a hurry to move back but it would be good to have her house straight again.

A movement on the other side of the croquet lawn caught Hattie's attention and she saw Bill by the pond.

Melissa appeared to be walking away. Bill lowered his head and Hattie saw his shoulders droop as he slumped onto a bench.

Suddenly, the penny dropped and Hattie nodded as she thought about Bill's body language whenever he was in Melissa's company. Initially, Hattie had thought his change was down to settling into the Boomerville way of life, but, by the look of things, their quiz captain had a crush.

Who would have known that the rude and introverted man that had arrived on Boomerville's doorstep a few weeks ago would come out of his shell so much? The Shaman was obviously working his magic and whatever sticks and herbs he was shaking at Bill during their morning meditation sessions, they were clearly hitting the spot. The man had mellowed beyond recognition, but love was cruel and in Bill's case, unrequited.

Hattie had a feeling that there may be trouble ahead.

A rumbling tummy reminded Hattie that it was time for lunch. As she made her way to the kitchen Hattie thought about Melissa, who, unlike Bill, seemed to be making no progress whatsoever and spent her days holed up in her room, or at the pool, with only occasional trips to the restaurant when Hattie insisted that she dine amongst others and not on her own. There was nothing Hattie could do to peel the guest away from a small corner table but at least it was better than a room service tray.

Thank goodness that brute of a husband hadn't turned up again. Malcolm was menacing and Hattie didn't fancy another encounter. He paid Melissa's hotel bill each week but Hattie had a feeling that this wouldn't continue. Perhaps Malcolm was keen to keep Melissa somewhere he could keep tabs on her?

She reached for a loaf of bread and cut a wedge, then sliced cheese and a tomato and made a sandwich. As she ate, she decided that it was time she had a word with Melissa and stirred her out of her lethargy. The woman needed a change to get back in the land of the living. This was one boomer who wasn't coming out of their comfort zone under Jo's carefully planned regime.

Hattie finished her snack and yawned.

She was tired after a late night. One of the guests had celebrated a birthday and together with a group who attended regular sessions with the Shaman, they'd partied hard. Elderly hips had swung and arthritic legs had danced like demons around his tepee, under the light of the moon and a roaring camp fire. It had taken Hattie several attempts to insist that they totter off to bed in the early hours and she knew that there'd been several guests on the missing list that morning.

Hattie had also caught up with Jo and heard about progress in Ireland. Her mind spun as she absorbed the plans that were taking shape. The opening event was fast approaching. It looked set to be a grand affair and Jo insisted that Hattie join them. Needing no encouragement, Hattie had agreed; she'd swim to Ireland if she had to, for it was a shindig not to be missed and she'd already worked out staff rotas to cover her absence.

But now it was time to get back to work.

Hattie hurried through the house. As she skipped down the stairs at the back of the hotel she bumped into Melissa. 'Ah, just the woman,' Hattie said. 'I want to have a word with you.'

Melissa shrank back. She tried to move away but

Hattie blocked the doorway. Taking her arm, Hattie steered Melissa into the dining room and sat them both at a corner table.

'We'll be nice and comfortable here. I expect you're hungry after your swim.' Hattie nodded to a passing waiter. 'A club sandwich and some coffee, please.'

'I'm not hungry,' Melissa said and gripped her bag to her knee. 'My towel is wet and I need to change.'

'Plenty of time for that.' Hattie took the bag and hooked it over the back of her chair. 'You look like a film star in that lovely leisure suit.'

'Hardly,' Melissa said and touched nervously at the soft velour jacket.

'Oh, I think you catch a fair bit of attention and pink suits your complexion.'

'I don't know what you mean.'

'Many a man would be happy to do a few lengths alongside you in the pool.' An uncomfortable image of Bill in speedos flashed through Hattie's mind.

Coffee arrived and Hattie poured. 'Now,' she began, 'what are we going to do about Malcolm?'

Melissa flinched and stared at Hattie.

'He's paying your bills but I don't think he's going to go away.'

'I keep thinking he's going to walk through the door and drag me back to Cheshire.'

'That's not going to happen while you're under our roof.' Hattie patted Melissa's hand. 'But you're not making any progress; you haven't joined in with any classes and the whole point of Boomerville is to expand your mind and get you to come out of your comfort zone to try new things.'

Melissa hung her head and Hattie had to lean in to hear.

'I'm scared,' Melissa whispered. 'I think he'll find me wherever I go and I don't see the point of running.'

'Nonsense, you can't let a man ruin your life. Take control. Life's too short.' The food arrived and Hattie pushed a plate in front of Melissa. 'We all have our downs but we climb back up.' She touched Melissa's hand. 'You have everything to live for.'

Melissa stared at the sandwich.

'If you can't find a new lease of life her at Hotel Boomerville, perhaps we should send you over the water to Boomerville Manor. Jo needs some bums in beds.'

'I don't understand.'

'There's a new Boomerville about to open in Southern Ireland, with a grand party, and guests can stay for a long weekend. It would get you away from here for a bit.'

As Melissa digested Hattie's words, her face lit up. 'Do you mean that I could go too?'

'Aye, why not?'

'Oh, I've always wanted to go to Ireland.' Melissa picked up a knife and fork. 'It sounds such a beautiful place and I met lots of Irish people when I worked on the cruise ships; they're so friendly.'

She began to tuck in to her sandwich.

'That's settled then.'

'Are you sure it would be alright?'

'Just so long as there's no nonsense about staying in your room while you're there,' Hattie said. 'There's taster sessions over the weekend and I expect you to join in.'

'Oh, Hattie, I can't wait.'

Hattie watched Melissa munch on the club sandwich. She'd brightened beyond recognition. Perhaps she felt trapped here, Hattie thought, with the menacing shadow of Malcolm hovering like the grim reaper.

Hattie was pleased with her idea and decided to call Jo immediately. Raising her cup, she smiled at Melissa. 'Here's to Ireland,' she said.

16

Malcolm Mercer lay on a lounger by the pool at his luxurious villa in Marbella and thought about his wife, who was still holed up at the hotel in Cumbria.

He glanced at his Rolex. They were an hour ahead in Spain but he knew that Melissa was awake, dressed and about to take her daily swim. He glanced at his phone and read a text message from a staff member who confirmed this. It was useful to have spies wherever he needed them and he knew that Melissa was unaware that she was being watched. The young waiter whom Malcom had approached at Boomerville was keen to trade information and his daily report earnt him more than his weekly salary. It suited Malcolm to know where Melissa was and he was happy to leave her there for the time being. The silly bitch thought that she'd got away from him but no one left Malcolm of their own free will.

When he was ready, he'd make her pay for her attempt to make him look foolish.

Malcolm had spent his childhood in care and his teenage years in various institutions. Systematically bullied throughout the years, as he clawed his way through business, he'd vowed to never let anyone get the better of him again. Drugs had killed his mother, an addict who'd abandoned him as a baby and he'd never known his father.

As the sun seared into his tanned skin, Malcom shrugged and walked over to the side of the pool. Sessions in the gym kept him toned and he knew that he looked good for a middle-aged man. Stretching his muscular body, he dived into the deep blue water.

As he swam, Malcolm thought about Melissa's pale skin and how much he enjoyed beating his fists into it. There was a time when he'd stroked it with passion, but his business was in trouble and without the buzz of success, she was an easy target for his frustration. He felt a ripple of pure pleasure when his rage exploded and she quivered before him.

Pleasure that he'd previously felt when sealing a high-risk deal.

Malcolm turned and broke into a backstroke, squinting his eyes against the sun. As he swam, he had much on his mind. Business deals had become difficult and it was taking all his expertise to keep things stable.

But his thoughts soon strayed back to his wife.

It seemed an age since he'd met Melissa in a nightclub on the Costa del Sol. She was fresh, beautiful and looked like a model, her legs long and her body shapely. When she sang, she had the voice of an angel and her vulnerability had captured not only his attention but the eye of every man in the room. When she'd stepped off the stage, Malcolm had determined to make her his own and had swept Melissa off her feet. Several romantic encounters later and it took little persuasion to encourage her to give up her seasonal cabaret job and stints on cruise ships. In a few short weeks, Malcolm had asked Melissa to marry him and she'd readily accepted his proposal.

Malcolm moved through the water with ease. He could almost see Melissa sitting on the steps, her toes splashing water as he swam and her hair a golden halo against the Mediterranean sun. With a smile full of love, she watched her new husband in their pool. He'd been on his own for more than a year when they met and all traces of his first wife, Allegra, had been removed from the villa. He'd let Melissa spruce the place up and add new furnishings, for she'd a good eye for décor and had created inviting homes, both in Spain and Cheshire.

But as he turned and began a crawl, a ghost-like apparition of Allegra had taken Melissa's place on the steps, her dark eyes taunting as she tossed her head back and her thick black hair fell across her Spanish skin. Malcolm felt as though Allegra was with him in the pool as her long shapely legs began to descend into the water, her beautiful body submerged, hair momentarily floating on the surface. He pounded the water, breathing heavily, pushing his body until his muscles ached and the vision faded.

Allegra had been killed in a freak accident some distance from their home, near Elviria, on the A7 road. She'd been driving from Marbella to Malaga, alone at the wheel of her luxury sports car. Mystified, the Spanish police found no explanation as to why she'd spun off the road and careered down an embankment, on a sunny spring day, when driving conditions were perfect. The car was so badly damaged that a fire crew and paramedics struggled to reach Allegra, where they discovered horrific injuries and she was pronounced dead at the scene of the crash. Following his mother's death, their son, Giles, went completely off the rails and Malcolm needed a firm hand to keep him occupied in the family business in the years that followed.

Malcolm reached the steps and climbed out of the water. He picked up a towel and put thoughts of Allegra out of his mind. He knew that at some point soon, he would need to deal with Melissa. The silly cow should be grateful to him, not running away to some godforsaken pit to bury herself in the north of England with a bunch of tired old losers, only fit for euthanasia.

A maid appeared with coffee and croissants and placed them on the table. Malcolm finished drying his skin and tossed the towel to one side. He stared out across the misty mountains and let his gaze wander over the hillside, which rolled towards the sparkling expanse of sea, and remembered how much Melissa had enjoyed sitting on this terrace with a glass of chilled wine, telling him how much she loved him and how lucky she was to live in such splendour.

The maid poured coffee and retreated across the patio to her kitchen. Malcolm took a sip of the strong dark liquid and as the bitter caffeine kicked into his veins, he smiled.

Melissa would never see this view again.

~

IN IRELAND, the gates were open and a sign had been erected at the end of the driveway at Boomerville

Manor. Suspended high and swaying gently, solid gold letters stood out against a glossy black background, surrounded by a fancy border. Jo and Finbar admired the handiwork as Declan and his sons hammered the final nails and turned the last screw.

'It's a fine sight,' Finbar said. 'With parties and dancing and things to learn, your boomers will flood through these gates and your coffers will soon overflow with euros.'

'I do hope so,' Jo replied. The budget she'd set aside was diminishing and it was becoming clear that the sooner they got this show on the road and the manor open, the better.

The sign had caught the attention of several passing vehicles and local motorists stepped out of their vehicles, curiosity piqued, to greet Finbar and enquire what all the fuss was about. A tractor too had pulled up and now blocked the road. The driver jumped down to slap Finbar on the back and greet Declan and his sons, who'd all stopped work to join in with the craic. Finbar, in full flow, invited everyone to spread the word and bring their family and friends to the grand opening in seven days' time.

Jo decided to leave them to it and eased away. But as she walked back to the manor her mind was preoccupied.

Earlier that morning, Pete had called but she'd been in the shower at the time and had missed him. As Jo listened to his message, she'd felt her blood begin to boil. The arrogant bastard sounded cheery and full of himself. Pete hoped that things were progressing in Ireland and thanked Jo for being so understanding about Amanda. He wanted Jo to know that Amanda had moved in and things were going well. Jo had been inclined to delete the message at that point, but gritting her teeth, she'd continued to listen Pete drone on. He'd arranged to have Harry pick up the belongings she'd left at Pete's home and drop them off with Hattie.

Jo was furious as she pounded across the grass. Pete obviously didn't want a meeting with Hattie and had got Harry to do his dirty work. Nor did he want to run the risk of Jo meeting up with Saint Amanda. He was covering his back, by arranging to get Jo's things out of the way. Well, he could get stuffed. Jo *would* turn up, on the pretext of having left something, and she'd give him a piece of her mind in front of Amanda.

But as she approached the manor, Jo knew in her heart that she wouldn't do anything foolish and make a scene. There was no point. It was over. The only heart that was broken was her own and single-handedly she would pick up the shattered pieces. Pete had moved on and had a new love in his life.

'Have you come to inspect progress?'

Jo looked up to see James at the door. He was smiling and his eyes, grey with flecks of silvery light, were gentle as he stood to one side.

'Yes,' Jo said. 'Have you time for a chat?'

'Of course,' he replied as they stepped into reception and made themselves comfortable on chairs by the desk.

'Have you any idea how many people will turn up for the opening?'

James was working hard on the arrangements but told Jo that so far he had no idea of numbers. On the day, Boomerville Manor would be an open house. They discussed the tours around the reception rooms and bedrooms, which would take place hourly. In the garden, several marquees would be erected for stalls, and James had arranged for a stage to be built.

'Finbar is waiting for confirmation from five local bands who will play during the afternoon and evening and we have two Irish dancing troupes who've agreed to come along too.'

'The locals need to know that they can bring a picnic and enjoy free entertainment.'

'I've added that to the advertisement for the Kindale News.'

'I pray that the weather holds and we're blessed with sunshine; Declan and his sons have worked so hard to prepare the grounds.'

As they both edited and revised their notes, Jo said, 'We're trying to achieve in a few weeks what would normally take months of planning.'

'I'm sure it will all come together perfectly.'

Satisfied that James was up to speed, Jo nodded when he asked if she'd like a cup of tea and as he headed for the kitchen, she flicked the computer on and checked the bookings. All of the sixteen bedrooms were now booked for the opening weekend and several locals, curious to see what was on offer, had reserved tables in the restaurant. A mailshot had been sent to former Boomerville guests and combined with a social media campaign to raise awareness of the new business in Ireland, Jo hoped that in time, rooms and courses would steadily fill.

She noted that Finbar's singing classes were popular and James' public speaking course was also selling, as were Connor's cookery classes. Declan's gardening group seemed to be a hit, much to his delight, for

Declan had dreams of hosting his own horticultural show on RTE, Ireland's national broadcaster.

Jo made a note to check that the dining room had everything necessary to cater for larger numbers. She'd bought extra tables and chairs from an antique dealer in Cork and the eclectic mix of furniture worked well in the lovely panelled room, where French windows surrounded by climbing wisteria cameoed a view of the lake. Scented blooms hung heavily over the terrace and Declan had placed earthenware pots of sweet-smelling flowers beside pretty ironwork tables and chairs.

But best of all was that Hattie would be there too. Jo knew that her friend would enjoy every moment and bring life to the proceedings, as well as being a great support.

A message appeared in Jo's inbox. It was from Hattie, listing her flight time. To Jo's surprise, Hattie was due to arrive later that day.

'Can't hang about any longer,' Hattie had written, 'rotas and the running of things all covered. There's a flight to Cork with my name on it, leaving at lunch time, see yah later.'

Jo's heart leapt, Hattie was on her way! She would have to camp down in the room Jo was using in the manor. A cottage in the grounds, that Jo planned to use for friends and family, hadn't been used for years and was due to be decorated but with time running out, it wouldn't be ready for the opening.

Jo glanced at her watch. There was just time to find a spare bed and move it to her bedroom. It would need making up and she must clear some wardrobe space, for Hattie was sure to arrive with an outfit for every occasion.

'We've an early arrival,' Jo said as James returned with their tea. 'I'll be leaving for Cork airport in a little while; Hattie's on her way.'

'It will be a pleasure to make her acquaintance.'

'I'm not sure that Boomerville Manor is ready for Hattie, so brace yourself, James, because we're about to find out.'

17

Hattie perched on a stool in the departure lounge at Manchester airport and nibbled on a packet of nuts. She licked salt from her lips and reached for the gin and tonic that sat on the bar beside her. An announcement called for the last passengers for Cork to go directly to the departure gate, where their flight was ready to leave.

'Don't want to miss this baby,' Hattie said and smiled at the barman.

'Have a great time,' he replied and scooped her generous tip.

'You can be sure of that.'

Hattie finished her drink and swung her bag over her shoulder. Dressed in a navy jumpsuit and glittery trainers, she began to walk through the terminal.

It was a lovely day and as she waited to board, she looked out of the windows to see sunshine glinting off the smooth metal of the plane on the tarmac outside. She visualised the soft sandy beaches of southern

Ireland and the dramatic coastline, edging the green and lush countryside of Kindale.

This wasn't Hattie's first trip to Ireland.

Many years ago, she'd visited the area around Dublin, to spend time on a farm with a friend, who became more than a friend until his untimely death. You never know what life is going to throw at you, she thought as her ticket was checked; another chapter was about to unfold and Hattie wanted to be along for the ride.

The flight took off on time and as Hattie settle down for the journey that would last just over an hour, she thought about the business she'd left behind. Hotel Boomerville would function while she was away; the staff were efficient and everyone knew what they were doing to ensure the smooth running. Melissa would check out in a few days and head to Ireland too. Hattie hoped that the trip would stir her into making decisions about what to do with the rest of her life and how to break completely away from her bullying husband. Hattie felt sure that they hadn't seen the last of Malcolm, but for now, Melissa was safe.

There had been much interest in the Irish venture. Audrey and the Boomerville Babes wanted to know if the lake was suitable for swimming and Harry was keen to learn if there were many pubs in the area. Alf said he fancied a break and put himself forward as an additional handyman, should the need arise, while Biddu offered to cook an Indian themed evening. Bill was grumpy when he learnt that Melissa was leaving and Hattie wondered if the quiz captain would cancel his booking and head home. Lucinda announced that she was being abandoned and with both Hattie and Jo away, she would need to spend more time with the Shaman to recharge her artistic batteries. Hattie knew that it was Lucinda's way of telling Hattie that she had no intention of running classes in their absence and would be smacked off her face for the foreseeable. Just as well that Hattie had a local artist on standby to replace the tutor.

Hattie was hungry. She ordered a coffee and a bacon roll and as the cabin attendant placed her food on a tray, Hattie's thoughts strayed to Pete and she wondered if Jo was still pining for her lost love. Hattie had asked Harry to drop by Pete's place on the pretext of checking that his friend was well. In truth, Hattie wanted a head's up on Amanda. Was she still amazing after a few days on Pete's muddy old farm? Exactly how good did Jo's replacement look when it came to dealing with damp dogs, muddy wellies and tinkering about with tractors? Hattie hoped it wouldn't last five minutes and Amanda would soon tire of AGA duties, cooking casseroles and the role of country wife, and Pete, when he removed his rose-tinted glasses, would wonder what the hell he had done when he ditched Jo.

Hattie expected a full report from Harry and hoped that she'd hear from him soon.

Harry's first teaching session at the hotel had been a great success. Most of the Boomerville guests had been keen to attend "Personal Protection & Self-Defence" and, going forward, Hattie suggested that Harry added more content on burglar alarms and neighbourhood watch and less martial arts. Jo would be mortified if she knew about the car full of boomers that Hattie had taken to Accident & Emergency in Marland, following the session.

Thankfully no bones were broken and discs had all been manipulated back into place.

The bacon roll was delicious and Hattie licked her lips as she finished her coffee. She looked out of the window as the plane cruised over the Irish Sea, where foam crests danced over the inky surface, and thought that Harry certainly had his uses, both in and out of the bedroom. Hattie was pleased to know that he'd tracked down the tenants who'd wrecked her house. They were living at an address in the north east and Harry's Geordie colleagues were keeping an eye on the new residents of a house in Newcastle and, as a favour for Harry, would personally ensure that any invoices Hattie sent would be delivered by the boys in blue. The damage to her property in Marland plus vet's fees for Teddy had mounted and Hattie wanted the scum bags to pay up.

The flight landed and Hattie disembarked. She found a trolley and collected her luggage then strode out of the terminal and into the arrivals area.

'Hattie, over here!' Jo called out and in moments the two friends were embracing.

'Just look at you, all Irish and countrified,' Hattie said as she stood back and stared at Jo, who was dressed in leather boots, jeans and a Barbour jacket, her chestnut hair scooped under a tweed cap. Jo returned the stare as she took in Hattie's jump suit, unzipped to reveal mounds of cleavage and a wide belt that strained at her shapely waist.

'Let me introduce you to Finbar,' Jo said. 'He's waiting by the car.'

Finbar held up a hand and waved. 'How's it going?' he asked and came forward. 'Welcome to Ireland.'

Hattie noted Finbar's handsome face and fiery green eyes. Magical eyes, Hattie thought in appreciation. 'Jo didn't tell me how attractive her world-famous singer was.'

'Ah, there's lots for you to learn.' Finbar beamed at Hattie's compliment as he packed her bags and guided the women into the vehicle then climbed in behind the wheel. 'We'll begin by teaching you how to drive on the Emerald Isle.' Finbar cranked the gears and hit his foot to the floor. 'Hold on tight,' he called out over his shoulder and in moments, they were careering away from the airport.

'Bloody hell,' Hattie said as she strapped herself in.

'It's only just begun.' Jo gripped the side of her seat. 'But I'm so glad you're here, it wouldn't have been the same without you.'

'Me too,' Hattie said as she braced herself into a bend. 'This is going to be a very special opening.'

～

BILL SAT on his usual bench in the garden at Hotel Boomerville and flicked a stone into the pond. He looked up to see Audrey, who was making her way to the pool, and called out a greeting.

'Why don't you join us?' she asked. 'We could do with a man on the team to assist with the lifts, and the ladies would love it.'

Bill ignored the remark and turned away. The thought of getting into the water with a gaggle of farmers' wives was Bill's idea of hell and he'd no intention of getting involved. If Melissa was a team member, he might reconsider. He'd seen her go to the pool earlier and knew that she'd be doing her daily laps. As Audrey disappeared, Bill stuffed his hands in his pockets and scuffed at the gravel underfoot. He'd heard from the other residents that Melissa was due to check out soon. She was travelling to Ireland to book into the new Boomerville and the thought of never seeing her again dismayed him more than he cared to admit.

A woman like that would never look at you, Bill Bradbury; you'll never have a woman, you're boring and brainless!

With a sigh, he shrugged and looked around to see Alf pottering about on the lawn. He'd laid out a croquet set and now, bent double, carefully placed the hoops in position.

'No classes today?' Alf called out. He straightened up and, reaching for a cigarette from behind his ear, lit up.

'No. I was due to be in metalwork but Lucinda cancelled.'

'Aye, she's taken a few days off.' Alf puffed and blew smoke rings. 'She's in with the Shaman, I hear.' He nodded towards the tepee in the meadow and gave Bill a wink.

'That woman is mad.'

'Oh, aye, barking, there's no doubt of that; she scares the living daylights out of me.'

Ness lay at Alf's feet, her tail thumping on the soft grass. The dog rolled over and he reached down to scratch her belly.

'Are you staying much longer?' Alf asked. 'You're

one of the long-term residents, they should give you a badge.' He chuckled. 'I Survived Boomerville!'

Bill stood up. He wasn't going to sit around here all day and have this damned handyman make fun. 'No,' he said. 'I shall be moving on.'

The conservatory door opened and Bunty and Teddy ran into the garden. The dogs shot across the lawn, tumbling over Ness and making circles around Bill's ankles.

'Bloody animals,' Bill grumbled as Teddy jumped up, but the dogs' attention was diverted and they ran past Bill.

He turned to follow their path and saw that Melissa had appeared and the dogs hurtled towards her. Bill was motionless as he stared. Sunlight kissed her wet hair and she laughed as she leaned down to stroke the playful animals. Bill had the urge to reach out and stroke the damp locks.

'You'll be leaving us, then?' Alf called out to Melissa. 'Moving on to pastures new?'

'I'm going to Ireland,' Melissa said as she scooped Teddy into her arms. 'I can't wait, there's going to be taster sessions for the new classes and trips to restaurants in Kindale.' Melissa ruffled the fur on Teddy's ears and he licked at the skin on her hand.

'Aye, it's a big affair.' Alf nodded. 'Lots of fancy folk from the area for the opening event and music all day long, I hear.'

Bill collapsed back on the bench. His lips were pressed tight as he listed to Alf and Melissa.

'Why don't you come?' Melissa said.

Her face was a picture as she smiled at Alf and Bill

wished that he could paint it. He wished too that he could join in the conversation.

You're nowt, Bill Bradbury, a nothing, an insignificant little man. No one wants anything to do with you!

Bill closed his eyes and thrust his hands over his ears to try and block the sound of his mother's voice.

'Are you alright?'

Bill looked up. Melissa stood before him, concern on her face.

'Yes, fine,' Bill said. 'Just a bit of a headache.'

'Have a game of croquet,' Alf said and thrust out a mallet. 'Why not try something new.'

'Well, perhaps,' Bill stuttered and, summoning up courage, he turned to Melissa. 'Would you join me?'

'Oh no, I'm sorry but I need to dry my hair.'

Deflated, Bill watched Melissa move away, Teddy still in her arms and Bunty padding behind.

Alf placed the mallet with the others, in a neat stack by the bench. 'Another day, old son,' he said.

No one wants you. You're a stupid man if you thought you had any friends.

This time, Bill knew in his heart that his mother was right.

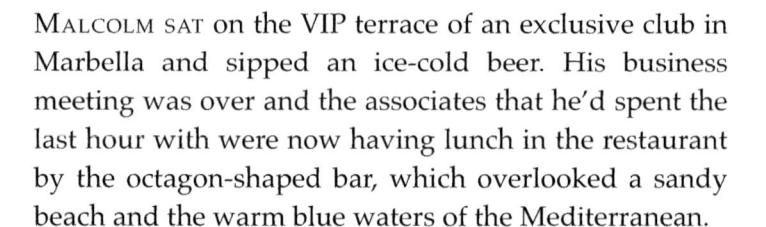

~

MALCOLM SAT on the VIP terrace of an exclusive club in Marbella and sipped an ice-cold beer. His business meeting was over and the associates that he'd spent the last hour with were now having lunch in the restaurant by the octagon-shaped bar, which overlooked a sandy beach and the warm blue waters of the Mediterranean.

Malcolm wasn't hungry. He'd made his excuses and left the other men to wine and dine the afternoon away, in the company of the many models and money-grabbing beauties who strutted around the complex, on the look-out for a lonely millionaire to spend the afternoon with.

He checked his phone for messages.

There was a text from his informant in Cumbria. Melissa had left the pool and returned to her room, where she'd ordered a light lunch. The waiter went on to say that things were changing at the hotel and a group was planning a trip to Ireland. Melissa was going too. Malcolm's wife had arranged to check out in a couple of days.

Malcolm typed a reply. He wanted to know her travelling arrangements, where she was staying and when she was due to arrive. He wasn't going to let her slip away and disappear.

Checking his watch, Malcolm smiled; he had another meeting to go to, this time in one of the secluded cabanas, hidden by a wall of palm trees. It was patrolled by beefy security guards and was discreet amongst a thick hedge of pink hibiscus.

Someone paused on the path and a shadow fell over Malcolm. He looked up to see a woman wearing stilettos and the briefest of bikinis. She was tall, striking and had the looks of Russian royalty and as she removed her designer sunglasses she raised a perfectly-shaped eyebrow, then walked away.

Malcolm allowed a little distance then reached into his pocket until his fingers brushed against a small gold tin. He remembered the woman's words from their last encounter, when her seductive foreign lilt had whispered in his ear, 'Cocaine, my dahling, is a pleasure we must not resist - my sugar rush, my bliss, it makes the perfect kiss.'

He stood, took a last sip of his beer, and followed her to the cabana.

18

The kitchen at Boomerville Manor was buzzing. Chef Connor had his fiery red hair tucked under a colourful bandana as he bent down to reach into an oven for yet another tray of scones. Freshly baked and ready to eat, their surface was golden brown.

Hattie hovered nearby. She held a pot of jam and a knife.

'If you eat any more, there'll be none left for the opening,' Connor said as he slapped the hot scones onto a stainless-steel table and loaded them onto a wire cooling rack.

'You won't miss a couple,' Hattie said and helped herself from the top of the pile. 'There's hundreds stashed in the freezer now.'

Connor raised a muscled arm and loosened the top button of his chef's jacket then took a scone too. Splitting it open with a sharp knife, he took a bite.

'These will be popular on the day, cream teas for everyone.' Hattie licked jam off her lips.

'Move yourself,' Connor said as he finished his scone in two mouthfuls. 'A man has work to do here.' He wiped his brow with a beefy hand and smoothed his palm along the folds of a crisp white apron. Nimble on his feet, despite being a giant of a man, the chef eyeballed Hattie.

'Aye, you've certainly got your work cut out with guests arriving tomorrow and the opening party only two days away.'

Hattie heard the point of the knife being tapped on the table and decided not to push her luck with another scone. She flicked crumbs off her blouse and nodded to the assistant chefs, who were scurrying around the kitchen. The young apprentices were prepping for the workload ahead. With the restaurant and hotel soon to be fully functional, there was much to be done. Hattie decided to leave them to it and pop back a bit later, when Connor had more recipes for her to sample.

As she hurried through the manor, she greeted staff who were busy with final touches. There was a strong smell of beeswax and the furniture shone, cushions were freshly plumped and muted light from table lamps softened the corners of rooms, where curtains hung in generous folds around mullioned windows. Bedrooms were ready with bathrooms gleaming and toiletries, towels and luxuries all in place. Hattie stopped to chat to the florist, who'd arrived with buckets full of flowers and was now creating arrangements throughout the manor.

It was just like old times, Hattie thought, as she went in search of Jo.

Starting a new business was so exciting, but as Hattie reached reception, she wondered where Jo was and, flicking the computer screen to the security camera settings, her eyes scanned the images of the house and grounds. The camera found Jo in the garden, pacing the lawn, clipboard gripped tightly in her hand.

Hattie turned the cameras off and opened the front door to run across the lawn until she came alongside Jo.

'Everything in order?' Hattie asked.

The two women studied the whirl of activity. James was issuing instructions as workmen set up a stage in front of the lake and several marquees had been erected around the lawn.

'It's bedlam,' Jo said. 'Everyone in Ballymegille has their own way of doing things and I may as well throw my lists away.'

Jo's face was flushed and her hair dishevelled, sprouting wildly as she ran her fingers through the thick copper locks. She chewed at her lips as she watched scaffolding being manoeuvred into place, scraping ruts in the lawn as it was unloaded from a truck.

'Declan will be furious when he sees the damage to his garden,' Jo said, her forehead creasing.

'Nonsense, nature soon restores itself,' Hattie replied. 'It all looks very organised to me.'

She waved to James, who returned the greeting as he issued instructions to the stagehands.

'By heck, you picked a good 'un there,' Hattie said.

Tall, handsome and efficient, with the sleeves of his perfectly-ironed shirt rolled to the elbow, James was in his element, at the cutting edge of an event.

'I'm sure that your manager has managed many a celebrity A-list party in his time. Imagine the capers and carry-ons he's witnessed working for the hoi polloi.' Hattie took Jo's arm. 'Let's leave him to it.'

They sat on a bench on the edge of the lawn; shaded by the low hanging branches of a willow tree, it was a perfect spot to observe the preparations.

'I bought you something to eat,' Hattie said, 'get your laughing gear around this.' She reached into a pocket and held out a crumbling scone, sticky with strawberry jam.

Jo stared and pulled a face. 'Where on earth have you dredged that from?'

'Off the cake mountain that Connor's building.'

'I hope the rest is more appetising.' Jo took the scone.

'I think you're starting to panic, but there's no need, we always get there in the end.'

'It's all very well saying that, but I'm absolutely knackered and, on top of everything else, I haven't slept in days.'

'I've slept like a baby.'

'Yes, you have.' Jo rolled her eyes. 'You've snored every night since you arrived. I'm not complaining but I've had to take a quilt and sleep on a sofa in the lounge.'

'You should have given me a poke, that usually calms it down.'

'Hattie, a double decker bus driving over your head wouldn't stop your snores.'

'Aye, well, I've been tired too.'

'I know, don't think I don't notice how hard you've been working, and I do appreciate all your help.'

Hattie's snores created sleepless nights for Jo, which in itself was an ordeal, but even as she settled far away on a sofa, her restless mind still hadn't found the sleep that she yearned for. Persistent thoughts of Pete and his new love played on her mind and time and time again she imagined him with Saint Amanda, hand in hand as they wandered through his garden or sitting together on a wooden seat as they looked out over the Cumbrian fells, arms around each other as the sun set on another happy day. As her wounded pride mixed with anxiety over the opening and everything that had to be done before the guests arrived, Jo was exhausted.

'I must be getting old,' she said. 'I used to be able to exist on very little sleep but right now I feel like I could lie down and not get up for a week.'

'Just a bit of nervous tension.' Hattie picked a crumb of scone from a tooth. 'I'll make you one of my pick-me-ups, that will sort you out.'

'The last time I had one of your potions, I didn't sleep for four days.'

'Then it's time I made you another one.'

Jo closed her eyes. One of Hattie's pick-me-ups was exactly what she needed to keep her going. In the last couple of weeks, the days had flown and with Hattie alongside, they'd burned the candle at both ends, pulling out all the stops to get Boomerville Manor operational.

Soon her dream would be a reality.

'Blimey,' Hattie nudged Jo, 'there's wagon loads of gear heading up the drive.'

They stared as dust swirled under the tyres of the laden vehicles and James directed the convoy across the gravel.

'That will be the carousel, helter-skelter and coconut shy.'

'A fairground.' Hattie clapped her hands.

'I think we've taken on too much,' Jo said as they watched the massive wagons roll across the grass. 'What if no one turns up?'

'Don't be so daft, half the county will be up for this event.' Hattie was confident. 'Live music, open-air bar and free entertainment, what's not to like?'

'Let's hope so; I've overstretched the budget and we can't afford to have a flop.'

'You've got a great team and with the hotel full, everyone is bound to have a good time.'

'Thank God there's plenty of volunteers to help.'

'Good old Finbar.' Hattie smiled.

At Jo's request for help, Finbar had swung into action and performed magic.

His cousin, a person high up on the local council, soon had the paperwork arranged for the event, including licenses, and Finbar's friends in health and safety had sourced a volunteer team to man the grounds, directing the public and checking security. In return they would enjoy free food, music and a day out. His contacts on the committee of the local Round Table had confirmed that they would be able to arrange stalls, offering everything from tombola to home-made cakes, and all proceeds would go to local charities. The local Women's Institute would be on hand to serve scones and tea.

Jo's phone buzzed. She reached into a pocket and stared at a text.

'You're not still mooning over Casanova back in Cumbria, are you?' Hattie asked.

'No, it's the balloon company confirming a time to decorate the marquees.' Jo tapped a reply. 'I'm too busy to think about Pete.'

'Well, you can bet your life he won't be thinking about you and it's no good sitting here, worrying yourself stupid about the opening.' Hattie stood up.

'I can't help but worry.'

'Well, I'm having none of it, so get off your arse.' Hattie tugged Jo to her feet and frog-marched her towards the manor. 'You can sleep for a week when this is all over, but for now you have to make it a success.'

Hattie's enthusiasm was working.

'You're absolutely right, as always.' Jo relaxed her shoulders. 'It's all in the preparation and we *are* well on the way.'

'That's my girl.' Hattie nodded. 'By the way, the florist is here and is working in the lounge; do you want flowers in the bedrooms too?'

'Yes, absolutely. I'll attend to it.'

'Good, and can we go through the final restaurant checks while the staff are setting things up.'

'Let's do it now.'

They'd reached the front door.

'When's Melissa arriving?' Jo asked.

'Tomorrow, she's all packed, I spoke to her earlier.' Hattie began to study her fingernails.

'Have you asked Finbar to meet her flight?'

'Leave it all to me.'

Hattie guided Jo into the manor.

As she waited for Jo to finish her conversation with the florist, Hattie thought about the arrangements that were taking place in Cumbria. Melissa wouldn't be travelling alone. Hattie knew that it wasn't a good time to explain this to Jo as she'd only go off in a panic, worrying about accommodation and extra mouths to feed.

Hattie smiled as she envisaged the excitement at Hotel Boomerville.

'Why are you smiling?' Jo asked.

'Nothing for you to worry your pretty head about.'

Jo looked doubtful. 'I think I will have one of your pick-me-ups,' she said.

'Good idea,' Hattie replied. 'I'll knock up a pitcher of the stuff and have a couple of glasses too.'

∽

MALCOLM SAT at a table on the terrace of his villa, where an umbrella shaded him from the glaring sun. The heat was at full blast and his deeply tanned skin glistened as he lifted a cold beer to his lips. He watched his son, Giles, in the pool. The boy leaned lazily on the tiled edge, waist deep in water and held a mobile phone to his ear. He smiled as he listened to the caller.

Malcolm stared at the boy's naked back, the shoulders hunched, accentuating strong arms and torso, his skin olive and smooth. Giles had a sharp jaw and chin, sculptured cheek bones and cold grey eyes, full of intensity.

He was the image of his mother.

'Giles!' Malcolm called. 'Come over here. I want to talk to you.'

Giles turned. He smirked as he reached for his sunglasses and tipped them above his nose to squint in the direction of his father's voice. Replacing the shades, he turned away and continued his phone conversation.

Malcolm was furious.

Throwing back his chair, he let it crash across the terrace as he stormed over to the pool. 'Speaking to your dealer?' he yelled. He grabbed the phone and tossed it high in the air.

The phone spiralled then dropped like a stone into the pool.

'Don't ignore me!' Malcolm yelled. 'Get the hell out of the water.' He struggled to resist the urge to wrench Giles by the shoulders and drag him across the terrace.

The boy was impossible. Since Allegra's death, he had been uncontrollable and, most worrying of all, seemed oblivious to his father's threats and commands.

'Don't get your blood pressure up,' Giles said as he climbed out of the pool. He stretched then walked slowly to the upturned chair and picked it up. 'What do you want?'

Malcolm took a deep breath. He felt like punching Giles. Or, at the very least, slapping the sneer off his face. But violence had no impact and however much Malcolm threatened, Giles paid little attention.

'I want to talk to you.'

'Oh, yeah? Got a job for me?' Giles sat down and tapped his fingers on the table. 'Am I to be pimping our wares across Spain or doing a Gibraltar trip with a delivery to the UK?'

He glared at his father.

Malcolm paced. Giles was obviously as high as a kite. His eyes were red, the pupils wide and dilated. Cocaine was no longer a recreational drug for his son; the boy was addicted to the deadly white powder and the confidence that it gave him. But this high would be short-lived, and paranoia would soon set in. Malcolm had seen it all before.

He sighed. Giles was no longer safe in the business. He was a loose cannon. There was no room for anyone who didn't have total loyalty to Malcolm. Not even his son. Business was bad enough without the pressure and worry of Giles.

For years, Malcolm had dominated the Costas with his legal and illegal dealings and had made a fortune in the process. His enterprise was the go-to-team for anything not readily available on the open market. A highly profitable drug and gun empire ran alongside his more transparent businesses, of holiday time-shares in Spain and Ireland. But the time-share holdings were drying up. People weren't as naive as they had been in the past and new laws tightening the process had slowed things down. It was getting harder to launder money through that business. Added pressure came in the form of drug barons from Eastern Europe, muscling in on the prime pickings that Malcolm had, at one time, solely enjoyed. These days he was under more pressure than he'd ever experienced and had much to lose.

But Malcolm was a fighter. He'd pulled himself up from the backstreets of Birmingham and wasn't prepared to go back. Whatever the cost, no one stood in his way.

'You're a mess,' Malcolm said. He stood before Giles, his shadow covering the figure sprawled on the chair.

'Who made me like this?'

'You've only yourself to blame.'

'Of course.' Giles wiped a hand across his nose. 'All kids grow up with a mother who is shit-scared of her husband and then mysteriously kills herself.' He laughed as he met Malcolm's angry gaze without fear.

'Your mother's death was a tragic accident.'

'And I had a diet of sweeties that ensured I never felt the heartache, every drug available to dull the pain. Daddy's shop was always open.'

'Not anymore. You've only yourself to blame for your habit, no one forced you.'

'But no one stopped me!' Giles shouted. 'You're a bloody awful father and I wish you were dead!'

Somehow, Malcolm restrained himself. He turned and walked away. As he left, he called out, 'We need to get you in rehab, think about it, you can't carry on this way.'

'The phone is waterproof!' Giles called out. His shoulders shook and he began to laugh.

But the laughter soon turned to tears as his father disappeared into the villa. Anguish flowed out of every pore in his body and Giles slumped painfully to the ground. He gripped the legs of the chair as a violent shaking took over and he wept with grief.

As he had for his beloved mother.

19

Melissa woke early and slid out of bed to draw back the curtains in her room and look out at the view. As dawn rose above the misty fells in the distance and the world came into focus, the sky was filled with soft tones of pink, peach and gold, promising a glorious morning.

She felt excited.

Today was the start of infinite possibilities and as she prepared to leave Hotel Boomerville, she felt that a fresh page might also turn in the story of her life. It was up to her what she wrote on it, and having heard nothing from Malcolm, Melissa felt a glimmer of hope that he would, at long last, leave her alone. As the sky turned to blue and sunshine peeped through silvery swirls of marshmallow cloud, she turned away from the window and made a cup of tea. Sipping the warm, comforting liquid, Melissa determined to stop daydreaming of a life without her husband and make a fresh start.

In a short while, she would embark on a journey to

Southern Ireland. She'd told Hattie that Malcolm wasn't to be billed any further, nor was he to have any forwarding address. He could send someone to collect her car but mustn't be told where she was.

Two letters, that she'd written earlier, lay on her dressing table, both addressed in her neat handwriting. The first, to Malcolm at Pendleton House, explained that she wanted to break all communication and start again on her own. She asked that he no longer contact her, nor try to find her. The second was to Patrick and she'd written lovingly to reassure her son that she was well and to give him her temporary address in Ireland. As Melissa picked the letters up and tucked them in her pocket, she hoped that Malcolm would do as she asked. She planned to stay in Ireland and if she enjoyed her time there and liked the area, she'd look for work and settle down. It didn't matter what she did, she'd happily work in a café or restaurant.

Anything to be free again.

She'd packed the evening before and her cases stood by the door of her bedroom. An outfit for travelling hung in the wardrobe, alongside shoes, handbag and coat. Hattie had kindly helped Melissa deposit her money into a new account and sort out a bank card. She'd make her limited finances stretch while she gained her independence. There was no point in asking Malcolm for a divorce, nor would she expect a settlement. She couldn't bear the thought of any further communication with him but, in time, when he'd calmed down, perhaps they *would* discuss divorce. God willing, he'd remarry and sort out the legalities, for she'd happily agree. But in the meantime, Melissa had letters to post and was about to begin a new adventure.

She couldn't wait.

~

IN THE ROSE ROOM, damask curtains, flowing full-length across a thick-pile carpet, were pulled back to reveal two sets of French doors either side of a marbled fireplace. White roses, arranged in tall vases with long trails of ivy, filled the mantel, their scent heady and strong as warm air breezed across the garden before seeping through open doors and into the room. The tables were neat with crisp white linen and shining silverware and a buffet, heavy with cereals, fruit, crisp bacon, thick sausages, tomatoes, mushrooms and all the components of a hearty feast, was ready for the early risers.

A young waiter stood in the hallway. He rang a gong to announce to the guests that breakfast was now being served and looked up as Melissa appeared.

'Good morning, John,' she said.

'Good morning,' he replied, 'are you joining us for breakfast?'

'Yes, absolutely, I've a long journey today but I'm just going to walk to the shop to post these letters.'

'Can I take them for you?'

'Well, if it's no trouble, that would be very kind.' Melissa reached into her bag and finding a five pound note in her purse, held it out with the letters. 'They need stamps but keep the change.'

John took the money and tucked it in his back pocket. He held the letters and opened the front door. 'Back shortly,' he said and with a smile, strode off to the village shop.

The front door opened almost immediately and Melissa was greeted by Audrey and the Boomerville Babes.

'Ready for the off, old girl?' Audrey said as she beckoned the Babes into the hallway and indicated that they deposit their luggage. Bags of various shapes and age were heaped in a pile as the Babes unburdened themselves.

'Yes, I can't wait,' she said. 'I was about to go for breakfast before we set off.'

'Bloody good idea, we should all fuel up for the journey.' Audrey tucked her arm through Melissa's and with instructions for her gals to follow, led the way.

∽

BILL STOOD in his bedroom and looked around. His cases sat by the door, packed with all the belongings he'd bought with him to Hotel Boomerville and now he wondered if he would ever see this room again.

You're a damn fool, Bill Bradbury! Get yourself off home and take care of the house; it'll go to wrack and ruin if you keep away any longer.

He shook his head to clear his mother's venomous words. Bill had tossed and turned all night as her petulant whine disturbed his sleep and there were times, as the darkened hours dragged, when he'd contemplated heading straight back home when dawn broke. Throughout his life, his mother had been full of malice but recently, her ghostly ranting had stepped up, coinciding with Bill's taste for new experiences, and he felt as though her spirit was with him wherever he went. It was an uncomfortable condition and he wished he could be rid of it.

Deprived of sleep and grumpy, Bill had risen early. He'd soaked in a bath and taken his time as he washed, shaved and readied himself for the day ahead. Dressed in comfortable cords and a short-sleeved shirt, Bill slipped his feet into a pair of trainers and chose a light-weight jacket.

This is your last chance! If you follow your stupid plan you'll soon be broke and homeless!

'Bugger off!' Bill yelled. 'Bugger off, you old crone, I'm going.' His words bounced off the walls and Bill felt a sudden calmness. No voice rang in his ears and no image of his mother's contemptuous face haunted him.

He opened the curtains and looked out.

It was a lovely day, a perfect day for a new adventure. Bill had never had any experiences that he could call an adventure and coming to Boomerville had been an undertaking he'd thought would be short-lived.

But here he was, packed and ready to head off to Ireland!

Bill's decision had been impetuous. When he'd heard that Melissa was leaving and having seen the expression of pity on Alf's face, Bill suddenly found a desire to break out of his crusty old shell. Possibly born out of anger, and fear of missing an opportunity, he'd raced into the hotel and put a call through to Hattie. To his surprise, she'd agreed to his request.

'You'll have to rough it a bit,' she'd said, 'but if you're prepared to muck in, I can sort out a bed.'

Hattie had explained the travelling arrangements and to his delight, Bill realised that the trip wouldn't be as expensive as he'd anticipated. She'd also told him that his car could be safely parked at the back of the hotel, alongside Melissa's, while he was away.

Although the trip to Ireland was a spur of the moment decision, Bill felt guilt at being away from the house where he'd grown up for so long. Determined to make arrangements, he'd put a call through to his mother's solicitor, who had a set of keys to the house, and asked if they could send someone round to make sure that the place hadn't been broken in to. After a lengthy conversation, the solicitor had agreed to Bill's various requests and assured him that everything would be taken care of.

Now, dressed for the journey and ready to depart, Bill found that he was ravenous. He'd settled his account the previous evening and knew that an early breakfast had been arranged. As he stood by his cases and prepared to leave, he closed his eyes, made a crude gesture with his finger and thought of his mother.

'Ireland here I come!'

With a smile, Bill gathered his luggage and set off in search of his breakfast.

~

SITTING at a table beside the buffet table, Audrey and the Babes were tucking in. Melissa sat with them. She'd chosen a bowl of fresh fruit, natural yogurt and a croissant and when Bill came into the room, she looked up. The man seemed self-assured today, as he took a plate and piled it high with bacon, two eggs and a juicy Cumberland sausage.

'Stock up for the journey if you're joining us,' Audrey called out. Her mouth was full of muesli and she flicked stray oats from her lips. 'Room for another one, over here.' She indicated to a place at her table.

Melissa smiled as Bill sat down. 'Are you coming to Ireland too?' she asked.

'Yes, I thought it might make a pleasant change.'

'I'm so excited,' Melissa said as she licked thick creamy yogurt from her spoon. 'I can hardly wait, I've always wanted to go to Ireland. Have you been there?'

Bill found it difficult to concentrate as he watched Melissa. Her tongue was pink and wet as she licked her spoon, savouring each mouthful. Her actions fascinated him.

'No, I haven't. Hattie seems to need a hand for some sort of fete she's organising, so I thought I'd step in and help out.'

'That's very kind of you.'

Melissa touched Bill's hand. An electric shock charged his skin and he felt his face burn. Unable to speak, he kept his head down and chewed robotically.

'Don't forget to pack a snack for the journey, you might need a stomach settler on the crossing.' Audrey spread butter on layers of bread, sandwiching slices of bacon. 'It might be choppy.'

'I need to get my things.' Melissa wiped at her mouth with a napkin, folded it neatly then stood. 'See you shortly.'

Bill watched her walk through the dining room, her neat figure sashaying through the tables. He stared at the napkin, seeing the indent made by her lips, and longed to tuck it in his pocket. Instead, he pushed his plate away and wiped his hands on his trousers, then picked up a croissant and wrapped it in a serviette. Bill had never been on a ferry, nor even a boat, and he wondered if he would feel seasick. Better to be prepared and have something to nibble on, as Audrey had advised.

Leaving the Rose Room, Bill went into the conservatory. In the garden, birds were pecking at seed on a table and swallows, pale against the blue sky, swooped low over the pond. As he watched the early morning activity, Bill felt a moment of panic. What the hell he was doing? But it was too late to change his mind, his bags were packed and he'd settled his room account. He had to check out.

Taking a last look at the garden, Bill turned and wandered through the bar and along the corridor to the front of the hotel, where luggage was stacked in the hall, including his own battered cases.

Alf stood by the door. At his feet, three dogs sat patiently.

'Are you here to wave us off?' Bill asked. He stared at the handyman who was smartly dressed in tweeds and waistcoat, his brogues polished. Bill noted a red silk hankie in the breast pocket of Alf's jacket. Compared to his own casual attire, Bill felt shabby.

'Not exactly,' Alf replied. 'Hattie has given me a job.'

'And what might that be?'

'I'm your tour guide for the duration.' Alf doffed his new cap.

'You're coming to Ireland?'

'At your service.'

'But what about Ness, and Bunty and that little one…Teddy?' Bill nodded towards the dogs who all sat up, tails thumping, at the mention of their names.

'Passports packed, microchipped and ready for the off.' Alf smiled and reached down to cuff the animals' ears. Smartly kitted out in matching fleecy jackets and pristine leather leads, their jewelled collars shone.

'Are they allowed to travel?"

'Aye, lad, 'tha needs to get out more, dogs are touring the world these days.' Alf shook his head. He was surprised that Boomerville's leading quizzer wasn't aware of the regulations required for animals to cross the Irish Sea. Alf personally thought that Hattie was insane to fork out the hefty fees for passports and injections, but she'd been insistent that the dogs came along too.

'Oh, don't they look adorable.' An excited voice could be heard and Melissa appeared. Bill stood back as she leant down to pet the animals. 'Can Teddy sit on my knee?'

'Just make sure he's strapped in,' Alf said and handed Melissa Teddy's lead. 'Do you want to look after Bunty?' Alf raised a bushy eyebrow and nudged Bunty towards Bill.

'Piss off,' Bill mumbled crossly.

Audrey, heading up her well-fed Babes, came storming down the hallway. 'Has our transport arrived?' she asked.

'Aye, it's pulling onto the driveway now.' Alf opened the front door. 'You lasses make yourselves comfortable, leave the cases to me.'

A single decker vintage bus chugged through the gates. It was bright green in colour with gold lettering embellished along the sides, announcing the name, 'William's Luxury Wheels.'

Gravel flew as the driver braked and the vehicle came to a halt.

'Morning Willie,' Alf called out. 'Shall I start packing 'em in?'

Audrey and the Babes had joined Alf on the drive. They waved in front of their faces as smoke, billowing from the ancient exhaust pipe, whirled around the coach.

'Willie's Wheels,' Audrey said, her tone reverent as she watched an elderly gentleman step down from the bus. He was smartly dressed, with a coach driver's hat perched on top of a full head of silver hair. His uniform jacket was embellished with an armoury of medals and badges.

'Audrey, my dear,' Willie said, his eyes half-closed, 'the last time I saw you was…'

'The golf club dance, 1987,' Audrey whispered as she took Willie's hand and climbed aboard the old transport vehicle. 'You took me home.'

'And we didn't surface for three days.' Willie smiled.

Audrey coloured, her cheeks red where fine veins stood out, the blush heating her neck as it spread. 'A long time ago, before I was married.'

'Anytime you want to rekindle the flame…' Willie winked.

Audrey let go of his hand and pushed him away. She glanced around to wave the Babes onto the coach. 'Come on, girls, let's get a good seat.'

The Babes trooped up the steps and spread themselves out, packing hand luggage into overhead storage racks, all in agreement that they were travelling in style.

Melissa let Willie help her too.

'Now, miss, you make yourself comfortable, here, behind me, where you'll have a good view.' Willie produced a travelling rug and tucked it over Melissa's knee. 'The little dog will be cosy on the seat next to you.' Willie placed Teddy on another rug and strapped him in beside Melissa.

Bill stood on the drive and stared at the transport. Surely they weren't going to make a journey of nearly five hundred miles, not including the sea crossing, in this run down old heap?

'A fine sight,' Alf said to Bill. 'She's a T499 with thirty-three seats, built in 1938.'

'She's a death trap.'

'Ran a route through East London, via Aldgate and the city.'

'Became an ambulance during the war.' Willie joined them. He took a cloth from his pocket and gently rubbed the paintwork. 'She worked through the Blitz recovering casualties.'

'Dear God,' Bill said. 'I hope there's no casualties today.'

'Nah, Bessie is as sound as they come.' Willie caressed a silver bumper. 'She ran her final days as a passenger carrier in Staines, before I got my hands on her.'

'What year was that?' Bill asked.

'1956.'

Bill closed his eyes and calculated that even if Willie was a lad when he purchased the coach, their driver for the day was an old man, well in his eighties.

'All aboard Bessie the bus,' Alf called out. He hopped onto the running board then spread himself out on the opposite seat to Melissa, with Bunty and Ness alongside.

As Willie packed their cases into a side compartment, Bill cautiously stepped up. Looking around, he noted that the only spare seats were at the back of the bus and he'd have to run the gauntlet past the Babes to get on and off. Reluctantly, he moved away from Melissa and made his way down the aisle.

Suddenly, a car appeared at the front of the hotel. It skidded to a halt then reversed into a parking space. The driver leapt out.

'Thought I'd missed you!' Harry shouted as he raced around to the trunk and grabbed his bag. 'Didn't fancy the drive all on my own.' He wore an old cable knit sweater, jeans and a battered Barbour jacket and carried a checked scarf. 'Have you got room for a little one?' he asked as he took Willie's hand and shook it.

'Aye, hop aboard,' Wille said and grabbed Harry's bag. 'Hattie said you might be able to make it.'

'Just a moment!'

Heads turned to see Biddu's taxi, hurtling through the gates. Biddu braked heavily and leapt out. He opened a rear door and retrieved a large hamper. 'We don't want anyone feeling hungry on the journey,' Biddu said. 'Hattie told me to make sure you have plenty of grub.' He handed the hamper to Willie, who stored it alongside the cases in the side of the bus, then slammed the cover shut.

'Driver!' Lucinda made a late entrance from the doorway of the hotel. She held a cigarette holder in one hand and an umbrella and carrier bag in the other. A heavy carpet bag hung from her bony shoulders. Blowing smoke rings into the air, she stepped in front of the coach and tapped the bonnet with her umbrella.

Willie, fearful of damage to his paintwork, wobbled

towards her and grabbed the offending object. 'I'll pack that,' he said, 'you climb aboard.'

Lucinda flicked her cigarette out on the drive and eased herself onto the coach. Her carrier bag clinked as she weaved down the aisle and found a place on a seat behind the Babes. Dressed in a thick velvet coat, which she removed and rolled, Lucinda placed the pillow against the window and lay her head on the soft fabric. Closing her eyes, she began to snore.

'Three sheets to the wind already,' Harry said. 'We're in for a rocky ride when she wakes up.'

'Wagons roll,' Willie called out as he slid into the driver's seat and started the engine.

'Chocks away!' the Babes sang out.

Alf reached for a map book. 'Let's hit the highway,' he said.

'Oh, how exciting.' Melissa cuddled up next to Teddy.

Bill was on the back seat and as Willie careered out of the gates and onto the busy road, he was thrown from one side of the coach to the other. 'Bloody hell!' he exclaimed and grappled about for a safety belt. As he fastened it, a voice whispered in his ear.

You're a stupid fool, thinking you can make friends with the likes of these people! And you'll be a sick as a dog crossing the water and wish you'd gone home!

Bill had a feeling that his mother was probably right. An aroma of spicy curry was seeping through the seat cushions and as Bill's stomach heaved, he wondered what the hell Biddu had packed in the hamper, which now lay simmering above the engine of Bessie the bus. God forbid that his Delhi belly return and disgrace him before they'd even got on the motorway. He stared miserably out at the countryside which stretched ahead like a huge quilt of brown and green squares, stitched together with hedgerows, reminding him of the faded old eiderdown on his mother's bed.

The old woman would forever taunt him.

As Bill thought of the long journey ahead and they sped through Cumbria to make their way south into Wales, to Holyhead to catch the ferry to Dublin, Bill felt miserable. He knew that he'd never been a good traveller and would probably be sick all the way.

'Slide along, old son,' Harry called out. 'Alf said there was plenty of room at the back.' He grabbed a seat and plonked himself down.

'If you like white-knuckle rides,' Bill grumbled.

'I've got something here that will ease the journey and steady your nerves.' Harry held up a canvas bag. 'And as I'm off duty, I thought we'd get stuck into a few beers and start the holiday as we mean to go on.' He reached into the bag and produced two cans. 'Got a couple of bottles of the hard stuff too, if you fancy a shot.' Harry grinned and fastened his seat-belt.

'Is someone handing out drinks?' Audrey swivelled round and, seeing Harry about to open a can, she clapped her hands together. 'What a splendid idea.'

The Babes rummaged in their bags and produced an assorted collection of home-made liqueurs and plastic beakers. Bottles of all shapes and sizes, containing sloe gin, damson vodka, blackberry brandy and nettle wine, soon exchanged hands.

'Anyone fancy a sing-song?' Audrey said as she knocked back a damson vodka.

At the front of the bus, Alf spread out his map book. He looked up as Willie cranked through the gears, slowing down to turn off the main road and onto the motorway.

'Stick with my instructions,' Alf said. 'I'll tell thee where to go; it's a long way and these lasses will no doubt want plenty of comfort breaks.' He cocked his head and looked in Willie's rear-view mirror. 'As will the Nolan sisters on the back seat.'

Harry and Bill held a beer in each hand and whisky chasers in the other. Bill, who'd relaxed considerably in the miles covered from Marland to the motorway, took alternate swigs of his drinks. His face beamed as he joined Harry and the Babes in a rousing rendition of "I'm In the Mood for Dancing".

'I hope young Hattie knows what she's in for,' Willie said as he thrust into top gear and perilously changed lanes.

'Aye, no doubt she does,' Alf replied as the coach rocked and the occupants cheered.

20

Across the sea in Ireland, Boomerville Manor was up and running. Earlier that morning, Jo had opened the doors to the public and already interested locals were arriving for coffee and snacks. Smartly attired in a formal suit, James was supervising the staff and there was an air of excitement as he issued instructions in readiness for hotel guests, who would arrive during the course of the afternoon.

In the kitchen, Connor was taking deliveries of fresh produce as his team began to prep food for the day ahead. Rock music played in the background as the commis chefs, with rolled up sleeves, worked in time to the pulsating beat. Housekeeping staff worked their way through each bedroom, applying the finishing touches with baskets of fresh fruit and bowls of carefully arranged flowers. Pillows were plumped and curtains hung neatly as welcome cards were placed alongside county magazines and folders of local information.

Jo was in the garden with Declan and Finbar. With two days to go before the public would descend on the manor for the day, she was concerned that all her preparations were on schedule. With her clipboard gripped tightly, she stared at her list and made copious notes.

'We're on top of it all,' Finbar assured Jo as they watched a truck arrive with portable loos, which were unloaded and placed behind the stage area. 'You've nothing to worry about.'

Jo admired Finbar's optimism but she had her doubts; there was still so much to be done.

She watched Declan, in overalls and wellingtons, stride across the grass to issue instructions to his sons. Jo couldn't tell the twins apart. Tall and strong, they wore identical checked shirts, scruffy jeans and their hair was as thick and sandy as their father's. As one raked gravel on a path and the other trimmed the edges of the lawn with an industrial strimmer, Jo noted that the menacing piece of equipment was almost as large as the operator.

'Don't be holding it at such an angle!' Declan yelled as the strimmer hit the gravel, pebble dashing the rake-holding son.

Jo winced as the twins argued and their father cursed.

'I've sorted the running order for the entertainment,' Finbar said. 'We'll finish the night with the headline act and I'll sing the closing numbers with him.'

'That's a good idea,' Jo said. 'I hope we get enough people here to enjoy it.'

'The place will be packed. Desmond Drecker has a massive following and he'll have all his relatives here too.'

Jo nodded as Finbar highlighted the merits of Desmond Drecker, a singer from the local pub, Father Ted's, who, like all the others who'd agreed to play on the night, wanted to see the manor get off to a good start and had offered his services free of charge. The pub was providing an outside bar and the landlord, Ted, had agreed that a percentage of profits would go to the area's hospice. The Round Table too would contribute from their various fund-raising stalls.

'Have you seen Hattie anywhere?' Jo asked.

'She was heading towards the old cottage about an hour ago.' Finbar nodded in the direction of the end of the garden, where the slated roof of a building peeped out from thick bushes and overhanging trees.

'What on earth is she doing down there?'

'Stretching her fine legs and taking some exercise,' Finbar said. 'If you're worried, I'll stroll that way and see if I can find her.'

'That would be a help; she's in charge of the restaurant tonight and needs to get a move on. I need to talk to Connor and make sure that he has everything ready for dinner. It has to be perfect.'

'Don't be worrying yourself, we're sucking the diesel now.'

'Er, yes, quite.'

Puzzled, Jo stared at Finbar. His hair shone in the sunlight and his teeth gleamed as his handsome face broke into a smile. Tucking his hands into his pockets, he turned to stroll away and search for Hattie.

~

AT THE END of the garden, Hattie was preoccupied and didn't hear Finbar as he approached the cottage. She wasn't expecting visitors and as her brain wrestled with the tasks in hand, she was unaware that he'd made his way down the uneven path to the open door.

Hattie stood in what once had been a parlour and admired her handywork. The room had been swept clean, with windows washed and surfaces dusted. Devoid of furniture, the linoleum floor was cracked in places and curled away from the edge of an old tiled fireplace. An iron latch held the windows together as trees brushed against glass as thick as a beer bottle. Like the stone walls, the windows, though old, were made to last.

Hot and dusty, Hattie had knotted a scarf around her head and damp curls poked out, clinging to her forehead. She looked around and nodded; it was the last room in the cottage to have her broom and mop treatment and she was satisfied with her efforts. In the kitchen she placed her cleaning materials next to an old stone sink and, running water from a creaking tap, she washed her hands and face, lifting the skirt of a grubby apron to dry her skin. She removed the apron, glanced at her watch and tutted, knowing that she needed to get back to the manor. Jo would be wondering where she'd got to and would no doubt be having kittens, as her nerves built for the evening ahead.

It was time for a pick-me-up and Hattie closed the kitchen door to step into the hallway.

'What's a pretty girl like you doing in an old place like this?'

'Jesus, Finbar!' Hattie gripped her chest and staggered back. 'What in the devil's name are you doing standing there and scaring the living daylights out of me?'

Finbar appeared from the shadow of the doorway. As he moved forward, he held out his hands. 'I've been sent as a search party and here you are.'

Hattie knocked his hands away and was angry as she stormed past. 'I'm not lost and I don't need anyone to come looking for me.'

Curious to see what Hattie was up to, Finbar stuck his head around the parlour doorway. 'What would you be doing in here?' He sniffed as a strong aroma of cleaning products wafting through the room. 'This place hasn't been lived in for years.'

'None of your damned business,' Hattie snapped. 'Now come away and we'll go back to the manor.'

They left the cottage and as they stepped into the sunshine, Finbar tapped his nose.

'Don't worry,' he said. 'You may be acting the maggot but whatever your secret is, you can rest assured that it's safe with me.'

'Aye, well that's as may be, but you mustn't tell Jo where I was.'

As they walked side by side through the garden, Finbar began to whistle.

Digging about in her pocket, Hattie found her mobile phone and stared at the screen. She'd had a message from Alf that the Cumbria party had managed an early start and were making their way by road from Marland to Holyhead, then a ferry across the Irish Sea, to arrive in Dublin before heading south via Cork to Kindale. Alf reckoned that the journey would take about ten hours, plus stops. Hattie calculated that by late evening, the manor would have many more guests to accommodate.

Jo was going to have a fit.

Oh well, she thought, there was no point in enlightening her friend until she had to.

~

IN THE MIDDLE of the Irish Sea, a twin-hulled Catamaran with six hundred passengers on board was hurtling across the water. Mid-way between Holyhead, on the island of Anglesey, and Dublin sitting on the east coast of Ireland, the high speed craft pitched and rolled against the breakers, whipped up by gusting winds. Despite the warmth from the sun hovering above in a glorious June sky, the sea was choppy as the boat crashed through the waves.

Gathered on bench-style seating, in clustered groups, the party from Cumbria were enjoying light snacks. Audrey and her Babes were tucking into the sandwiches she'd prepared earlier, with the addition of ice-cream and cake from a self-service brasserie, while Willie poured himself a cup of tea and ate from a foil wrap containing a selection of samosas from Biddu's hamper. Alf stood at the bar with Harry, both savouring a pint of Guinness and as the boat sliced through the sea, they gripped their glasses and held on tight.

Melissa was worried about leaving Bunty, Ness and Teddy on the coach during the crossing and had volunteered to stay with them. With a bowl of fresh water, doggie treats and Melissa's undivided attention, the animals were happy and contented.

In the gift shop, Lucinda was examining a display of

watches as an assistant hovered, inviting her to try anything that caught her eye. With a disdainful glare, she waved the man away and turned from the cabinet, wrapping her velvet coat tightly around her thin body. She reached into her bag for cigarettes and a holder.

'You can't smoke in here,' the assistant said, a look of horror crossing his pale face as he watched Lucinda remove a cigarette and place it in the holder. 'I'll report you.'

'Don't flap,' she replied, holding the smoking apparatus aloft. 'Which way to the open deck?'

'Up the stairs.' The man shook his head, muttered about the rudeness of passengers, turned his back and locked the cabinet.

On deck, she lit her cigarette and exhaled with pleasure as sea spray whipped at her hair, loosening it from the chignon knotted at her neck. Salty particles caressed her face and she smiled as she strode along the deck. It was good to be out in the fresh air and away from the confines of Boomerville, where there were times when the ageing artists nearly drove her round the bend. If it wasn't for her need to be earning, with no home that she could call her own, Lucinda would be travelling, experiencing cultures and countries that were on her list of things to do before she died. This trip to Ireland might be a new adventure; who knew what would happen on the Emerald Isle?

There was no one about as Lucinda made her way, but turning at the stern she noticed a figure hunched as he gripped the railing, his body sagging as a bout of nausea passed.

Lucinda recognised Bill immediately. The stupid fool would get swept overboard if he continued to stay in that position. 'Take my arm!' Lucinda yelled, her voice fading into the wind.

Bill's head slowly turned and his bleary eyes focussed when he saw Lucinda coming towards him. Like a bird of prey descending on its catch, Lucinda hovered then pounced, releasing Bill's balled fists from the railings and scooping him up.

'Hold on tight!' she said as she manipulated Bill to a bench, tucked between buoyancy aids, in a sheltered section of the deck. She sat him down, and pushed his head between his legs.

Bill felt as though his neck had been broken. But the pain was marginally less that the searing ache in his stomach, where alcohol sloshed about with Biddu's biryani and a spicy onion bhaji.

'I'm going to be sick again,' Bill mumbled, rearing up against Lucinda's hand.

'No, you're not.' Lucinda pushed harder. 'Take deep breaths.' She fumbled about in her bag with her free hand until her fingers found a small phial. Flipping the cap, she shook two tiny tablets out and drove them between Bill's clenched lips. 'Swallow.'

A few moments later, she loosened her grip and Bill straightened up. He blinked his eyes in disbelief as he looked around and stared at Lucinda.

'What the hell have you just given me?'

'A potion in the form of a pill, from the Shaman. I never leave home without them.'

'It's a miracle.' Bill stood and put his hand in his pocket. His fingers found a napkin containing a crumpled croissant and with inordinate haste Bill shoved the doughy pastry into his mouth and began to munch.

He turned and looked out to sea. In the distance, a

dark outline was emerging. Bill wiped crumbs from his mouth and smiled. 'I can see Ireland; we'll be there soon.'

'Then I suggest you make use of the time left and clean yourself up.' Lucinda stared at the stains on Bill's jacket. 'Vomit stinks,' she said and, gripping her bag, she moved away.

21

In the candlelit dining room at the manor the atmosphere was jovial. Many returning visitors were familiar with the Boomerville experience, some had even met before on previous stays at Jo's hotels and were excited, knowing that they were lucky enough to have secured a place for the opening weekend.

Guests had arrived during the afternoon and after settling into their rooms, they'd been briefed on the activities planned over the next two days. They'd explored the house and grounds in the company of James, before taking tea and cake in the lounges. Now, refreshed after their journeys, they chatted about their stay and the next day's classes. On Saturday they had invitations to the opening party, followed by an exclusive dining experience in the evening, where Connor would showcase a taster menu of his signature dishes. On Sunday, classes would resume again and after a hearty breakfast on Monday, they would depart.

The manor would close and re-open the following weekend.

Connor and his team had pulled out all the stops for the guest's first evening in the restaurant. The menu, printed on headed paper, offered a selection of local dishes.

<u>DINNER in the FLATTERLY ROOM</u>
West Coast scallops *with artichokes*
Pumpkin soup *with burrata & seeds*
Chicken liver pate *with toasted sourdough and apple puree*

∽

Glazed Duck Breast
Salsify, roasted beetroot & plum sauce
Beef Striploin
Cep mushrooms and smoked oxtail
Kindale Cod
Black bacon & lemon butter sauce

∽

Raspberry Cake *with passionfruit sorbet*
Salted caramel ice-cream *with peanut brittle*
Chocolate fondant *with blackberry cream*

∽

Irish cheeses
Apple chutney, oat crackers

'By heck, its making my mouth water,' Hattie said to Jo as they stood by the door and watched guests tucking in, as staff whirled by.

'Dining is like theatre,' Jo said. 'Timing is critical and guests need to be entertained with each course.'

'Well, you've pulled off a great show tonight, just look at the smiling faces.'

The two women studied the guests. With tongues loosened with pre-dinner cocktails and wines accompanying the meal, their happy faces reflected the ambience of the evening. For their first night at Boomerville Manor, they'd been seated together on a long mahogany table, the centre filled with flickering candles, white-petalled lilies and an assortment of foliage from the garden. Glasses clinked and conversation became animated as each course arrived.

'They'll sleep like babies,' Jo said, noticing one or two yawns as coffee was served.

'Well, not just yet.' Hattie nudged Jo's arm and inclined her head to the doorway where Finbar had entered the room.

Immaculately dressed in a smart lounge suit, he held a microphone as he came forward.

'What the devil's going on?' Jo turned to Hattie, her eyebrows raised.

'I thought the guests might enjoy a bit of after dinner entertainment.'

'Bloody hell, Hattie, you could have told me.'

'Aye, well, you'd only have said no.'

'I most certainly would.' Jo looked at her watch. 'It's nearly ten o'clock and we've a busy day tomorrow; I'm sure both guests and staff would appreciate an early night.'

'That's a matter of opinion.'

They watched as Finbar introduced himself and as he walked around the room, shaking hands with the guests, a waiter produced a fiddle and began to play, then Finbar began to sing, 'As I was goin' over, the Cork and Kerry Mountains...'

A bottle of whisky appeared and shots were poured. Everyone raised their glass and joined Finbar in the chorus.

> Musha rain dum a doo, dum a da
> Whack for my daddy, oh
> Whack for my daddy, oh
> There's whiskey in the jar

'OH, Lord, and there will be far too much whisky in the guests if the night carries on like this.' Jo shook her head. 'Really, Hattie, do we need to get everyone absolutely slaughtered on their first night?'

'Ease up, loosen your knicker elastic, you're in Ireland now, the guests expect a bit of craic on their first night.'

Finbar held his hands up and smiled, relishing the hearty applause. 'More!' a guest called out as another put his fingers to his mouth and let out a piercing whistle.

'Looks like we're in for a session,' Hattie said. 'You stay here and keep an eye on things and I'll go and check the bedrooms, to make sure housekeeping have turned the beds down.'

Jo hardly heard. She was distracted by Finbar who'd taken the hands of a middle-aged widow from Warrington and was now encouraging her to join him in a duet. As Finbar and Fiona became Kenny and Dolly, Hattie hurried from the room, to a chorus of 'Islands in the stream, that is what we are…'

Hattie sped along the corridor and made her way to the front door. She reached into her pocket and looked at her phone. Alf had messaged to say that they had left Cork half an hour ago and would be arriving at any moment. As she stood on the step and looked out into the night, James joined her.

'Have you mentioned the new arrivals to Jo?'

'Er, no, I thought you might break the news, but she knows Melissa is due at any time.'

'Very good,' James said. 'Refreshments are ready and a light buffet is laid out in the music room.'

'You're a star.' Hattie turned and looked at James and saw that his eyebrows were raised. 'It'll be alright, honestly. I had to do it like this or Jo would never have agreed to it.'

'As long as you know what you're doing.'

A horn tooted in the distance and they both turned as the lights from Willie's coach came into view. It flew along the drive and came to a sudden halt, twenty feet from the door.

'Tell her now,' Hattie urged and raised her hands in greeting.

With a nod, James disappeared.

'Hattie!' voices yelled from the coach, as Willie eased himself out of his cab and trudged over.

'Tha's looking grand.' Willie clenched Hattie in a bear hug, his hands encircling her waist.

'Good to see you, Willie,' Hattie replied, removing herself from his grip. 'Shall we get this lot unloaded?'

Alf was first out of the coach. He placed his cap on his head and stretched his arms. He grinned when he saw Hattie. 'Nice place.'

'Aye, belting, now let's get everyone in.'

Hattie approached the coach and as the party from Cumbria descended, she was caught up in a confusion of kisses, hugs and excited greetings from Audrey and the Babes. Harry and Lucinda joined in, followed by Bill, who cautiously came forward to shake Hattie's hand.

'Glad you could make it,' Hattie said. She stared at a stain on Bill's jacket and pulled a face. 'Bumpy crossing?'

Suddenly, everyone stopped. They turned to the doorway where a figure stood, mouth agape as she stared at the new arrivals.

Hattie closed her eyes and crossed her fingers, waiting for Jo's reaction. But as she held her breath and said a prayer, Audrey and the Babes began to sing.

'For she's a jolly good fellow! For she's a jolly good fellow...'

Alf stepped forward and grabbed Jo's hands, his voice singing out too.

'For she's a jolly good feeeelloow, and so say all of us!'

Jo was surrounded. She looked confused as she stared at the number of people standing on her drive. She'd been expecting Melissa to arrive, on her own, in a taxi, but to her astonishment and horror, she saw that she had many more bodies to find beds for.

As silence fell and everyone waited for Jo to say something, Hattie opened her eyes. She turned to the coach where Melissa stood on the top step, fiddling with three leads as she unleashed Bunty, Ness and Teddy.

Bunty hurled herself forward and leapt on Jo, her tongue licking and tail wagging with absolute joy to be reunited with her mistress and as Teddy followed suit, Jo's face softened.

Hattie let out a sigh of relief and whispered a prayer to the guardian angel of the canine world as she watched Jo lean down and embrace the dogs.

It was going to be all right.

'Refreshments are being served in the music room,' James said, 'if you'd all like to follow me.'

'Aye, leave your luggage, we'll sort all that out,' Hattie said and began to usher everyone into the manor. She stood by the door and watched the last of the party follow James.

'You bugger,' Jo said as she joined Hattie. She held Teddy in her arms and reached down to stroke Bunty's head. 'Where in God's name are we going to put everyone?'

'Well, Melissa is in the manor, as planned,' Hattie replied, 'and I've sorted beds out for everyone else, so don't be worrying yourself, just think of all the extra help you've got on hand.'

'I suppose James is in on this too?'

'Couldn't have done it without him.'

'By the look of things, we're in for a long night.'

'I thought that Finbar could bring the hotel guests

into the music room too, so that the staff can get the dining room ready for breakfast.'

'You've thought of everything.'

Hattie linked her arm through Jo's. 'Don't I always?'

'Don't you just.'

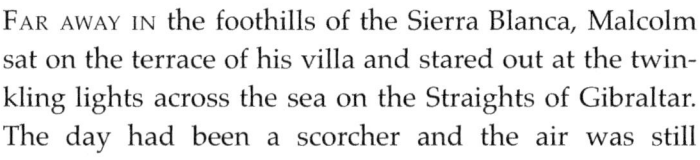

~

FAR AWAY IN the foothills of the Sierra Blanca, Malcolm sat on the terrace of his villa and stared out at the twinkling lights across the sea on the Straights of Gibraltar. The day had been a scorcher and the air was still muggy, despite a cooling breeze blowing in from the valley.

Malcolm studied his Rolex. It was past midnight, but he wasn't tired.

Earlier, he'd heard Giles' Ferrari roar down the driveway as his son headed off to the nightlife in Marbella, no doubt squandering god only knew how much money on Cristal Champagne and lines of coke. They'd argued incessantly throughout the day and Malcolm had found it difficult to focus on his work as Giles winged and moaned and made a nuisance of himself.

A bottle of cognac sat on the table and as he sipped from a cut-glass goblet, Malcolm wondered what he was going to do about Giles. The boy was a loose cannon, staggering on life's tightrope, his addictions spiralling out of control. Every morning, Malcolm expected the Policía to appear at the villa bringing news that Giles was locked up or laid out on a slab in the mortuary.

Allegra would be turning in her grave.

Her precious son was finding life difficult at home with his father and Giles wasn't leading the life that she'd planned for him. Allegra had had high hopes for Giles and had wanted him to train to be a doctor or pilot, anything that was the polar opposite of his father's career. But despite an expensive education, Giles had been expelled from his boarding school and the only option that he'd been remotely interested in was to work with Malcolm, an arrangement doomed from the start.

Malcolm sighed.

Giles had never been an easy child and was far too spoilt, his every whim catered for by his overprotective mother. Her death had devastated the boy. He didn't speak for months and when Melissa came along, she tried in vain to ease Giles out of his despair; no amount of counselling had made any difference and Giles was as cold towards his stepmother as he was towards his father.

Malcom finished his drink. His phone lay on the table and he picked it up, his fingers scrolling through messages until he found what he was looking for. As he re-read the words from the waiter in Cumbria, Malcolm's grip tightened.

The bitch was on the move.

Melissa had packed up and headed off and stupidly, his wife thought she'd got the better of him. The letters that she'd written to Malcolm and Patrick had been scanned and forwarded and as he read the words, he tensed. Did she really think that he wouldn't come after her? Was Melissa so stupid that she expected Malcolm to let her go and move on with her life? She'd even suggested that he take her car back and sell it, after all, the log book was in his name.

He re-read Melissa's letter to Patrick and laughed. The silly cow had sent her forwarding address and given her son her new number. She wrote fondly that she was missing him and hoped that he'd come and visit when she was settled. For she intended to settle in Ireland if she liked the area around Cork and Kindale and seemed to think she'd make friends and be able to start her life again in a completely new environment.

Malcolm threw the phone across the table and poured another cognac. Melissa was clueless! She had no idea that Malcolm had financed Patrick's business, after paying for a three month spell in the Priory. Patrick's addictions had been almost as bad as Giles' and he'd come to Malcolm begging him not to tell Melissa, for he feared it would break his mother's heart. Melissa had enough hang-ups about Patrick's upbringing and not being there for him when she worked on the cruises.

The thought of her son as a drug addict would be too much for her to bear.

Well, all that was about to change!

Malcolm tossed back his drink and stood up. He had much to do.

Screw his family. All any of them ever wanted was more than he could give. Melissa may think she'd escaped from her marriage and whatever hell she thought she'd been living through.

But little did she know that hell was only now about to begin.

22

Breakfast at Boomerville Manor the following morning was a subdued affair. With many guests opting to have the meal served in their room, the kitchen was busy making up trays and staff hurried about to deliver them. In the dining room, the stalwarts who'd made it to the buffet table were piling their plates with carbohydrates in an effort to quell hangover headaches and sickly stomachs.

Hattie had risen early and after sneaking down to the kitchen to knock up a couple of glasses of her pick-me-up, she'd taken one to Jo and placed it on the table beside Jo's bed.

Jo woke up as she heard Hattie moving about. 'What time is it?' she asked.

'Time to let these two daft mongrels out,' Hattie replied and reached out to nudge Bunty and Teddy off the bottom of Jo's bed. 'I'll see to it.'

Dressed in jeans, t-shirt and glittery trainers, with the dogs close on her heels, Hattie hot-footed across the dew dampened lawn and hurried along the path to the cottage. As she stood in the doorway, she cocked her head to one side, listening for signs of life.

'Kettle's on, if tha' fancies a brew,' Alf called out.

Hattie left the dogs moseying about the garden and crept down the hallway to enter the kitchen where Alf, fully dressed, stood by the stone sink with a pint of milk in his hand. Ness sat at his feet, thumping her tail. Willie was draped across a pine chair by a wobbly table. He wore old-fashioned combinations that had seen much better days and with his tussled hair and two-day stubble, looked much the worse for wear.

'That was some party,' Alf said as he brewed tea.

'Best fun I've had in years,' Willie said.

'How did you sleep?' Hattie asked.

'Not so bad once we got used to things.' Alf handed a mug to Hattie. 'Had a bit of trouble getting old Willie here on his feet this morning, but with the help of Audrey and the Babes, we managed it.'

The door leading to the parlour crashed open and Harry, dressed in nothing but his boxers, staggered in.

'Christ, Hattie,' Harry said as he rubbed his puffy eyes and yawned, 'you could have warned us about the beds.' He took the drink that Alf held out, and sat down on a spare chair. 'I know you said we might be roughing it a bit, but ex-army, WWII camp beds?'

'And mine was broken,' Willie added.

'Oh, stop moaning, you've a roof over your heads, haven't you?' Hattie flopped down. She'd wondered how the Cumbrian party would fare with the sleeping arrangements and, looking at the state of Harry and Willie, it hadn't gone well. 'It's all I could get from the local boy scouts; you're lucky they had sleeping bags too.'

'I'm not complaining,' Alf said, 'but I'm ready for some breakfast.'

'Go and see Connor in the kitchen; he'll look after you.'

Hattie had warned Chef to expect additional guests for breakfast and knew that there was a mountain of bacon butties, slabs of black pudding and thick Irish sausages in a hot cupboard, waiting for the cottage residents to descend.

'Where's Audrey and the Babes?' Hattie asked as she finished her tea.

'They're out getting some exercise; Audrey said they needed to keep fit.' Alf took Hattie's mug and rinsed it under the cold tap.

'Has anyone seen Bill?'

'Out cold in the top bedroom, we had to carry him back.'

'And Lucinda?'

'She's insisted on having her own room and has set up in the parlour, but she looked in earlier and has taken her paints and says she has a class this morning.'

'Oh Lord, I'd forgotten about that.' Hattie scratched her head. 'There's taster classes all day and I'm supposed to be organising them. I'd better be off.'

'Let us know how we can help, there's plenty of willing hands here.' Alf nodded towards Willie and Harry. Both groaned and held their heads in their hands.

'Keep hold of the dogs for a bit, if you will? Bunty and Teddy are in the garden. I'll catch up with you later.'

Hattie left the cottage and headed for the manor. It was another beautiful day and, by the look of things, the forecast was correct and the weather was going to hold for the party tomorrow. The early sunlight was soft, giving way to the first rays of the day that shone across the grounds, outlining the silent silhouettes of fairground rides, an empty stage, marquees and stalls. All was motionless, waiting for the activity that was about to come. Clouds, white and fluffy, danced across a blue sky as a rabbit hopped along the lawn, its white tail bobbing.

On the lake, spray suddenly flew outwards and loud splashy strokes circled the centre of the water.

'What on earth is going on?' Hattie said as she set off towards the commotion.

'Easy does it…and flip!'

Eight pairs of legs kicked in unison as Audrey's Babes flipped upside down and performed a handstand routine. Audrey, standing nearby on the wooden jetty, clapped her hands.

'Marvellous, girls!' she cried. 'You've finally got it.'

Whatever it was that the girls had got, Hattie hoped that it didn't include hyperthermia. She stared at the mottled flesh and purple thighs that disappeared into the water. Moments later a floral display moved along the surface, in a figure of eight, as the Babes emerged, their flowered rubber headgear held high.

'Very nice,' Hattie said as she joined Audrey on the jetty.

'We'll make an interesting contribution to the entertainment tomorrow.' Audrey gestured to the Babes and they swam towards her.

'Er, yes, that sound fabulous; does Jo know?'

'Not yet, but I thought that she might include synchronised swimming as a course.'

Hattie thought that Jo would sooner include bungee jumping off the top of the Friary, rather than risk her boomers' lives in the freezing cold, muddy depths of the murky old lake.

'Aye, good idea, stick it in the suggestion box.'

They watched the Babes help each other as they scrambled out, their shivering bodies brushing against reeds and grasses on the edge of the lake. Audrey handed out towels and began to pour hot tea and brandy from a flask.

'Did you sleep well?' Hattie asked as the Babes stripped off and climbed into matching tracksuits.

'Like logs,' Audrey said. 'It's a fine little cottage you found for us.'

'As long as you're cosy.' Hattie turned to leave. 'There's breakfast for you all if you make your way to the manor.'

'Splendid!' Audrey slapped Hattie on the back. 'Come on, girls!'

Hattie steadied herself and as the Babes trooped past, made a mental note to add to her shopping list that day. She'd need to find somewhere that sold lifebelts and must ensure that St John's Ambulance, Ireland had a defibrillator on hand tomorrow.

In the meantime, with taster classes to prepare, she'd go and find Jo.

~

ON THE FIRST FLOOR, in a bedroom named the Peacock Room, floral curtains were drawn back to reveal a view of the lake. In the distance, Audrey and her Babes could be heard splashing about in the water as birds circled overhead. As the sun rose and streamed through the latticed window, it cast honeycomb shadows on the blue-gold carpet. Fingers of light splayed out, embracing the solitary figure of Melissa, who sat on a chair by the rosewood dressing table, staring into the bevelled mirror. The face that stared back was pale, eyes wide and startled.

Melissa looked as though she'd seen a ghost.

She closed her eyes and, gently rocking, bit her lower lip as her fingers twisted around a silver bracelet on her wrist. Melissa was lost in thought and as her mind wandered, the years melted away.

At twenty-two, Melissa was talented and pretty, with a love of the entertainment industry. Her parents' hotel had given her the first taste of performing and her job as a dancer fulfilled all of her dreams as she travelled the world on luxury liners. Now, far from the stage at the tired seaside hotel in Newquay, where her parents had spurred Melissa on, she had an opportunity to rise up from the ranks of dancer, in the troupe who performed each night in the Starlight Room on board the Crystal Royal. The female vocalist, who headlined the show, had a throat infection and was confined. That afternoon, the cruise director had been holding auditions for anyone who wanted to step in and take the vocalist's place. Melissa knew every word of the act and sensing a chance to break out of the faceless ranks, took her chance.

She stood on the stage and sang the poignant words of a popular song that was in the charts and part of the evening entertainment. 'Tell me, how am I supposed to live without you?'

The cruise director and casting coach had both

smiled. She'd nailed the words of the song and to her delight, Melissa was successful.

A few hours later she whirled onto the stage in a dazzling silver gown and stood alongside the cruise line's resident entertainer. They sang her audition song together, then, as they moved through the numbers, their footsteps and harmonies in perfect time, passengers gave them a standing ovation and it was an elated Melissa who took four curtain calls before leaving the stage.

Later that night, it was an elated Mel, as she was known on the ship, who lay in the narrow bed in the cabin of the resident entertainer and stared into his fiery green eyes. Magical eyes, flecked with gold, they twinkled in the dim light and captivated her, as the ship sailed through the tranquil Caribbean Sea.

The relationship lasted for two weeks.

During that time, the cruise visited many beautiful islands and travelled as far as South America, before heading back to Barbados where she would disembark at the end of her contract, to fly home. The entertainer had three more months at sea when they said goodbye, on a scorching hot day, as the ship docked in Bridgetown.

'Here's lookin' at you, beautiful Mel,' he'd called out as she climbed into a taxi.

Melissa knew that she'd never see him again. Life at sea was fickle - a different destination every day. New passengers, fresh crew. The chance of ever meeting again was doubtful. They made no promises, arranged no further contact. Both were young, with the world at their feet.

Until Melissa got home and realised she was pregnant.

Melissa opened her eyes and looked at her reflection. Her head shook in disbelief. She'd never seen nor contacted Patrick's father in all of her son's twenty-six years. Her only memory was of his eyes. The eyes that had captivated her as she sang and danced by his side.

Magical eyes. Eyes that she'd suddenly and shockingly recognised, that belonged to a man who'd entertained everyone with his songs and tales the night before.

Eyes that belonged to Finbar Murphy.

23

'You look fabulous!' Hattie exclaimed. She stood by the reception desk in the hallway and watched Jo as she came down the stairs. 'Where the devil did you get that dress?'

Jo stepped onto the polished parquet flooring and, taking hold of her skirt, did a twirl. The dropped shoulders of the cap-sleeved gown were flattering and scarlet suited her auburn hair and creamy skin.

'I found it in a vintage shop in Cork; you don't think it's too tight?'

Hattie walked around Jo and studied the nipped in waist which flowed to a full skirt just below the knee. 'Nope, it's perfect.'

'I'm not sure if I can walk in these shoes.' Jo looked down at her matching suede stilettos.

'Well, you should try because they look great.'

'I thought we should make an effort, with this being the first full day.'

In truth, when Jo had opened her wardrobe that morning she'd thought about Pete. The dress was as good as giving him a one finger salute. Anguish was turning to anger and, determined to stop moping around and pull herself together, she had grabbed the dress and put it on.

As she touched the silky fabric, Jo realised that the dress made her feel good again; she actually felt quite sexy.

'Is that a smile on your face?' Hattie raised her eyebrows and gave Jo a wink. 'Time you got back in the saddle, a red-hot affair would do you good.'

'And who would I have an affair with?'

'You should get in touch with Long Tom, that was the best medicine you ever took, a two-week tumble with Mr Rock and Roll and you'd soon got over your grief and had the rest of your life planned out.'

'That's never going to happen because, one, he lives in Los Angeles.' Jo held up her hand and counted her fingers. 'And two, he's probably married again and three, he'd never look at an old crone like me when he has La La Land lovelies at his fingertips.'

'I'm just saying,' Hattie shrugged, 'he looked at you once.'

'Well, it's never going to happen again.' Jo sighed and wondered what she would do if Long Tom were to walk through the door. She'd put him out of her mind when she'd chosen Pete and look where that had got her.

Deciding to change the subject, Jo stared at Hattie's outfit and smiled. 'My goodness, I wouldn't have known you.'

Hattie wore a severe black dress. Well-cut and tailored, it had a round collar and neat cuffs.

'Aye, well don't let appearances fool you.' Hattie

tugged on the zip at the neck of the dress and pulled it down to her chest. Red lace peeped out over a mound of cleavage. 'Where are my shoes?' She shuffled barefoot to the desk and reached under to retrieve a pair of animal print kitten heels.

'A transformation.' Jo smiled.

'I want to keep the punters happy.' Hattie reached into her bra and pulled out a lipstick. In moments her lips puckered pearly pink. 'None of that trout pout for me,' she said.

'You do look remarkably good for your age.' Jo studied Hattie's skin and ran her fingers over her friends smooth forehead. 'Hardly a line.'

Hattie turned away. She'd no intention of letting Jo in on the fact that she'd been taking regular trips to a Botox clinic since Hugo's death, and the results, in Hattie's opinion, had taken years off. She wouldn't mind a bit of lipo-suction on her tummy too. Hattie sucked her stomach in and wondered if the miracle pants that squeezed her backside and crushed the flesh around her ribs, would be bearable all day. It would be a miracle if she still had them on by teatime.

'The taster classes kick off in an hour.' Jo sat at the desk and studied the day's schedule.

'Aye, I'm about to do a check and make sure the instructors are ready and prepared.'

Four classes were to run that morning, each lasting for two to three hours. They would be repeated after lunch.

As the weather was fine, Lucinda would be hosting students by the lake. Easels and paints were being set up and placed in position to catch the best of the morning light. James had arranged chairs in one of the lounges and would take the class for Public Speaking, while Declan and the twins were ready to welcome gardeners to the vegetable patch with forks, trowels and long handled dibbers, to learn all about the business of "The Birds and the Bees in the Garden".

'Let's hope there's no repercussions,' Hattie said, as she leaned over Jo's shoulder and studied the title of the gardening class.

'I'm more concerned with twisted knees and arthritic backs,' Jo replied. 'There's a community hospital in Kindale, but the nearest Accident & Emergency is in Cork.'

'A long way to go if your dibber gets stuck.'

'Do you think it was a good idea to let Finbar host a singing class?'

'You've played a blinder and judging by the reaction of every female in the place, who was still doing an Irish jig with him at three o'clock this morning, I'm sure his classes will be booked out for months.'

'He is popular with the ladies, isn't he?'

Hattie's eyes were dreamy. 'I'd give him a go,' she said.

'Hattie,' Jo said, 'there'll be no fraternising with the staff. Remember what happened with Paul the Potter.'

Hattie sighed as she remembered more than Jo had ever known. The pottery wheel had taken a frenzied spin back at Boomerville in Cumbria when Paul, the traumatised potter, had ended up in hospital. But he'd soon got over his injury and they enjoyed more than moulding clay pots in their out of hours liaisons.

She picked up a clipboard. 'We need to press on; there's a ruck of outsiders joining the classes today and by the look of things, some of them are starting to arrive.'

They looked out to the driveway, where cars were assembling. The occupants, a mixture of middle-aged residents from the surrounding area, keen to try the new classes, were greeting each other as they headed towards the front door.

'Coffee and biscuits are being served in the lounge that overlooks the lake.' Jo stood. 'Can you direct everyone to assemble in there?'

'On my way,' Hattie replied and with a broad smile stepped out to welcome the new arrivals.

～

BILL HAD A STONKING HEADACHE. It was all he could do to lift his head from his rolled-up jacket and sit up. His bed rocked as he wriggled out of his sleeping bag. Bill's mouth was dry and his tongue felt thick; he was sure his breath was foul too.

You stupid man! Getting yourself hooked up with this lot; it'll end in tears!

'Morning, Mother,' Bill said out loud as he sat up and rubbed his eyes. He was parched and as he was overtaken by a yawn that made his jaw ache, he looked through bleary lids for a glass of water.

You deserve to be dead, not just hungover!

'You'd like that, wouldn't you?' Bill sighed, the old woman was off to an early start today. 'Six feet under, alongside you.'

You're bringing a bad name to the family, get yourself home – away from this evil place!

'The only evil thing here is your bloody ghostly

presence,' Bill said. 'Now bugger off and let me get on with my day.'

The door of the bedroom opened and Alf came in.

'Talking to yourself, old lad?' Alf asked. 'That's a bad sign.' He held out a plate stacked with a bacon sandwich and two fat sausages. 'I thought you might be ready for a bite to eat.'

'My mouth's as dry as dust.'

Alf took a bottle of water from his pocket and handed it to Bill. 'There you go, that will whet your whistle.'

Bill flicked the top and glugged the water down in one. Licking his lips, he reached out and took the plate. 'Thank you, I needed that,' he said.

Harry appeared in the doorway. He had a towel wrapped around his waist and his hair was wet. He nodded when he saw Bill. 'Good night, last night, eh?'

Bill, who had a mouth full of sausage, nodded.

In truth, the previous evening had been one of the best nights of Bill's life, as had the journey to Kindale. Once Bill had overcome his queasiness on the ferry, he'd loved every second of the ride. The repartee with Harry, as they enjoyed drinks and a sing-song on the back seat of the bus, was second only to the feeling of being part of a team, with Alf and Willie, as they chaperoned Audrey and the Babes to dinner, and the unexpected dance with Finbar and the hotel guests. Bill had never been so happy, as he'd found himself participating in a Irish jig with a lady from London, and the group hug at the end of the Gay Gordon's had left him exhausted but ecstatic. As the Cumbrian party staggered across the lawn and headed back to the cottage, in the dead of the night, it was a happy Bill who'd fallen onto his camp bed, breaking one of the supporting legs, as Alf and Harry slid him into a sleeping bag before collapsing, head over heels, themselves.

For the first time in his life, Bill felt as though he had friends. It was a curious feeling but one that felt good. Very good.

'The shower's cold,' Harry said and looked at Bill, 'but it will wake you up.' He rummaged in his case for clean clothes and laid them out on his camp bed.

Finishing his breakfast, Bill put the plate to one side. He realised that other than a pair of faded old Y-fronts, he was naked. Alf and Harry must have removed Bill's clothes when they put him to bed. Two days ago, that fact would have horrified Bill, but today he felt proud that in his drunken stupor, they'd taken care of him.

Alf was leaning on the windowsill, looking out at the garden. The art class was underway by the lake and he could see Lucinda, dressed in a multi-coloured smock, as bright as the sunshine, cigarette and holder a silhouette, as she walked from easel to easel inspecting her students' work. Birds were singing in the surrounding trees and Bunty, Ness and Teddy lay on the lawn below, tummies turned to the sky. Audrey and the Babes had settled on a selection of rickety old chairs, eyes closed, enjoying the sunshine.

'It's a fine setup Jo's got here,' Alf said, straightening his back. 'There'll be plenty of jobs to do in a bit, but Willie says he'll take us and the Babes on a ride out to Kindale, if you lads are up to it?'

'That sounds grand.' Harry zipped himself into a pair of camouflage shorts and pulled a creased T-shirt over his head. He smoothed the cotton fabric, where a slogan read, "Free Hugs".

'I'll be ready in five minutes.' Bill stood up. Slightly dizzy, he rocked as he reached for a towel and soap bag, but steadying himself, he thrust his shoulders back and strode confidently out of the room.

'Bathroom's on the left!' Harry called out. He didn't enlighten Bill as to the shower arrangements, which consisted of an old rubber hose, attached to two dripping taps, over a rusting iron bath where the water ran as cold as a river.

'Willie's ready,' Alf said as he gazed out, seeing exhaust fumes swirl in the sky on the other side of the manor.

'I'm coming too,' Harry said as he flicked a comb through his hair and slipped his feet into a pair of sandals.

They called out to Bill that they would wait for him by the coach. Bill muttered a response through chattering teeth as he shivered under the shower. Alf went into the kitchen, collected the leads, and whistled to the dogs. Outside, Harry told Audrey and the Babes that their passage to paradise awaited them.

'Splendid,' Audrey said as she gave Harry a hug and slapped him on the back, sending him teetering through the gate, and with the Babes bringing up the rear, they set off.

∼

IN THE MUSIC ROOM, Finbar was enjoying himself. Seated at the grand piano, he tinkled the ivories as he waited for his class to arrive. To be sitting on the stool where the great Long Tom had composed many a tune was, in

Finbar's book, to be in the presence of greatness and he felt honoured and inspired.

The acoustics were perfect.

Tears pricked at the corner of his eyes as each note, pure as a mountain stream, felt like a heartbeat, his pulse, his reason to be on this wonderful planet.

Music had always been the biggest part of Finbar's life and he'd been singing for as long as he could remember. From his mammy's knee, to the choir at the Catholic church, he'd been in a local folk band as a teen, followed by gigs in working men's clubs and pubs throughout the country. His granny had taught the young Finbar how to play the piano and, although she couldn't read a note of music herself, she'd saved up to send him to lessons with the formidable Caitlin O'Connelly, who taught at the Cork School of Music. Caitlin was a demon when it came to getting things right and Finbar still remembered the pain of her cane as it whacked across his young knuckles when he played a wrong note or got the timing wrong. It was useful to play an instrument, despite the fact that his main role was that of vocalist, an entertainer, the man who captivated an audience during the cabaret nights on cruise ships and in the clubs of the Spanish Costas.

Finbar considered himself to be an artist and now, as everyone arrived, he gave them a warm welcome. He ticked off names on a list of attendees and frowned when he saw that one guest was missing.

Melissa Mercer had yet to show.

Finbar couldn't hold the class up and indicated that as they were ready to begin, everyone should make themselves comfortable on the chairs arranged in a semi-circle around the piano. He turned as the door opened and an elderly woman appeared. She carried a leather satchel and she stepped into the room without a word.

'Ah, good morning,' Finbar said, 'ladies and gentlemen, I am pleased to introduce you to Miss O'Connelly, who will be accompanying us on the piano today.'

Miss O'Connelly sat down. Taking sheets of music out of her satchel, she placed them on the piano. Her fingers smoothed her dark woollen dress and she straightened the lace at the neck before patting a long grey plait neatly into place. Finbar noted thick lisle stockings and leather lace-up shoes. Caitlin's appearance hadn't changed, despite her ninety years on earth, but her once flawless complexion looked more like an overstored apple and the skin on her wrinkled hands was as transparent as tissue.

Finbar listened to each individual voice then split the group into sections. With only three men in a class of eighteen, he was grateful that the old boys could actually hold a note. They would give depth to the performance that he intended to present on stage, the following day.

'Now I know that we've only just met,' Finbar said, 'but we've a concert tomorrow, here at the manor, and I thought it would be a grand surprise for Jo, to have the Boomerville, "A Choired Taste" up on stage too.'

There was a ripple of excitement as the singers nodded and nudged each other. Finbar's idea had met with approval.

'We need a couple of numbers that will entertain the audience, so we're going to have to practice like crazy to get this right.' Finbar searched their faces. 'Are you with me?' he asked.

There was a cheer and Miss O'Connelly began to play a selection of melodies that Finbar had chosen earlier.

As he handed out sheets of paper with the words to all the songs and listened to the group as they joined in, Finbar soon had his choice. He looked at his watch. It was going to take a big effort to get this lot tuned up, word perfect and ready to perform the following evening, but Finbar loved a challenge and he'd make it his mission to ensure that the concert was the best event the area had seen in years.

An occasion to store in everyone's musical memory bank.

24

Jo and Hattie sat on their favourite bench in the garden. The weather was sultry but their position was shaded by the overhanging willow tree. Bunty, Ness and Teddy sat with them. The dogs panted and Bunty idly flicked a fly from her face with a hot and heavy paw, while Teddy snuggled into her belly. A chorus of birdsong chittered from nearby hedgerows as Declan's mower hummed in the background, adding the finishing touch to the lawns, in readiness for tomorrow.

Jo loosened the belt on her dress and Hattie kicked off her shoes.

'I shouldn't have had that extra slice of quiche at lunch.' Hattie fiddled with the edge of her miracle pants, trying to ease flesh back into the constricting elastane. 'This is the most unforgiving garment I've ever worn.'

'Take it off,' Jo said as she watched Hattie writhe in pain, 'before you crack a rib.'

'Aye, that's a good idea,' Hattie stood and, thrusting

her hands under the hem of her dress, she hooked the offending pants with her thumbs and began to tug.

'Be quick,' Jo sat up. 'Willie's back and the bus is spilling everyone out.'

Willie's Wheels had ground to a halt at the front of the manor and the first to be seen were Audrey and the Babes, clutching carrier bags.

'Yoo, hoo!' Audrey called out and she headed their way.

'Shite,' Hattie hissed as she pulled at the pants. But the shapewear was refusing to budge and having ridden to her thighs and gone no further, Hattie's hands were stuck. Teetering about on one foot, she suddenly fell to the floor.

'Oh heck!' Jo exclaimed and seeing Alf and Harry coming towards them, leapt to her feet and attempted to help.

'You're making it worse!' Hattie tried to stand but her legs were stuck, and rolling onto her tummy, she shuffled to the side of the tree.

'Glorious day,' Audrey said as she reached the bench. 'I say, is everything alright?' She stared at the prostrate form on the floor.

'Hattie's got her support pants stuck and there are men approaching.'

'Understood.' Audrey dropped her bags. 'Mayday, ladies!' She waved her hands and pointed to Hattie, who was now purple in the face and cursing.

In moments, the Babes had formed a human shield, removed Hattie's pants and pulled her back to her feet.

'Crisis averted,' Audrey said, retrieving her shopping as Hattie folded her pants, hid them beneath her, and flopped down on the bench.

'Have you bought anything nice?' Jo asked.

'Just a few finishing touches for our outfits for the big day tomorrow. What's the drill for this afternoon?'

'I'd hoped that you might dress the stage and marquees?'

'What in?' Audrey looked puzzled.

'If you borrow some secateurs from Declan, you'll find lots of greenery in the garden and perhaps you could drape it artistically?'

'Ah, gotcha.' Audrey nodded. 'Most of the gals create arrangements in the church back home, consider it done.' She turned to the Babes. 'Pronto! We have a mission.'

Jo watched them head off. She hoped that there'd be something left of the garden after the floral team had finished snipping.

'Be it on your own head,' Hattie said, as if reading Jo's mind. 'Look out, it's the Three Musketeers.' Hattie stared as Alf, Harry and Bill appeared. 'Where's Willie?'

'Polishing his pistons,' Harry said. 'They've been playing up today.'

'Did you enjoy your trip to Kindale?' Jo asked.

'Aye,' said Alf, ''tis a grand place. There's a pretty little harbour with fishing boats and yachts, galleries, shops and plenty of pubs too.'

Hattie eyed the logo on Harry's T-shirt. 'You can't possibly expect anyone to want a hug with you in that state?'

Harry looked hot and sweaty. 'You'd be surprised.' Harry smiled. 'The Irish lasses are very friendly.'

'Or blind,' Hattie said. She turned to Bill. 'A letter came for you today, by courier. It's in reception. I signed for it.'

'Thank you,' Bill replied, 'it's from my solicitor. I asked him to do a report on my house, as I've been away for so long.'

'Well, don't forget it and let me know if you need any help with anything, properties need carefully managing when you're not there.' Hattie thought of her own house in Marland and the terrible state she'd found it in.

Jo handed a list to Alf. He nodded his head as he read it. 'Leave it with us,' Alf said and passed the list to Bill.

Bill looked puzzled, manual work wasn't his forte. 'Soon have this lot done,' he said, determined not to let his new mates down.

'I'd better go and check on Lucinda,' Jo said and she looked at her watch.

To Jo's horror, Lucinda's art students had been stoned when they returned to the manor for lunch. Covered in paint, they'd all laughed hysterically as they fell into the dining room, clutching their etchings. Jo told Lucinda that she didn't want a repeat performance in the afternoon class, most of the boomers were on medication and she feared for their health.

But Hattie had told Jo to back off. 'Take a chill pill,' she'd said. 'Pot, paint and penicillin works wonders at their age.'

Reluctantly, Jo had agreed.

'Aye, let's get cracking,' Hattie said. 'We can't stay here gossiping here all day, there's lots to be done.'

'Did you forget something?' Harry reached down and took Hattie's support pants from the bench.

'Shite,' Hattie mumbled.

'Hang on to 'em,' Alf chuckled. 'We need an extra awning for the stage.'

Hattie swiped at Alf's head and snatched her pants.

'See thee later.' Alf whistled for the dogs to follow and together with Bill and Harry, set off.

'Have you seen Melissa today?' Jo asked as she watched Hattie retrieve her shoes.

'No, I haven't and she went to bed early last night.'

'Do you think she's heard from Malcolm?'

'Unlikely, he won't know she's here.'

'I think one of us should check and make sure she's alright.'

'Aye, leave it with me.'

They'd reached the door of the manor and as they stepped in, a clock on the slender mediaeval tower of the church in the distance chimed twice.

Jo paused to listen and turned to Hattie. 'Only twenty-four hours to go,' she said.

~

BEHIND THE LOCKED door of her bedroom, Melissa sat on her bed and wondered what to do. After the shock of the previous evening, her instinct told her to hide away. Terrified of mixing with the hotel residents and seeing Finbar again, she'd ignored the housekeeper's earlier knock on the door.

Her room could wait; it didn't need servicing.

As the morning passed, Melissa ran herself take a warm soapy bath. She took care when styling her hair and to pass the time and organise her thoughts, gave herself a manicure and face-pack. Anything to keep occupied while she decided what to do. She wondered if Finbar would remember the nervous young singer who'd joined him on stage all those years ago. Did he ever think about their time on the cruise and would he recognise her now?

Melissa could see that the years had been kind to Finbar.

Middle-aged but still handsome, as soon as he'd appeared the previous evening, she'd known that Finbar was the man who'd stolen her heart and left her with a lasting souvenir of their brief encounter. What on earth would he say if he ever found out that he had a twenty-six year old son, when he'd never been given the opportunity to get to know him?

When she'd discovered that she was pregnant, Melissa's parents had nagged and cajoled their daughter, in their quest to find out who the father was. Melissa had refused. She'd wanted Finbar to find her but she'd never heard from him again and instead, as her belly swelled and her future looked uncertain, she'd kept the secret to herself, realising that Finbar was a nomad with no intention of settling down. Surrounded by beautiful women wherever he went, why on earth would he take up with a silly young girl who'd been foolish enough to get herself into trouble? It would never have worked and despite her parents' protestations, Melissa was adamant that it was in everyone's interest that child and father never know each other.

Until now. The shock of seeing the only man that she'd ever slept with, until Malcolm came along, had sent Melissa into a spin.

She decided to skip classes that day and go for a walk to clear her head. As she ran down the stairs to the hallway, James, sitting at the desk in reception, called out a greeting.

'Hello, may I get you anything?'

'Oh no, I'm fine,' Melissa replied. 'I've had a terrible migraine and needed to lie down, it must be all the travelling.' She crossed her fingers and hoped that James would accept her explanation. 'I thought I'd pop out for a walk.'

'Do you need any medication?' he asked.

'No, a walk will sort me out.'

'Very well, it's a lovely day, can I supply you with a map?'

'Oh no, thanks, I'm not going far.'

'Flatterly Friary, the old monastery nearby, is interesting; the place is in ruins but you can still walk around the extensive grounds.'

'Thank you, I might do that.'

'Turn right when you get to the road, keep going and you'll see the entrance on the left.'

Melissa thanked James again and hurried past. She hadn't a clue where she was going but the need to arrange her confused thoughts into some sort of working plan was suddenly critical and she picked up her pace as she headed down the drive.

It was bright outside and Melissa reached into her bag for her sunglasses. As she came to the end of the driveway, she turned right. A long stone wall ran the length of the road, as far as the eye could see and Melissa assumed that the derelict monastery lay beyond. With no desire to scramble over a tumbled-down building, she kept going.

There was little traffic on the road and the countryside stretched ahead. Fields, dotted with animals, rose and fell like waves on an ocean and again she was reminded of being at sea. She wondered if, after all these years, Finbar would recognise her. Melissa knew that he was Patrick's father, she could see it in their eyes. They shared the fiery green that sparkled and held beauty, undeniably captivating. His poise and stance too. Of similar height and build, both father and son had thick wavy hair, the colour of jet, Finbar's tinged at the sides with grey.

Melissa thought of Patrick and wondered if he'd received her news. In her letter, she'd asked him to call as soon as he'd read it and hoped that she'd hear from him that day. He'd be pleased that she'd left Malcolm, she was certain. Perhaps he'd come and visit her soon.

An engine sounded and Melissa turned to see a bus heading towards her. The destination sign read, "Kindale". Deciding to check out the local town, she held out her hand.

The vehicle stopped and the door swished open.

'Where to, miss?' the driver called out.

'I'd like to go to Kindale.'

'I'll get you there in ten minutes, hop on.'

Melissa paid her fare and as she settled on a seat by a window, her tummy rumbled and she realised she was hungry. With luck, there would be a decent café in the town and she could grab a coffee and a bite to eat.

For now, she'd try and relax and worry about what to do about Finbar when she had a full stomach and a clear mind.

～

MALCOLM SAT by the window in the foyer of Kindale House Hotel and yawned. After reading Melissa's letters, it had only taken him moments to decide to track her down. Since leaving him, the senseless bitch had got a taste for freedom and with her confidence growing daily, he intended to halt her progress, before she got out of hand. Malcolm hadn't slept and now, as he waited to check into a room, he sipped a coffee hoping that the caffeine would ease his tiredness, following his early flight.

He'd packed a case with haste and woken his housekeeper to tell her that he would be away for a few days. After checking online, Malcolm had bought his ticket at the airport and the six-thirty flight from Marbella to Cork had been half-empty, with a few hungover stragglers from a stag party sleeping off their excesses. In less than three hours, he landed in Ireland and gaining an hour with Ireland's time behind Spain, a taxi had sped him to Kindale House Hotel in the centre of the town.

'I hope you enjoy your time in Ireland,' the driver had said, as he deposited Malcolm's cases by the desk. Turning to the receptionist, he smiled. 'Good morning, gorgeous Kathleen, make sure you find this gentleman a fine room, he's had a long journey.'

Malcolm gave the driver a generous tip then signed the registration form. He waited as Kathleen checked the reservation. 'Your room isn't available yet but we'll take care of your luggage if you'd like to relax in the lounge. I'll give you a shout when its ready.' As she took Malcolm's form, Kathleen turned to call out to the driver. 'Take care of yourself, Finbar,' she said.

Malcolm ordered a club sandwich and as he ate, he

looked out of the window and watched the world go by. Kindale House Hotel was perfectly placed in the centre of the town, with a green area to the front, surrounded by shops and galleries. Families sat on the grass, enjoying ice-creams, while several young boys kicked a ball. Ahead, on the other side of the road, lay the sea, where boats glistening in the sunshine were moored, as gulls circled overhead in lazy arcs.

At the bus-stop, a queue had formed on the pavement, as people waited to be whisked off along the Wild Atlantic Way, a scenic journey of soaring cliffs, hidden beaches and beautiful bays.

Malcolm finished his meal and pushed his plate to one side. He wiped his mouth with his napkin and looked out of the window to see a bus come to a halt and several passengers get off. A lone woman crossed the road and as she stood on the green, studying the many cafes and shops, Malcolm leaned forward.

He could hardly believe his eyes!

There, within yards of the window, stood Melissa. Her hair shone in the sunlight and as she held onto her bag and looked around, he studied his wife. With her shoulders square and back straight, Melissa radiated a confidence that he'd not seen in a long time and it was all he could do not to run out of the hotel and pound into her with his fists.

'Excuse me, sir,' a voice called out, 'your room is ready.' Kathleen held out a key. 'We hope you enjoy your stay.'

Malcolm stood. He shot another glance at Melissa then turned and snatched at the card.

'Thank you, Kathleen,' he said. 'I'm sure I will.'

25

Jo woke early. She'd been awake for some time and had a fluttering feeling in her stomach, making sleep impossible. Sliding out of the covers, she took care not to disturb Bunty and Teddy and tip-toed past Hattie, who was slumbering in the opposite bed. Crossing the room, Jo gently pulled the curtains back and the glorious sight beyond the window made her gasp. The sun had begun to rise, filling the baby blue sky with shades of orange and pink as puffs of cloud swirled by. The grass, mown short, dazzled diamonds with dew.

It was postcard perfect and Jo was delighted. The weather could not be better for their special day. 'Thank you,' she called out to the heavens.

'Talking to yourself?' A voice came from beneath the covers of the opposite bed and a tousled head appeared. Bleary eyed, Hattie sat up.

'Oh Hattie, do come and look at the beautiful morning.'

'Bleedin' hell, it's six o'clock, I've only been in bed five minutes,' Hattie said and she yawned.

'Five hours, actually, and you went out like a light.'

'Hardly surprising, I was knackered; I don't know where the oldies get their stamina from.'

'It's a big day today and the guests are excited.' Jo looked out at the marquees and staging area. 'The party in the cottage went on 'til very late.'

She looked beyond the lake, which glistened like a mirror, to the cottage nestling in the trees. During the night, faint sounds of music and laughter had drifted over the garden as the cottage residents continued their merry making.

'There'll be some sore heads this morning.' Hattie rubbed her eyes. 'I'll send over a batch of my pick-me-up.'

'You might need to double the quantity to breathe life into Willie, he was out for the count after dinner.' Jo opened the wardrobe door and began to rifle through the garments. She chose a silky blue dress and placed it to one side. 'I hope Melissa joins in today; she isolated herself yesterday.'

'Aye, I thought it seemed strange that she went for a walk and a poke around the shops in Kindale.'

'She missed the singing class too; she was looking forward to that.'

'Perhaps she wants to find her feet.'

'Maybe, but I'm still worried; try and keep an eye on her, if you get the time.'

Teddy was awake and had slid from the bed to wriggle around Jo's toes. His teeth tickled her skin and she leaned down to scoop him up.

'Okay,' Hattie replied as she got out of bed. 'But it's a big day today, try and enjoy it.'

'I will, once it's all over.' Jo was thoughtful as she rubbed Teddy's head. 'Do you know, I hardly think of Pete at the moment.'

'Thank God for that.'

'In fact, I feel quite angry about the way he treated me.'

'Hallelujah!'

'I think that in some ways, he might have done me good.' Jo put Teddy on the floor and reached out to stroke Bunty. 'You can lose your confidence in a relationship.'

'Only if the relationship isn't working.'

'Maybe it wasn't and I just didn't see it, but I am beginning to feel better about myself.'

'So you should, with everything that you've achieved, and I told you your broken heart would mend if you kept busy.' Hattie picked up a towel and opened the bathroom door. 'I'm first in the shower, tell Connor to save me some breakfast.'

∼

IN THE COTTAGE, there was little sign of life. With no curtains to shield sun from the windows, Audrey and the Babes had draped towels and, in the parlour, Lucinda had pinned her smock to the pelmet where it hung, like an abstract painting, in a kaleidoscope of colour.

Lucinda was dead to the world and her snores thundered off the thick stone walls, vibrating sound to the floor above where Harry, Bill and Willie, windows open wide, snored too. In the opposite room, the Babes were also sound asleep. Like cramped sardines in an oversized can, their camp beds lay in uniform lines with Audrey's positioned under the window. There was hardly room to stand between overflowing suitcases and swimsuits laid out to dry.

In the kitchen, Alf had been up for more than an hour. He'd taken his morning walk and as he passed the front door of the manor, Jo appeared with Bunty and Teddy, who, seeing Ness, had bounded across to join him. He'd given Jo a thumbs up and now was busy mixing meat and biscuits into three dishes.

A KETTLE WHISTLED on the ancient gas stove and Alf poured boiling water onto tea in a large china pot and placed it on one side to brew.

'Is there anything to eat?' Harry came into the kitchen. He looked surprisingly fresh and wore a T-shirt bearing the slogan, "I'm Not As Drunk As You Think I Am".

'A slice of toast, if you can manage the cooker.' Alf dug in his pocket and flicked a box of matches over to Harry. He cut a wedge from a loaf of bread and placed it on the wire rack.

'Shit!' Harry yelled as a blast of gas ignited and sent him staggering back from the grill. 'It's burnt my hair.'

Alf passed no comment as he slid the bread under the flaming jets.

'That cooker must be from the 1950s,' Harry said as he stood over the sink, rubbing his uneven fringe.

'A classic; they don't make them like that anymore.'

'Thank god.' Harry stared at fragments of singed hair scattered over the stoneware.

Alf turned the bread and when it was golden brown, placed it on a plate and spread butter thickly. 'Shall I pour you a cuppa?'

'Did someone say tea?' Lucinda stood in the doorway. She wore a long, silk kimono and dragged on a cigarette. Her hair, not confined to a chignon, was wild.

'Is that the smell of breakfast?' Audrey slithered past Lucinda, who made no attempt to move, and reached out to pick up the toast. 'Delicious,' she said and turning to Harry asked, 'What have you done to your hair?'

Harry ignored Audrey and taking more bread from Alf, began to slice, as footsteps pounded down the stairs and the Babes flocked in, followed by Willie and Bill.

As tea was poured and a makeshift breakfast enjoyed, the group discussed their activities for the day. Willie asked Harry and Bill to help with washing and polishing his coach, as Bessie the Bus would be on display that afternoon. Audrey and the Babes had work to do on their outfits and Lucinda said that she needed to have a lie down. She'd had an exhausting time with classes, the day before.

Alf clattered mugs and plates into the sink and turned the tap. Water, the colour of rusting iron, trickled over the debris. 'We'd best all crack on then,' Alf said and began to wash.

∼

Melissa sat in the dining room and forced herself to eat a bowl of cereal. It had been an effort to dress and come down, but she knew that Hattie would be on the warpath if she didn't put in an appearance.

'We missed you yesterday,' Hattie had said when she'd called Melissa at an unearthly hour. 'I wanted to make sure that you're up and ready to enjoy the celebrations today.'

Melissa had told Hattie that she'd wanted a quiet time to herself the previous day and would, of course, be joining in with the activities planned.

'That's good, we don't want you moping about, worrying that Malcolm will appear at any moment,' Hattie said. 'He doesn't know where you are; you can relax and have a bit of fun.'

If only she could!

Melissa finished her breakfast and left the dining room. She still hadn't a clue what to do about Finbar and the only decision she'd made was to stay out of his way.

She walked through the hallway and into reception. There were no classes today and guests were free to do as they liked. Wandering out to the driveway, she stopped when she saw Willie cleaning his coach. Harry held a sponge and was soaping the paintwork, while Bill gripped a hose and sprayed.

They all looked up when Melissa appeared.

'We missed you yesterday,' Bill called out, his new found confidence shining.

'I had a quiet day to myself,' Melissa replied.

'Want to help?' Willie asked.

'Well, er, I was looking for Teddy.' Melissa faltered. 'I thought I'd take him for a walk.'

'He's with Alf near the lake, fixing up some bunting,' Willie said. 'If you'd be kind enough to do the woodwork on the inside?'

'Yes, of course.' Melissa took a duster and polish from Willie's wrinkled hands. 'Anything I can do to assist.'

~

FINBAR WAS in the music room where Miss O'Connelly sat at the piano, her fingers travelling confidently over the keys, as the students sang their hearts out. They'd nailed the two songs that Finbar wanted to perform that evening and he was delighted.

'May the wind always be at your back,' Finbar said and clapped his hands, 'you're all to be congratulated.' He went around the room shaking hands. 'Now make sure you're ready on time tonight and I'll see you all on stage.'

'Break a leg,' someone called out.

'We can do it!' shouted another.

Finbar walked over to Miss O'Connelly and after conferring for a few moments, raised his hand to say goodbye to the group and left the room.

He walked down the hallway and into reception and noting that there was no one about, headed outside. 'The quiet before the storm,' he said to himself as he wandered over the drive, where a coach was being buffed and polished.

'Top of the mornin' to you, lads,' Finbar called.

As he acknowledged their greetings in response, he looked up. A woman was on the coach and she appeared to be cleaning the woodwork trim that ran throughout the interior. Strands of strawberry blonde hair had come loose from combs holding it away from her pretty face. Finbar watched her stretch and bend, noting her neat figure as she faced the window and began to wipe the glass.

Suddenly, as if magnetically drawn, she stopped. Their eyes met and Finbar felt as though he'd been struck by a bolt of lightning. The woman's eyes were as blue as a tropical pool and he had the urge to dive in.

Glued to the spot, he gazed back.

But in what seemed like only seconds, she turned and fled. He heard her steps crunch as she hurried across the gravel and disappeared into the manor.

'Wait!' he called out, but it was too late.

Finbar realised that Bill was standing next to him, the hose still gripped in his hand.

'She's fragile,' Bill said, 'let her be.'

The hose in Bill's hand splashed water onto Finbar's legs and shoes and he jumped back. As he looked at Bill in amazement, he saw something menacing in the man's eyes.

Now was not the time to be making enquiries about the mysterious blonde.

'I'll be on my way,' Finbar said, shaking his trouser leg. 'You're doing a grand job, lads.'

He turned and set off. There was much to be done in the stage area; groups who'd perform later had arrived and begun sound checks and rehearsals, and as compere for the evening, in charge of just about everything to do with the show, Finbar needed to be on hand.

As he walked across the grass he nodded to members of the Round Table, who were setting out their stalls in the marquees. He smiled when he saw

Audrey and her Babes, trooping towards the lake, clad in dressing gowns and carrying flippers.

'Will you be havin' a livener, Finbar?' Ted called out from the pub as he set up the bar.

Finbar shook his head and carried on. His mind was full of things that he had to do but there was one thing that he needed to add to his list.

The woman with the blue eyes was familiar. He couldn't for the life of him think where he'd seen her but, sure as saints were saints, Finbar knew that it wasn't the first time they'd met. As he waved a hand in greeting to the guys and girls gathered in groups, Finbar vowed that, just as soon as he could, he'd track her down and find out who she was.

26

The gates of Boomerville Manor were opened to the public at precisely two o'clock and as volunteers directed cars to park at the bottom of the drive, families and friends who'd walked to the event from Kindale and the surrounding area began to pile in.

On stage, The Bothy Brothers, a local folk band, played catchy tunes as a troupe of young Irish dancers performed. In distinctive costumes, their leather ghillies, laced from ankle to toe, were soundless as they made their way around the platform.

On the carousel, garishly-painted wooden horses began to turn. From the top of the helter-skelter, cries of excitement could be heard, as children clinging to straw mats whooshed down at speed, twisting and turning until, ejected like bullets from a gun, they ricocheted across the grass. The ladies from the Women's Institute were busy in the refreshment tent, serving cakes and scones and at Father Ted's a queue had formed as Ted and his team kept up with the demand for beer.

Lucinda, revived from her morning's sleep, had set up an easel and stool. She was busy face painting and her paint-daubed smock billowed around her bony body. She held her cigarette holder aloft and blew smoke in the face of any whingeing child that didn't like her creations.

'Bleedin' hell,' Hattie said as she walked through the crowd with Jo. 'I hope Lucinda's using water based paints that wash off.'

'I don't remember agreeing to let her loose on children.' Jo was perplexed as she stared at angry looking tigers and wild orangutans. 'Why couldn't she stick to painting butterflies and fairies?'

At the coconut shy, Harry and Alf were hurling hard wooden balls. Neither had a good aim and as balls went flying, visitors scattered.

'Let me show you how to do it,' Bill said and stepped forward. He tossed a ball between his hands and eyed a coconut. Taking a run, his arm swung in an arc and the ball pelted through the air. It hit a coconut hard.

Alf and Harry were open-mouthed as the nut fell to the floor.

'Where did you learn to throw a ball like that?' Alf asked.

'I've never done it before.' Bill beamed as he collected his prize.

'You'll have to join a cricket team.' Harry patted Bill on the shoulder. 'Is there one local to you at home?'

Bill mumbled that he had no idea. He didn't want to think about Creston and the dismal old villa, it would put a dampener on the day.

You see! It's not just me who thinks you should be away from this place and facing up to your responsibilities.

As Bill gripped the coconut, he imagined it was his mother's head and squeezed tightly.

The house is going to rack and ruin and it's all your fault! Galivanting and squandering your money.

'Enough!' Bill shouted and he flung the coconut some distance away.

'Steady on, old son,' Alf said in alarm and took Bill's arm. 'You could kill someone doing that.'

Hearing Alf's words, Bill thought of his mother. "Kill" was too kind a word and he didn't dare voice what he really felt.

'Fancy a beer?' Harry asked.

'That's a grand idea, let's go over to Father Ted's, then see how Willie is getting on.' Alf led Bill away.

On the stage, Finbar had gathered the Mayor of Kindale and was ready to make an announcement. James, looking cool in a short-sleeved cotton shirt and smart dark trousers, was escorting the mayor during the afternoon and stood to one side.

'Ladies and gentlemen,' Finbar began, 'it gives me great pleasure to ask Madam Mayor to officially open this wonderful event.'

Jo and Hattie had been commandeered to assist on stage and they held either end of a ribbon as Finbar handed the mayor a pair of scissors. Suited and booted in a tight linen suit, the robust lady mayor was flustered as she stepped forward. Her chain of office, the work of fine Irish craftsmen, appeared cumbersome, as the heavy gold links shone in the searing sunshine beating down on the stage.

'Well,' the mayor began, 'the good Lord has shh…

ertainly blessed this event with a hot day for the shelebrations.' She took a lace-edged handkerchief from her pocket and wiped her brow.

'Is she pissed?' Hattie whispered, as James edged forward.

'But before I cut the wibbon, I'd like to congratulate the new owner of Fllaaatterly Manor, or Boooooomerville Manor, as I understand it is now known.' She turned to Jo and laughed. 'Jo Docherty is bwringing jobs to our area and pwoviding a woooonderful place to benefit from unusual classes.' She looked ahead at the audience, closing one eye as she focussed. 'And I will sooon twreat myself to a fine meal in the Fllaaatterly Woom Westaurant.'

There was a cheer from Father Ted's as friends of chef Connor raised their glasses.

'It gives me gweat pleasure,' the mayor continued, 'to officially announce that this event is now ooopen and I welcome everwyone to Booooomerville Manor.'

She sawed at the ribbon, as James steadied her from behind and Jo and Hattie held tight. There was a polite round of applause. Finbar clapped too then took the microphone from the mayor.

'Folks,' he said, 'we've a grand line-up of entertainment which carries right on into the evening and, to kick-off, I'd like you to all make your way to the lake, where in thirty minutes time, the Boomerville Babes will present an aquatic performance.'

'That will be interwesting,' the mayor said to Jo and Hattie as they helped her down from the stage. She continued to dab at her face with her hankie. 'But I need a dwink before I wander into the lake.'

James stepped forward. 'May I suggest tea and scones in the refreshment tent?' he asked.

'Something stwonger,' the mayor replied. 'Father Ted's pleeese.'

Jo and Hattie watched the mayor as she reached out and grabbed the arm that James held out.

'I think the mayor may have had a livener before she arrived today,' Hattie said as she watched the woman, teetering on her heels, being led away by James.

Jo was far more interested in the activity by the lake. 'What the devil is going on with Audrey?' she asked Hattie. She had her hands on her hips and a murderous look in her eyes. 'I don't remember agreeing to any aquatic performances.'

'Ease up,' Hattie replied. 'Perhaps you should join the mayor and chill out.'

'What if someone drowns?' Jo looked anxious. 'The lake's freezing cold and god knows what's under that murky water.'

'Eight Babes wearing rubber bob hats.' Hattie grinned. 'It'll bring the house down; stop panicking, Audrey has it sorted.' Hattie put her arm around Jo's shoulders and moved her along. 'Wild water swimming is all the rage these days.'

Jo felt like drowning Hattie in as wild a stretch of water as she could find, but at this part of the programme, she knew that there was little she could do to change things.

'I'm starving,' Hattie said. 'Let's grab a scone and a piece of cake to keep our strength up.'

'I think I'll join the mayor at Father Ted's.'

'An even better idea.' Hattie saluted Jo. 'Father Ted's it is.'

MELISSA HAD MADE her mind up. No matter what complications came her way, she would never divulge her secret. Having thought long and hard, she knew that it would be impossible to avoid Finbar during her time in Ireland. Matters may even be made more difficult if he knew about Patrick and she decided to stay in the area, for Finbar was a local here and it seemed that his days wandering around the globe, with a microphone in his hand, were over. She'd checked online and discovered that he had a taxi business and also advertised himself to host events and sing in pubs and clubs. He had a steady life in Kindale and there was almost certainly a Mrs Finbar Murphy somewhere in the wings, possibly a dozen younger Murphys too.

The best thing to do was to ignore him and make sure that they never became friends.

Melissa's decision was further endorsed by a conversation she'd had with Patrick earlier that morning. Her son hadn't responded to her letter and she'd decided to give him a call. He told her that he hadn't received her letter, perhaps it was delayed in the post.

'I'm really pleased for you, Mum,' Patrick had said when she told him her news. 'A fresh start in Ireland sounds like a great idea.'

But Patrick sounded worried and Melissa could detect anxiety in his voice.

'Are you alright?' she asked. 'Is something bothering you?'

'No, it's okay, just a bit of pressure at work, that's all,' he'd replied, 'nothing for you to stress about.'

They'd spoken further and Patrick said that he was

glad that she'd decided to leave Malcolm, for he'd thought that his mother hadn't been happy for some time.

If only Patrick knew the truth, Melissa mused as she selected an outfit and began to get ready for the opening event. She'd never told her son about the beatings, the pain and humiliation that she'd endured for the last couple of years. But he must have detected something during his phone calls, and on the rare visits to Cheshire or Spain.

Melissa knew that Patrick didn't like Malcolm and hoped that now, with her marriage at an end, she'd see more of her son. How wonderful it would be to be free to go and stay with him and have him here, in the home that she hoped to create.

But now was not the time to be making a shocking announcement. Patrick seemed to have worries of his own and what would be the benefit of telling him that his father had suddenly turned up? It was, she decided, a subject to be left well alone. No one need know and in that way, no one would get hurt. Finbar and Patrick would carry on with their lives, none the wiser.

Melissa chose a pretty lemon-coloured dress. It had been expensive and she'd bought it in a designer boutique in Marbella. Knowing it was unlikely that she'd ever spend that sort of money on clothing again, and with the wonderful weather in Ireland, she decided to make sure it got plenty of wear.

Beginning today.

Sleeveless and straight, the dress stopped just above the knee and was cut low at the back. She remembered the last time she'd worn it. Malcolm had taken her to a restaurant in Marbella; it was her birthday and he'd presented her with an opal pendant. Melissa loathed the pendant and although she knew that opals were supposed to be lucky for some, it certainly hadn't been lucky that night. The beating she'd received was severe with Malcolm yelling that she wasn't grateful for his gifts.

But now, as Melissa stared at her reflection in a full-length mirror on the wall, she smiled. She didn't look too bad for her age and, best of all, she was free.

She smoothed on coral lipstick and sprayed perfume. With her hair pinned up and a few strands astray, Melissa was satisfied with her appearance.

Slipping her feet into a pair of gold sandals, she looked out of the window. The garden was crowded and she could hear music coming from the direction of the stage. Melissa felt a flurry of excitement and vowed that she was not only going to enjoy today, but every second of her stay at Boomerville Manor.

~

BILL WAS FEELING BRIGHTER. His mother had stopped nagging and at that moment wasn't haunting him from beyond the grave. Although, Bill chuckled to himself as he stood at the bar in Father Ted's, she'd certainly be turning in her grave if she could see her only son with Harry and Alf as they bought a round of drinks for a group of pretty girls from Kindale. Bill had even told a joke and to his astonishment the girls had laughed; one had even slapped his arm and said what a grand fella he was.

'And do you dance, Bill?' the redhead asked. She

was older than the others, but not unattractive. He could feel her heat as she came close.

'No, but I'm sure you could teach me,' he heard himself saying and took a long drink of his pint.

It must be the Guinness.

He felt confident and quite lightheaded and as Alf handed out shots, he raised his glass. 'Sláinte!' he shouted as the shots were knocked back.

'Sláinte is táinte,' the girls said. 'Health is wealth.'

The redhead had taken hold of Bill's arm and as Alf shared another joke, Bill felt her fingers wriggle into his own. He realised that he was actually holding hands with a woman, for the very first time in his life. Her body was warm and her breasts, large and soft, rubbed against his skin. Bill began to feel hot; a sweat had broken out on his forehead.

Harry, wearing a T-shirt with the slogan, "God is Busy, May I Help You?" was about to order another round and as he turned to the busy bar, he caught sight of Melissa.

'Melissa!' Harry called out. 'Come and join us, I'm getting the drinks in.'

Melissa walked over to the group and thanking Harry, was about to order a mineral water but a shout, above the noise, made her turn.

'Bugger off!' Bill said. 'Leave me alone!

The redhead suddenly dropped his hand.

Bill's face was crimson and he was angry. He could hear his mother's relentless voice, taunting him.

The devil is watching your carrying on, with drink and women and reckless behaviour; it's straight to hell, that's where you're going, Bill Bradbury!

Incensed, Bill turned to the redhead and realised

what he'd done. Flustered, he tried to explain. 'I'm so sorry, I didn't mean to startle you, I had a voice in my head and...' he trailed off.

The woman's look of horror, as she backed off, said it all.

Bill was a misfit and he always would be.

Alf put his hand on Bill's shoulder. 'Why don't you give the shots a rest for a bit, old son,' he said as the redhead and her party picked up their drinks and stormed off.

Bill was deflated. His earlier excitement had diminished, as fast as a candle blown out in the wind. He felt ashamed as Alf and Harry stared at him and to his dismay, Melissa had appeared from nowhere and was staring at him too. Tears welled at the corner of his eyes and threatened to spill over. Dear God, please don't let him cry in front of his new friends.

'I'd like to go and see what's happening at the lake.' Melissa stepped forward. 'Will you walk with me?'

She spoke softly and Bill could see her delicate fingers reach out. Dressed in lemon with her velvety blonde hair piled high, her eyes kind and lips smiling, she looked like an angel as she slipped her hand into the crook of his arm.

It was too much and to Bill's dismay he heard a snuffle and realising that the sound came from his own throat, hung his head in shame. But the tears that he'd fought to keep back were now flowing and Bill couldn't control his heaving shoulders. Sobs tore through his body and he was incapable of controlling himself as Alf and Harry came forward, their words sympathetic.

'Come on, old son, we all do daft things,' Alf said. 'We know you couldn't help it.'

Together with Melissa, they guided him away from the pub and across the lawn, to a corner of the refreshment tent. A chair was found and gentle hands lowered Bill into it. Melissa forced a cotton hankie into Bill's fingers and he heard Alf whispering to a group of concerned ladies from the WI.

'It's the heat, he's just a bit overcome, that's all.'

'Shall we get help from the St John's Ambulance team?' a lady asked.

'No need, we'll take care of him, it's cool in here.'

A glass of water was held against Bill's lips. 'Try and have a drink,' Melissa said, as Bill's sobs began to subside. 'It'll help.'

'Everything alright?' Hattie, having seen a commotion at the other end of the bar in Father Ted's, had left Jo to the company of the mayor, who was hosting her own entertainment, as she encouraged drinkers to join with her in a chorus of, "The Rocky Road to Dublin".

Alf took Hattie to one side.

'Bill's upset, he thinks he's offended us.'

'And has he?'

'No, not at all, we've sort of got used to Bill shouting out.'

'Ah, that.' Hattie nodded her head. 'I've heard him too. It's as if he's talking to an imaginary person.'

'Or they're talking to him.'

'We all have our demons, maybe Bill's evil spirits are a little livelier than ours.'

'I'll keep an eye on him, he's not a bad sort and he's been grand company over the past few days.' Alf looked over to the corner, where Bill, still clutching Melissa's hankie, was looking a bit brighter. Melissa had conjured up a cup of sweet tea and was encouraging him to drink.

'If you can get him to his feet, there's an activity about to start over at the lake that will take his mind off things.'

'Oh hell,' Alf said. 'Is Audrey about to launch her Babes?'

'Off the end of the jetty by the look of things.'

'Save us a place, we're on our way.' Alf gave Hattie a smile. 'Come on, Bill,' he called out, 'there's a bench by the lake that's got our name on it and a surprise in the water that you won't want to miss.'

27

Malcolm had hired a car and, having been given directions for Ballymegille, was soon driving through the gates of the manor. He followed instructions given by a tall, ruddy-face youth with a head of flaming hair. An identical youth in a matching checked shirt, worn under a visibility waistcoat, directed him to an empty space. Malcolm parked his car, turned off the ignition, and reached across the passenger seat to retrieve a Panama hat. Placing it on his head, he adjusted his Ray-Bans then checked his reflection in the mirror. Satisfied with his appearance, he picked up a small leather bag and climbed out of the vehicle.

Peeling off a pair of leather gloves, he placed them in the bag and slung the strap over his shoulder.

The ground was dry underfoot and with the temperature rising, it was busy on the driveway as people made their way to grounds of the manor. Dust began to settle on Malcolm's Louis Vuitton suede loafers and he silently cursed as he joined a line of excited children and parents, dressed in shorts and casual tops. His Armani chinos would soon be grubby too, if he didn't get off this dusty path and onto the grass.

It didn't take long to walk to the manor and at the main entrance, Malcolm was directed to the event by a middle-aged, craggy-faced supervisor. Casual in jeans and a jacket, his fiery locks were scraped into a pony tail. His jacket was printed with the word, "Steward" across the back.

'Hey, Declan,' a woman wearing a white apron leaning out of a van selling ice-cream called out to the man. 'Will you have an ice to cool you off?'

'No, Marie, I'm just fine, but you could take a couple of cornets to the lads on the gate.'

Several children ran forward, surrounding the van.

'To be sure, just as soon as I've served this lot,' Marie replied.

'Here's a programme of events,' Declan said and handed a leaflet to Malcolm. 'Enjoy your day.'

Malcolm studied the leaflet as he wandered across the lawn. He couldn't imagine why on earth Melissa would want to be involved in this hillbilly scenario, when she had classy events in Cheshire and Marbella at her fingertips, from golf tournaments and polo to exclusive charity dinners.

The sooner he found her and talked some sense into her dense blonde head, the sooner they could get away from the back of beyond and return to their normal lives. His business needed time and attention and although Malcolm was confident that he could sort out any of his current difficulties, time away was money and he needed to get back.

The place was packed as Malcolm negotiated his

way through the crowds. People gathered around the many stalls and there was a queue at the tombola stand and coconut shy. He'd no desire to stop and pin a tail on a donkey, nor have his face painted by a weary looking woman who sat on a stool, with a cigarette held high. Malcolm noticed a white-haired, elderly man sitting on the steps of a vintage bus. He drank a pint of Guinness and appeared to be enjoying the attention that his vehicle was receiving from like-minded enthusiasts who made appreciate noises as they admired the paintwork and stopped to ask questions. A tug of war was taking place on one side of the lawn and Malcolm was horrified to see that the average age of the competitors appeared to be over sixty. He witnessed a similar sight at a three-legged race, that had just ended with a pile of happy pensioners falling over the finishing line. Afternoon tea was being served in a refreshment tent, but Malcolm was thirsty and with no appetite for scones or cake, he searched for a pub.

Father Ted's was doing a brisk trade and it was several minutes before Malcolm reached the bar to order a drink. A substantial woman with a beehive hairdo, wearing a crumpled suit with a magnificent chain of office around the folds of her neck, sat on one end of the bar and saluted him with her drink.

'Don't mind our mayor,' Ted said as he lifted a mat and wiped a sticky surface, 'she does a grand job.' He smiled as the mayor began to sing. 'Now, what can I get you?'

'Just a cold beer.'

'Coming up.'

Malcolm paid Ted but as he sipped the froth at the rim of his glass, he noticed a commotion at the other end of the pub. People stood back and a red-haired woman led several girls away from a man, who called after them. He appeared to be apologising.

Malcolm removed his sunglasses and stared at the man. To his astonishment he recognised him. It was the little creep who'd bent Malcolm's arm at Hotel Boomerville in Cumbria. What the hell was he doing here? He watched as two men stepped forward and took the arms of the man, who was clearly upset.

Suddenly, a flash of lemon fabric caught Malcolm's eye as a woman leaned in to talk to the person in distress.

A smile crept across Malcolm's face.

The last time he'd seen Melissa in that lemon dress was when she'd worn it to the restaurant Paco Jiménez, in the Plaza de los Naranjos, in the old town of Marbella. They'd gone there to celebrate her birthday and Melissa had looked beautiful in the candlelight of the sophisticated surroundings. Her face had lit up when he'd presented her with an expensive opal pendant, jewellery that complemented the dress perfectly. But last week, when Malcolm rifled through Melissa's belongings in Spain, he'd discovered that the silly bitch had left all her jewellery behind. He wondered if this implied that she intended to return? Was all this Irish nonsense just a fantasy, no doubt bought on by menopause or some other female failing, or had she deliberately left without her precious jewels?

As he watched his wife leave the pub, accompanying the men, Malcolm silently cursed. Whatever her plans, how dare she think that she could get away from him! He made the rules and called the shots in this marriage.

As he drank his beer, he was determined that the only way she'd part from his company would be in a wooden box.

∼

Finbar stood on the side of the stage. As he waited for the current act to finish their gig, he thought about the woman he'd seen earlier. There was something about her that was familiar and appealing and he couldn't for the life of him work out what it was. Since his marriage had ended, many years ago, he'd gone back to his bachelor days and women came and went in Finbar's life. If he was truthful, they always had; being married hadn't stopped his philandering and it was no wonder that his wife had upped and left him.

As he watched the young lads performing on the stage, Finbar's mind was elsewhere. It was unfortunate that he'd never had any kids of his own, but perhaps the good Lord knew what he was doing, for Finbar felt sure that he wouldn't have made a very good father. He'd rarely been at home and spent his money on fripperies, like his beloved boat, that was moored in the harbour in Kindale. His dear mam cost a packet too, especially since she'd gone completely doolally, and in need of Finbar's finances to support her round-the-clock care.

The act was winding up and as the group belted out their last chorus, Finbar checked his headpiece for sound and moved onto the stage. As he stepped out, a glimmer of lemon, soft in the sunlight, caught his eye. It was the woman, moving through the crowd. Wearing a sleeveless dress, cut low at the back, her blonde hair was piled high and with sunglasses perched on the end of her pretty nose, she didn't look Finbar's way.

'I'll find you,' he whispered.

The Rolling Tones, a group of nine teenage boys from the local high school, completed their set and took a bow and Finbar invited the audience to give the band one last round of applause. When the enthusiastic clapping from friends and family had died down, Finbar helped the lads pick up their gear and make their way off the stage.

Finbar checked the running order. There were forty minutes before the next act was due and he just had time to hurry over to the lake, start the music and watch the Boomerville Babes, who were about to begin their performance.

Perhaps the lady in lemon would be there.

~

A CROWD SURROUNDED THE LAKE, where Jo stood with Hattie and waited anxiously.

Jo wondered what the hell Audrey was up to.

'You know I would never have agreed to this.' Jo was cross and she folded her arms. 'I'm praying that Audrey keeps it short and no one gets injured.'

'I can't wait,' Hattie said. 'I'm thinking of joining the Babes when I get back to Cumbria.' She looked around and was pleased to see the many folk that had gathered to witness the water event.

'God help us,' Jo replied and was about to remonstrate further, but stopped when she heard music suddenly blast from a boombox, placed on the end of the jetty.

Audrey, to the accompaniment of the band of the Royal Irish Regiment, stepped out. She put her best foot forward and keeping time with the bugles, pipes and drums, marched smartly across the wooden boards.

'What the hell has she got on?' Jo's jaw dropped as she stared at Audrey.

Wearing nothing but a flesh-coloured bodysuit and several tired gladioli pinned in her hair, Audrey raised a hand. On her command, drums thundered and the Babes, each to a beat, began to shoot through the air, flying high over Audrey's head.

'Are they naked?' Jo's eyes were wide as she stared in horror. The start of the routine seemed endless as eight middle-aged bodies flew past before plunging deep into the lake.

Parents gasped and covered their children's eyes.

Hattie, however, was laughing. Audrey had played a blinder, having concealed a trampoline in the bushes, to bounce the Babes into the water. Their bodysuits, on loan from a theatrical costume supplier in Kindale, hadn't quite achieved the desired effect of turning the babe's bodies into the smooth stems of flowers, which now created a bouquet effect on the surface of the lake, as eight capped heads emerged. Rubber lilies, daffodils and daisies, glued to the caps, moved in a circle to join with sunflowers, carnations and tulips.

Bugles and pipes played the tune, "An English Country Garden", and Finbar began to sing.

'There is joy in the spring
When the birds begin to sing
In an English Country Garden…'

With Audrey directing, the Babes produced their most dazzling routine. Fishtail moves turned into Flamingo spins and sixteen legs performed the more complicated "Egg-beater", which whisked up a considerable lather on the lake. The entertainment ended with a breathtaking series of well-rehearsed backflips, projecting the Babes, with Audrey's assistance, into a sitting position on the edge of the jetty. Their flowery heads bounced as they synchronised the crossing of their legs, whilst smiling and waving to the applauding crowd.

'Let's hear it for the Boomerville Babes!' Finbar called out.

'I want to join in!' The mayor, now barefoot, wobbled perilously close to the jetty. But James was by the mayor's side, kitten heels in hand, and he took a firm hold and guided her to the safety of the lawn.

'Someone find some towels and cover them up,' Jo said. She shook her head as eight seemingly bare bottoms, of all shapes and sizes, faced the crowd as the Babes turned and stood to pose for a photographer from the Kindale & County News.

'That will fill the classes for months to come,' Hattie said, still clapping her hands.

'If we're not closed down,' Jo snapped. 'I hope there's no one here from Health & Safety.' She turned away. 'I'm going to check on things at the manor.'

'Aye, I'll come with you, we don't want any strangers wandering about the place,' Hattie said.

Finbar leapt back on the stage and announced that it was time for the next act.

Jo and Hattie side-stepped the many picnics that

had appeared, as visitors laid rugs on the lawn and made themselves comfortable for further entertainment. They unpacked baskets and bags containing sandwiches and snacks and began to tuck in.

'Families and friends, saints and sinners,' Finbar called out, 'will you please put your hands together for the one and only, Molly Malones!'

A female folk group took to the stage. The oldest, grey-haired and dressed in clogs and a smock, made herself comfortable in a rocking chair and began to squeeze an accordion. Three middle-aged woman, in denim dungarees with daisies weaved into their waist-length locks, waved to the audience and held fiddles and bows aloft. The youngest musician, a child wearing a patchwork dress, held a recorder.

'It can only get better,' Hattie said. She winced as the child began to play, her recorder screeching into a microphone.

'I thought Finbar said he'd organised quality entertainment,' Jo shouted as she stuck her fingers in her ears.

'I don't know what you expect in return for a scone and a cup of tea but there's plenty more to come.'

They'd reached the pub where Alf, Bill and Harry, clutching bottles of beer, sat on a bench, enjoying the sunshine.

'Everything alright?' Hattie asked Harry, yelling above the din on stage. She nodded her head towards Bill.

'Right as rain.' Harry gave a stupid grin as Hattie stared at his T-shirt.

'"God is Busy May I Help You?"' Hattie shook her head. 'Have you been on Lucinda's whacky baccy?'

But Harry wasn't taking the bait and, still smiling, turned away.

'Where's Melissa?' Hattie asked.

'She said she wanted to have a walk to see the stalls,' Alf said.

'Are you coming?' Jo tugged on Hattie's arm.

Pleased to see that Bill had recovered from his earlier outburst, Hattie noted the contented grin on his face as he watched the world go by.

'Aye, let's leave the Three Musketeers to struggle through the rest of the day.' She nodded to Jo. 'Lead on.'

∼

MALCOLM WAS INFURIATED. It was nigh on impossible to catch Melissa on her own and as he trailed behind his wife, keeping a safe distance, with his hat low and Ray-Bans in place, he attempted to look as inconspicuous as possible. Melissa was bound to create a scene when he caught up with her and for his plan to work, it wouldn't do to have any kind of commotion.

Malcolm intended to use information that he'd kept quiet for some considerable time. A secret weapon that would disarm Melissa. When she heard what he'd got to say, Melissa would be back in their marriage as fast as it took to book a seat on a plane to Spain. She'd had her moment of glory, her escape from routine and he'd allowed his wife what he considered to be a holiday on her own, but enough was enough, and now it was time to go home.

Malcolm would be back in control.

But first, he needed to get Melissa alone. He couldn't run the risk of being arrested if he had to bundle his wife out of the manor and wrestle her into the car. He knew that the hotel manager, the overweight cow from Cumbria, whom he'd seen wandering around the grounds, would be on his case faster that a dose of the clap.

He followed Melissa from stall to stall and sighed with frustration as he watched her win a prize on the tombola and almost hit a coconut at the coconut shy. She'd even had a ride on the carousel, her shapely legs astride a brightly painted wooden horse, while Malcolm hid in the shadows and looked on. If only she'd go into the manor and up to her room. Once he had Melissa on her own, he planned to break his news and, without any fuss, they'd pack her things and be on their way.

He watched his wife wander over the lawn and settle down to watch the performers on stage.

Malcolm looked at his Rolex. It was only a matter of time.

28

Jo and Hattie sat on opposite beds in Jo's room, both nursing a mug of iced tea. The room was dimly lit, the only light from a lamp on Hattie's bedside table. Heat still hung heavy after a day of clear blue skies and scorching sunshine and they'd kicked off their covers, to rest their weary bodies on cool cotton sheets. Hours after the last act had left the stage and members of the public had been directed to their vehicles, the two women were exhausted.

Bunty and Teddy lay on the floor, on a rug under an open window. Their eyes moved beneath closed lids and noses twitched, as they set off on their nocturnal journey. Bunty had one large paw in the air and another wrapped around Teddy, as they slept the sleep of two very hot and weary woofers.

'I think you can safely say that you have a success on your hands,' Hattie said. She reached out to the bedside table, picked up a bottle of rum and poured a good measure. 'The opening event could not have given Boomerville Manor a better start.'

'My head is buzzing with it all,' Jo replied. 'I don't think I'll ever be able to sleep.'

'Have a knock-out drop.' Hattie tipped rum into a glass by Jo's bed.

'I thought Finbar's choir was very good,' Jo said, 'they bought the house down at the end.'

'Aye, it was good to see the audience on their feet.' Hattie tugged the waistband of her pyjama shorts suit. She was hot and the fabric clung. 'Watching Caitlin O'Connelly turn into the Big Bopper was a sight I never thought I'd witness.'

'She's remarkably nimble for a ninety-year-old.'

'Amazing that she can play the piano with her feet, despite the lisle stockings.'

'She made Little Richard look like a novice.'

Jo took a sip of the rum. The alcohol was soothing and she began to relax.

'Desmond made a marvellous Elvis.'

'It's his signature act.'

'What a shame that his catsuit split; I hope he'll be able to get it repaired.'

'Remind me to check on the members of the choir tomorrow,' Jo said. 'I think there'll be some very stiff legs.'

'Stiff legs?' Hattie sat up. 'More like dislocated knees and slipped discs; I've never seen so many pensioners doing a Chuck Berry duck walk.'

'I hope they're all okay.'

'I think you might be organising a couple of trips to Kindale Community Hospital in the morning; you could use Willie's bus, there's plenty of room.'

'For wheelchairs and stretchers?' Jo smiled. 'And

thinking of guests who let their hair down, do you think the mayor will have a hangover tomorrow?'

'Hangover?' Hattie turned, wide-eyed. 'I've never seen anyone consume so much booze and still stay upright.'

'James certainly had his hands full.'

'In more ways than one.'

The pair began to giggle as they remembered James, engulfed by the mayor, chain of office still in place, rocking and a reelin' across the drive, as he led her to a taxi and carefully folded her in.

'She'll be working again tomorrow.'

'Another day, another function,' Hattie said. 'She's very popular with the locals and never misses an event. Ted's profits would plummet without her.'

Jo dabbed at her brow with a tissue. She slid out of bed and walked over to the open window. Carefully avoiding the dogs, she looked out into the night where the lake glinted in the moonlight. 'I think I'll forgive Audrey for the aquatic show,' Jo said. 'She put an awful lot of effort into creating that performance.'

'Everyone loved it; you should think about wild water swimming classes and making use of the lake.'

'I wouldn't go that far.'

'I also think you should give Finbar a pay rise; he was the star of the show today.'

'Yes, he was good, wasn't he?' Jo smiled. 'He kept the whole thing flowing and was brilliant with the audience, telling jokes and keeping everyone entertained.'

'The man is a marvel, an all-round entertainment act. Serious eye-candy too.'

～

As Jo and Hattie talked long into the night, exhausted guests slept peacefully, beneath cosy covers in their comfortable bedrooms, and with the kitchen closed and staff at home replenishing their energy for the next day, the old manor house was silent. Tomorrow, the marquees and stage were to be dismantled and the garden returned to its original use.

Declan and his helpers would be busy.

The occupants of the cottage on the other side of the garden were sleeping soundly too. Outside, pinned to a long washing line, hung eight flesh-coloured bodysuits. Like sausage skin corpses, their lifeless limbs dangled in the oppressive night air.

Lucinda, normally the last to bed, had turned in early and slumbered in an alcohol-induced stupor. She was worn out by the endless procession of children, who'd been eager to be turned into tigers, witches and werewolves. Her finances were replenished and after donating a percentage of her takings to the Round Table charities, it was a satisfied Lucinda that had crawled into bed. Her snores thundered through the ceiling of the parlour to the bedroom above where Alf, Willie and Harry were also comatose.

Bill, however, was wide awake.

Despite fatigue clinging to his weary body, he was too tired to sleep. He felt as flaccid as an old lettuce as he lay on his sleeping bag, on the battered camp bed, while perspiration, clammy and warm, glued his body to the sticky fabric.

He reflected on a day full of confusing emotions. It had started well but by the afternoon, Bill had made a fool of himself and he was angry. His bloody mother, with her voice constantly in his head, had made him look stupid and now, everyone knew that he talked to a dead woman. They must think he was mad. Bill couldn't believe that he'd cried, and in front of Melissa of all people. Whatever must she think of him?

But as his mind churned, he remembered Melissa's kindness. She'd touched his arm and spoken softly when he was upset, and, as if reading his thoughts, had known what to do. He still had her hankie in his pocket and knew that he'd never return it. It was the one small thing that he could hold on to and fantasise over. She'd held a cup of tea to Bill's lips and it had been all he could do not to kiss her fingers, to smell her skin and drink in her flesh. Her soothing words had stemmed his tears, as if the incident was nothing. Melissa had made him feel as though it hadn't happened at all. Later, when he sat outside the pub, on a bench with Alf and Harry, he'd held a bottle of beer in one hand, while caressing her hankie in his pocket with the other and soon he'd forgotten his outburst and a smile had returned to his face.

Bill sighed in frustration. He knew it was no use. There wasn't a snowball's chance in hell of getting any sleep that night. He reached for his trousers and shirt.

As Bill crept down the creaking stairs, the very fabric of the building seemed to rise and fall to a cacophony of snores that echoed from each room. Even Ness, asleep by Alf's bed, didn't look up as Bill crept past. Outside, the air was cooler and it was a relief to be away from the stuffy bedroom.

Bill had no idea where he was going.

But as he put one foot in front of the other and

headed across the grass to the cottage gate, his mother was wide awake too.

Now look at the mess you've got yourself into, Bill Bradbury! You've make a fool of our family! Only a baby blubbers. Whatever were you thinking?

Her voice droned on as Bill walked towards washing hanging on a line.

Unexpectedly, he took a step back and his heart raced, eyes wide, as he saw eight lifeless bodies hanging limply in the velvet dark of the sticky night. But as his eyes adjusted and a colourful towel brushed his face, he remembered Audrey's Babes and the aquatic performance.

Bill puffed out his breath in relief. He opened the gate and entered the grounds of the manor and as he headed towards the lake, he put his hand in his pocket and found Melissa's hankie.

You need to stop thinking of that blonde-haired slut! Take that piece of rubbish out of your pocket and throw it in the water.

On and on, his mother's voice whined, almost in time to his footsteps and Bill felt more miserable than ever.

The water ahead glistened in the moonlight and Bill stopped to stare at the ripples on the surface. Reeds swayed by the grassy banks, where the neatly cut lawn, cool and damp underfoot, created a pathway to the edge of the lake.

As if in a trance, Bill suddenly had the urge to keep walking.

Until the water was over his head.

~

Malcolm had parked his car down a lane, unseen from the main road. He'd tucked it beside a rickety old gate that looked as though it hadn't been opened in years. Weeds clung to the rotting wooden struts and the hinges were rusty, nails aged.

It was an ideal spot to lie low.

For the past four hours Malcolm had rested, and now, refreshed from his catnap, he flexed his fingers and smoothed the leather that covered his gloved hands. Frustrated that he'd been unable to get Melissa on her own earlier, he took the keys out of the ignition, unlocked the car and slipped silently out of the vehicle. His body, having been cramped behind the wheel, was stiff and Malcolm stretched out his arms and rolled his head to ease the muscles in his neck. He opened the trunk and reached into a holdall, digging out a black hooded tracksuit. Shrugging off his crumpled clothes and dusty shoes, he slipped it on, adding a pair of soft-soled trainers.

With his preparations in place, Malcolm checked the contents of his bag, adjusted the strap to fit snugly, and slung it across his body. As the moon disappeared behind clouds the colour of soot, he walked away from the car and onto the main road, where the entrance to Boomerville Manor lay only a few yards away. Blanketed by darkness, Malcolm moved swiftly.

He knew that Melissa would be sleeping, weary from her busy day.

Silhouetted by the night, the empty fairground rides and stalls appeared as a monochrome photograph as Malcolm stole into the garden. Aware that the property would have security cameras dotted about and the front door was certain to bolted and locked, he kept close to the shadows of the lake. He edged his way to the rear of the building, heading to the room that opened onto the lawn. Earlier in the day, he'd noticed that the French windows would be the easiest point of access. He had a metal file in his bag and a set of master keys that had been useful on many occasions.

Once he'd gained access, he'd soon find Melissa for the stupid woman had written in her letter to Patrick that she was staying in the Peacock Room.

There was an open space between the lake and the stage and keen to take cover, Malcolm sprinted across the lawn. But visibility was poor and he didn't see the coconut that had rolled onto the damp grass. As the arch of his foot landed on the hard round surface Malcolm was unable to stop his ankle twisting beneath him and he fell, with a thud, to the ground.

The pain was excruciating and unable to control himself, he cried out, gripping his foot and biting down hard on his lip, as he writhed in agony.

∼

AT THE EDGE of the lake, Bill was waist deep in water. He looked straight ahead as his mother's voice urged him to go deeper. He felt his legs tire and weeds tangle around his feet, dragging him further into the muddy depths. Bill was calm as he listened, seduced by the sudden softness of her words.

That's the way, my darling son, just a little bit more, let the water take you, soon you will see the glory and be with me, safe and happy, on the other side.

But suddenly, a shriek pierced through the darkness. The howl was so shrill, it woke Bill from his stupor and he turned. Was it an animal in pain?

Perhaps one of dogs had got out.

Fearing that it might be Teddy, Bill could only think of Melissa and how devastated she would be if anything were to happen to the puppy.

Stop, stop! You stupid boy, turn back!

Bill ignored the haunted voice. Finding strength that was driven by fear for Melissa, he grabbed at the reeds and, with gargantuan effort, pulled himself out of the water and up the side of the bank. He crawled to his feet, trousers and trainers weighed down with water, senses alert, listening for movement and signs of life.

Suddenly, a shape, only yards away, rolled from side to side. In the dark, Bill couldn't make it out. It was too big for Teddy but perhaps it was Bunty? He forced himself forward but as he got closer, Bill realised that the shape had arms and legs. His heart was pounding and he hesitated. This wasn't looking good; why on earth would anyone, clad in black clothing, be out here in the middle of the night.

Bill was about slink off but as he started to turn, the figure turned too and rose unsteadily to its feet. The hood covering the stranger's face fell away and as their eyes met, Bill felt his heart pound and his body begin to shake.

'You,' Bill whispered.

'Well, if it isn't the besotted little prick who twisted my arm.'

'W…what are you doing here?'

'I'd have thought that was obvious.' Malcolm felt for

the bag still strapped across his body, and slid a hand into the soft leather folds.

At that moment, the moon reappeared from behind dark clouds and Bill's hand flew to his mouth as a beam of light caught the glint of steel in Malcolm's hand.

'Still panting after my wife?' Malcolm said and he moved forward. 'Like a sweaty stinking dog.'

Bill couldn't stop the uncontrollable whimper that came from his throat. He felt the veins on his forehead pulse beneath the skin.

'You'll never have a woman like that, you sad, sick little man.'

Bill was gulping down breaths in an effort to focus. But Malcolm had moved closer and in a flash, raised his arm to pounce, but then stumbled. The steel file slipped from his hand and, falling forward, he collapsed onto Bill and they crashed to the ground.

Bill fought hard, knowing that his life depended on it.

But to his surprise, he realised that after the initial collision, Malcolm wasn't putting up much of a fight, in fact, he'd staggered to his feet and now was motionless.

Lights had come on in the manor and illuminated the lawn. In the distance, a dog barked. Someone had heard them!

'You stupid arsehole!' Malcolm hissed; he groped about until he found his file and slid it into his bag. Then, raising his arm again, he aimed a punch at Bill's head. It landed full on and sent Bill flying backwards.

The last thing that Bill remembered was a sickening crack as his head hit the hard surface of the lawn. It was followed by a sharp pain in his neck and he felt something warm ooze along his collar bone.

As his eyes began to close, his mother's voice whispered,

Come on, son, just let yourself go, here I am, waiting. Just waiting for you…

29

Jo and Hattie were still chittering about the events of the day when suddenly Bunty began to bark. They turned to look at the dog, who'd woken from a deep sleep and now lumbered across the room to the open window. She placed her paws on the sill and nudged her head through the curtains, thumping her tail as she looked out, and barked again. Teddy, also awake, clawed at the curtain.

'What is it?' Hattie whispered. She put her drink down and, eyes wide, sat very still.

'I don't know,' Jo replied, easing herself out of bed. She moved over to the window, scooped Teddy up, and gave the older dog a nudge. 'Shush, Bunty, what's the matter, what can you see?'

Jo twitched the curtain and peeped out.

'Is someone there?' Hattie leapt from her bed and turned the main light on.

'I can't tell, it's so dark in the garden, but Bunty must have heard something, she never wakes up in the night. I ought to go and have a look.'

'You're not going on your own,' Hattie said. 'I'll come with you and we'll take the dogs.'

Jo put Teddy down and grabbed a dressing gown as Hattie opened the bedroom door.

'Are you going like that?' Jo asked.

Hattie was wearing her pyjama shorts suit. The vest-like top did little to support her chest and the shorts had risen high. She rummaged about in a pile of discarded clothes and found a sweatshirt. Tugging it over her head, she pulled it on.

'That barely covers your bottom,' Jo frowned as she tied a silk cord, securing her gown tightly around her body.

'I don't think an intruder would be remotely interested in my backside; come on.'

Together with the dogs, they hurried along the hallway and down the stairs.

'We'll go through the kitchen.'

Jo reached into her pocket for a set of keys and unbolted the kitchen door and together, they crept out. Floodlight fell across the lawn as the dogs raced ahead. Bunty had her nose to the ground as she examined the damp grass, while Teddy, excited to be awake in the middle of the night, pounced and circled.

'Probably a squirrel,' Hattie said as she stood on the patio, hands on her hips.

'I wish I'd put my slippers on.' Barefoot, Jo hopped up and down.

'Aye, well, there's nothing to see, let's go in,' Hattie turned back to the kitchen, but as she reached the door, Bunty began to woof again. The bark was loud and now, Teddy joined in.

'Bugger, they'll wake everyone up,' Jo said. 'I'll have to go and fetch them.'

'Well, put something on your feet.' Hattie reached into the kitchen doorway, where several pairs of kitchen clogs were lined up, 'Connor won't mind,' she said and thrust her toes into soft rubber. 'They're too big, but will have to do.'

Bunty's barking became louder as they got closer to the lake and Jo began to slow down. 'Bloody hell, Hattie,' she said, 'I think there's someone there.' She stopped, her arms folded tight as she stared into the dark and tried to make out a motionless shape.

'Well, whoever or whatever it is, it isn't moving.' Hattie said. 'Hush up, Bunty, Teddy!' she called out but as she ran across the damp grass, her foot slipped in the oversized clog, and she slid along the ground, almost careering into a body.

'Move the dogs!' Hattie screamed to Jo. 'There *is* someone here.' She scrambled to her knees and with her heart pounding, peered at the shape on the ground. As her eyes adjusted to the shadowy surroundings, Hattie gasped. 'Oh, Lord, it's Bill,' she whispered, 'and he's hurt.'

'What's happened?' Jo was breathless as she gripped Bunty and Teddy by their collars.

'Get help, anyone, Alf, Harry…'

'I think they're already here.' Jo looked up.

Two figures were pounding towards them.

'We saw the lights and heard the dogs, what's happened? Is someone hurt?'

Hattie was relieved to hear Harry's voice.

'It's Bill,' she said, as Harry, wearing boxers and a crumpled T-shirt, knelt down beside her. 'He seems to be out cold and I think he's bleeding, there's blood on the ground.' Hattie touched her knees; her fingers were sticky.

'Is he dead?' Jo whispered.

'Let me see.' Harry took Bill's wrist. 'No, he's alive, but his pulse is very faint.' Harry stared at Bill. 'Where's the blood coming from?'

Hattie pulled her sweatshirt off and bundled it into a ball. 'It's here; he's got a bad cut on the side of his neck.' She placed the sweatshirt over the cut and pressed hard.

Alf reached into his pocket for his mobile. He dialled the emergency services. 'Ambulance, please.' Ness, who'd raced behind her master, sat at his feet. 'Help is on the way,' Alf said. He picked Teddy up and placed the bouncing puppy under his arm.

'Try not to disturb anything.' Harry looked around at the area where Bill lay.

'Do you think he's been attacked?' Jo sounded anxious.

'Difficult to say.'

Hattie's knees had cramped and as she shuffled about she knelt on something sharp. 'Ouch!' she cried out and with her free hand groped along the ground. Her hand fell on something hard and jagged. 'What the devil is this?'

'Let me see.' Harry took the object and as he felt the husky surface, he shook his head. 'It's a shattered piece of coconut,' he said, 'and its covered in blood.'

'Bill must have slipped and fallen onto it.'

'Keep back,' Harry said and motioned to Jo and Alf. 'Go and get blankets.' He touched Bill's cold body and to his surprise discovered that Bill's trouser were soaked. 'We need to keep him warm until the ambulance arrives.'

Placing his fingers back on Bill's wrist, Harry held his breath.

There was a very faint beat.

'Keep pressing on the wound,' Harry said to Hattie, 'you're doing a great job.' He patted her leg. Despite the mugginess of the night, her skin was cold.

'Don't worry about me, I can keep this up for as long as it takes,' Hattie whispered. 'Just do everything you can to keep Bill alive.' She nodded towards the motionless body.

Harry leaned in, his mouth almost touching the injured man's ear. 'Listen to me, my friend, I'm here to help. I'm not going to let you go, don't give in to the voices in your head. Keep fighting, old son.'

~

MALCOLM LEANED HEAVILY against the tiled wall of the shower cubicle as water sprayed against his skin. Taking a bar of soap, he rubbed it against his body and scrubbed.

What a bloody stupid waste of a trip, he thought to himself and as his tense muscles eased and his body began to relax, he thought of Melissa.

He'd trailed after her for hours, enduring the ridiculous event that she'd come all this way to be a part of, but at no point did he have an opportunity to get her on her own. All day, she'd been in the company of others, whether fooling about on the stalls or sitting with a crowd watching the entertainment. There hadn't been a moment when he could speak to her and break the news that he knew would keep her in their marriage.

He unhooked the shower head and held it to his throbbing ankle, turning the water so it ran ice-cold for several minutes. The pain was intense but he hoped that it was only a sprain and not a break.

Now, as Malcolm hobbled out of the shower and began to towel his body, he felt angry. His plans had been scuppered and he would need to rethink. If only that idiotic little man hadn't appeared on the lawn! Malcolm would have been able to slip the latch on the French windows at the back of the hotel, and sneak into the building. He'd soon have found the Peacock room and picked the lock. With Melissa terrified out of her wits at the intrusion, he would have told her his intentions, then packed her case and got her out of the manor.

But as things had turned out, he'd achieved none of that and now, there was every possibility that he'd killed a man.

As Malcolm began to dress, he went through the events that had happened hours earlier. He felt certain that no one had seen him, neither during the day, nor at night. He'd been cautious when following Melissa and had had no interaction with anyone. Even the barman wouldn't remember him in the pub, there'd been far too many people buying drinks. He was sure too that no one had seen him return to the manor and creep about the garden before hastily leaving, even though his injury had meant progress to his car had been slow, each step painful.

Malcolm had travelled to Ireland on a false passport, one of many that he held in different names. He'd used a different identity when he checked in the hotel and another to hire the car. Now, he needed to pray that the creepy little man was dead. God forbid that he make a recovery, for there was every chance he'd remember Malcolm's face and he'd be charged with a vicious assault.

He needed to get out of the country. Fast. Once back in Spain, he'd get an alibi from his housekeeper. She'd do anything for the large amount of money that he paid her, and more than once had turned a blind eye to Malcolm's wrong doings.

Malcolm dug into a hidden section of his suitcase. His fingers groped for a tin and he flicked it open. Taking the last two tablets, he placed them on his tongue and reached for a glass of water.

Morphine. Daddy's little helper.

It had come in useful on more than one occasion when he'd needed to quieten Allegra and now he was thankful that the strong drug would help him overcome the pain in his ankle, and enable him to get onto a plane. If only he had more to get him through the journey.

His fingers touched the steel file, safely tucked away, then he selected a passport. Picking up his mobile, he dialled the number for Aer Lingus. There was a flight in three hours and as he made his reservation, he thought about Melissa and felt his anger rising. The stupid bitch would rue the day that she'd left him! He couldn't make her travel with him today, it might run the risk of his cover being blown, but why was he waiting? He may as well break his news and ruin what remained of her stay in Ireland.

He flicked through his contacts until he came to the

number for Melissa's new phone. The waiter in Cumbria had soon located it, from the guest information form at the hotel.

Malcolm smiled. As soon as he'd had a sandwich and was ready for the off, he'd call Melissa.

30

The show must go on, Hattie had reminded Jo, when they eventually got back to their bedroom to change out of their dishevelled clothes. Despite the commotion in the night, classes had taken place during the day as planned. Finbar's group were in a buoyant mood and celebrated the choir's success from the previous evening with sherry and a sing-song. Lucinda had set up easels and displayed a still-life arrangement on a table in the lounge where items of fruit lay next to a jug, a bowl and a bottle and under the careful eye of their tutor, budding Boomerville artists were hard at work on their masterpieces.

In the kitchen, Connor was utilising a section to run a bakery class and clouds of flour swirled across the table as the bakers laughed and chattered, pounding dough, elbow deep in brioche and baguettes.

'Do you think Bill's going to pull through?' Jo looked up as Hattie came into reception. She was checking the bookings for the restaurant that evening and as she sat at the desk, she bit at the corner of a nail. She looked anxious as she waited for Hattie to reply.

'I've no idea but you should be thanking your lucky stars that the Garda don't suspect foul play,' Hattie replied.

Harry had been insistent that Jo call the police, following Bill's accident. 'Just to put your mind at ease,' Harry explained. But despite Harry's misgivings, the Garda were satisfied that Bill had been alone and they found no evidence of anyone else being involved. They concluded that he was probably sleep walking.

'Everyone says that Bill heard imaginary voices.'

'Aye, and that he'd probably gone for a nocturnal walk around Ballymegille to get away from them, then tripped on that wayward coconut, falling hard and banging his head.'

'I suppose the shell *would* break if you stepped on a coconut.'

'Aye, but like the Garda said, it's unfortunate that he rolled on one of the pieces and it pierced his neck.'

'Well, there's no reason to suspect anything else, strange things do happen and everyone was asleep.'

'We were up,' Hattie raised an eyebrow, 'so was Bill, no reason why other's weren't about too.'

'Please don't go looking for something sinister to have happened,' Jo said. 'It was just an unfortunate accident and thank god Bunty barked and alerted us.'

'I guess we'll never know, until he recovers.' Hattie shook her head. 'And I'm wondering why the legs of his trousers were wet; it was a bit late to go paddling.'

'Yes, that did seem odd.' Jo opened a drawer in the desk and rummaged about for a nail file.

Hattie looked at her watch. 'Well, as we're taking it

in turns to sit with Bill, I'll be off and relieve Melissa for a few hours.'

'I've arranged for Finbar to drive over to the hospital and bring her back in his taxi.'

'That's a good idea. I'm in for a long stint. I'll call by the kitchen and pick up a sandwich, I'll get one for Melissa too, she's bound to be hungry.'

'Good idea, and I'll let everyone in the cottage know what the doctor said, they're all very concerned about Bill.'

'Let James take some of the strain today.' Hattie studied Jo. 'You look done in and you've missed a night's sleep.'

'I won't be able to sleep and I can't help but think that it was such a terribly sad way to end what had been a great day.'

'Listen to me.' Hattie placed her hand on Jo's shoulder. 'There are folks staying here who've paid good money for the privilege and we're open to the public for food, drinks and meals too. You have to keep smiling, whatever happens.'

'I know, but they're also my responsibility when they're staying under my roof and I feel obligated to look after them and ensure that their time here is, at the very least, in a safe environment.'

Hattie sighed. It was impossible to cheer Jo up. The guests came first, no matter what. She was relieved when James came in.

'Ah, James,' Hattie said. 'I was just saying that Jo could do with a siesta and as I'm off to the hospital, I wonder if you could take over here for a bit?'

'With pleasure,' James said. 'Take as much time as you like, everything is in hand. The guests have a tasting menu to look forward to in the restaurant this evening. The kitchen is prepared and I'll host the pre-dinner farewell cocktail party in the music room.'

'I'll just have a couple of hours' rest and then be around to help later; thank you, James. What about transport for the departures tomorrow?'

'Also, all in hand,' James replied. 'House guests will checkout and leave after breakfast.'

'And then you'll have breathing space for a week or so, until you open full-time.' Hattie watched James as he headed to the restaurant to arrange the seating plan for the evening. 'He's a star. I hope you're keeping him on.'

'I would if I could but soon he'll be heading back to a more glamorous lifestyle.'

'What? Waiting on an old rock star hand and foot? I doubt it.'

'Life in Los Angeles or Ballymegille?' Jo raised her eyebrows.

'Aye, I take your point.' Hattie turned. 'Now go and get your feet up and I'll see you later.'

∽

FINBAR WAS cheerful as he left his singing class. The group had been on top form and although they were only temporary members of his choir, he was going to miss them when they left Boomerville and their holiday at this beautiful place was over. He'd no doubt that many would return and if Jo was kind enough to keep him on, he hoped that he'd meet them again in the years to come.

He loved everything about the experience Jo had

created in the tiny hamlet of Ballymegille and as he headed to the carpark be thought about business at Boomerville Manor. It was going to be a success and he was proud to be a part of it. The staged event had been a blast and reminded Finbar that there was nothing he liked more than standing in front of an audience, entertaining the crowd. Some of his best memories were from the times he'd been on the cruise ships, seeing the world. With a frequently changing passenger and crew list, there had always been women to flirt with too, both on and off stage. He'd seen the world, and he'd loved every single moment.

But life was quieter now. He had a successful taxi business and in between journeys around the county, filled his time with any gigs he could pick up. Working at the manor would boost his income too.

Finbar started the engine and reversed. As he turned the car around, his phone buzzed. It was a text from his mother's carers with a shopping list to be done that day. Finbar sighed. The old girl's care was costing him a bomb. His sister was in England, married with a large family and unable to help and his only other sibling, an older brother who lived in Dublin, said that Finbar should put their mam in a home and let the state contribute. But Finbar had seen the inside of some of the old folks' homes and anyway, he'd made a promise that he'd never do that.

Not that she'd know, he thought, as his foot hit the accelerator and he sped off the drive onto the main road. She was away with the fairies these days and didn't even recognise her own son. But as long as she was happy in her own way and safe and comfortable, Finbar would keep his promise, whatever the cost.

It was another hot day and as he raced inland to join the N71, which would take him to Cork University Hospital, Finbar turned up the air conditioning. He wanted his vehicle to be as comfortable as possible for his passenger, who would no doubt be weary after her bedside duties. He'd heard that one of the guests, the strange little guy who'd sprinkled water on Finbar's trousers, had taken a nasty fall and was receiving treatment. Finbar felt sad for the bloke and hoped that he'd make a full recovery and be back at the manor soon. But one man's bad luck was another's good fortune and it was an eager Finbar that went to collect his ride.

Melissa Mercer was the name of the passenger that Jo had instructed Finbar to collect and bring back to the manor.

The illusive lady in lemon.

He checked his watch as he pulled into the hospital waiting area. Bang on time. He'd been told that she'd come out of the main hospital entrance to find her lift. The doors to the hospital swished open and Finbar searched the faces of the folk who stepped out. Melissa was nowhere to be seen. Pulling into a parking bay and flicking the lock, Finbar walked towards the doors.

Perhaps she was waiting inside.

~

Melissa stood in the foyer of the hospital and looked out of the huge glass doors. Jo had called to say that she'd sent a taxi to collect Melissa and Hattie was also on her way to sit with Bill. She'd met Hattie outside the ward and given her an update. There was no change in Bill's condition and the doctors were considering surgery to remove a hematoma. Hattie had presented her with a sandwich and a slice of cake and now, as Melissa stared out at people coming and going, the foil-wrapped package felt heavy in her hand.

The last thing on her mind was food.

Her major concern was that Finbar, who she could see on the other side of the doors, was heading towards her. What was she to do? Melissa looked from side-to-side but there was nowhere to escape and even if she did, how could she possibly explain?

The doors opened and Finbar stepped in. He had no difficulty in locating Melissa and with a cheery wave, he called out,

'Hi there, Melissa, I'm your lift back to Ballymegille; Jo at Boomerville Manor sent me.'

'Oh hi,' Melissa said and, keeping her head low, moved towards him.

'The car is right outside,' Finbar said. 'Can I carry anything for you?' He looked at the package in her hand.

'No, I'm fine, thank you, go ahead and I'll follow.'

Finbar rushed forward to guide her through the door. 'I'm right here,' he said and as they reached the vehicle, he held open the passenger door. 'You jump in, I'll pay for the parking.'

'I'll sit in the back.' Melissa was curt.

'Just as you like, make yourself comfortable, there's a bottle of cold mineral water in the seat back.'

Melissa watched Finbar queue at the pay station, then return to the car.

'Soon have you back at Boomerville,' he said as he started the engine.

· · ·

For the duration of the journey, Finbar did everything in his power to make conversation. He admired Melissa's outfit and asked if she was enjoying her stay in Ireland. Was she happy at Boomerville Manor? Had she made any friends? What did she think of the restaurant and had she enjoyed the stage show? Finally, he tentatively asked why she hadn't come to his singing classes, despite being booked on the course.

But it was of little use.

Melissa's answers were monosyllabic, she was curt and every response was short. By the end of the journey, Finbar knew no more about her than he had at the beginning and as he pulled up at the front of the manor and turned off the engine, she was out of the car and through the door before he had a chance to help her.

Had he done something to upset Melissa or was the woman just rude? Finbar was mystified. He still had a feeling in the back of his mind that he'd seen her somewhere before, but he was damned if he could place her. Perhaps her bad manners were due to the fact that she was worried about the bloke in the hospital, maybe he was more than just a friend? It still didn't excuse her.

But God loves a tryer and Finbar was determined that he would try again.

In the meantime, he had shopping to do and several more fares to take care of before the day was done.

~

Melissa peeped out of the curtains in her bedroom and watched Finbar's car pull away. As dust swirled from the surface of the tyres, she couldn't believe that she'd been so bad mannered. The poor man had done everything possible to make her journey comfortable and enjoyable but she'd snapped at each of his questions, making it clear that she had no desire to talk. She'd kept her head down too and huddled in a corner, hoping that his delicious fiery green eyes didn't seek her out in the rear view mirror. Instead of thanking him for his time and kindness, she'd run into the manor without so much as a goodbye.

He must think that she was a stuck up bitch with a capital "B".

Melissa turned from the window and sighed. Finbar reminded her so much of Patrick that she felt a physical pain. Kind, funny and attractive, she longed to spend time with this man who'd magically reappeared from her past. It was no good denying it, Melissa yearned for his company. He'd made her feel so special all those years ago, when she'd twirled in his arms and they'd danced across the stage.

She felt her cheeks flush.

How could she ever forget the nights in his cabin? Lying together on the narrow bed, as the liner surged through the Caribbean sea, their bodies entwined, exhilarated and happy, following hours of love-making. Melissa touched her palm to her heart and closed her eyes.

The years had seemed to melt away when she saw Finbar. Gone was the nightmare marriage with Malcolm and the terror of being trapped at the hands of a monster. She sighed and toyed with the ends of her hair. But how on earth would she explain that she couldn't come to Finbar's singing classes, when they were to have been a highlight of her trip?

Melissa opened her eyes. The package of food that

Hattie had kindly prepared sat unopened on her bed. She'd no appetite and tossed it into the bin.

Sitting in the hospital, with the nurses hard at work as she stared at Bill, hoping that he'd wake up, Melissa had sipped a cup of cold weak tea and nibbled on a chocolate biscuit. It had been all she could manage as she watched Bill sleeping; the tubes and machinery that surrounded him made her feel quite queasy. His face was a mess, swollen and with bruising beginning to show around his eyes; she'd felt so terribly sorry for him. He didn't seem to have had a very happy life and now, having made the courageous leap into something new, a brave decision given his circumstances, he'd met with an unfortunate accident and by the look of things, was very poorly.

She stroked his hand, willing him to wake up and get better. He'd been so protective when Malcolm turned up in Cumbria, if only she could help him now. The nurses had said that, although asleep, Bill might be aware that someone was sitting by his bed.

She'd decided to talk to him.

'Bill,' she'd begun, 'it's Melissa. Can you feel me touching your hand?'

She'd carried on, whispering to Bill about Boomerville Manor and how everyone was so worried for him but there was no response and she'd been relieved when Hattie turned up to take over.

Now, as the afternoon turned into evening, she knew that she couldn't stay in her room. With Finbar off the premises, perhaps she'd go down to dinner to take her mind off things. It would be good to find Teddy too and take him for a walk. Shrugging off the dress that's she'd worn all day, Melissa slipped into a pair of smart black trousers and a white silk shirt. She reached for a pair of animal print pumps and as she pulled them on, sighed with relief. At least Malcolm hadn't contacted her. Her husband was far away and had no idea where she was. How wonderful it was to be out of his clutches and not living in an environment of constant fear.

Melissa brushed her hair and tucked the shining locks behind her ears. She reached for a lipstick and carefully applied a coat of red gloss. The bright colour gave her confidence and she decided that she'd have a glass or two of wine with her dinner to celebrate life without Malcolm.

As she picked up her bag and moved across the room to the door, her mobile began to ring. Perhaps it was Patrick! Feeling suddenly excited to speak to her son, Melissa held the phone to her ear.

'Hello?' The phone was silent. Puzzled she looked at the screen and saw that the number was withheld. 'Patrick, is that you?' she asked.

The voice that replied was cold. Melissa recognised it instantly and, unable to speak, felt her knees give way as she sank onto the bed.

'I know that you can hear me, you stupid bitch,' Malcolm said, his tone low and menacing. 'I'm only going to say this once, so listen carefully and do exactly as I tell you.'

Melissa felt beads of sweat on her forehead. She slapped her hand to her mouth to silence an uncontrolled whimper.

'You son is a junkie,' Malcolm began. 'A coke head, heroin too.'

Melissa gasped.

'It began in Marbella, at your perfect villa, when he

went out on the town with Giles.' Malcolm paused to let the words sink in. 'You were so wrapped up in yourself, you never noticed and of course, never knew that it got worse.'

'W...what are you saying?' Melissa's voice trembled.

'I'm saying that eventually I put precious Patrick in rehab. When you thought that he was touring the Far East looking for suppliers for his business concept, he was in fact, locked down in a clinic in East London. When he came out, I put up a considerable amount of cash to get his business off the ground.'

'I thought he had a bank loan.' Melissa shook her head.

'That's how stupid you are; banks don't loan to junkies with a poor credit history.'

'I... I don't understand?'

'Although I helped Patrick, I did it for you. That ended when you left me. I've called the loan in and your perfect son is crapping himself. His business is about to go under.'

'But why?'

'I don't like it when women walk out.'

'I c...c...can't come back.'

'Then you'll destroy your son.' Malcolm laughed. 'I'm about to send him a package of the white powder to help him cope with his stress and I've no doubt that junkie boy will soon be out on the streets.'

'You bastard.' Melissa's breath came in a burst. 'How could you do that?'

'Come home, Melissa.' Malcolm's voice was hard. 'I'll give you two days to get your pathetic arse on a plane and back to Spain. When you step through the door at the villa, I'll reinstate Patrick's loan.'

'Please, Malcolm.' Melissa ran her fingers through her hair. 'There must be some other way.'

'My offer is final. Come back or I'll destroy Patrick.'

The line went dead.

Melissa's body was shaking and the phone fell to the floor. She lay back on the bed and curled into a ball, her fingers squeezing a pillow, as tears cascaded down her face. How the hell had she not known that Patrick was taking drugs? How could she possibly have missed the signs?

But as her body was wracked with sobs, Melissa knew the reason.

She'd tried so hard to hide her unhappiness when Patrick came to Spain, that she'd failed to be aware that he was being led astray by Giles. Melissa had worn kaftans and loose clothing around the villa, anything that would hide the scars and bruises from the beatings that Malcolm systematically inflicted, to areas of her body that couldn't be seen.

Now, the cold-hearted bastard was giving her no choice. If she didn't go back, Malcolm's actions would kill Patrick; the only person that she truly loved and had in her life.

Her baby, her boy, her beautiful son.

The pain in her chest was unbearable and her heart felt as though it would explode at any minute. But despite her agony and frustration, Melissa knew that her fate was final.

She had to go back.

31

Harry was thoughtful as he stared out of the kitchen window, waiting for the kettle to boil. What had happened during the night seemed a very odd business and his policeman's instinct told him that there may be more to the incident than met the eye.

He'd had to agree with the Garda that Bill had clearly tumbled and fallen badly. It was bizarre that it was a coconut that had caused the fall, and the chances of Bill cutting his neck on a slither of the hard, wood-like casing were incredibly slim. But strange things did happen and when the Garda learnt that Bill had taken to talking to himself recently and often acted strangely, they didn't think it at all hard to believe that the man was out walking in the middle of the night.

The kettle whistled and Harry poured boiling water over tea in the pot. As he stirred and replaced the lid, Alf wandered into the kitchen.

'Fancy a brew?' Harry asked.

'Aye, nice and strong,' Alf replied and sat down.

'Where's Willie?'

'He's taken the Babes into Kindale; the mayor has asked Audrey to put on a special Sunday show in the outdoor swimming pool this afternoon; it's been on the local radio.'

'They'll be famous in no time.'

'Audrey's wondering how she can get them on Britain's Got Talent.'

'I'm sure she'll find a way.' Harry picked up two mugs of steaming hot tea and joined Alf at the table.

'Any word on Bill?' Alf asked.

'Still unconscious; he won't be travelling back with us, that's for sure.' Harry spooned sugar into his mug. 'Hattie is with him now and I'm thinking I might have a trip over there in a bit. I'm waiting to hear if Finbar is free to take me.'

'You've got doubts; are things not as straight forward as the Garda think?'

'It just seems a bit weird to me.' Harry sipped his tea. 'Bill was very down yesterday; he was upset about shouting at the lass in the pub.'

'The voices in his head?'

'Yes, they must have been worse.'

'He seemed to cheer up.' Alf frowned. 'He was smiling and drinking a beer with us.'

'I think that was a front; I think he's depressed.'

'So, what exactly are you saying?'

'It wouldn't surprise me if the voices led him into the lake last night.'

'Eh?' Alf raised his eyebrows.

'Why was he wet from the waist down?'

'Perhaps he fell in?'

'Possibly, that's an option but I favour the first.'

The door to the garden was ajar and Alf looked up as Ness scratched at the paintwork then nudged her way in. She trotted across the tiled floor and placed her head on Alf's knee.

'This one wants a walk,' Alf said. 'I'll go and find t'others. I'm sure Bunty and Teddy could do with a stretch.'

'I'll catch up with you later.' Harry stood too and, taking the empty mugs to the sink, rinsed them under the tap. He watched Alf wander through the garden and out of the gate, Ness bounding ahead, but Bill's accident was still playing on his mind. He'd give Finbar another ring and see if he could get over to the hospital.

If Bill had woken up, he might be able to have a word with him.

Harry wiped his fingers on his T-shirt and decided that he'd better get changed. Hattie would kill him if he turned up in these scruffy clothes.

Taking the stairs two at a time, Harry reached the bedroom he was sharing with Alf, Bill and Willie. He'd better tidy Bill's stuff up too, he thought as he looked at the untidy mess around Bill's bed and, reaching for Bill's suitcase, set to.

∽

MALCOLM HOBBLED INTO CORK AIRPORT. He'd dropped the hire car off and taken a courtesy bus to the departure area and now, as he stood in a queue, waiting to check in for the early evening flight to Malaga, his ankle throbbed.

It was agony and he was beginning to panic.

If he couldn't walk onto the flight he might be

stopped and refused a seat. The morphine was helping the pain but he'd need more tablets as soon as the flight landed and he got back to the villa. If only this damn queue would move and he could sit down. It seemed to be families who were travelling and Malcolm silently cursed; all he needed was a three hour flight amongst screaming kids. He leaned to one side to see if check-in was fully operational and sighed; only one member of staff on the desk.

Malcolm shuffled his case forward. At last, he could check-in.

The assistant took Malcolm's passport. Glancing at it, he asked Malcolm to lift his case onto the baggage conveyor belt then wrapped an identification tag around the handle.

'Travelling alone today, sir?'

'Yes.'

'I hope that you enjoy your flight with us. You need to proceed to the departure lounge, where your gate number will be called.'

Malcolm took his passport and his case disappeared.

As he turned to leave the desk, the man called out, 'Your flight is running a little behind schedule; please keep an eye on the departure boards.'

'How behind?' Malcolm snapped.

'There will be an update soon.' The man looked beyond Malcolm. 'Next passenger, please.'

Malcolm shrugged; the first place he'd stop when he got through to departures would be the airport bar. Cursing with pain, he shuffled away.

Hattie had finished her sandwiches before she came into Bill's room and now, as she sat beside his bed, she surreptitiously took a bite of cake. It was delicious. Connor's carrot cake should win an award. Perhaps they could market it too. She wiped crumbs from her mouth and taking an antibacterial wipe from her bag, cleaned her fingers.

'Now, Bill,' she said, 'it's time you woke up and gave us a smile.' She reached out and stroked Bill's arm. 'Everyone is wanting to hear some good news, that you are awake and having a cup of tea with me. They're looking forward to having you back at Boomerville and all the Babes want to sit next to you on Willie's coach, on the journey back.'

Hattie carried on, her constant flow of words uninterrupted, as nursing staff came and went. She'd been keeping it up for the best part of two hours, when Harry appeared in the doorway. He wore a navy, short-sleeved T-shirt and combat trousers. The T-shirt had an official looking badge on the front, with the slogan, "F.B.I."

'F.B.I?' Hattie raised her eyebrows as Harry stepped into the room.

'Female Body Inspector.'

'Dead bodies?'

'Very funny.' Harry sat down. 'How is he?'

'Still out cold.' Hattie sighed. 'I'm worn out with conversation; nothing seems to work to wake him up.' She turned to Harry. 'Did you bring anything to eat?'

'No, Finbar gave me a lift and we stopped at a pub on the way. I've had a lovely fish chowder with sourdough bread.' He patted his stomach.

'Alright, don't rub it in,' Hattie said. 'What brings you here?'

'I wanted to have a word with Bill, when he wakes up.'

'You don't think his fall was an accident?'

'Do you?'

'To be honest, no.' Hattie shook her head. 'It doesn't make any sense.'

'I've checked the CCTV cameras at the manor and there's nothing on them.'

'They won't record that far into the garden.'

They continued to chat, their voices lowered, as they watched Bill for any signs of movement. The monitor beside his bed pulsed steadily as fluids dripped from an elevated bag.

Hattie sat forward. 'Look!' she whispered. 'I think his eyelids are moving.' She reached out to hold Bill's hand as his fingers began to twitch.

'Bill,' Harry whispered. 'Bill, old son, can you hear me? It's Harry and I'm here to help you.'

Bill's eyelids flickered. He slowly opened his eyes.

'Bill,' Hattie said, 'you're back with us.' She beamed and, holding his fingers with one hand, tenderly rubbed his arm with the other.

'What happened, can you tell us?' Harry leaned in close.

'M...m....m...'

'What's he trying to say?' Hattie looked from Bill to Harry.

'Shush.' Harry held up his hand.

'Mal..colmmm..'

'Malcolm?' Harry asked.

'Punched.' Bill's voice was faint.

'Malcolm hit you?' Harry urged.

Hattie felt Bill's hand move in her own; he seemed to be trying to grip her fingers.

'Bill,' Harry repeated, 'please try and concentrate; are you trying to tell me that Malcolm punched you?'

But Bill's eyes had closed.

Harry leaned further, his ear close to Bill's mouth; his eyes became wide as his listened to the words Bill whispered.

'What did he say?' Hattie said.

Harry moved back, tears in his eyes. 'He said, "Thank you for being my friends."'

Hattie felt Bill's hand go limp. Suddenly the monitor began to beep loudly and zigzag lines raced across the screen. In the distance an alarm could be heard.

Footsteps pounded down the hall and nursing staff raced in.

'Please leave the bedside,' one of the team said to Hattie and Bill. 'You can wait in the relatives' room.'

∽

HATTIE AND HARRY held onto each other, as the clock on the wall ticked loudly. The repetitive movement of the clock's minute hand moved slowly around a yellowing dial.

'Why are they taking so long?' Hattie asked.

'Let them do their job.'

'Bill said that Malcolm punched him; I think he was trying to squeeze my fingers to tell me.'

'I know, let me think.' Harry stood and began to pace the room.

'Well, think a little bit quicker because if Malcolm

was at the manor last night, he could still be in the area.'

'And that means Melissa is in danger too.'

'Correct.'

'You should be a detective.' Harry leapt to his feet. 'Get Jo on the phone, I need to speak to her.'

Jo answered almost immediately.

'Jo, it's me, Harry, is Melissa with you?'

'Well, erm… yes and no.'

'What do you mean?'

'She's packing and is about to check out, she won't tell me why, she just says she has to leave,' Jo said. 'I'm about to call Finbar to take her to the airport.'

'Don't let her go!' Harry yelled.

'What? Why?'

'Malcolm is in Ireland and we think he was at the manor last night.'

'Oh, good Lord.'

'Find Alf and Finbar and tell them not to let Melissa out of their sight.'

'Are you sure?'

'On police instruction, she is *not* to leave!' Harry handed the mobile back to Hattie and dug out his own phone.

He dialled the number for the local Garda and spoke quickly.

'What shall we do?' Hattie asked.

'You stay here and let me know as soon as you hear any news on Bill's condition; I'm going to look for Malcolm.'

Harry took Hattie in his arms and gave her a hug, then turning on his heel, opened the door and raced out of the hospital.

∽

MELISSA'S HEART was hammering as she threw her clothes into cases. She piled everything in a haphazard pile and flicked the locks. She'd called the airport and there was an Aer Lingus flight leaving that evening; she'd booked a ticket and if she was quick, she'd be at the airport in time to catch the plane to Malaga and then get a taxi to the villa. With any luck, she'd be there in the early hours of the morning. The sooner she made the trip, the sooner Patrick would be spared from Malcolm's mission to ruin him.

She looked out of her bedroom window and saw Finbar's taxi pull onto the drive. As he leapt out of the vehicle, Finbar looked up. Their eyes met and for a moment, as if in a trance, she held his gaze. He held his hand up and waved and the spell was broken. She moved away and caught sight of herself in the mirror on the dressing table. Her shirt was crumpled and tearstained, her hair disarrayed.

But it didn't matter. She had to catch that flight.

Melissa moved across the room and wedged the door open. She picked up her bag and slung it over her shoulder then taking the two cases, lugged them down the stairs.

'Let us help you,' someone said.

Melissa was halfway down and looked up as Alf and Finbar came up the stairs. Both took a case and guided her towards reception, where Jo was waiting.

'Come and sit in the lounge,' Jo said.

'What's going on?' Melissa looked from one to the other.

'I'll explain in a moment.' Jo held Melissa's arm and walked her down the hallway.

'But I don't understand. I need to go, I have a plane to catch.'

'You can't leave at the moment,' Jo said and held Melissa's hand, as she sat beside her on the sofa. Her voice was soft as she continued. 'We think that your husband was here, at the manor, last night.'

'What?' Melissa's eyes were wide. She shook her head in confusion and looked from Finbar to Alf.

'We can't be certain but for your own safety, it's best that you stay here with us, until we know.'

'But what makes you think that Malcolm is here?'

Jo gave Alf a sideways glance.

'Bill?' Melissa asked. 'Has this got something to do with Bill?'

'Bill regained consciousness a little while ago.' Jo took a deep breath. 'He mentioned Malcolm's name.' She omitted what Hattie had already told her, that Malcolm had punched Bill, doubtless causing the injury to his head.

'Bill's better?' Melissa asked.

'No, not yet.'

Jo saw little point in upsetting Melissa any further, and until they knew more about Bill's condition, she'd say nothing else.

James came into the room, followed by a waiter who carried a tray. 'I thought everyone might benefit from a cup of tea,' he said, 'or something stronger?'

32

Harry sat in the back of a police vehicle as the driver held his foot to the accelerator. Blue lights flashed, as a siren speeded them through Saturday traffic in Cork. The journey from the hospital to the airport was a distance of seven and a half kilometres and in traffic-free conditions, would take no more that fifteen minutes. But with traffic heavy today, the driver had to use all his skills to negotiate a way through at speed.

The inspector who sat with Harry gripped his seatbelt as they flew around a bend. 'I hope that you're right about this,' he said.

'I'm sure that Malcolm Mercer is booked on the Cork to Malaga flight and if what Bill Bradbury told me is true, he is responsible for a crime which I would class as attempted murder.'

The inspector's phone rang and he took the call as Cork airport came into sight. Harry watched the man's face, as he listened to the caller's words.

He hung up and turned to Harry. 'There's no one on the flight with that name.'

'Are you sure?'

'Of course we are, a Melissa Mercer is listed, but not Malcolm.'

'He could be using a false passport.'

'Or he might be sitting on his patio in Spain.'

'I'm certain he's here,' Harry said. 'I know it's just a hunch but the casualty has confirmed my suspicions.'

'We've got the local Garda checking around the manor; if he's there, we'll find him.'

The police vehicle came to a sudden halt outside the departure area and Harry and the inspector leapt out.

'The flight has been delayed, don't rush,' the inspector said. 'If your man *is* here, we'll find him.'

Together with two Garda, they spread out. There was no sign of Malcolm in the departure area, nor at the boarding gate.

'He must be here,' Harry said to himself. He stood with his hands on his hips and looked around. Passengers looked up when they saw the Garda, curiosity raised, boredom broken as they waited for their overdue flight.

Harry's phone rang and he reached into his pocket.

'Yes,' he said as he held it to his ear.

He listened carefully, letting the words sink in, then discontinued the call.

Now, more than ever, he wanted to find Malcolm Murdering Mercer.

~

Bill Bradbury died at precisely five-forty-five in the afternoon. He'd suffered a major cardiac arrest. A doctor told Hattie that Bill may have had a weak heart and the fall could have been a traumatic episode that heightened underlying problems.

It was still bright outside as Hattie stood by Bill's bed and stared at his body.

Late rays of sunshine shone through the windows of the room where Bill had spent the last few hours of his life. Now, his head lay on a pillow, hair ruffled, skin bruised, with bandages seeping bloody red still strapped to the wound on his neck. But Bill felt no pain as nurses removed the tubes and leads that had monitored his failing body.

Hattie turned.

She nodded as a nurse touched her arm and asked her if she was alright.

'Could I have a few moments?' Hattie asked.

'Of course, just call if you need anything. I'll pop back with a nice cup of tea in a few minutes.'

Hattie stooped, her shoulders lowered as her chest caved. Her arms hung slack by her sides. 'Oh, Bill,' she whispered. 'I fear that we let you down.' She felt hot tears trickle over her face and slumped on a chair.

She held her head in her hands and wept.

Death wasn't kind. It snatched when you least expected it.

But as Hattie's sobs subsided and she reached into a pocket for a tissue, she suddenly felt as though she was floating, her body enveloped in warmth. Wide-eyed, she looked up and gazed over at where Bill lay. The man looked almost handsome, his skin smooth, lips smiling and he wore an expression of peace, as though the last piece of his puzzle was finally in place. A voice nearby seemed to be whispering and Hattie tilted her head.

It was my time but I didn't go alone, for my friends were with me. My friends, my friends.

Hattie shivered.

She stood and reached for her phone. She must call Harry but before she dialled, she leaned over and placed a kiss on Bill's cheek. 'Sleep well, old son,' she said.

33

Melissa held a cup of tea in her hands. The china was warm and felt soothing as her cold fingers wrapped around the prettily decorated cup. Finbar paced beside the window, occasionally stopping to look out. Jo had disappeared to take a phone call, while Alf sat beside the fireplace, the dogs sprawled at his feet.

Bunty suddenly lumbered to her feet. She placed her head on Alf's knee and began to thump her tail. Teddy woke too and began to run in circles as Ness pricked up her ears, her eyes watching Alf.

'I'd better let these 'un's out,' Alf said. 'I'll not be long, don't go anywhere.'

Melissa and Finbar were alone.

She hadn't spoken to him since Jo had led her into the room and now the silence was thick, suspended in a confusion of unanswered questions.

Finbar had his back to Melissa. He stared out to the garden, where workers stacked staging onto a truck and dismantled the marquees. Despite James' offer of a strong drink, Finbar had stuck to tea, not knowing when he would be needed behind a wheel. He held a cup in his hand and sipped as he watched the activity outside.

Melissa felt foolish and sank deeper into the sofa. Mortified that she might be the reason for so much commotion, she wished that she could put the clock back to this time yesterday, when she'd been so happy as she'd wandered around the garden, enjoying the opening event. She reached out to place her cup on the tray and as she sat back, crossed her fingers. Waiting to hear news about Bill's condition and Malcolm's whereabouts was excruciating, but God willing, Bill would make a full recovery. She shuddered when she thought of Malcolm. Where the hell was he and what mayhem was he creating now?

Melissa raised her head and glanced at Finbar. There was so much that she wanted to say to him but all would go unsaid. She was aware that Finbar didn't remember her. Many years had passed but she'd thought that something might have sparked in his mind. Clearly, their time together had meant nothing and she had been just another blonde in his bed.

Another cruise, another caper. Another faceless encounter that had come and gone.

As she stared at Finbar's strong shoulders and straight back, she wished that she could go and wrap her arms around his body, nestle into his neck and feel his arms pull her into him. But that could never happen and now, as Melissa waited, a sense of impending doom made her heart race.

She should have taken James' offer of a stronger drink.

FINBAR WAS ROOTED to the spot, his legs unable to move and his body taut, as he watched Declan and the twins straightening the garden. Benches were being put back in place and flower urns reappeared on patios, as borders were tidied and plants watered. A couple of garda from the local police were walking around the lake and bushes beyond. Perhaps they were searching for Malcolm.

But in his thoughts, Finbar was on a ship.

Thousands of miles away, a young vocalist, touring the Caribbean islands as a guest entertainer. He'd fallen in love and it had knocked him sideways. The girl was a dancer, she could sing too. From their very first night on stage together, he'd been head-over-heels and their romance was like a magical merry-go-round for two fantastic weeks. But as quickly as she'd come into his life, she'd disappeared. Her contract had ended and she'd been flown back to Britain, leaving him alone, on the quayside in Bridgetown, as he watched a taxi take her to the airport in Barbados. He'd tried to contact her and had found her parents' address. But his letters were returned and when he phoned their hotel in Newquay, her father had bluntly told him that he was to stay away. Finbar was a no good philandering waster and his daughter would set her sights higher than an Irish tinker.

And now, after all this time, here she was.

When their eyes had met that morning, as he stood on the driveway and looked up to her room, the years had dissolved. There was his Mel, the name she'd used then. Older but still beautiful. The only girl he'd ever loved. No one had touched his heart in the years that had followed and despite many attempts, Finbar had never felt that way again.

But she knew who he was, and for that reason Finbar was acutely aware that Melissa was avoiding him. She couldn't look him in the eye nor hold a conversation. Their relationship must have been an embarrassment to her and something that she'd buried. The coincidence of running into each other again had unsettled her and she'd made it obvious that she'd no intention of speaking to him. Finbar wondered about her husband. Malcom, they called him, a man whom he'd been told wanted to track down his wife and posed a possible threat. Finbar would do what was needed to protect Melissa and if she refused to have anything to do with him, he'd accept that it was the way she wanted things to be. He'd no choice but to respect her decision and let things lie.

His heart was heavy, as Declan, on the other side of the window, gave him a thumbs up and waved.

With a sigh, Finbar forced a smile and waved back.

THE DOOR to the lounge opened and Jo came in. She was overtaken by the dogs, who, fresh from a walk in the garden, bounded across the floor and settled themselves on a rug.

'Any news?' Alf asked as he followed Jo into the room.

'Yes,' Jo said. 'I do have something to tell you.'

She sat down beside Melissa and took her hand.

Finbar turned, his attention captured. He waited to hear what Jo had to say.

'Malcolm hasn't been found yet but Harry is confident that it won't be long, so try not to worry, you're quite safe here.'

Jo gave Melissa's hand a gentle squeeze.

'Any news of Bill?' Melissa asked. 'Is he awake? Has Hattie spoken to him?'

'Yes, I believe that Bill did wake up, for a brief moment, this afternoon.' Jo's voice was quiet.

Alf and Finbar were still. Neither moved a muscle as they waited to hear Jo's words. Melissa sat forward; she brushed hair away from her eyes and stared at Jo.

'I'm afraid that I have some very sad and upsetting news,' Jo began. 'Unfortunately, Bill died a little while ago.' She paused to let the words sink in. 'He suffered what the doctors described as a major cardiac arrest.' Jo hung her head. 'It was very quick, he wouldn't have been in any pain.'

'Oh, no,' Melissa whispered.

'Bejesus,' Finbar said.

'Aye, now, that's bad news.' Alf's mouth fell open and, blindly, he felt for the arm of a chair and sat down. 'The poor old lad,' he said and shook his head.

Ness crept towards Alf and laid her head on his knee.

'It's certainly not the news we wanted.' Jo stared at her fingers and felt hot tears behind her eyelids.

'I can't believe it,' Melissa said, shaking her head. Her face had paled and when she spoke, her voice cracked. 'Is...is M...Malcolm behind this?'

'I don't know, we're waiting to hear from Harry.'

Jo was reluctant to discuss the manner of Bill's death. It would only upset Melissa further. She gently removed her hand from Melissa's and stood up. 'I think we could all do with a strong drink,' she said. 'I'll be back in a moment.'

~

HARRY STOOD in the departure lounge, opposite gate number eight. He watched the two Garda as they circled the area, while the inspector spoke to an attendant, who held paperwork attached to a clipboard. Together they checked the passenger manifest for the outgoing flight to Malaga.

The inspector looked up and catching Harry's attention, shook his head.

'Where are you, you bastard?' Harry whispered to himself as he searched the faces of passengers, mostly parents with families, waiting for information regarding the delay. Malcolm wasn't among the faces that stared back.

Harry went over to the inspector and the attendant. 'How many men booked on this flight are travelling on their own?'

'I'll just check,' the attendant said, 'the flight is only half full.' She ran her fingers over the manifest. 'Two,' she replied. 'Would you like me to ask them to come forward to check their boarding pass?'

'Yes, please.' Harry looked around again, his eyes searching for Malcom. 'We need to move away, he won't come forward if he sees us.'

A staff member, wearing a uniform with a smart apron, came towards him and Harry asked, 'Is there anywhere else I could sit while I wait to board this flight?'

'Yes, of course, sir, you could go to the Aspire

Lounge, there's a bar there that serves drinks and complimentary snacks,' the man said, 'but you'll have to upgrade to use the lounge.' He pointed ahead. 'If you go to the desk, you can pay there, it costs twenty-five euros.'

Harry thanked the man. Of course! Why on earth hadn't he thought of it? If Malcolm *was* travelling on a false passport and waiting to catch this flight he wouldn't want to draw any attention to himself. There was every possibility that he was keeping cover in a corner of the airconditioned bar.

'This way,' Harry called out to the inspector and garda and indicated that they follow.

Harry entered the lounge first and stopped. He looked around at the elegant surroundings where cool white furnishings blended with soft sofas in greys and pale blue.

There was no sign of Malcolm.

Harry slowly began to walk the length of the room.

Behind a screen, in a discreet corner that overlooked the airport tarmac, where flights were being prepared, a man was talking into a mobile phone. He wore a pair of Louis Vuitton suede loafers and, as he spoke, reached down and rubbed at a swollen ankle, oblivious to the men nearby.

Harry couldn't see the man's face but he nodded to the inspector and the two garda and together, they stood back.

The man had finished his call and was reaching for a glass of brandy when a voice over the public address system announced, 'Would passengers Thomas and McLaren please come to boarding gate eight.'

Harry braced himself. He was sure that the man

who'd finished his drink and now placed an empty glass on the table, was Malcolm. Time seemed to stand still as Harry waited.

The man made no effort to move as the minutes ticked by.

'Would passenger Thomas, that is, passenger Michael Thomas,' the voice repeated, 'please come to boarding gate eight.'

Harry heard the man curse. He watched as passenger Michael Thomas slowly and painstakingly rose to his feet then reached down to grab his bag. As he moved forward, he stumbled and cursed again. Turning to leave the bar, he hopped on one foot.

Harry moved forward and stood in the aisle, blocking the man's way.

'Malcolm Mercer?' Harry asked, his hands by his sides as he stared eye to eye.

'Sorry, mate?' the man said.

'Malcolm Mercer, I have a strong suspicion that you are travelling on a false travel document.'

'You've got the wrong guy, here, check my passport.' He winced as he shifted the weight on his foot, to reach into his bag.

'No need,' the inspector stepped between them. 'It's him,' he said. He turned to Malcolm and took his bag. Laying it out on a table, and ignoring Malcolm's protests, he carefully searched through the layers until his fingers found three passports. Flicking them open, the inspector smiled. 'Same face, different names.'

Harry watched as Malcolm shrugged his shoulders. 'What exactly am I supposed to have done?' he asked.

'Malcolm Mercer, I am arresting you on suspicion of attempted murder,' the inspector began. 'You do not have to say anything, but it may harm your defence if you do not mention when questioned, something you later rely on in court. Anything you do say may be given in evidence.'

He took Malcolm's arm and began to lead him away.

As they moved forward, Malcolm stumbled and cursed again.

'Stepped on a coconut by any chance?' Harry asked.

'Go to hell,' Malcolm hissed in reply.

34

Mid-morning, on a wet and windy Monday at Boomerville Manor, there was a steady pounding of rain on the windows either side of the heavy oak door, as residents gathered in reception to settle their bills and say their goodbyes. With the weekend party over, Jo and Hattie shook hands with departing guests, while James, holding an umbrella, organised cases to be loaded into vehicles waiting on the driveway.

'I think you can safely say that the weekend was a success,' Hattie said, as they stood in the doorway and waved to those departing. 'Everyone enjoyed Connor's wonderful dinner on Saturday night and most have rebooked and promised to tell their friends.'

'That's a relief.' Jo sighed. 'A miracle really, considering we've had a murder and a missing person terrorising us.' Her mood was as gloomy as the weather.

'You don't know that it was murder.' Hattie took Jo's arm and led her back into reception. 'Bill died of a heart attack.'

'But remember what might have caused it.'

'There's no evidence of that and anyway, Malcolm is locked up, he won't pose a problem to Melissa anymore.'

'I feel so sorry for Bill.' Jo sighed. 'He really didn't deserve to die in the way that he did.'

'It could have happened anytime; Bill may have been living with a heart condition, try not to upset yourself.'

'I can't help it; he was staying under my roof and in my care and whatever happened during the night that led to his fall and ultimate heart attack must have been so distressing for him.'

'Well, you're going to have to come to terms with the fact that we may never know.' Hattie shrugged. 'But Harry can give us an update when he gets here.'

The door opened and James appeared. He shook out his umbrella and placed it in a stand. 'The weather has certainly taken a turn,' he said, running his fingers through his hair. 'That's the last guest on their way; might I suggest coffee?'

'I think that's an excellent idea,' Jo said. 'We can discuss the weekend and debrief in the lounge.'

Hattie looked at her watch. 'Aye, there's a couple of hours before Willie's Wheels roll again; everyone in the cottage is all packed up and ready to set off for the seven o'clock ferry.'

'Why don't you ask them to join us?'

'I'll give Alf a shout.' Hattie reached into a pocket and dug out her phone.

Alf answered almost immediately.

'Coffee and cakes for you and the Babes, bring

Lucinda over too.' Hattie hung up. 'They're loading the bus and will be with us in ten minutes.'

'Perfect,' Jo replied. 'James, could you ask Connor to make sure that he's prepared supplies for the Cumbrian party; they'll need a snack to take with them on their journey.'

'I'll attend to it now.' James nodded and headed off to the kitchen.

'You've got to make him an offer he can't refuse,' Hattie said as she watched James retreat. 'He's a massive asset to your business.'

'There's not a prayer that he'll stay on.' Jo sighed. 'I've had a chat with him and I know that he's keen to catch up with his employer.'

'As keen as you might be?' Hattie raised an eyebrow.

'I don't know what you mean.'

'Come off it.' Hattie smiled. 'If Long Tom placed a Cuban heel over this threshold and gave you a nod of his Stetson, you'd melt like butter and pool into his roving arms.'

'That ship has sailed,' Jo said and walked ahead. 'And I'm too old.'

'Rubbish, you're as old as you feel and feeling Long Tom's lanky body and arms around you would do you good. We all need a bit of romance in our lives.'

'There isn't a cat in hell's chance that it's ever going to happen, so will you pipe down.' Jo stomped into the lounge.

As she looked out of the window, she saw a bedraggled group walking across the lawn. With Bunty, Teddy and Ness at his feet, Alf held an umbrella for Lucinda. The artist appeared to be in no hurry as she took a drag on a cigarette and blew smoke rings into the cloudy sky, from where steady rain pummelled down. Willie followed, loaded down with Lucinda's bags.

'Lady Lucinda's holding court,' Hattie said as she joined Jo and looked out.

Audrey and the Babes had towels around their shoulders, their flowery rubber caps were pulled tight, squashing wet weathered faces, as they sloshed over the grass.

'Audrey's aquatic show was a winner yesterday,' Hattie commented as she watched the Babes jog behind Audrey, in perfect formation. 'The mayor rang earlier,' she continued, 'she's asked them back for an autumn display; she said it was a tremendous success and there wasn't a spare seat at the pool. The locals loved it.'

'Did they raise money for a local charity?'

'They did more than that,' Hattie said. 'They raised the mayor, as part of their act, wearing multi-coloured Lycra, over a trembling tower of Babes. It bought the house down.'

'Oh Lord.' Jo shook her head as she imagined the show. 'Was the mayor sober?'

'As pissed as a fart, she went face down in the shallow end. It took four lifeguards to lift her out and five to resuscitate her.' Hattie chuckled. 'The audience filled the collection buckets to the brim with euros. Willie said he'd never seen anything like it.'

There was a tentative knock on the door and Jo and Hattie turned to see Melissa peep round the doorway. 'Hi, Melissa, come in and join us,' Jo called out.

'I wanted to say goodbye to everyone,' Melissa said as she came into the room.

'Perfect timing, they're on their way, grab a seat.'

'How are you feeling?' Hattie asked.

'Better since our chat last night.' Melissa smiled. 'I don't know how I'll ever thank you both for what you've done for me.'

'Nonsense,' Jo said. 'We can't wait to have you as part of the team here and you're more than welcome to stay in the cottage.'

The previous evening Melissa had asked if she could speak to them both. She'd decided that it was time to make her mind up about her future. News of Malcolm's arrest had been a relief and now, confident that she could make plans to rebuild her life, she'd asked Jo if there was any chance of work at Boomerville Manor. She would clean, wait on tables, change beds, anything to give her an income.

'The way things are looking,' Jo had said, 'we'll be busy after we reopen next weekend and could certainly do with an extra pair of hands.' Jo offered Melissa the position of general assistant, which would encompass everything from learning all about reception to working in the restaurant. 'It will be a great help to have a versatile person on hand, if you don't mind learning the ropes.'

Hattie suggested that Melissa move into the cottage and Jo agreed.

'I may need spare bedrooms for family and friends from time to time,' Jo said, 'but we can sort that out later. Hattie can give you a hand to decorate this week and I'm sure that I can find decent furnishings to tide things over.'

'Aye, she'll not want to sleep on a camp bed.' Hattie had nodded in agreement to the plans.

Now, as they waited for everyone to join them, they spoke about Bill.

'What about his funeral?' Melissa asked.

'We'll know more in due course,' Hattie replied. 'The police in Creston, where Bill lived, have traced a lady who cleaned for Bill, and his mother when she was alive. She seems to know who their solicitor was.'

'Does that mean that there's a will?' Melissa looked puzzled.

'Oh, yes, there's a will.'

Jo was about to ask Hattie how she was so certain that Bill had written a will, but the door to the lounge was suddenly flung open and a dishevelled group trooped in.

'Damned dismal day out there,' Audrey said, shrugging off her towel. 'The lake's a mud bath, good job we're not performing.' Mounds of mottled pink flesh appeared as soggy blouses were unbuttoned and flesh rubbed down. Willie, who was still reeling after the weight of Lucinda's luggage, looked fascinated as chafed bottoms bounced into dry tracksuits.

'Where's Alf?' Jo asked.

'Drying the dogs off in the porch,' Willie said and took a handkerchief out of his pocket to dab at his damp face.

James came into the lounge, followed by a waiter who pushed a trolley laden with coffee and cakes. Connor had added plates of sandwiches, mini cheese pies and hot sausage rolls.

Lucinda, who was a dry as a bone and sprawled on a sofa, looked up and eyed the offering. 'Any gin to be had?' she demanded.

'Tonic and ice?" James asked.

'Easy on the tonic.' Lucinda yawned then puffed on the unlit cigarette in her holder.

Alf and three damp dogs joined them. Bunty leaned on Melissa's legs and eyed a sausage roll as Teddy jumped onto her knee. Ness, glued to Alf, demolished a crust and was patiently waiting for her master to drop another into her mouth.

James returned with Lucinda's drink and was followed by Finbar, back from his airport trip.

'I've come to say goodbye to you all and wish you a safe journey,' Finbar said.

'Hell of a fellow,' Audrey boomed and slapped Finbar on the back. 'We'll miss you.'

Finbar hugged the Babes and shook Alf and Willie's hand.

Hattie was enjoying a slice of Connor's carrot cake when the door opened again and Harry walked in. He wore a T-shirt with a slogan stretched tightly across his chest that read, "You're Using My Oxygen".

Hattie rolled her eyes and shook her head. 'Now then, Sherlock, what have you got to tell us?'

'I think you all need to sit down.'

'Are you going to tell us a story?' Lucinda asked.

'Aye, it will sound like a story, I'm afraid.' Harry frowned.

'Tell us the good news,' Hattie said, 'that Malcolm is safely locked up and, with any luck, the Garda have thrown away the key.'

'If only that was true.' Harry walked over to the trolley and poured himself a cup of coffee. He stood in front of the group, as the many expectant faces stopped eating and drinking, waiting to hear his news.

'Malcolm has been questioned all night, about Bill's

death,' Harry began. 'He says that he knows nothing about it and was asleep in bed at the time.'

'Where was he asleep?' Jo wanted to know.

'He'd booked into a local hotel, Kindale House, under a false name. The receptionist confirms that he was staying there.'

'I've a feeling that I took him from the airport to the hotel.' Finbar frowned as he remembered. 'I'm sure he was the man you've all described.'

'The inspector has repeatedly asked him why he was in the area and Malcolm says that he came here to reunite with his wife.'

'So why didn't the damned man make an appearance?' Audrey asked.

'He says he had second thoughts.' Harry sighed. 'He decided that if Melissa was happy, the kindest thing he could do was leave her alone.'

There was a collective intake of breath and heads turned to look at Melissa.

'That's simply not true,' Melissa whispered.

'In other words, complete bollocks.' Hattie looked at Melissa. 'He want us to believe that he came all this way and decided not to take you back? Stuff and nonsense, if you ask me.'

'Well, the inspector has no proof. There's no evidence of Malcolm being here at the manor, or most importantly, of him attacking Bill.' Harry looked around. 'In fact, he has absolutely no reason whatsoever to suspect Malcolm of any wrongdoing.'

'But what about travelling on a false passport?' Alf asked.

'Yes, that's a different matter and it's a serious offence.'

'So, he's locked up and will be charged?'

'He's been charged.' Harry paused. 'But, I'm very sorry to have to tell you…'

'What?' they all chorused.

'He was up before a judge this morning and Malcolm has been let out on bail.'

Melissa gasped. The cup in her hand rattled against the saucer and Jo leaned in to steady it. There was a murmur of disbelief as Harry continued.

'It was the judge's decision and someone here in Ireland has put up bail,' Harry said. 'Malcolm is now residing in a hotel in Cork and has given the police his address. He has strict instructions not to leave the county.'

Hattie caught Jo's eye and they exchanged an anxious glance.

'I hate to add further bad news.' Everyone turned to look towards Willie. 'If we don't leave now, we're going to miss the ferry.'

35

It was a sombre party who gathered on the driveway to say goodbye to the visitors from Cumbria. Melissa stood next to James and watched as Willie stacked and packed luggage. Surrounded by Audrey and the Babes, she hugged each member of the aquatic team, who all wanted to wish her well, in her new life in Ireland.

'Don't forget us!' Audrey called out. 'There's always a place in the squad whenever you come back to Cumbria.' Turning to James, Audrey gave him a hearty slap on the back. 'We hope you'll still be here when we visit the manor again,' she said. 'It would be a dreadful loss if you decide to move on.'

Audrey wrapped her arms around Jo and Hattie to give them a hug, then Alf took her arm and guided her up the steps and onto the bus.

'By heck, is that a tear I see in Audrey's eye?' Hattie asked, as the Babes followed their captain and made themselves comfortable.

'I do believe it is,' Jo said as she waved.

'I've no doubt you'll be needing my services again,' Lucinda said. 'And if I'm to split my time between Cumbria and Ireland, I must insist on a pay rise.' She took a deep drag on her cigarette and exhaled slowly.

Smoke hung in the air above Jo and Hattie's heads. Lucinda turned away and, ignoring Willie's frown, pinched the end of her cigarette and climbed aboard the bus.

'She'll be lucky.' Jo shook her head.

'Lady Lucinda lives very nicely,' Hattie said.

'Free board and lodgings, a generous salary for her classes and a regular allowance from her deceased fiancé.'

'She's not the only one you've given a life-line to.' Hattie nodded towards Melissa, who was saying goodbye to Alf.

Surrounded by Ness and Bunty, Alf held Teddy in his arms and Melissa was stroking Teddy's head, nuzzling into his face as his little tongue licked rapidly, tiny teeth nibbling her fingers.

'Melissa deserves a chance too and I'm happy that I can offer her an opportunity to start a new life.'

'You'll have to tear that dog away from her,' Hattie said. 'She's terribly fond of Teddy.'

Jo reached out and stroked Teddy too, then kissed Alf on his cheek and thanked him for all his help over the last few days.

'Aye, no problem, glad to have been here,' Alf said.

Bunty, seeing Jo, wandered over to her side. She plonked herself down, her weight pinning Jo's foot and looked up with pleading eyes, the irises as chocolate as her thick fur. She panted and thumped her tail.

'Am I to leave the lass with you?' Alf asked.

'Yes, of course.' Jo reached down and stroked Bunty's head. 'I can't bear to be parted from my girl again.'

'What about this little terror?' Alf held Teddy out. The puppy's paws air-walked as he wriggled in his quest to be released from the firm grip that held him.

Jo took Teddy and looked over to where Hattie was standing. Their eyes met and Hattie smiled and nodded her head.

'I think that there's one place where this little fella will feel comfortable.' Jo turned to Melissa. 'Would you like some company in the cottage?'

Melissa's eyes were wide. 'W...what do you mean?'

'We know that you adore Teddy and the feeling is obviously mutual.' Jo handed the dog to Melissa and he snuggled into her arms. 'He'll be a companion for you and can play with Bunty when she's here.'

'But... I'll be working?' Melissa stroked Teddy's head.

'We'll sort it all out.' Jo smiled. 'Now let's get everyone on their way, Willie has started the engine.'

As diesel fumes billowed from the back of the bus and the engine fired up, Harry handed his bag to Alf. 'Stick this on the back seat for me,' he said. 'I'll be along in a moment.'

Another bag lay at Harry's feet and, with care, he reached down and picked it up. Walking over to Hattie, he handed it to her.

'This is Bill's,' he said quietly. 'I packed all his stuff up, there wasn't much.'

'I'll look after it.'

'What will you do with it?'

'There's a few things I have to sort out for Bill, don't worry.'

Harry pulled Hattie into his arms. 'Look out for Melissa,' he whispered into her ear. 'Keep her safe while that bastard husband is in the area.'

'Don't worry,' Hattie said. 'I'm moving into the cottage with her; Malcolm won't get near Melissa while I'm on the premises.'

'I'm sorry about Bill and I'm sorry that I couldn't keep that piece of shit locked up.'

'Malcolm will get his comeuppance one day.'

'But sadly, not on my watch.'

'You never know where Malcolm will turn up.' Hattie pulled back and placing her hand on Harry's chest she gave him a little shove and said, 'Now move on, I'm using your oxygen.'

'When will you be back?' Harry asked as he turned to leave.

'In a week or two; I've things to sort here, then I'll think about heading home.'

'I'll look forward to it.'

'Aye, as will all the boomers waiting for round two of your Pensioner's Personal Protection classes; now be off with you.' Hattie stepped back.

'Wagons roll!' Willie yelled as Harry hopped on board and Alf closed the door.

The passengers glued themselves to the windows, as the coach roared into life and surged forward. They waved their hands and called out last goodbyes.

'See you soon!' Melissa cried, holding Teddy's paw to wave, as Alf held Ness and waved her paw too.

'Have a safe journey,' James said as he directed Willie to negotiate the vehicle around several parked cars, narrowly missing paintwork. As Willie hit the accelerator, gravel flew from under the tyres, flying towards Finbar's taxi.

'Goodbye!' Jo held both hands up.

'Missing you already!' Hattie blew kisses into the air.

Finbar stood on the doorstep. 'Slan agaibh,' he called out. 'May the road rise to meet you.' He looked over to Melissa and, for a moment, their eyes met. But as the coach gathered speed behind her, and headed down the driveway, Finbar turned away.

The rain had stopped and as Willie's Wheels left the manor, the clouds above parted and sunshine beamed down, casting a glow on the bushes and trees that lined the drive. Connor and his team waved colourful tea-towels, while the housekeeping girls held white aprons aloft, the strings dancing in the breeze. Declan and the twins appeared from the hedgerows. They raised spades and rakes in salute and when the elderly bus reached the end of the drive, a rainbow appeared above the gates.

Jo watched as the bus began to turn. 'Travel safely everyone,' she whispered, as it disappeared out of sight.

∽

MALCOLM TAPPED the keys of his laptop as he stared at the screen. The information he required was clear and he made a mental note of the details displayed.

There were at least ten sailings a day by ferry from Dublin to Holyhead.

He closed the laptop and reached for its case to pack it away. He yawned and shook his head to try and rid himself of the tiredness caused by his throbbing ankle and two nights without sleep. The last twenty-four hours had been a nightmare. The Irish inspector had been determined to get something to stick and now, Malcolm thanked God that he'd not left any incriminating evidence to place him at the scene at Boomerville Manor, when he'd encountered Bill. He couldn't give a damn that the strange little man had died. It was a life that wouldn't be missed.

Malcolm ran his hands through his hair.

It had been a worrying experience and he'd had to think on his feet. He'd known that he'd never escape the charges made for travelling on false documentation, but he'd barely believed his luck when the judge had agreed bail. It was highly unusual, but with overflowing prisons and the justice system stretched, the decision to allow Malcolm to reside at a temporary address in Cork, until his hearing, was a welcome piece of news and a huge relief.

But it hadn't come about by chance, nor had Malcolm caught the judge on an "off" day. With a phone call permitted, Malcolm had called an underworld contact who'd swung into action and arranged the best legal defence. Bail had been set and paid by the contact. It was a hefty amount which would rise by a considerable sum.

For Malcolm intended to skip bail and be out of the country in the next twenty-four hours.

He needed to free up funds to repay the contact and knew that if he reneged on the deal the consequences would be dire. He also had to hand over the deeds of his time-share properties in Ireland, as payment for getting him out of the mess.

Malcolm sighed and looked at his watch. He had much to do.

His business interests were thoroughly tied up and he'd always ensured that the names, details and company holdings were so complicated that none could ever be traced back to him. Melissa's marital home, the property in Cheshire, was registered in an off-shore trust and it would take a clairvoyant to untangle the paperwork trail that led everything back to Malcolm.

Once he got to Spain, Malcolm intended to transfer the time-share titles to his Irish contact and pay off the debt for helping him. He would also liquidise all his assets and relocate to South America as fast as possible, before an extradition order, which would be issued for his arrest, caught up with him.

As he stared out of the window of his hotel room and looked down on the dull grey streets of Cork, Malcolm smiled. He fancied somewhere new. Several business connections had made a similar move and were now reaping their rewards much further afield. Spain was becoming tiresome and with Eastern European magnates moving fast to dominate a lucrative market that he'd previously had exclusivity over, he knew in his heart that it was time to call it a day. There was a safe in Spain that contained everything he needed to start a new life and with sexy South American senoritas on hand, he'd no doubt that his future life would be comfortable.

And as for Melissa?

Malcolm felt a vein pulse in his neck. He clenched his knuckles and heard them crack. If only it was Melissa's neck between his fingers! He'd squeeze the air out of her body and enjoy the sight of the stupid bitch pleading for her life. His heart pounded as he thought about his wife and he knew that he wouldn't let her get away. Melissa would never have the freedom she craved and when things had settled down, he'd ensure that his Irish contacts dealt with her. Whatever price he had to pay would be worth it and he smiled as he thought of the deceiving cow, her rotting body buried deep in a turf bog.

Malcolm vowed that he would have his revenge, no matter how long it took.

Turning back from the window, he checked the time again. A condition of his bail was to report to the police station each day at two o'clock in the afternoon. If he left now, a train would have him in Dublin in less than three hours. He could pick up a car and be on a late ferry to Holyhead, enabling him to drive through the night to Manchester airport and get the first flight out to Spain. He'd be long gone before he'd even been missed.

Malcolm gathered his things. His underworld contacts had also arranged more fake identification and with access to the best forgers in Ireland, it had been arranged in a matter of hours.

Now all he had to do was make that ferry in time.

36

After days of hot sunshine, the weather in Ballymegille was uncertain. The sun briefly put in an appearance but now, as the afternoon faded, the sky had darkened and steel-black clouds drifted ominously overhead.

'It looks like we're in for a downpour,' Hattie said, as she stood by the window in the study.

'It'll do the garden good,' Jo replied. 'The lawn's very tired after the weekend.'

'Aye, but it will soon spring back with a decent drop of rain.'

Jo sat at her desk and studied the paperwork spread out before her. Bunty lay by her feet, eyes closed and sound asleep. Every now and again, Jo glanced at the screen on her computer and made notes.

'Have you paid the mortgage off after the weekend's takings?' Hattie asked.

'Hardly, but we've broken even, thank goodness, and bookings are steadily coming in.'

'The place will fill up now, mark my words.'

'I'll keep my fingers crossed that you're right; we re-open at the weekend and with a substantial payroll and suppliers bills, the manor needs to be running on a high occupancy.' Jo put down her pen and noted that Hattie was dressed in paint-splattered overalls, a knotted scarf covering her hair. 'Are you going out?'

'Eh?' Hattie glanced down at her outfit, 'like this?'

'It's very attractive,' Jo teased. 'The boiler suit fits you snugly, you'll be quite a hit in Kindale.'

'Don't be so daft; I found it in the cottage and thought I'd make a start on the painting.' Hattie ran her hand over the coarse fabric. Buttons were missing at chest level and her cleavage spilled out.

'Why not wait until tomorrow? We've never stopped for days.' Jo yawned and sat back. 'Willie's Wheels should be boarding the ferry soon. Harry said he'd call me once they were underway.'

'Well, there *is* something that I need to do.' Hattie moved away from the window and shifted from one foot to the other. She clutched a large brown envelope in her hand.

'Is something wrong?' Jo asked. 'You look anxious.'

'I need to talk about Bill and what arrangements we're going to make for his funeral.'

'Yes, we must; is it a conversation that you want to have now?'

'I'd like to get on with things,' Hattie said, 'and I need James and Melissa in here too.'

'Very well, I'll call them.' Jo picked up her phone and began to tap numbers.

As she spoke, there was a knock on the door.

Hattie smiled when she saw Finbar. 'Come in,' she said, 'grab a seat and make yourself comfortable.'

'I don't want to disturb you.' Finbar nodded when he saw Jo. 'I just wanted to know if you have a timetable for me, for singing classes next week; I need to work the taxi business around it.'

'Yes, of course, but I'm about to talk about Bill and you may as well stay to hear what I've got to say.'

'But I hardly knew the man. I'd only made his acquaintance briefly.' He thought of Bill's angry face when he'd sprayed water on Finbar's trousers.

'I'd like you to help with the funeral.'

'Ah, of course, then I'll be willing to do what I can.'

The door opened again and James entered the study. He greeted everyone and took a seat.

'We're just waiting for Melissa,' Jo said.

'She's here now.' Hattie looked out of the window to see the hunched figure of Melissa, braced against heavy rain. She held an umbrella in one hand and Teddy's lead in the other as the puppy skipped happily alongside.

A few moments later, Melissa had shrugged off her damp coat, allowing James to hang it on the back of the door as she sat down in a sagging armchair. Teddy ran over to Bunty and snuggled up. In moments, the little dog was asleep. Melissa flicked wet hair off her face and glanced nervously at Finbar, but he didn't look her way. His eyes were firmly fixed on Hattie, as she began to speak.

'Thank you all for being here today,' Hattie began. 'It's a strange task that I'm about to undertake, and not one that I ever envisaged having to do.' She stood before them and ran fingers through her tousled hair, tucking it beneath the scarf. 'Bill, as you know, was a solitary sort of chap when he came to stay at Boomerville and at first, I did wonder if he would ever fit in.' She paused. 'But as time went on, I think he began to feel that he was, possibly for the first time in his life, making friends.'

Melissa looked out of the window and as rain cascaded from the sky; she had a tear in her eye. 'Poor Bill,' she whispered, 'he must have felt so lonely.'

'Let's try and remember him in his last days, with Alf and Harry and everyone, enjoying the opening and having a good time,' Jo said and handed Melissa a tissue.

'But whatever are we to do?' Melissa dabbed at her eyes. 'He doesn't have any family or friends to arrange his funeral.'

'Well,' Hattie took a deep breath. 'I think I can answer that question.

'After I left for Ireland, Bill telephoned me and set a process in motion; we had several later chats.' Hattie paused and stared at the envelope in her hand. 'He'd been in touch with his solicitor, in Creston.' She ran her finger along the seal and pulled out several sheets of neatly typed paper.

'A will?' Jo gasped.

'Aye,' Hattie sighed. 'Bill wanted his solicitor to check on his house but more importantly, to make sure that his affairs were in order, should anything happen to him while he was away.'

'But how did he know he was going to have an accident?' Melissa asked.

'He didn't, of course, but we know that he was hearing voices and perhaps he had a premonition.' She shrugged. 'Bill asked his solicitor and me to be his executors and arranged to have his will sent to me here.'

'But who witnessed it?'

James sat forward. 'I did,' he said.

Hattie saw Jo frown. 'Now don't be getting all bent out of shape,' Hattie said. 'I couldn't ask you to be a witness, you would only have worried and you had enough on your plate; James here was the obvious choice.'

She patted James on the shoulder.

'So, let's talk about the funeral.' Hattie took a deep breath. 'Bill wanted to be cremated in the nearest crematorium to the last place he visited,' she paused, 'which I believe will be in Kindale.' Hattie looked at Finbar. 'As you know everyone locally and how things work around here, I was hoping that you'd be able to put us in touch with whatever authorities need to be notified to make the arrangements?'

'It will be my honour,' Finbar said.

'His ashes are to be scattered at my discretion.'

No one spoke. They sat quietly and waited for her to continue.

Hattie turned to Jo. 'I thought we could have a little send-off here?'

'Yes, of course.'

'So, now we come to the matter of Bill's will.' Hattie ruffled the papers. 'Bill and his solicitor gave permission that I read it, should anything happen to him whilst he was away.' She put the papers in order and skimmed through the wording. 'Well,' she began, 'there's not a lot to say.' Hattie looked up. 'Bill had a Victorian villa in Creston, which is in Merseyside, as you probably know. His solicitor says that it's a big place and despite not having had a thing done to it in years, will fetch a tidy sum.' She wriggled her shoulders and stretched her neck. 'There's an amount of cash in a bank account too, but I believe this has dwindled considerably, owing to Bill's fees at Boomerville.'

'No doubt he's left everything to a charity.' Jo nodded. 'I wonder which one will benefit.'

'No, he hasn't, surprisingly,' Hattie replied, 'and I think what I am about to say is going to be a bit of a shock.'

'What on earth do you mean?'

'Bill has left his entire estate, which is house, contents, money in the bank and his car,' she paused and stared at the expectant faces, then with a beaming smile, turned and faced Melissa. 'You, my dear, are the sole beneficiary of the estate of William Arthur Bradbury.'

There was a silence in the room as everyone turned to Melissa. Her eyes were wide and she held her hand to her mouth as she whispered, 'You must be mistaken, that can't possibly be true.'

'I can assure you that there's no mistake.' Hattie fiddled with the paperwork and produced a small envelope. She handed it to Melissa. 'Bill included this with his will, to be given to you in the event of his death.'

One word was neatly handwritten on the front of the letter. It simply read, *Melissa*.

'I think you should read that on your own.' Jo stood up and put her arm around Melissa.

'And I think we could all do with a stiff drink,' Hattie said, stuffing the papers back in the large brown envelope. 'James, be an absolute darling and dig out some gin, make it large ones all round.'

As James disappeared from the room, Finbar's phone began to ring. Hattie turned and watched as he dug in his pocket.

With a polite, 'Excuse me,' Finbar answered the call and left the room.

'Everything alright?' Hattie asked, when he returned.

'Er, I'm not sure.' Finbar looked anxious. 'It's Mam, I've to get home.'

'Can we do anything?' Jo walked with Finbar to the door.

'No, it'll be fine,' he said. 'I'll be in touch as soon as I can, about Bill's funeral arrangements.'

'Please let us know about your mother,' Jo said. 'Ring me if there's anything that you need.'

As Finbar left the room, Melissa called out, 'I hope that your mam will be okay.'

But Finbar didn't hear her. He was already at the end of the corridor and heading for the front door.

∽

FINBAR STOOD beside his mother's bed and reached down to take her hand. The old girl's eyes were closed and her neatly brushed hair was as white as the delicately embroidered pillow case, where her head lay. Skin that had wrinkled with age appeared smooth and she wore an expression of peace and tranquillity. Her fingers were cold and Finbar had the urge to rub them warm. But he didn't move, there was no point. No amount of rubbing would breathe life back into these bones.

The old lady had been dead for almost an hour.

Finbar felt hot tears burn the skin on his cheeks; he swayed slightly and squeezed his eyes shut. He'd known that this day would come but in his heart, he hadn't prepared for it and now he felt an overwhelming sense of grief for this woman who'd been such a large part of his life.

'The doctor is here,' the carer said and touched Finbar gently on the arm. 'I've made you a cup of tea but you might want something stronger.'

Finbar looked up as Doctor MacKinley stepped into the room.

'I'm sorry for your loss,' the doctor said. 'Your mam was a fine woman.' He reached into his bag for a stethoscope. 'If you'd care to step outside, while I just do what's necessary.'

Finbar nodded and as if in a trance, walked away from the bed.

'Have a drop of this.' The carer held out a glass of whisky and led Finbar to a chair. 'It was very peaceful,' she said softly. 'We'd had a little bit of tea and I'd settled her; I went to do the dishes and when I came back, she'd gone.'

'I wished I'd been here,' Finbar said and he took a slug of the whisky.

'Sometimes it's better when you're not, that's when they want to slip quietly away.' The carer poured a drink for herself and took a sip. 'The priest has been held up but he's on his way.'

'Natural causes,' the doctor said, as he came into the sitting room. 'She had a good innings.'

The carer poured the doctor a drink too and they sat in silence as they sipped the smooth malt.

'I'll sort out the death certificate and other formalities.' Doctor MacKinley placed his empty glass on the table and stood. 'You must make arrangements as soon as you can.'

The doctor left the house and moments later, a knock sounded on the door and the carer let the priest in.

Finbar thought about the doctor's words. With Bill's death and now his mother, he'd plenty of arrangements to make and he closed his eyes and remembered happier times with his mam.

∽

MELISSA STARED at the letter in her hand. She ran her finger over the lettering on the front and wondered what had been going through Bill's mind when he'd put pen to paper.

She was struggling to deal with the events that had taken place over the last couple of days. First Bill's shocking and unexpected death, then the terrifying news that Malcolm was in the area. When she'd been told that her husband was under arrest, she'd allowed herself to relax, despite the distress of Bill's demise. But that moment of calm had soon passed and now, to her horror, Malcolm was out on bail and free to find her.

It was equally as staggering to learn of the contents

of Bill's will. Melissa could scarcely believe that the sad and sometimes angry man who'd been around during her time at Boomerville had left all his worldly possessions to a woman he barely knew.

She heard a movement on the other side of the door. Hattie, determined to shadow Melissa until they knew where Malcolm was, had allowed the guest a few moments to herself. Now, with Hattie stationed outside, Melissa knew that it was no good putting things off, she had to read the letter. Her fingers shook as she carefully unfolded a single sheet of paper. Written on one side only, the handwriting, in black ink, was neat.

Hello Melissa,

I hope that I haven't given you a shock. If you are reading this then I am no longer alive and my mother has finally had her wish granted.

You probably know that I've been hearing voices in my head. My mother's voice to be exact. How I wish I'd been strong enough to leave her years ago, but I wasn't, and now I've no doubt that whatever has happened to me is divine retribution for what I have done.

You showed me great kindness when I struggled with the real world at Boomerville. I've only ever known feelings of anguish in regard to another person, but for once, I felt happiness when you were around. I know that you would never have considered a man like me, but all that I wanted was to be in your company.

I hope that I've left enough equity for you to make your life easier. If your husband persists in pursuing you, perhaps my estate will enable you to make a fresh start.

Please know that you were loved, whatever love is.

I never knew love as a child, or as an adult, which is why I pushed my father down the basement steps. He died instantly and his death was recorded as accidental. My mother died of natural causes, well, that's what the death certificate said, and I suppose that at her age, no one would have reason to investigate further. But in truth, she suffocated and it was my hands that held the pillow.

I have no regrets, other than not being able to get to know you better.

But as I said before, you would never look at a man like me.

The letter was unsigned and Melissa tossed it to one side, as if the paper was burning her fingers. She felt sick and wondered if what she'd read was the truth. Had Bill really killed his parents or were the voices in his head playing games?

What on earth was she to do?

A gentle knock sounded and Hattie came in. 'Harry's just called,' she said and, reaching down, she picked up the discarded letter. 'Everyone has arrived at the ferry and they're about to sail; would you like to come down and have a drink with Jo and me?' She tucked the note in its envelope and placed it on a table. 'I'm sure you could do with one.'

Melissa felt dizzy but she stumbled to her feet. 'Yes, please,' she said and taking Hattie's arm, allowed herself to be led out of the room.

'We'll get you packed up and moved into the cottage tomorrow,' Hattie continued as they headed down the stairs. 'It will be fun decorating and I'm looking forward to staying there too.'

But Melissa had hardly heard a word that Hattie had said. Her thoughts were on Bill's letter and the predicament she found herself facing. She gripped the banister, took a deep breath, and forced herself to concentrate.

God willing a solution would present itself in the next day or two.

37

In contrast to the outward expedition, the travellers aboard Willie's Wheels were subdued on their return journey and as the coach sped along the motorway that took them from Kindale to the ferry terminal in Dublin, the occupants stared out at the soggy countryside as it sped by. Willie sat forward to look beyond wipers that beat rhythmically across the windscreen, where spray from vehicles ahead clouded his vision. He was deep in concentration, brows furrowed, lips pursed, as he focussed on the busy road.

Alf sat with a map book open on his knee, Ness snuggled beside him.

On the back seat, Harry huddled into a corner. Beside him, the space was wide as a chasm and as he looked out to see rain fall steadily on lush green fields and pastures dotted with animals, he was conscious of the empty seat where Bill should have been.

Harry thought of Malcolm.

The bastard was out on bail and free to roam the streets and carry on with his life.

Harry hoped that Hattie had taken precautions to protect Melissa, for he was convinced that Malcolm was behind Bill's death and he feared that if Melissa wasn't careful, Malcolm would, in time, be responsible for her death too. Harry sighed with frustration. Was he right? His policeman's intuition had kicked in and it had never let him down in the past.

Unable to rest, Harry decided to join Alf at the front of the coach. He pulled himself up and gripped the seat backs to move forward. Lucinda was on the seat in front and Harry saw that she was sound asleep, her cigarette holder clutched between her teeth. With limbs sprawled in an ungainly fashion, her eyelids flickered and as her chest rose and she breathed out, a loud snore trembled through her body. Hearing the noise, Audrey turned and gave Harry a nod then looked around and checked the Babes. Many were also asleep as they sat or lay on the hard upholstery.

'Have we got far to go?' Harry asked and took a seat next to Alf.

'Not long, we'll soon be in Dublin, the ferry signs are starting,' Alf flicked his wrist and looked at his watch. 'Plenty of time to board, old Willie has done us proud.'

'The weather's grim,' Harry said as rain hammered on the roof of the coach.

'Aye, it'll be a bit choppy, that's for sure.'

'Don't worry lads,' Willie said, 'the Stena Voyager is a fine boat and will sail the sea with ease.'

Willie manoeuvred the coach towards the terminal and after following the required checks, his passengers were soon aboard. Settling Ness on a blanket, with one of Alf's old sweaters, they left her on the coach and walked along the car deck to wander around the boat.

'Shall we find seats in the bar?' Audrey asked. 'We can all brace together if the crossing is rough.'

Everyone agreed that her suggestion was sensible and they settled to order drinks and snacks. As the ferry sounded its horn and left the port of Dublin, the journey got underway and they sailed into open sea, the boat bumping through the waves as a strong wind blew and rain lashed down.

'Brandy will settle any poorly tummies,' Audrey said and knocked back a double. The Babes followed suit as Lucinda sipped a red wine and Alf supped a pint. Harry joined Willie and ordered a mug of strong coffee; he had no need of spirits to get him through the journey and wanted to stay alert.

Audrey, to pass the time, read clues from a crossword and as everyone chipped in with their answers, Harry thought of Bill. Quizzes were one of the few things he'd seemed to enjoy. He remembered Bill's last few days in Ireland. If he'd only woken up when Bill went for a walk during the night, he might have seen what had happened and been there to help. He sighed as he looked around the crowded bar, wondering what all these folks were travelling on to. Had Bill lived, and been with them now, he might have taken the Boomerville philosophy to heart and travelled on to enjoy a better life too.

As Harry reminisced and looked at the many faces, he noticed a man on his own, making his way across the room to the bar. He wore a baseball cap that covered his forehead and kept his head low. The man skirted the throng but as he moved forward, Harry suddenly felt goose bumps shiver across his arms and his pulse began to race.

The man was limping!

'You bastard,' Harry whispered and rose slowly to his feet.

Alf looked up and following Harry's gaze, placed his half-empty pint on the table. 'Is it him?' he asked.

'I'm almost certain,' Harry replied, 'but be very careful, Malcolm is dangerous.' He felt his fingers clench into fists.

'Wait till he's got a drink and turns back, we can get a better look at his face,' Alf said.

And as if by telepathy, one by one, the Cumbrian party slowly rose to their feet.

~

MALCOLM WAS HOT AND BOTHERED. His ankle was throbbing and pain shot through his leg as he hobbled through the crowded bar. He'd only just made the connection, after his train from Cork to Dublin had been delayed and he'd had to run to find a taxi to make the ferry on time. If only he had a couple of morphine tablets to hand to ease his agony; the painkillers he'd picked up at the station were hardly making any difference. The bag that he carried felt heavy and cumbersome, even though he'd left most of his clothes in his hotel room.

But a couple of large brandies would help.

Malcolm kept his head low as he waited to be served and when he reached the counter he knocked back the drink that the barman poured and asked for the same again. Handing over cash, Malcolm paid for his drinks and gripping his bag, turned to find somewhere quiet to sit.

He reached the edge of the room. A chair was vacant by a small table, littered with empty glasses and debris. As Malcolm was about to sit down and clear a space for his glass, he heard a voice call out his name.

Malcolm froze. Moving slowly, he turned.

He was almost surrounded, as Alf and Willie stood alongside Lucinda, Audrey and the Babes. Harry, who'd spoken, stepped forward.

Malcolm felt his breath quickening and darted his gaze to a door a few feet away. As Harry suddenly lunged towards him, Malcolm threw his drink and the glass hit Harry on the forehead, the brandy blinding as it splashed into his eyes. Seizing the opportunity, Malcolm grabbed his bag and sped to the door. Pulling it open, he ran through.

Outside, the deck was soaked.

Rain fell in sheets, making visibility almost impossible as darkness closed in. Malcolm hobbled ahead, moving swiftly despite the pain, determined to find somewhere to hide.

But the door to the bar had opened again and Harry, wiping his eyes with his sleeve, appeared, surrounded by the Cumbrian party. Lucinda was the first to go forward. She'd removed her shoes and flung them in her bag. Holding her cigarette holder high, she shouted for the others to follow.

They clung on to each other and felt for the railing as they crept along the deck.

Further ahead, Malcolm had reached what looked like a lifeboat drill point. Large box-like casings, screwed down tightly, lay to one side, away from the walkway, and edging his way around them, he crouched down. With any luck, his followers, unable to see, would keep going.

'He's disappeared.'

'Where can he have gone?'

'He must be further ahead.'

'Or he's jumped overboard.'

Malcolm hardly dared breathe as he heard their conversation, shouted into the wind. His position was crippling but as he eased himself around to shift his weight, he caught his ankle. White-hot pain seared through the bone and he was unable to stop himself from crying out.

'He's here!' Lucinda yelled and doubling back, ran barefoot around the casings. Wind tore at her hair and her eyes were wild, as she came face-to-face with the runaway.

Malcolm struggled to his feet and stumbled, reaching blindly for the railing as he saw Lucinda lunge forward. Brandishing her cigarette holder, she thrust it towards his face.

'Get off!' Malcolm shouted and letting go of the railing, held his hands in front of his face.

Suddenly, his ankle gave way as a huge wave hit the side of the boat. The Cumbrian party stared in horror as they saw Malcolm's Luis Vuitton loafers slip on the soaking wet deck, sending him spinning backwards. The boat dipped and, as if in slow motion, and unable to save himself, Malcolm fell backwards over the railing and disappeared into the Irish Sea.

'Oh my God,' Lucinda gasped.

All eyes turned from the black void overboard. They searched each other's faces, unable to speak. Alf reached down to take Malcolm's bag, which skidded across the deck.

'Leave it,' Harry commanded. 'Everyone back in the bar.'

~

MALCOLM FELT excruciating pain in his ankle as he lost control of his feet. As the boat dipped, the wind, battering his body, seemed to lift him off the deck, high above the railing, to soar into the black of night. He felt himself fall and as he plunged down, he heard a voice in his ear.

'Not such a brave boy now, my husband,' Allegra whispered. *'Now you die too.'*

When Malcolm's body hit the freezing cold water, the swell sucked him under. As he began to lose consciousness, he thought that he was behind the wheel of a sportscar, speeding out of control down a mountainside. As the vehicle careered, his feet thrashed to connect with the brake, but as the current of the sea carried him deeper, nothing could stop his imminent death. His lungs were full and about to explode and his last thoughts, in the final seconds of his life, were of regret for tampering with the brakes of Allegra's sports car.

~

WILLIE STARTED the engine of the coach, thrust into first gear, and moved the vehicle slowly forward to rumble down the slope from the truck deck of the ferry, and onto the tarmac of the terminal at Holyhead. It was still dark outside as Alf studied the map and guided Willie onto the A55 which would take them through Wales, to join the motorway north to Cumbria.

No one had uttered a word since returning to the bar on the boat and now they all sat in silence, staring blindly through the windows, as the coach began to pick up speed.

Harry, having moved Ness to one side, sat on an aisle seat, next to Alf.

'Willie,' Harry spoke softly, 'I think it would be a good idea if you stopped at the next service station.'

'Aye, I can do that,' Willie replied.

A few miles further on, neon lights appeared and he pulled off the main road. The service station was brightly lit and two wagons refuelled at the pumps, but there were very few vehicles on the forecourt as the coach slowed and Willie brought it to a halt.

Harry stood and turned to the group.

'We need to discuss what happened back there,' Harry began. 'I know that you're all in shock and many of you will be angry because I didn't report the incident.' He looked around at the faces, their eyes fixed on Harry, as they waited for him to continue. 'I just want you all to bear in mind that Malcolm had come to Ireland to abduct Melissa, possibly kill her, who knows?' He paused. 'I am absolutely sure that he had something to do with Bill's death and for that, I am struggling to forgive myself.'

'The man was no good,' Willie spoke up.

'Drugs and all sorts of bad dealings, I've heard,' Alf said.

Audrey stood. She paused to smooth the jacket of her velour tracksuit, adjusting the zip at the neck then patting her hair into place. Standing tall with straight back and shoulders, she looked around the group, staring intently at each person. 'I don't know what you're talking about,' she finally said as she turned to Harry. 'The crossing was a bit choppy but it was uneventful as far as I'm concerned.'

'Nothing to report,' the Babes said.

'Very humdrum, I slept throughout,' Lucinda added.

Willie and Alf looked at each other and nodded.

'As far as this group is concerned,' Audrey said, 'I'm sure we'd all like to get on with the journey and be on our way.'

Willie started the engine and as Harry sat down, he heard Audrey call out.

'I speak on behalf of everyone on this coach, when I say that what happened on the ferry crossing, stays on the ferry crossing, and that's our final word.'

~

HATTIE STOOD in reception with a phone in her hand and held it close to her ear. Harry had called and explained that the party from Cumbria has just arrived back. As the sun was rising over the Lake District fells, Willie's Wheels pulled onto the driveway at Hotel Boomerville and the weary passengers, having retrieved their luggage, had departed for their homes.

Hattie didn't say a word as Harry told her about the details of their journey. She nodded to herself as he told her about their encounter with Malcolm and what had happened.

'Did anyone else see anything?' Hattie asked.

'I don't think so, I checked for CCTV but there didn't seem to be any in that area and it was pitch dark and stormy.'

'His bag will be found, there will be something in there to hopefully identify him; it will look like a suicide, given his circumstances.'

'I doubt it, if he was travelling on false paperwork again.'

'Well, don't beat yourself up, Malcolm slipped and fell overboard; it's as simple as that.' Hattie spoke quietly. 'None of you pushed him.'

'That's true.'

'Get back to your life and carry on as normal,' Hattie said. 'Not many folk will be in a hurry to solve the mystery of Malcolm Mercer's disappearance.'

'His underworld contacts won't be too pleased.'

'That's not your problem.'

'You're right,' Harry said, 'but can you find a way of easing Melissa's mind without telling her what happened?'

'Leave it with me.'

Hattie hung up. She wanted to punch the air and dance a jig.

News of Malcom's demise was shocking, but it was also a huge relief and this meant that Melissa could, at last, get on with her life. She'd feel comfortable travelling to see Bill's solicitor in Creston, to sort out her inheritance, and wouldn't fear for her safety twenty-four hours a day.

Hattie tugged on the collar of her overalls and scrunched her hair into a scarf. She was going to spend the day making a start on painting the rooms in the cottage and hoped that Melissa would join her. Whatever she decided to do with the money that Bill had left her, Melissa still needed a roof over her head, for the time being at least.

The rain had stopped and the sun was shining. Hattie knew that she needed to tell Jo that Malcolm was no longer a problem and made a call to her friend.

Jo listened carefully. 'It's not rocket science to work things out,' she said, 'but my lips are sealed and we won't speak of it again.'

Jo had taken Bunty for a walk by the estuary and wouldn't be back for a while. It gave Hattie a chance to get started on the cottage; she knew that Jo would never agree with the colour scheme Hattie had planned and it was best that her friend was out of the way.

Hattie opened the front door and looked out.

A car was coming up the driveway and she recognised Finbar's taxi. She wondered what he wanted, for the manor wasn't opening again until the weekend. But Hattie was pleased that he was here; she hadn't spoken to him about his mother's death and having grown fond of Finbar, wanted to commiserate.

The vehicle pulled up and Finbar climbed out.

He opened the door to assist the passenger and curious, Hattie stared as two feet appeared. Laced-up brown leather brogues and a pair of wheat-coloured cords came into view, and when Hattie recognised the tweed jacket and checked shirt, she blew out a breath and tutted.

'Bleedin' hell,' she said, with her hands on her hips, feet planted firmly on the drive, 'if it isn't "Yours Truly" himself.'

'Hello, Hattie.' The man nodded. He appeared

nervous as he paid his fare and picked up the holdall that Finbar had retrieved from the trunk.

'Don't go driving off,' Hattie said and indicated that Finbar should head into the manor. 'There's coffee in a pot in the kitchen, this gentleman won't be stopping for long.'

'That's for Jo to decide.' The man was brusque as he stepped forward, and made his way to the front door. 'Where is she?'

'She's walking the dog and won't be back for some time.'

'Then I'll wait.'

'There's a bench over there.'

'Are you serious?'

'Aye, I am, use it.'

Turning her back on the visitor, Hattie reached into her pocket for a bunch of keys. With Finbar inside, and standing patiently in the hall, she closed the door then fiddled about until she found the key that she wanted. She turned it in the lock and when certain that the man couldn't get in, shook her head.

'Bloody Pete Parks!' Hattie swore and, taking Finbar's arm, guided him into the bar.

38

Hattie and Finbar sat in the music room. Hattie had positioned their chairs by the window and on a nearby table had placed a selection of Irish gins, a bucket of ice, limes, lemons and several bottles of tonic water.

'Here's to your mam,' Hattie said and raised her glass. 'I'm sure she was a wonderful lady.'

'To Mammy,' Finbar replied and took a long slug of his drink.

Hattie, still in her overalls, kicked off her trainers and raised her feet to place them on a footstool and, with an arm either side of her chair and legs stretched, sighed with pleasure. There was nothing quite as satisfying as relaxing with a lovely tipple and good company, she thought to herself as she gazed out at the garden, where Declan and the twins were mowing the lawn. Bugger the painting, she'd get round to that later. A little while ago, she'd seen Melissa and James, pots of paint in hand, head to the cottage, with Teddy in tow. She'd let them get on with it. For now, it was a joy to sit with Finbar and listen to him reminisce with stories about his mammy and their life in Kindale.

'She must have been quite a woman,' Hattie said and looked across at Finbar.

'She certainly was, until the devil dementia got a hold.' He stared at a distant point in the garden. 'Mammy was the one who encouraged me to travel and see the world; without her saving up and paying for my singing and dancing lessons and insisting that I audition, I would never had taken the opportunities that came my way.'

'Another drink?' Hattie leaned across to pour and as she added ice, lime and gin to Finbar's glass. 'What job did you like best?'

'The cruise ships were most fun, a different port each day, so many beautiful countries to see.'

Hattie thought about her cruising days with dear Hugo and nodded.

'Did you know that Melissa worked on cruise ships when she was younger?'

'I had an inkling.'

'I don't suppose your paths ever crossed?'

'It's hard to say.' Finbar was evasive. 'You meet so many people in that sort of job.'

Hattie took a sip of her drink and savoured the hint of juniper, lemon and coriander on her tongue. Cork Dry Gin was delicious. She thought about Finbar and the way he looked at Melissa. Hattie had caught stolen glances from both, when the other wasn't looking.

Was there something unspoken in the air?

Pete came into view and they watched him pace around the garden. With his hands in his pockets and shoulders hunched, Hattie wondered if he felt as fed up as he looked. She'd called Jo and told her of the visitor and Jo, although surprised, was angry.

'Damn the man!' Jo had cursed and assured Hattie that she'd make him wait. There was a famous tourist spot that she'd been meaning to visit since her arrival at Ballymegille and she'd taken Bunty over to the Old Head of Kindale, which had an interesting fort, a stunning view of open sea and masses of space for the dog to have a run.

Hattie chuckled as she watched Pete slump down on a bench. Jo's excursion should take up three hours at least. Hattie thought that she ought to go out and rescue him, it was hot outside and he must be gagging for a drink and a bite to eat, after his flight and long journey from Cumbria, but she decided to let him wait for a while. After all, he'd hardly shown Jo any courtesies when he'd dumped her so unceremoniously.

'Shall we try the Wild Burrow?' Hattie drained her glass.

'Why not?' Finbar replied and reaching out for a blue bottle, twisted the foil seal. 'You should visit Rabbit Island while you're here, it's just off the west coast of Cork; this craft gin is distilled there, and the botanical ingredients grow locally.'

Finbar poured and added ice.

'Easy on the tonic.' Hattie snuggled deeper into her chair and smiled.

What a perfectly blissful way to spend the afternoon.

~

MELISSA PICKED up a cloth and wiped her brow. The cloth was splattered in paint, but she didn't notice as she dabbed at perspiration on her forehead and face. The weather had picked up again and the sun, scorching an overgrown patch of garden beyond the open window, was hot as it struck the leaded glass, heat seeping across the sill and into the stuffy room.

Melissa stood back.

The walls were now a shade of delicate lemon, as soft as the creamy butter from the local dairy. Having earlier scrubbed and rubbed until every surface and tile shone, the kitchen was transformed. Melissa couldn't wait to add delicate voile curtains and an old pine dresser, that James had found in an outbuilding. It would be perfect for the pretty pottery and delicate china that she knew she'd find in the many antique shops in Kindale.

For Melissa had made up her mind to stay in Ballymegille.

If Bill's inheritance was really hers, she'd capitalise the asset and have something to fall back on, but for now, she'd set her heart on making a home in Ireland. She needed to be with people and the job that Jo had offered at the manor was ideal. Everyone here seemed to care about her and they'd promised to ensure that Malcolm, wherever he was, wouldn't be allowed to come near. Even now, as she worked in the cottage, she knew that James was looking out for her, as he painted the parlour walls.

Melissa picked up her brush and dipped it into a pot of paint. She frowned and chewed on her lip as she ran the brush along the edge of wall around the window and thought of Patrick. They'd spoken at length the previous day and he'd assured her that he'd not seen or heard from Malcolm for more than a week.

To begin, the conversation had been difficult.

Patrick was reluctant to tell his mother about his business problems, lack of cash flow and dependence on Malcolm. But as each explained their situation and many unanswered questions began to fall into place, they found themselves crying with relief and angst, as the truth came out.

'I wish you'd told me about your drug problems.' Melissa spoke softly, cradling the phone as though Patrick's hand was in hers.

'I couldn't, Mum, you were too wrapped up in your life and I thought you'd be furious with me.'

'I *was* too wrapped up, but only in trying to protect you from seeing the abuse that Malcolm inflicted on me.'

'He offered me rehab and cash to start my business, I had to take his offer.'

As Melissa continued to paint the walls around the kitchen window, she remembered her shock when Patrick explained that he had to store drugs on his premises. It was part of the deal, as the goods came into the UK from Spain to be distributed by Malcolm's network.

'Are there drugs there now?'

'No, the premises are clean, I've not had any contact for several days.' Patrick sounded anxious and told his mother that Malcolm had removed all monies from the joint business account he had with Patrick and now he was unable to pay his creditors. In a hushed voice he'd told Melissa that Malcolm had even sent a packet of premium quality coke, confident that Patrick would start using again.

'What did you do with it?'

'I trashed it.'

'Thank God.'

'I'm not going down that road again.'

'I can help you, but you *have* to get away from him, pay your staff off and close the business, don't worry about money.'

'I can't just disappear, he'll track me down, he has contacts everywhere, never think that you can get away from Malcolm.' Patrick sounded flat. 'He has to have the last word or action.'

They'd ended the call, promising to speak the next day.

Melissa felt her hand shake and paint splashed onto the window. 'Damn!' she cursed and reached for the cloth to wipe it away. Where the hell *was* Malcolm?

She shuddered as she realised that it was inevitable that he would track them both down, no matter how safe she felt at the manor.

As long as her husband breathed air into his bullying body, Melissa and Patrick would never be free.

~

Jo STOOD on the headland and looked out to sea. The view was stunning, as waves rolling in from the vast Atlantic Ocean crashed against towering cliffs, hundreds of feet below. She'd walked for almost an hour, on a circular route that took in the Old Head of Kindale, a large promontory that jutted out from the spectacular coastal path. Bunty padded alongside, occasionally running ahead to chase a gull or pick up the scent of a rabbit.

The weather was wonderful and with the sun hot and wind warm, Jo felt her skin tingle. For the first time in weeks, she relaxed.

She smiled when she remembered Hattie's call and couldn't believe that Pete had turned up at the manor. The audacity of the man! Jo knew that she would have to face him and in a while, she'd head back and do the right thing. Pete would have a bite to eat and get whatever he needed to say off his chest, and then, to put the matter in Hattie's words, she wanted him to pack up and piss off.

Jo never wanted to lay eyes on Pete again.

Let him go back and make up with Saint Amanda. Or spend his days alone in his farmhouse with only his vintage tractors to keep him company. There may be another woman to hook up with in time, but Jo was certain of one thing. It would never be her.

As she stared out at the Atlantic, she thought of an island so far away, across this vast sea, where the very same slate grey breakers rolled in until they crashed along windswept shores. The wild Atlantic east coast of Barbados was such a contrast to the tranquil Caribbean waters of the west.

Jo sat down with her knees drawn up and wrapped an arm around Bunty. As the warm wind caressed them both, she remembered a holiday that seemed so long ago, when she'd met a man named Long Tom Hendry and for four glorious days, he'd stolen her heart.

Hattie had always told Jo that to mend a broken heart you should engage in a fling, no matter how short. She maintained that dipping your toes back in romantic waters could help ease the pain of heartbreak. Jo had been grieving for the loss of John, her beloved Romany husband, who'd succumbed to a sudden and devastating cancer.

In Barbados, Long Tom had mended her.

She'd never forget John, but time spent with Long Tom had taught her that it was okay to move on and to enjoy herself.

To take a leap of faith.

They'd spent evenings on the veranda of an old plantation house, where he'd strummed on a guitar as they listened to the nocturnal chirruping of cicadas and the chatter of monkeys, hidden in branches that hung over sweet-smelling orchids, ginger lilies and gardenias in the garden below. In the day they'd wandered along the east coast to sit and watch rain fall like drift smoke on huge volcanic rocks, then they'd eaten at rickety rum shops, gorging on freshly caught fish with yellow rice and garlic-smothered plantain.

Jo hugged Bunty as she stared out at the sea, the very same sea thousands of miles away, where together with Long Tom she'd marvelled at humpback whales that leapt out of the deep waters. On the island, at night, he'd played a grand piano, positioned in the corner of their guest suite. As the stars sparkled in the ink-black sky, Long Tom had written a new song and now as she remembered, she sang the words.

'The sun is going down on this island so unknown,
We're out of sight and all alone,
Don't forget me!
Don't forget me.'

They'd made love in the mahogany four-poster, savouring the pleasure of two bodies, perfectly tuned in the act of passion, before watching the sun rise beyond open doors that overlooked a coast as dramatic as the one that now lay before her.

Salty tears spilled over Jo's windblown face and Bunty licked them away. As she reminisced, she wondered how she'd let Long Tom go. It had seemed so complicated at the time, his life so different to hers.

He'd promised to make her happy. He'd urged her to take a leap of faith.

But Jo had chosen Pete over the ageing rock singer. She'd settled for stability. Whatever that was. Life had continued and she'd settled into a routine, working long hours in her businesses and enjoying Pete's company for meals out, days away to vintage tractor rallies and someone to cuddle up to at night.

Jo looked at the horizon and the watery depths below the cliffs and wondered if Hattie was right. Had she bought Flatterly Manor on the hope that one day Long Tom would return? Perhaps, subconsciously, she had. But she knew in her heart that it was a fantasy. His life was on the other side of the world, in very different circumstances and now, their fleeting romance would be as forgotten as the many that had undoubtably followed.

As Jo nestled her head into Bunty's soft, silky fur, she wondered what would have happened if she'd taken that leap of faith.

A sudden, much cooler wind had whipped up and Jo stood, shrugging her shoulders. She looked at her watch and realised that she'd been out for far longer than she ought to have been. What on earth was she doing, day-dreaming about something that could never be?

The past was gone. Buried. Over.

It was the future that mattered and right now, she had an ex-lover to send on his way, a guest that needed a secure environment and a funeral to arrange. Not forgetting a new business to get open and operational.

'Come on, Bunty,' Jo called out and the dog ambled alongside.

Together, silhouetted against a sun slowly setting into the ocean, Jo and Bunty began to jog back to her car, as the orange and gold sky stretched far and wide over a land that she now called home.

39

Jo drove carefully along the narrow winding roads as she left the Old Head of Kindale behind. She wanted to detour through Kindale and pick up some shopping that she'd been meaning to do, but with time moving on, she knew that she needed to get back to the manor. Her car rattled as she drove and Bunty, who'd refused to get in the back, sat next to Jo, securely strapped in, barking at every passing vehicle.

The car had been purchased from Declan. It was slow and steady but battered both inside and out. Jo's dear dad had always told her that to be prosperous you have to look prosperous and she knew that she'd upgrade the vehicle as soon as finances allowed, despite Declan telling her that the old charabanc had many years of happy motoring to go.

As she pulled onto the drive at the manor, she saw Finbar's taxi neatly parked. Was Pete was still here? Jo wondered why he hadn't sent a text; that was his usual form of communication. Perhaps Pete thought that turning up in person would be the best way of winning her back, for there could be no other reason for his visit.

As she unbuckled Bunty and the dog scrambled over her knee, Jo climbed out of the car. A voice called out and she looked up to see Pete, crossing the lawn and coming towards her.

'Jo, it's me.'

'Hello, Pete,' Jo said. 'What are you doing here?'

'I thought that we could have a chat?' He reached down to ruffle Bunty's fur.

The dog sniffed his hand. Bunty recognised Pete but for reasons of her own, trotted off and away into the garden without a backward glance.

'We could chat on the phone.'

'Well, not properly, it's not the same as being together to talk.'

Jo didn't reply and there was an awkward silence as Pete scraped a hand through his hair and cleared his throat.

'Is that yours?' he asked, staring wide-eyed at Jo's car.

'Yes.'

'It's as vintage as my tractors.'

'Pete, I've really got nothing to say to you.' Jo sighed. She reached into the car to find her bag and Bunty's lead then closed the door and looked at him. 'But as you're here, I'm sure you could do with a drink and a bite to eat, then I'd be grateful if you could make arrangements to leave as soon as possible.'

'There's no need to be like that,' Pete began as he followed Jo into the manor. 'I made a stupid mistake but it's all over now, no harm came of it and I think we should carry on where we left off.'

Halfway across the hallway, Jo stopped in her tracks.

Had she really just heard the nonsense that was coming out of Pete's mouth? *Carry on where we left off?* She had her back to Pete and, taking a deep breath, she slowly counted to ten.

'We were good together,' Pete continued. 'All those years must mean something, it would be stupid to throw them away.'

He reached out and took Jo's hand, but she snatched it back.

'There was a time when I would have shouted and ranted and told you what I really think of you,' Jo said, 'but now, at my age, I simply won't get myself worked up.'

'Good, that's got matters out of your system.' Pete smiled. 'I knew you'd agree if I came all this way to see you.'

Jo felt colour creeping up her neck, her cheeks were hot and her pulse had begun to hammer in her temple. Was this man, whom she thought she'd known so well, really so insensitive?

Pete was walking around the reception area, taking in the antiques and polished furniture. 'It looks a nice set-up but you don't seem to be very busy; there'll be plenty of room for me to stay for a couple of nights.'

Having heard enough, Jo took another deep breath and braced her body. She was about to give Pete a piece of her mind with both barrels blazing, when the door to the music room opened and Hattie appeared.

'Ah, Romeo,' Hattie said, 'you've flown the love nest, where's Saint Amanda?' Barefoot and with a slight stagger, she stepped out and began to look around the room. 'Nope, I can't see her here.' Hattie pulled back a curtain and made a show of searching high and low. 'Did you leave her cooking casseroles and polishing your wellies?'

'Piss off, Hattie. I've been knocking on the front door for the last three hours; you could have let me in.'

Finbar stuck his head around the doorway and looked from one to the other. 'Is everything alright?' he asked.

Hattie swept her arm in an arc. 'Finbar, this is Jo's ex, Pete, who you met when you bought him here.'

The two men nodded in greeting.

'Pete has just called in, to hear Jo say that she wishes he'd hurry off back to Cumbria,' Hattie continued. 'She wants him to know that in her opinion, he is an arrogant shite, who thinks of no one but himself and if he is under the illusion that she would ever get back with him, he is very much mistaken.' Hattie took a bow. 'Am I right?' She looked at Jo.

'Yes, I couldn't have said it better myself.'

'But…' Pete stepped forward.

Jo put up her hand to stop him. Hattie, true to form, had said everything that needed to be said.

'While Pete checks his return flight, why don't we all have a drink?' Hattie linked her arm through Jo's and led her into the music room.

'I think you've started already,' Jo whispered. 'Is Finbar sozzled too?'

'He's just lost his mammy, have a heart.'

As Hattie mixed drinks, Jo spoke to Finbar and discussed how the funeral plans were shaping up. Pete took a seat and looked miserable as Hattie handed him a glass.

In the hallway, a bell rang.

'Someone at the front door,' Hattie said, slipping her feet into her trainers. 'I'll get it.'

'Ah, here's Melissa and James.' Jo looked out at the garden, where the pair of painters were walking across the lawn, heading for the kitchen door as Teddy ran ahead. Jo knocked on the glass and indicated that they should join her.

'We've an unexpected visitor,' Hattie said as she came back into the room.

'Who is it?' Jo asked, turning away from the window.

'I'll let him introduce himself; he's gone to freshen up.'

James followed Melissa into the music room and as Melissa settled Teddy, Jo introduced Pete, then asked James how the decorating was progressing.

Hattie pulled Melissa to one side.

'I've got news.'

'What sort of news?' Melissa, hot and covered in paint, was tired and still anxious.

'It's Malcolm.'

'What?' Melissa eyed the doorway. 'Is he here?'

'No, nothing like that.' Hattie stared directly into Melissa's eyes. 'Do you trust me?'

'Yes, of course, you're my friend.'

'Then I want you to believe me when I tell you that Malcolm will never trouble you again.'

'I don't understand?'

'Don't ask me any questions; I can't and won't answer them, but you have my word that Malcolm will never, ever come near you again.'

'I don't know what to say.' Melissa shrank back. 'Are you sure?'

'Certain.'

'But that's the most wonderful piece of news!'

'You can celebrate.' Hattie turned and led Melissa to the window.

Jo, aware that Hattie had told Melissa about Malcolm, needed no explanation when she saw the look of joy on Melissa's face. She held out a drink. 'Congratulations, here's to your future.'

'Oh my gosh.' Melissa let out a sigh. 'I don't know what to say.'

Finbar, aware that Melissa must have received good news, stood back and watched as Hattie and Jo raised their glasses and Melissa laughed. The tension in Melissa's face had lifted and for the first time since he'd seen her at the manor, she appeared to relax. The anxious woman, who'd crossed the lawn and entered this room, moments earlier, was gone. It was as though the years had lifted and now Finbar saw the young Mel, the girl that he'd fallen in love with. He looked at his glass and wondered if he'd had too much to drink. He'd enjoyed Hattie's company and her ability to let him talk comfortably about his mammy, aided by several large gins, but now, he longed to speak to Melissa. But knowing that she'd only rebuff him, Finbar turned away.

He was about to say his goodbyes and make tracks to walk home, when the door opened and a young man entered the room.

Heads turned and conversation stopped as everyone stared at the stranger.

'Oh, my goodness,' Melissa said. Her hand flew to her mouth and Hattie reached out to grab her glass.

'Hello, Mum,' the young man said.

'P...Patrick,' Melissa ran forward and threw her arms around her son. They hugged and tears flowed, both oblivious to the onlookers.

Jo turned to Hattie and took her hand.

'It can't be...' Jo whispered.

'I think it could,' Hattie replied.

As the two women studied Patrick they turned to look at Finbar.

Finbar was silent. He stood quite still, the colour draining from his face. James moved forward and reached out to grasp Finbar's shoulder but his arm was pushed away as Finbar continued to stare. Pete, ensconced on a sofa, looked from one face to other, baffled by the change in atmosphere but aware that something momentous was taking place.

Melissa, still holding Patrick, let her hands drop to her side. She turned to face Finbar, her eyes imploring as she studied his stricken face.

'Is it true?' Finbar whispered. 'You have a son?' His brain whirled as he stared at the young man, calculating his age, and also the number of years since his encounter with Melissa, on the cruise.

'Yes,' Melissa replied.

'Mum,' Patrick interrupted. 'I don't understand.' He looked confused as he looked at the familiar features of Finbar's face.

'Bleedin' hell,' Hattie whispered to Jo as they stared at Finbar and Patrick. 'They're like two peas in a pod.'

'Patrick,' Melissa put her hand on his arm, 'I want you to meet your father.'

Tears streamed down Finbar's face. His felt his legs begin to give way and his body felt like jelly, but as confusion left the face of the young man before him and he smiled, Finbar moved forward and held out his arms.

'My dad?' Patrick asked. 'Are you really... Dad?

'Yes,' Finbar replied and he stepped forward, pulling Patrick into his embrace. 'My son,' he whispered, 'my darling, darling son.'

40

'Well, you couldn't have written that one,' Hattie said to Jo, the following morning as they sat up in bed, both nursing a cup of hot tea and a hangover.

'Did you have any idea that Finbar was the father of Melissa's son?' Jo rubbed her sore head.

'Aye, I had a feeling that there was something between them, with neither one speaking to the other, there had to be an explanation.' Hattie reached out and took a drink of water.

'Patrick is a fine looking man.'

'The image of his father.'

'I thought Finbar was going to collapse when he realised that Patrick was his son.' Jo yawned and rolled her shoulders from side to side.

'I've never seen a man look so happy.'

'And as for Pete, ' Jo said, 'I've never see a man look so miserable. I don't think he'll be too long before he's up and off, this morning.'

'Aye, back to Saint Amanda.'

'If she'll have him.'

Both women giggled.

Finbar, Melissa and Patrick had had a lot of catching up to do and they'd been left in the music room while Hattie showed Pete to a room and Jo and James prepared a meal. Later, everyone sat around the kitchen table, as Jo served spaghetti bolognaise and James poured wine. Hattie, still in her overalls, had encouraged Finbar and Melissa to take to the floor and show everyone what had created the magic, all those years ago. Jo grabbed her laptop and after searching online, soon found the song that Melissa said was her audition piece on the cruise ship, when she'd met Finbar.

Finbar had stood up, taken Melissa's hand, and led her to the centre of the kitchen.

Jo started the music and everyone watched, spellbound, as the pair harmonised perfectly, remembering every word as they gazed into the other's eyes.

'Tell me, how am I supposed to live without you?'

'It's no wonder this lad here came into the world nine months later,' Hattie said and patted Patrick on the back. She slid off her stool and indicated that Jo should crank up more hits from the 90s, so that they could all have a dance. Barefoot, Hattie led the way as hips wriggled and heads bobbed to songs from Madonna, Billy Idol and Jon Bon Jovi. James kept the wine flowing in perfect time to his own version of the "Electric Slide" and they'd finished in the early hours, with Hattie's rendition of "The Macarena", and Finbar's energetic "Mambo Number Five".

'Do you think that Finbar and Melissa will make a go of things?' Jo wriggled on the bed and plumped up the pillows.

'Aye, they're a match made in heaven, with a lot of catching up to do.'

'Do you think I've lost my newest member of staff, before she's even started work?'

'Maybe. But you've a hotel to get open in a couple of days and a funeral to arrange.'

Jo walked slowly over to the window to see Pete placing his case in a taxi. 'I ought to go and say goodbye,' she said as she watched her old flame glance at his watch, indecision furrowing his brow.

'Just give him a knock on the glass.'

'No, I can't be so rude, I must go down.'

Jo ran along the corridor and down the stairs, Bunty by her side. She'd have to hurry to catch Pete; his flight was at lunchtime and she knew that he needed to get away if he was to make it in time. Realising that she was barefoot, Jo slid her feet into a pair of wellingtons, that stood on a boot rack by the front door. Bunty nuzzled the muddy rubber, as Jo pulled the boots on then hurried down the steps and ran out across the gravel, where the taxi had begun to pull away.

'Pete!' Jo called out and held up her hand.

He turned his head and seeing Jo, asked the driver to stop the car and got out.

'Don't go without saying goodbye.'

'I thought you were having a lie-in.' Pete stared at the woman whom he'd travelled across the sea to win back.

What a bloody fool he'd been.

Pete shook his head and reached out. 'I'm so sorry, Jo,' he said. 'I really have messed things up, haven't I?'

'Yes, I'm afraid you have.' Jo took his hand.

'You're a still a beauty.' Pete stared at her thick

auburn hair, longing to lift it from her shoulders and feel it soft on his face. His eyes travelled over her slim, shapely body, under the soft silk of her nightgown. He looked at her feet, encased in muddy wellingtons. 'But always the country girl at heart.' He smiled.

'Goodbye, Pete.' Jo leaned in to kiss his cheek.

'Goodbye, lass,' Pete whispered. 'Good luck, I hope you find happiness.' He had tears in his eyes and not wanting Jo to see, quickly turned.

Jo watched until the vehicle become a distant speck on the drive. She reached down and stroked Bunty's head, then whispered, 'And you,' as the taxi disappeared onto the main road and Pete faded from her life. 'I hope you find happiness too.'

∽

MELISSA LUXURIATED in the soft downy duvet which covered her naked body. She stretched, her movements cat-like as she slowly opened her eyes.

'Good morning, beautiful lady,' Finbar's rich voice whispered softly in her ear. 'Did you sleep well?' His arm snaked around her waist and Melissa felt herself being pulled into a warm and loving embrace.

'Never better,' she said and nuzzled her head into Finbar's shoulder, kissing the deeply tanned skin. 'I think that's the best sleep I've had in years.'

'The first of the rest of our lives.'

Melissa pulled away and turned to look at Finbar. 'Do you mean that?' she asked.

'Today might be our last tomorrow,' he replied, his smile slow and lazy. 'I'm never going to let you go again.'

Melissa lay back. Her fingers tingled and she felt a lightness in her limbs, as though she was weightless. The feeling, so unfamiliar, almost made her cry.

She was happy and deeply in love.

Turning on her side, she traced the outline of Finbar's handsome face. His eyes were closed, breaths deep, as he relaxed and sleep returned.

Melissa wanted to pinch herself. She could hardly believe that things had turned out this way. Here she was, lying next to a man who'd earlier told her that he would always love and protect her and never let her out of his sight again. Finbar was overcome with the news that he had a son and the fact that all these years had passed didn't seem to matter to him. He'd assured both Melissa and Patrick that they had a lot of catching up to do and the rest of their lives to do it.

He'd explained that when he'd left their cruise, he'd tried to contact her, but never managed to get past her father. Thinking that Melissa didn't want anything to do with him and had forewarned her father, Finbar eventually gave up.

'I suppose Dad thought that your lifestyle would never support me,' Melissa said as they sat in the music room with Patrick. 'Working on cruises meant that you'd always be away.'

'He assumed that I was no good, feckless and fancy-free,' Finbar had sighed. 'But if he'd only given me a chance, I'd have got a shore job and married you.' He looked fondly at Patrick, 'Especially with a baby on the way.'

They'd discussed Patrick and his future and when Melissa shared details of her conversation with Hattie, Finbar had nodded his head.

'Something has happened to Malcolm, that's for sure,' he said. 'No doubt, in time, we'll learn more, but for now, you have to accept what she's said.'

'I hope he's dead.' Patrick was adamant. 'The man has ruined me.'

'He nearly ruined us both.' Melissa placed her hand on Patrick's arm. 'But don't worry, you can start again and, with my inheritance, I can help you.'

She'd wanted to know what had happened to Giles and Patrick said that he'd spoken to him the previous day. Giles too, wondered where his father was.

'Not that I really care,' Giles had said. 'The man murdered my mother and I wish that he was ten feet under.'

Melissa thought that Giles and Patrick could well have had their wish granted.

She'd been pleased to hear that Giles was moving to Antigua, to live with a man he'd met in Marbella. It had been love at first sight, Giles told Patrick.

Melissa traced the shape of Finbar's lips and leaned in to kiss him. His eyes slowly opened and he wrapped his arms around her. She felt the strength of his loving body; it seemed to pulse into her own. As their glances met and she looked deep into the pools of Finbar's fiery green eyes, magical and flecked with gold, she almost purred with happiness.

'The first day of the rest of our lives.'

41

On a sunny day in late September, the garden at Boomerville Manor was still colourful despite the few short months of summer having flown by. Pots of geraniums brightened up the patio and hanging baskets trailed the last blooms of the year. Declan and the twins knelt by the borders, their trowels and forks working feverishly, as they dug up annuals to plant pansies, daisies and wallflowers, to flower alongside daffodils and bluebells in the spring. In the distance, the clock on the mediaeval church tower, at Flatterly Friary, could be seen from the avenue that led to the manor.

It struck twelve times, the chime resounding across the quiet countryside.

On the driveway, Jo and Hattie stood with a group of friends. Subdued and silent, they'd dressed in muted shades, expressing their respect. Hattie in a dark cashmere coat, held a wooden box in her gloved hands. On the smooth polished surface, lay a gold plaque, engraved with the words, "William Arthur Bradbury".

'Everyone ready?' Hattie looked up at the assembled party.

'We'll all follow Hattie,' Jo said. She took her friend's arm, and they began to walk through the garden, treading softly across the grass.

The trees had begun to shed their leaves, creating a carpet of reds and golds and the sky was cloudless, the sun bright and warm on the perfect autumn day.

Connor and his chefs had joined with the girls from housekeeping and they lined the pathway, their heads bowed in respect. Declan had stopped digging and together with his sons, they stood and removed their caps.

'This is it,' Harry said. He lowered his head, his hands hanging loosely by his side as he stood at the spot where Hattie had found Bill, many weeks ago. 'Let's have a few moments of silence, while we remember our friend.'

The garden became quiet; not a sound could be heard and even the birds seemed to cease singing.

'Thank you.' Harry raised his head. 'And now we'll follow Hattie to the lake.'

Lucinda took Alf's arm and stepped forward, forming a procession behind Finbar and Melissa, with James alongside Willie. Everyone walked slowly and when they reached the jetty, they stopped, forming a semi-circle at the edge of the lake. The silver blue water in the light of the noon sun was calm and as flat as a mirror.

Hattie kept walking and stepped up and onto the wooden boards. A faint wind ruffled the curls in her hair as she turned to face everyone.

'We're all here today on behalf of our dear friend,

Bill,' she began. 'Bill asked me to leave his ashes at the last place he visited, and that's why we're here at the lake.'

Hattie looked at the faces turned towards her.

'We paid our respects to Bill at the crematorium, some weeks ago, and today, many of you have travelled a long way to see him in what will be his resting place, to say a final goodbye.'

Heads nodded as they listened to Hattie.

Finbar reached for Melissa's hand and cupped it in his own. Alf glanced down to see Ness, Bunty and Teddy sit side-by-side, their coats shining, tails still.

'So, with no further words, I'm going to hand Bill over.'

Hattie turned and faced the water and held the box out at arm's length.

The surface of the lake began to ripple and, gliding towards the jetty, what appeared to be a large bouquet of pretty flowers, moved forward. When it reached Hattie, the flowers came together and a body was thrust high, breaking the surface, as Audrey, in colourful Lycra, was raised up, her arms outstretched. She took the box and as she was lowered, her Lycra-clad, rubber-capped Babes surfaced too.

They swam backwards and formed a circle to escort Audrey to the centre.

The onlookers began to clap as Audrey raised Bill's remains then slowly disappeared, to deposit the box at the bottom of the lake. A breeze suddenly blew, breathing softly through the trees, as everyone stared at the surface.

In the years to come, whenever the group gathered,

they would remember the moment when a voice seemed to whisper from the water,

'Thank you for being my friends.'

~

IN THE DINING room at Boomerville Manor, drinks were being served from the bar and a tasty buffet was laid on a long table. Guests, who'd come together to celebrate Bill's life and give him a good send-off, helped themselves to delicious delicacies. A roaring log fire burned, the ribbons of flame illuminating the cosy ingle-nook fireplace, in the centre of the room where Audrey and her Babes, now groomed and wearing their best dresses, supped glasses of damson gin and chatted with Declan and the twins. Willie, keeping close to Audrey, had a whisky in his hand and reached down to stroke Ness, who lay beside Bunty and Teddy. Asleep on a thick rug, they were curled in a furry pile, basking in the heat from the fire.

'I think that went rather well,' Hattie said to Jo, as they sipped sherry and watched the guests' interactions.

'Yes, I agree,' Jo replied. 'I'd like to think that if Bill was here today, he'd enjoy his own party.' She saw James beckon her. 'I'll be back in a moment,' she said.

Harry, holding a sausage roll in one hand and a pint in the other, wandered over. He wore a T-shirt under his suit jacket and Hattie, who reached out to move the lapels of the suit to one side, read the slogan, "You Would Look Better Embalmed".

'Very funny,' she said and shook her head.

'I thought it was topical.' Harry bit into his sausage roll.

'No wonder you're still single.'

'So,' Harry said, 'the inquest concluded that he'd died of natural causes.' Crumbs from Connor's flaky pastry fell on his jacket and he brushed them away.

'Aye, that's what the death certificate has on it.'

'I'll never accept that.' Harry took a slug of his beer.

'I think you're right, but does it really matter?'

'No, not now the police say that Malcolm jumped off a ferry.' Harry looked at Hattie and smiled.

'I heard that they found a holdall on the deck. It contained Malcolm's wallet, fake ID and his British and Spanish driving licence together with a photo of Melissa, torn in two pieces, in a pocket on the side.'

'So I believe.'

'Another pint'?' Alf called out. He stood by the bar with Lucinda and shook an empty glass in Harry's direction. Lucinda held a large glass of red wine.

'I'll catch up with you in a bit,' Harry said to Hattie.

'No hurry.'

Hattie looked around the room and saw that Melissa stood alone by the window. 'Penny for your thoughts?' Hattie said, as she joined her.

'Oh, hello.' Melissa smiled. 'I was just thinking how lucky I am, to be living here in the cottage and working with you and Jo.'

'Perhaps not for long?' Hattie raised her eyebrows. 'What does Finbar want you to do?'

'We're not sure yet; he has his mother's estate to sort out and there's a sister and a brother to inherit too, but in time, we'll find a place together. I love being in Ireland.'

'You'll be able to form a singing and dancing duo and tour the pubs and clubs of the country, maybe go back on the cruises?'

'Oh no, I think we're too old for that.' Melissa shook her head.

'You're as old as you feel and anything is possible.'

'Yes, I think you may be right, being at Boomerville has taught me that.'

'Now, what about that lovely lad of yours?' Hattie asked. 'What's Patrick going to do?'

'He's gone back to London to sort things out, but now that we know that Malcolm is dead, he'll carry on with his business, with my financial help to get things going again.'

'Will you go back to Cheshire or Spain?'

'God, no.' Melissa shook her head. 'I should think the police and the underworld are crawling all over Malcolm's properties and investments; the further away I am from all that, the better.'

Melissa stared out of the window and looked over towards the lake. 'That was a lovely send-off for Bill,' she said. 'Was it really his last wish to be buried at Boomerville?'

'Where else would we bury him?' Hattie asked. 'I don't think it would have been right to send him back to Creston, where his parents are interred. I got the impression from Bill that if anything happened to him, he didn't want to be laid to rest with them.'

Hattie remembered her conversations with Bill, when his will was being prepared.

'Well, I think there's something I need to talk to you about.' Melissa dug in her pocket and bought out the letter that Bill had left for her. Her fingers began to open the envelope but before she could slide the contents out, Hattie took it from her hand.

'I shouldn't worry about anything in there,' Hattie said and slipped the letter in her pocket. 'Bill probably said a few things that he didn't mean to say.'

'Yes, but…'

'As his will is being processed and everything is in order,' Hattie put her arm around Melissa, 'I think that if I was you, I'd let the inheritance drop into your bank account, help that lad of yours and keep your memories of our friend Bill as happy as you possibly can.'

Melissa looked into Hattie's eyes and after a few moments said, 'Are you sure?'

'Quite sure.' Hattie pulled Melissa into a hug. 'Now, look who's coming across the room, it's your handsome crooner.'

Finbar held a drink in each hand and gave one to Melissa. 'Can I get something for you, Hattie?'

'I'll sort myself out, thanks, you two catch up with everyone.'

Hattie walked away but when she reached the fireplace, she dug into her pocket and took the letter out. As she stared into the fire, she scrunched the paper into a ball then tossed it onto the burning logs. 'God forgives you, old son,' she whispered, as the letter flared up and white hot flames extinguished Bill's confession.

∽

THE AFTERNOON WORE ON and with the passengers on Willie's Wheels not returning to Cumbria until the next day, and with no rush to go anywhere, the guests for Bill's send-off settled around the fire feeling relaxed and content, as they grazed on the buffet and drank from the bar.

Jo, who'd been in reception checking guests in, caught up with Hattie. Taking her arm, she pulled her to one side.

'Guess what?'

Hattie could see that her friend was excited. 'Astound me.' Hattie reached for a slice of apple cake and took a large bite.

'James has decided to stay on.'

'Eh?' Hattie mumbled, chomping her cake.

'Isn't it wonderful?'

'Aye, in actual fact, it is,' Hattie said and thought that with James in situ as full-time manager, Jo would be free to move around her businesses. 'So, he's decided not to go back to LA and work with his old boss?'

'Apparently not; Long Tom leads a quiet life these days and is settled in his house in Malibu,' Jo said. 'He lives with a couple of dogs and his music.'

'No need of a butler?'

'Not according to James.'

'Shame you never took that leap of faith all those years ago.' Hattie lowered her voice. 'You could be holed up in comfort, sitting on a sunny deck, listening to Long Tom tinkling on his ivories, whilst watching the surfers out in Malibu bay.'

'I don't know why you always bang on about that,' Jo said crossly, 'it was never meant to be.' She shrugged. 'Anyway, I'm too old, too set in my ways and don't have limbs capable of leaping anywhere these days.'

'Well, I think we should have a drink to celebrate.' Hattie strolled over to the bar and asked a waiter to open a bottle of champagne. 'In fact, let's have champagne all round!'

As glasses were filled and toasts made, Jo and Hattie stood to one side. They both surveyed the group before them and as if by telepathy, turned and smiled at each other.

'This all started with a funeral,' Jo said.

'Aye, Hugo's, not so long ago.'

'What are you going to do now?' Jo touched Hattie on the arm and spoke softly. 'Something tells me that you're going back to Cumbria but not to Hotel Boomerville.'

Hattie sighed. Jo knew her so well.

It was true, Hattie *did* feel that it was time to go back. Jo didn't need her in Ireland and now, with James in place and Jo having more free time to manage her properties, Hattie had to find something else to do. She hadn't told Jo that she'd recently learnt that she'd inherited a derelict cottage from an old aunt she hardly knew. It was in a village called Hollywood, not far from her house in Marland.

Hattie thought about the property in Marland. She'd put it up for sale for she had no desire to return there, since it had been trashed.

'Aye, it's time I made tracks,' Hattie said; she took a drink and felt the bubbles tingle on her tongue. 'In fact, I think I'll grab a seat on the coach with Willie and the gang, when they leave tomorrow.'

'So soon?'

'You don't need me, Jo; you're achieving your dreams, all by yourself.'

'I'll always need you, Hattie, no matter where I am.'

'But I need a dream.' Hattie raised her glass. 'Something new. Hollywood is calling me,' she smiled.

'Here's to dreams,' Jo said and toasted Hattie. 'And may our dreams always come true.'

∽

Three months later...

Jo strolled across the snow covered lawn at Boomerville Manor, where the trees edging the garden were almost swallowed in white. The ground underfoot was icy hard but the snow was soft as icing sugar, as it dusted the tops of Jo's walking boots, creating lace patterns on the edge of her jeans. As flakes drifted windlessly down, she turned to see pawprints crisscross the paths and called to Bunty and Teddy, who followed close behind.

The dogs wore red fleecy jackets, edged with Christmas ribbon.

Jo smiled. Hattie would have a fit to see the two daft mongrels dressed up like fancy baubles.

As she reached the snow-hugged manor, Jo opened the front door, banged her boots on the stone step, untied the laces and slipped her feet out, placing the boots on a rack. She stooped to remove the damp coats from the dogs and shooing them ahead, went into a utility room that led off the hall. She pulled the woolly hat off her head and slipped her coat on a hook above the radiator to dry.

'I'll be back in a bit,' she said as she stroked and

soothed, watching Teddy climb into Bunty's box and settle down.

The manor was strangely quiet.

Finbar and Melissa had joined with James to take guests into Kindale for a Christmas carol service followed by chestnut roasting, mulled wine and a festive fair in the town square and, for once, it was lovely to have the old place to herself. Lights from the huge tree twinkled in the reception area and as the day darkened, Jo flicked table lamps on in the corners of the room.

She padded softly along the corridor, in her thick wool socks, running fingers through her tousled hair. She was going to sit by the fire in the lounge and relax for a while, before getting changed to greet the returning guests. As Jo walked, she thought she heard a melody coming from the music room.

Had Finbar left a radio on?

She approached the door and gently turned the handle. As she stepped in, she thought that the room was empty, but as she looked over to the window, where the grand piano stood, Jo felt her heart stop. Her eyes were wide and mouth half-open as she stared at a man, sitting on a stool, his fingers moving confidently across the keys.

Outside, the wintery sun was falling into the sky. A golden glow, glimmering through the leaded windows, lit the room, silhouetting the man as he continued to play.

A Stetson lay on the lid of the piano and Jo caught a glimpse of intricately-tooled leather cowboy boots, softly touching the pedals.

Dressed in jeans, his hair thick on the collar of his

coal-black shirt, Long Tom Hendry looked up. His tanned face was still handsome after all these years and, dark eyes dancing, he smiled.

Jo felt her heart cartwheel in her chest.

'Hello, Jo,' Long Tom said. 'Are you ready to take that leap of faith?'

THANK YOU

TEDDY

I hope that you enjoyed reading this book. Word of mouth is crucial for any author to succeed with their writing and reader feedback really helps. If you enjoyed reading "Boomerville at Ballymegille" I would be so thrilled if you could leave a review on Amazon or Goodreads.

With love and happy reading
Caroline xx

If you enjoyed "Boomerville at Ballymegille"
now read:

HATTIE GOES TO HOLLYWOOD

HATTIE GOES TO HOLLYWOOD

A Cumbrian village…
A red-hot summer…
Three suicides…

Join super sleuth Hattie as tempers and temperatures rise in the Cumbrian village of Hollywood. With mischief and shenanigans aplenty, will Hattie discover the truth? A funny and intriguing mystery by Caroline James

When recently bereaved Hattie Mulberry inherits her aunt's dilapidated cottage in the Cumbrian village of Hollywood, she envisages a quiet life. But retired hotelier Hattie is bored and when her neighbour asks her to investigate a suspicious suicide, Hattie's career takes a new direction and H&H Investigations is born. During the hottest summer on record, Hattie discovers there have been three recent suicides in Hollywood and she determines to find out why. Temperatures rise as she throws herself into village life and, with mischief and shenanigans aplenty, Hattie has her work cut out. But will she establish the truth?

"Cosy crime, a Cumbrian village, friendship, romance & love – just perfect!"
27 Book Street reviews

"5 Stars! I loved everything about this book!"
Tessa Talks Books

"Great sleuthing, faultless settings, interesting characters & a super fun read."
Rachel's Random Reviews

CONTACT CAROLINE

Find out more about the author at:

www.carolinejamesauthor.co.uk
Twitter @CarolineJames12
Instagram as Caroline James Author
Facebook as Caroline James Author

FURTHER READING

All of Caroline's books are stand-alone reads but can be read in the following order:

Coffee Tea the Gypsy & Me
Coffee Tea the Chef & Me
Coffee Tea the Caribbean & Me
Jungle Rock
The Best Boomerville Hotel
Boomerville at Ballymegille
Hattie Goes to Hollywood

Printed in Great Britain
by Amazon

46081363R00239